PLAN OF ATTACK

"After fifty years of careful deliberation, it has been decided that the proper course of action is destruction of your race."

Pruit felt her fists clenching at her sides.

Kep spoke to the captive. "Please lay out the Lucien plan for me in detail."

"Within twenty-five years we will double the number of military spacecraft watching Herrod. During the same period we will increase infiltration of your cities with the aim of gathering information pertinent to our attack plans.

"By thirty years from now we will have all military ordnance in place and fully developed plans of attack. In the thirty-fifth year we will attack."

Kep continued on. "You are human, aren't you?"

"I have a human body, yes," the man replied.

"How do you feel about destroying your own race?"

"It is not my race, for I am Lucien," the man replied. "The destruction of your race will not be total," he continued. "We feel it is in our interest to preserve human genetic information so the race can be used if needed to serve Lucien interests."

RESURRECTION

Arwen Elys Dayton

A ROC BOOK

ROC
Published by New American Library, a division of
Penguin Putnam Inc., 375 Hudson Street,
New York, New York, 10014, U.S.A.
Penguin Books Ltd, 27 Wrights Lane,
London W8 5TZ, England
Penguin Books Australia Ltd, Ringwood,
Victoria, Australia
Penguin Books Canada Ltd, 10 Alcorn Avenue,
Toronto, Ontario, Canada M4V 3B2
Penguin Books (N.Z.) Ltd, 182–190 Wairau Road,
Auckland 10, New Zealand

Penguin Books Ltd, Registered Offices:
Harmondsworth, Middlesex, England

First published by Roc, an imprint of New American Library,
a division of Penguin Putnam Inc.

First Printing, June 2001
10 9 8 7 6 5 4 3 2 1

Cover art by Danilo Ducak

 REGISTERED TRADEMARK—MARCA REGISTRADA

Printed in the United States of America

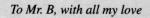

To Mr. B, with all my love

ACKNOWLEDGMENTS

I would like to thank Erich Von Däniken and Zecharia Sitchin for pointing the way to our possible pasts. No matter how far out their theories, they are at least looking for answers.

Thanks also to John Anthony West for leading the way by flashlight.

J. E. Manchip White and Guillemette Andreu have written excellent books on Egypt, which were helpful to me.

And thanks to Matt Bialer and Laura Anne Gilman for the grilling.

AUTHOR'S NOTE

I have been inconsistent in my use of ancient names. Some appear in the Egyptian pronunciation, some in the Greek. Both versions are generally accepted, and employment of one or the other is a matter of personal preference.

The Egyptian kings in this work are not referred to as "Pharaoh." Pharaoh, the literal meaning of which is "Great House," was not used of the king himself until the Eighteenth Dynasty.

Chapter 1

Four Years Ago

The feeling was gray, like dawn, but harder to define. Pruit was surfacing, moving through layers of awareness that seemed to wash over her in varying shades of light. It was minutes, or perhaps hours, before she was aware that she was surfacing. First there was awareness after a fashion, and this was followed by her own knowledge of that awareness, but between the two were infinite levels of gray.

At last she could feel her own chest moving, she could sense her muscles and the position of her body. She felt the warmth of liquid around her, and she remembered that she could see out of her eyes.

She opened them. She felt the biofluid, and it was pleasant. Through its slightly orange coloring, she could make out a shape above her. Niks. His face was too blurry to discern any expression, but Pruit knew he was smiling.

She saw him move an arm to the controls of her crib. There was a shift in the fluid, and in a moment she could feel it draining away. It slid off of her face and now she could see Niks more clearly. The plantglass retracted from the top of the crib, and she felt the brush of air from the ship. It seemed too cold. All over her body, bloodarms and feedarms were gently releasing her and moving back into the wombwalls of the crib, leaving no trace on her of their presence. A reedy breathearm withdrew from her throat, and she gagged.

She spit out biofluid and shakily reached for the sides of the crib. Niks took her hands and pulled her to a sitting position. He wiped her eyes gently and she looked at him.

"Hello, sleepyhead," he said softly. And he was smiling. He was in his early twenties, with copper-colored skin and hair that was reddish brown. His eyes were blue. This description accurately fit Pruit as well, except for her hair, which was shoulder length and slightly darker brown. It was a description that fit everyone they knew—relatives, friends, strangers in the narrow corridor streets of their home.

She saw that Niks was already dressed, and felt a moment of distress at his breach of regulation. He should have woken simultaneously with her, not first.

"Hello," she said, her voice scratchy. "Year fourteen?" Her mind was still waking up.

He nodded and helped her stand. The remainder of the biofluid slid off of her, back into the crib, to be reclaimed by the ship's central system. Niks draped a blanket over her shoulders, and Pruit stepped from the crib. She could already feel how weak her muscles were.

She surveyed their small ship. The cribs were in the very center, two oblong boxes, rounded at the edges, made of light brown solid-reed that had been specially grown in place when the ship was assembled. The inside walls of the cribs were a web of pinkish orange, from which extended the organic-looking, stemlike arms that entered their bodies and kept them alive through years of hibernation.

Along the ship's walls, on either side of the cribs, were the control centers, the computer systems that navigated the ship and monitored it second by second as it made its journey.

At one end of the oval ship were two bunks, stowed exercise equipment, and an open mat space for exercise. At the other end were the medical station, the food station, and a large dark structure, loosely the shape of a box, that stretched from floor to ceiling. This was the sentient tank. They would not need it until later in their trip.

Next to the tank was the shower, and Pruit walked carefully toward it. She and Niks said nothing else, not yet. He knew it took several minutes to become oriented after waking, and he gave her time to adjust.

She dropped the blanket and stepped into the shower. As the water sprayed out onto her face and body, she felt the same dread she had felt thirteen times before. It was an eerie sensation that started somewhere in the pit of her stomach. Another day, another year. Fourteen years. A few hours or days awake followed by a year of sleep, and each time they woke their world was farther away.

She washed herself, feeling how thin she was. Thin and atrophied. Niks had looked gaunt as well, his ribs plainly visible through his once muscular frame.

She finished her shower and he helped her into her blue one-piece undergarment and her white coveralls. He wore the same outfit.

"I feel very weak," she said. "How do you feel?"

"The same." He fastened the straps of the coveralls for her. She noticed that he did not caress her, and she was relieved. They should follow their regulations. There would be time for other things later.

"We're too weak," she said. "After our checklist I want to do a full medical." Pruit was the medical officer of their two-man crew. "We may have to make this a five-day." She was referring to five days awake, before returning to hibernation. Their usual stint was a single day or less, but five-days were required if their bodies needed extra time to recover. They had been awake for twenty days so far out of the fourteen years of their trip.

"We've already taken two five-days. Is that normal?"

"Normal?" She smiled, not cheerfully. "Fourteen years asleep, Niks. Almost anything would qualify as normal."

They took their seats at the control centers, on opposite sides of the ship, one of them sitting at each, and began their lengthy checklist.

"Checklist begin," Niks said. He was slightly her senior in rank and the technical captain of the mission. "Hull?"

Pruit sank her hand into the putty control pad and manipulated it. On the screens in front of her, rows of data popped up, displayed by varicolored reeds whose cells formed and reformed in nanoseconds to create the images required. The screens gave the impression that the images on them were growing, and this was close to the truth, for the cells regenerated themselves and reproduced, and were, even in their highly manipulated state, biological.

"Hull secure," Pruit said. "Three incidents in the last period. Two minor. One a level two. The hull was breached for ten seconds by debris. Then regenerated. The hull cell count has been normal since then."

"Crew radiation exposure?"

She manipulated the putty pad and new data appeared. "Minimal. The cribs were sufficient protection."

"Internal systems?" Niks asked, moving to the next item on the checklist. This was his to check, and he began a diagnostic test.

By the time they had completed the checklist, they had examined in detail every system of the ship. They encountered nothing unusual; things were running well.

"Good," Niks said, marking the list as complete on his screen and asking the computer to file it in the permanent log. "Time to eat."

Pruit made a face. It was nearly impossible to regain appetite within fifteen hours of waking, but they were required to feed themselves so their bodies would not become too dependent on intravenous nutrition.

They ate a small meal of reconstituted meat and vegetables, prepared by the ship's food processor. The flavor was good, but they could do little more than choke it down. They promptly threw it up a few minutes later, as had happened frequently on their recent wakes. More slowly, they ate again.

The chore of eating finished, they moved to the medical station, and Pruit began a waking diagnostic check. She compared this with the record from the crib for an accurate analysis of how well their bodies were adjusting to and recovering from the hibernation.

"We need a five-day," she confirmed, gently pulling the medical reader off of Niks's wrist. "We're losing resilience." Their bodies were manifesting hibernation exhaustion, a condition the doctors back home had predicted. Their body systems had operated so long at near death levels that they were now having difficulty attaining normal function. Their trouble keeping down food and their general wasted appearance were part of this.

Niks nodded and turned his head slightly, to address the ship at large. "Central, wake." It was a command, and it was followed by a chime.

"I'm here," a female voice said, emanating from the walls. It was the human voice they had chosen for the ship's central computer. Though Central was incapable of actual thought, the computer's artificial intelligence programming allowed it to carry on very natural conversations with the crew.

"Central, please review medical data. We're going to take a five-day," Pruit said.

"Correct," Central replied after the briefest of pauses, in which it scanned through Pruit's medical report and extensive medical archives. "That's advisable. Recheck medical daily with special attention to rates of metabolism."

"All right."

Pruit and Niks looked at each other, and something in their attitudes changed. They had reached the end of their immediate crew obligations. For the moment they were technically off duty.

"Fourteen years," he said quietly, sitting into a chair at the study desk by the medical station. "It doesn't seem real."

"You say that every time we wake."

"It's true every time."

She moved over to him and sat on one of his legs, putting her arms around his neck, feeling how narrow his shoulders had become. She had tied her hair into two braids, but it still looked brittle and unhealthy. There were dark circles under both of their eyes and their brown skin seemed ashen. She knew she must feel like a leaf, sitting on his knee, with her coveralls hanging on her body now, several sizes too large. "I know," she whispered. He put his arms around her. When their duties were finished, there was no routine to distract them from their circumstances.

"Pruit . . ." He leaned forward to kiss her. It was a kiss to pull comfort from physical contact, but as their lips touched, it turned into something else. She kissed him back, and it became a passionate kiss, both of them feeling the immediacy of desire. Their arms slid around each other more tightly, and she turned to sit astride him as the kiss deepened. She thought how remarkable it was, that despite the frail condition of their bodies, this passion was there every time they woke, urged, perhaps, by the fear of death.

In moments they were pulling off each other's clothes and moving to the bottom bunk, kissing, touching, caressing. Niks pulled the bunk down and pulled her down on top of him.

He turned his head away from her to address the ship. "Central, sleep," he said. A chime sounded, indicating the computer had stopped monitoring them, at least obviously.

He turned back into her kiss. "I love you, Pruit."

"I love you, Niks," she breathed.

Their bodies moved together, were together, and they were not alone in the vast reaches of space, they were not alone light-years from home, where their families were aging and the Lucien were setting in motion plans to prevent them from ever producing another generation to carry on. It would be years and years before they arrived home, if there was a home to return to . . .

They cried out together in the final moment, and then Pruit collapsed on top of him, and Niks let his head fall back onto the bed, both of them completely spent.

Later they lay side by side in the bunk, feeling the exhaustion that had been sinking into their bodies through years of false sleep. Pruit's head rested on Niks's shoulder. Niks was holding up photographs of home in their yearly ritual of remembrance. The pictures had been printed on a mat of light-sensitive plant cells. These cells created nearly perfect images with a hint of depth.

The photograph now in his hand was a picture of Pruit's family: her mother and father and her younger brother. They looked healthy and vibrant. And happy. The picture had been taken before they knew that Pruit would be leaving.

Pruit noticed that she and Niks no longer asked, "What do you think their lives are like now?" They had exhausted such questions during their previous wakes. Too much time had passed for the people captured in the pictures for any conjectures to be meaningful.

Niks flipped to another photograph. This one was him, standing between his mother and father. Then there was a picture of Pruit. She was riding up an escalator that stretched ten stories, and behind her, outside the city dome, stretched fields of radioactive glass. She wore a sleeveless shirt, and the lean lines of her arms were visible. She looked in top physical condition, healthy but not happy.

"Little sourpuss," Niks muttered affectionately.

He flipped the picture again, and now they were looking at Pruit's younger brother Makus. He was sitting at the family dining table doing homework. When she looked at him, Pruit saw a man in his late twenties, with children of his own, perhaps. And did he know what was coming? Had the Sentinel told anyone yet, or was it still a secret, a hidden cancer that would eat all of them alive just a few short years from now?

She suddenly grew tired of nostalgia.

"Let's put the pictures away," she said.

"We should remember."

"I do remember." She got up from the bunk and pulled her clothes back on. "And it doesn't help." She fastened her coveralls and pulled her hair more tightly into her braids. "Great Life! What did they tell them, Niks? What do they think happened to us? We're dead to them. And they don't know why we left."

Niks sat up and reached for his own clothes. "It's better if they think we're dead."

"I know!" Then, more calmly, "I know." This was a conversation that had repeated itself several times in their fourteen wakes. Frustration, suppressed most of the time, would now and then boil to the surface. It was good, a reminder that they still had an emotional connection to those left behind. "It's better if they don't know, since there's nothing they can do."

Niks did not respond. There was no need. Instead he stood and took her hands. "We should start our exercises," he said quietly.

With that they were back on duty, and they moved to the exercise mat to begin their first-day stretching routine. As they went through the motions together, arms and legs holding positions, reaching, energy concentrated and directed, they both felt their minds clearing. These were peaceful exercises, and they held the comfort of long familiarity. This was one of the first routines they had been taught as young children. The motions were a reminder of their peers, their fellow soldiers. Some of those peers might be alone together, also hurtling through space as Pruit and Niks were, though several years behind. The rest were back home on Herrod, brothers and sisters who bore the weight of the world.

Five days later their bodies had begun to recover. Pruit and Central agreed that it was safe to return to hibernation.

Naked, Pruit lowered herself into her crib. Her body looked much healthier that it had upon waking, but it would take more than five days to erase the marks of so many years asleep. That, however, would have to wait until their mission reached its next stage. The crib walls and floor felt dry against her skin, but they would soon be refreshed with fluid. She manipulated the controls on the outside crib wall, and the inner web kicked into motion. In moments, the reedy arms were growing out, seeking her body so they could put it under control.

Niks sat over her, still dressed, violating regulations again. They were supposed to enter hibernation simultaneously, each following the sleep checklist and verifying the other's motions. It was Niks's only quirk. He liked to be there when she woke and when she went back to sleep.

"We really should do this right," Pruit said.

Niks knew what she was referring to. "I'll just make sure you're safely sleeping."

She didn't protest. He never listened on this point, and in truth she was happy he was there. They were equals in almost everything, but sometimes he protected her in ways that were at odds with their positions and their lives. Secretly she enjoyed it.

The bloodarms gently entered her veins. The crib was filing with biofluid, warm and inviting. Niks leaned over and kissed her. A breathearm curled up her chest. She touched Niks's cheek and then leaned back into the crib, letting the breathearm find her mouth and snake down her throat. She suppressed the urge to gag and then felt herself relaxing. There was a gentle hiss of air as the plantglass slid into place above her. The biofluid covered her now, and she opened her eyes in it. There was Niks, a faint blur. And then her eyes closed and she was diving into darkness.

Chapter 2

Eighteen Years Ago

"It's so big," Makus said, looking out through the dome at the wastelands.

"That's why we're needed," Pruit said. "To protect everyone in the cities and all of that out there."

Makus was her younger brother, just thirteen. They were standing together in Evansquare, a large park up against the Kellersland city dome. Outside the dome the ground was covered with green-yellow glass, ugly and radioactive, stretching in every direction to the horizon. Much of the glass was perfectly smooth, but here and there it was broken by enormous piles of rubble, small at this distance, that marked the spots where great outdoor cities had once stood. That was in the ancient times, long before the bombs. It was late afternoon, and the green sky was darkening.

"It's hard for me to think about it," Makus said. He took a seat on the bench behind them and started eating the lunch they had brought.

Pruit joined him. "It's hard for all of us. But that's our job. Now it's your job too." She tried to say it with a smile but it was difficult. Makus had just been accepted into the Sentinel, the elite military organization which bore the ultimate responsibility for the future of their race, who were known as the Kinley. The job was not easy. She and Niks, now in their mid-twenties, had also joined the Sentinel at Makus's age.

"Yes, I know."

He said it heavily, and Pruit pushed him playfully on the shoulder, trying to lighten the mood. "This is a celebration lunch," she said. "Congratulations on being accepted. You'll get used to the responsibility soon enough."

At this, Makus cheered up and even smiled. "Thanks, Pru. Is Niks coming?"

"He'll try and make it. We've had a busy few weeks." She twisted her left shoulder, which was in a sling, recovering from a laser burn. She saw Makus glance at her, but he did not ask about the wound. He knew too well that she would not be able to tell him its cause. Her work in the Sentinel was almost always secret. "What about Mom and Dad? I haven't seen them for ages."

"They're sleeping," he said. "They've switched shifts."

Pruit nodded. Outside, she caught sight of a reclamation crew picking its way through the fields of glass. Reclamation of destroyed land and water was a constant and achingly slow project. "That may be one of your first assignments, Makus," she said, pointing at the squad. There were several members of the Sentinel, recognizable by orange-colored fullsuits, walking with the reclamation crew and carrying weapons.

Makus was silent and a sudden thought occurred to Pruit. She turned to him. "Makus, have you ever been outside?"

He shook his head. "No."

"I'd forgotten. Of course you haven't." Only members of the Sentinel, reclamation workers, and scientists went outside. "It's not as bad as it looks," she said, knowing this was a lie. "I mean . . . it's not pleasant, and it's hard to feel totally at ease in a fullsuit. But you'll get used to it. In the Sentinel you'll have a lot of work outside."

Makus looked outside again at the barren landscape. "It scares me a little. Like I'll be out there with all the ghosts. And sometimes I'll be walking right where the bombs dropped." He could even see one such location, a clearly defined bomb crater a few miles away.

Pruit followed his gaze. She had spent months outside, and the feel of her heavy boots walking across that ancient, poisonous glass was now an inherent part of her. "No," she said. "The ghosts have given up on it. It's just dead out there. I wish I could say the same for the Lucien."

The name affected both of them. Makus almost shivered. "Have you ever seen one?"

"You know I can't tell you," she said. The truth was she had never seen a Lucien. They were the silver, insectlike creatures who had rained fusion and fission bombs down upon Herrod five thousand years before and nearly wiped out all Kinley life. She had never seen a true Lucien, not in person, but she had seen their minions, she had seen humans who were bred in Lucien laboratories from stolen Kinley genetic material and used as spies.

Just then a large meteor shower streaked across the dusking sky, brilliant lines of fire cutting across the upper atmosphere. Impulsively, Pruit massaged her laser-burned shoulder. As she watched the meteors, she felt deep hatred of the Lucien. It was an emotion she had been aware of since childhood, perhaps before. It was not anger. It was much calmer than that, a hatred that had softly infiltrated every fiber of her, and it was matched by the thought that kept her living: they will not win.

"There's Niks!" Makus said, looking across the crowds in the square at a figure approaching. The glum mood that had settled on both of them lifted abruptly.

In a moment, Niks was there, dressed, like Pruit, in the informal fatigues of the Sentinel: pants of a lightweight material, dark red and falling to mid-calf, snug jersey with rank insignia around the collar, and flexible black boots, designed for running.

"Hello there," Niks said with a big smile, as he shook Makus's hand and drew the boy into an embrace. "Congratulations, Skinny! It's great to have you on the team."

Makus smiled back and saluted. "Thank you, sir."

"Sorry I'm late. But unfortunately Pruit and I have to go." He caught her eye and she saw that he was in fact quite perturbed about something, though he was covering well.

"I understand," Makus said, now holding himself a little straighter. Niks always had that effect on her little brother.

"Pru, our Chief is calling us," Niks said.

Pruit nodded and took one last bite of her lunch. Then she gave Makus a final hug. "Tell Mom and Dad hello," she said. "I may have a free day coming up to spend some time with them." Though somehow she doubted it. Then she moved off with Niks, leaving her brother staring out through the dome and contemplating the future.

Together she and Niks quickly crossed the park, threading their way through its heavy foot traffic, and made their way to the escalators which led up and inward to the stacked levels of Kellersland. The city was a dense warren of residential, business, industrial, and military sectors piled on top of each other and nestled beneath the dome.

"Urgent?" Pruit asked.

"Sounded like it," Niks said.

They rode the reed mat of the escalator up five stories then exited. A group of young schoolchildren ran through the crowds in front of them creating a momentary path. Niks grabbed Pruit's arm and followed in the children's wake.

Around them were faces of their fellow Kinley citizens, their skin a uniform copper color, and their hair, while varying slightly here and there, for the most part reddish-brown. Their eyes were blue or green, with blue the dominant color. Overall there was little variation from one person to the next. The gene pool after the Great War with the Lucien had been so small that all Kinley were as closely related as brother and sister.

They worked their way through a labyrinth of corridors. Beyond a security checkpoint, they passed down into one of the lowest levels of the city, far underground. Here they moved through narrow hallways, with ceilings that hung just a foot overhead. Stopping at several more security checkpoints to identify themselves, they were quickly passed along and in a few minutes had arrived in a small meeting room, where their commander, Chief Sentinel Guardian Haren, waited for them.

"Sir," they greeted him in unison, not saluting, for they were not properly uniformed for this, but standing at attention.

"Pruit, Niks," he greeted them. "Good. You're in time for a recap."

The meaning of this was not immediately clear to them, but he gestured, and they moved over to stand by him. He sank his hand into a putty control pad mounted at one side of the wall, and the wall itself seemed to dissolve, as the plantglass that comprised it changed color from a milky white to clear. It was one-way glass, and through it they could see a neighboring interrogation room. This room was all white, almost disturbingly so, and contained only a small white table, with chairs on either side. There were two men inside. One they recognized as Kep Tellie, one of the Chief's top aides. Kep's back was to them.

Across from Kep, and thus facing them, was a young Kinley man, wearing civilian clothes, and sitting up very straight in his chair. The expression on his face was unreadable. He was speaking, but his mouth hardly moved as he formed the words.

"We captured him five days ago," the Chief explained. "He managed to get into Marretland," one of the secondary cities on Herrod. There were only three cities and a few other outposts on the whole of the planet. "He was passed through with a reclamation crew, but he attracted the attention of a security guard in the park, if you can believe that." He said this last in a disgusted tone, and Pruit and Niks understood him immediately. The captive in there was not one of their citizens. He was a Lucien spy who had without apparent problem entered one of their cities and only by the merest luck been found.

Neither of them said anything. It was unnecessary. All understood what such an easy breach bespoke in terms of general security. If one spy could get in, a dozen could get in. Or more. Perhaps they were already here.

"We haven't tortured him," the Chief continued. "He sat in his cell for two days and meditated—in the way they do—then he started talking to us." Ordinarily, torture was necessary to extract information from such spies, but more often than not those Lucien humans somehow willed themselves into death before giving up information. A spy willingly speaking was a new thing.

The Chief used the putty pad again, and then spoke, and his voice was transmitted to the ear of Kep within. "Walk him through it again," he said.

Kep made no physical acknowledgment of the order, but as the Chief turned on the sound, allowing them to hear the conversation within the interrogation room, Kep addressed the prisoner. "I'd like to go over this again," he said patiently to the captive across from him. "Is that all right with you?"

The Lucien human's face did not change. "Yes," he said. "I will tell you again."

"Good. Tell me how you got to Herrod."

"I came in mimicking a meteorite. The landing was hard but bearable." This was the usual way for Lucien spies to arrive on Herrod. Because meteorites were so common and because the deserted area of Herrod was so large, it was impossible to track every impact with the surface. Pruit had received the laser burn on her shoulder while chasing and killing another such spy just weeks before. "I walked for three days and then fell in with a mining party when the shifts were changing," the man continued. He spoke Soulene, the modern language of the Kinley, very well. He had only the faintest of lisps on certain words to give himself away. He went on to describe how he passed undetected through the checkpoints leading into the city, using duplicated identity tags, stolen from a reclamation worker he had killed. Pruit and Niks blanched at his description.

"Tell me the purpose of your mission here," Kep said.

"I was sent to study your cities, especially their systems of defense. I was ordered to return with schematics of city construction if possible."

"Why would such information be needed by the Lucien?" Kep asked. He did an excellent job of keeping his voice level and pleasant, Pruit thought. It would have taken all her self-restraint to prevent herself from wringing the man's neck if she were sitting in Kep's chair.

"We seek information that will allow us to plan an effective attack on Herrod."

"Is this a contingency plan or a plan that has already been set in motion?" Kep asked.

"The plan is already under way. We are currently preparing for a devastating attack upon your planet." The captive's voice was level, somewhat thoughtful, but not colored by emotion.

Pruit and Niks both glanced at their Chief. He gestured for them to keep watching.

"Why?" Kep asked.

"Our Council of One Hundred has been watching your development very closely over the last two centuries. You have developed rudimentary space travel during this time and have begun to mine the asteroids that lie between you and the next planet in the system.

"You could conceivably develop ships to rival our own within the next two hundred years. We cannot allow this. Based on the history of our two races, we know the threat you pose to our continued survival. You nearly destroyed us once in the past and we will not allow this to happen again.

"After fifty years of careful deliberation, it has been decided that the proper course is destruction of your race."

Pruit and Niks gasped quietly in unison. After the Great War, Lucien civilization had recovered far more quickly than Kinley, and the Lucien had established a space-based blockade of Herrod. Lucien ships were constantly in orbit just outside the neighboring asteroid belt, watching the Kinley. If a Kinley ship ever ventured beyond the belt, it was summarily destroyed. The Kinley had accepted the blockade, for they had no choice in view of the Lucien's much greater space-faring power, but they had never suspected that their ancient enemies would grudge them even their meager existence on their own planet.

"The destruction of your race will not be total," the captive continued, in the same bland tone. "We feel it is in our interest to preserve human genetic information so the race can be used if needed to serve Lucien interests."

Pruit felt her hands clenching as he said this.

Without any apparent concern for the content of what the prisoner had said, Kep continued. "Please lay out the Lucien plan for me in detail."

"Within twenty-five years from now we will double the number of military spacecraft watching Herrod. During the same period we will increase infiltration of your cities with the aim of gathering all information pertinent to our attack plans.

"By thirty years from now we will have all ordnance in place and fully developed plans of attack.

"On the thirty-fifth year we will attack."

Pruit and Niks looked to their Chief desperately. His face was set in a contemplative attitude. He had already had opportunity to digest this information, and his shock, while still real, had somewhat abated.

Next door, Kep continued. "You are human, aren't you?" he asked the captive.

"I have a human body, yes," the man replied.

"How do you feel about destroying your race?" It was a tactic they often tried on Lucien spies—forcing them to exhibit emotion. It did not often work.

"It is not my race, for I am Lucien," the man replied. He paused, then for the first time his expression changed and took on a slightly pained look. "I have thought long about my feelings in this matter, and it distresses me that my mind is not fully my own. As a Lucien I know that you must be destroyed. We have our own future generations to consider, and this outweighs all else. You are not to be trusted. However, there is some part of me . . . some part beyond my control." He paused. His lisp had become stronger as emotion crept in, and the slight motions of his head and arms were more birdlike, just as a Lucien's would be. Under stress his Lucien upbringing became more apparent. He took a long, deep breath and composed himself. "Some part of me is saddened by what we must do, and though I betray my loved ones and myself, I have decided to tell you our plans. Perhaps you can put your houses in order and find peace for your souls before destruction comes. That would give me happiness."

Before she could stop herself, Pruit was pounding on the plantglass with both fists and screaming incoherently at the captive. Kep and the Lucien spy could not hear her voice, but her pounding shook the wall and the captive's eyes turned and seemed to look right at her.

She yelled at him, and her voice began to form coherent words. "No! No! No!"

Niks grabbed her shoulders and wrenched her away from the glass, shaking her. He yelled into her face, "Stop it! By all that lives, stop it, Pruit!" He shook her hard and she quieted, still breathing heavily. The Chief looked at her, but made no response to her outburst, perhaps remembering his own reaction when he first heard the Lucien's story.

"Stop it!" Niks said, now speaking more quietly. "That's not helping."

Slowly, Pruit nodded. "I'm sorry," she said. "He just . . . He just . . . How dare he? Put our houses in order, while he decides our fate . . ." With great effort she controlled herself and calmed. This was why they were an excellent team, she and Niks. Their skills were nearly equal, but while Pruit felt driven by dread and hatred and was sometimes overcome by these emotions, Niks was the one who pulled her back and steadied her, and even, most times, brought a sense of lightheartedness to their work.

"Your anger is justified," the Chief said softly. "Sit down."

They complied, and he sank into a chair facing them, switching the plantglass back to its opaque white setting, so Kep and captive were hidden from view. Pruit still felt her heart beating fast, but she made an effort to relax.

"It's time to be blunt and unemotional in examining this," the Chief said. "We have thirty-five years, and then, if their plan continues unabated, all of this will be gone." He made a vague, sweeping gesture that indicated the entirety of the city above and around them. "Our city domes are not built to withstand a nuclear attack. They will provide some moderate protection from distant blasts, but bombs dropped close to the domes, or on top of the domes, will quickly compromise them, and then the city can be destroyed easily by a follow-up explosion. They are hundreds of years ahead of us in spacecraft. We are ten million citizens, grouped into three cities. We require massive filtration systems for drinking water and breathable air. We are easy targets."

"Is there any chance of negotiation?" Niks asked.

"We don't want to let them know that we have discovered their plan," the Chief said. "And at any rate, we know their opinion of us. We are not considered a race of equal stature. We are not even considered sentient beings, not really. In a thousand years they have never answered a broadcast from us, and there is no reason this would change. We are pests to them, nothing more.

"The Sentinel Council has been in session for the last four days and has decided on our course of action. We will halt standard reclamation procedures immediately and turn our full attentions to burrowing deeper underground, creating shelters at a depth great enough to hopefully provide protection from a sustained nuclear attack. Concurrently we will begin a program to develop space-based defense. This is a double-edged sword, however, for it may make us appear an even greater threat to the Lucien."

He waited while Pruit and Niks thought these things over.

Then Niks asked, "How can that be sufficient to protect us?"

"It won't be. Even if we begin today, we will not be able to protect our population from any kind of sustained bombing. It is nearly impossible that we can survive the attack."

They stared at him. There was no sugarcoating here.

"Then what . . . How will we save ourselves?" Pruit asked at last.

The Chief hesitated for a moment, then reached into his breast pocket and drew out a small object, about the length of his index finger and not much thicker. He set it on the table and slid it toward them. Niks picked it up and he and Pruit examined it. It was a crystal, perfectly symmetrical, with four long faces that met at right angles, and faces of forty-five degrees that met in a point at each end. It was extremely hard. Along the length of it were four red bands. On close examination it was apparent that these bands were grown into and through the crystal itself. They made little red planes through the clear substance.

"You will remember this from history class," the Chief said. "Before the Great War, the Kinley ancients had many uses for crystals. They were able to manipulate them and grow them in ways we have never fully understood.

"The bands of red were created by inserting foreign atoms into the crystal as it grew—in this case iron and oxygen. By manipulating the pattern of these foreign atoms, they could use them to store information, vast quantities of it."

Pruit and Niks remembered all of this somewhat from their early education, but its relevance was not yet clear. Everyone knew the ancients had achieved many things the modern Kinley could only dream of.

"And the crystals," the Chief continued, "especially ones like this one, which is an artificial diamond, last almost forever—theoretically, of course, since in actuality most of them were destroyed in the Great War. They don't survive a direct nuclear attack."

He paused and they both held his gaze. Slowly, the Chief said, "These crystals were once taken elsewhere. Off of Herrod. Do you remember the story?"

Pruit and Niks were silent for several moments, thinking back to their early schooling. Then, with an almost religious sense of awe, Pruit realized what the Chief was referring to. As young children, they had studied what was known of the Kinley ancient history. In this history was the story of a small group of Kinley scientists who had built a ship that could travel the universe. They had set out for a planet nearly eight light-years distant. The war had come soon after, and they had never returned.

"The Eschless Funnel," Pruit breathed.

"The Eschless Funnel," the Chief agreed.

For that was the name of the engine within the ship that had allowed it to travel at speeds faster than light. If that history tale had been accurate, those ancient Kinley had unraveled the deepest secret of the universe and had built a ship with their knowledge.

"Did it really exist?" Pruit asked. For that ship and its crew and the Eschless Funnel were so far removed from modern Kinley civilization that they had the flavor of a creation myth, a story that could not possibly be real.

"Yes," the Chief said seriously. "We know that the Eschless Funnel did exist. There are many references to it, though no records of what exactly it was."

"Earth," Niks whispered. That was the name of the world to which those ancient Kinley had traveled.

"Yes, Earth. Earth is there, just as it was. And somewhere on Earth are the crystals that traveled with that ancient crew. Crystals that recorded the building of the Eschless Funnel ship and the science behind it."

Pruit felt a surge of hope within her. There was, perhaps, a doorway to the past, to the days before the Great War, when the Kinley were masters of all they surveyed and the future was wide open.

"If those crystals still exist," the Chief continued, "they would teach us the true nature of physics. They would vault us past Lucien technology, and enable us, perhaps, to win a war against them."

Pruit stared at him, then slowly said, "You want us to find the technology."

"Yes," the Chief said. "And bring it back. You two are young enough to make it through the trip without serious consequences to your health. And you have both proven your abilities as soldiers. I and the Council believe you are the right choice. Obviously, this is a last-ditch effort. But Kinley science achieved faster-than-light travel once. There is no reason we cannot achieve it again. We just need the key. And what better time than now, when it may be our only option?"

They almost laughed at the desperation of this plan, but neither thought of refusing.

As they lay together in bed that evening, their small suite of rooms on the very top level of Kellersland, they looked up through their plantglass ceiling at the dome canopy above. Through the dome they could see thousands of stars, spread out across the galaxy.

"I'm frightened, Niks," Pruit said, her arms twined about him under their light covers.

"Me too." He held her to him, his lips in her hair. "But if someone will go, I'm glad it's us. No matter how desperate it is."

"Yes," she whispered back. She wouldn't have it any other way.

Chapter 3

Adaiz-Ari and Enon-Amet walked side by side down a wide hallway with an enormous arched ceiling. The ceiling was of a polished aluminum alloy that shimmered in the white light of the artificial suns outside.

Adaiz was human, a man in his twenties, bred in a Lucien laboratory from human genetic material gathered from captured Kinley. At birth, when he had emerged crying from the Lucien incubator that had nurtured his prenatal development, he had been given to the father and mother of Enon-Amet, then a Lucien pup of three years, and Adaiz and Enon had been raised as brothers.

The racial difference between them had never been of any consequence to either. Like any younger brother, Adaiz had adored and emulated his older brother Enon, and Enon had treasured his unique sibling.

They passed guards standing at attention in front of high doors that led off from the hall, back into the meditation chambers and meeting rooms that filled the bulk of the Hall of Elders. Both Adaiz and Enon wore the uniforms of Clan Providence, the Lucien army, which left them bare to the waist. From the corner of his eyes, Adaiz caught glints of sunlight reflecting off the silver chest of his brother. Enon was slightly over six feet tall, average for a Lucien male.

A human seeing a Lucien for the first time would think them insectile, but this assessment would be incorrect. They were more akin to mammals than insects. Their most striking characteristic was their skin. It was silver and was partially reflective, as long as they were exposed to regular sunlight. Their coloring was caused by a subcutaneous layer of a silica solution that captured sunlight and employed it in biochemical reactions. Starved of sunlight, they became less and less reflective as their bodies sought to draw in all available light to perform these functions.

Their oval heads tapered to a narrow point at the place where a human's chin would be. Their mouths sat behind this point, at a place analogous to the underside of a human's chin. Two small slits above the tapered point made up the Lucien nose. Their heads were smooth and hairless, and on each side, above small, pointed ears, were remnant antlers, the legacy of some previous step in their evolution. The antlers were about four inches long and lay back flush against the sides of their skulls. They were made of soft cartilage and covered with brown fuzz.

Their arms were quite similar to human arms, but their legs had two knee joints, the upper bending forward, the lower backward. Their feet had long, splayed toes, three facing front, and two facing back. Their double knees and the shape of their feet allowed them to run quickly and jump quite long distances.

Enon's uniform consisted of loose elastic trousers which allowed for the bending of his double knee joints. There was a golden stripe running up the side of each leg, indicating that he was an officer. On his feet were soft, black sandals. His rank was indicated by bronze armbands on both of his upper arms. Enon had a regal carriage, and his silver head displayed a distinct facial bone structure that was considered quite attractive by the females of their race. His wide, slanted eyes were a black obsidian.

Adaiz wore an almost identical uniform, modified only to fit his human form. He had one fewer armbands than his brother, for he was of a lower rank. His upper body was tanned from its natural copper color to a deep brown. His eyes

were blue. His hair was reddish-brown and he wore it shaved
close to his scalp, with two longer, braided queues at the back
of his head. Far from being burdened by his human body, he
had turned it to his advantage by developing manual skills that
were difficult for Lucien to achieve.

Despite the difference in their heights and physical makeup,
the brothers' gaits were almost identical. Growing up as a Lucien, Adaiz had long since learned to modify the natural incli-
nations of his body to match those of his adopted race.

At the end of the hallway, they reached silver doors that
stood twenty feet high. Before these were two guards, wearing
the blue trousers of noncommissioned officers. They swung
the doors open to allow Enon and Adaiz to pass through.

The doors opened in on a tall receiving room, one wall of
which was a solid glass window, letting in bright sunlight. The
room was spare. There was a rug of woven fiber and several
low tables, at which visitors might sit until they were called.
Across from the great window was another set of doors, these
leading to the Triad chamber within. Near these inner doors
was a low desk, and behind this an officer sat cross-legged on
the floor, speaking in soft tones through a communicator at his
ear. As Adaiz and Enon entered, the officer politely excused
himself from the communicator conversation and stood, his
long legs unbending.

Adaiz and Enon drew themselves to attention and saluted,
by bowing their heads slightly, with their arms held before
their chests, the fist of one hand cradled in the palm of the
other. The officer returned their salute.

"Leader Enon-Amet, Officer Adaiz-Ari, you are expected,"
he said in the sibilant tones of Avani, the chief language of the
Lucien, designed for the natural lisps of the soft Lucien palate.
"The Medium Triad is engaged in a peaceful Opening at present. They will call you when they have surfaced. Please be at
your ease."

Enon and Adaiz nodded again, and withdrew to stand by the
window. An Opening was a form of meditation, a way of
clearing the mind and centering oneself. It was a common con-

clusion to deliberations of great weight, and the officer's mention of it indicated that the Triad had been discussing matters of import. "Surfacing" was the Lucien expression for returning to the world after meditation.

The two brothers stood at the window, their arms neatly held behind their backs, their posture upright and only a fraction more relaxed than it would have been had they been standing at full attention. They were, after all, in the antechamber of a Medium Triad, one of the highest ranking groups within Clan Providence. There were only five such triads within the whole of Lucien civilization.

"Younger Brother, it is indeed an honor that the Triad has asked to see us alone," Enon said. "I had expected other officers to be waiting with us."

"Yes, Older Brother," Adaiz replied. "An honor few of our rank have had." Adaiz had spoken Avani as his first tongue. He considered it his mother tongue, but his human mouth would never be able to pronounce all of the words correctly.

They said no more, preferring to hold themselves in calm awareness of their bodies, their minds, and their surroundings. The room in which they stood was over a hundred stories above the surface of Galea, the asteroid that was the primary Lucien settlement. Below them were spread the lesser buildings of Shekalla, the city over which the Hall of Elders towered. From this vantage, they could see past the great industrial zone, where all manner of consumer goods and industrial products were produced, past the shipyards where much of their space fleet was built, past the miles and miles of residential districts, with flowering trees and bathing gardens, to the edge of the city, where the agricultural district began. The layered green farms stretched to the visible horizon, lush with crops almost ready to be harvested. Below the top layer of these farms were underground hydroponic layers, where fish and vegetables were grown in an almost closed system, the unused portions of the vegetables being fed to the fish, and the bones of the fish being used to fertilize the vegetables.

Above it all was the canopy that stretched over the upper

surface of Galea and was anchored in encircling cliffs. The asteroid itself had once been bare metallic rock.

Looking up from the window, Adaiz could see through the canopy itself, out into deep space, populated with stars. Galea was almost at the edge of their star system, so far out from the sun that it appeared as little more than a bright star in the dark sky. To make up for this lack of a natural sun, the Lucien had created artificial suns, three bright balls powered by fusion. These small suns hung outside the canopy, evenly spaced along its breadth, and they moved slowly back and forth to create spaces of morning, afternoon, evening, and night.

As Adaiz looked up at the faint real sun of their star system, just visible between two of the artificial suns, he thought of Herrod and the human Plaguers far away, circling close to the warmth of that natural sun. He felt hatred welling within him, but he did not let the emotion gain a foothold. Hate was not useful. The Plaguers had made their choice millennia ago. Only barbarians would knowingly destroy an entire race. And now their fate was sealed.

There was a soft chime, and Adaiz and Enon turned to the officer, who was speaking again into his communicator. "Yes, sir," he said deferentially. "They are here."

He stood and beckoned them. "You will be seen now," he said.

Enon and Adaiz nodded, and followed him through the tall inner doors.

Within was a chamber with a glass ceiling that soared fifty feet above. The glass had darkened to mitigate the streaming light from the suns, and the chamber glowed with a muted brightness. The walls and floor were bronze. There was no rug, and nowhere to sit, save for three round daises, grouped in a tight knot in the middle of the room. These daises floated six feet above the floor, and perched on each was a robed figure, seated cross-legged and wearing the bronze headband of the Medium Triad rank. These Lucien had a tightening around their eyes and a dull cast to their skin which indicated their great age. Each of them held a shiny silver sphere in his left hand, another emblem of their rank.

Adaiz and his older brother approached, awed by this private audience with so august a group. Behind them the attending officer silently shut the doors.

The central member of the Triad spoke. "Leader Enon-Amet and Officer Adaiz-Ari, you are welcome to our chamber. Your superiors have spoken nothing but praise of your service to Clan Providence and the Lucien race."

The two of them bowed deeply in response to this high compliment.

"There is a matter of great import before us today," the center Lucien continued. "We have deliberated for many months and our minds are now clear. We have a course of action." His two companions flexed their remnant antlers almost imperceptibly in agreement. "You know well of our plans to dispose of the Plaguers. This plan continues on schedule. Indeed, the Council of One Hundred deliberated so long and so carefully on that plan that it is considered infallible. There is, however, a slight wrinkle.

"A clan member has turned treasonous and informed the Plaguers of our intentions. They know of the coming attack."

Enon's antlers pressed back along the sides of his silver scalp in an expression of surprise. Adaiz's human face mimicked this expression, which resulted in a drawing back of the muscles around his ears.

"We still do not know the reason our spy did this," the center Lucien continued. "Such a thing has never happened before. Still, the fact remains that the Plaguers know of our plans. Their response to this knowledge has been odd. Another of our spies informs us that in addition to building shelters deep underground and attempting to create space-based defense systems, they are mounting an unusual mission." The Triad member on the left reached forward to a small set of controls. On the wall behind the Triad, a map sprang up, projected by lasers. It was a star map, and on it Enon and Adaiz could see their own star system and another.

"They are sending a ship to this system, eight light-years away," the central Triad member said. "There they will retrieve a technology from their distant past." He continued to tell what little they knew of the Eschless Funnel. This little was nonetheless impressive. Current Lucien science did not even admit of the possibility that faster-than-light travel was possible. "If the Plaguers are convinced that this technology exists and are willing to spend their precious few resources to mount such a mission," he continued, "there must be some substance behind this improbable claim."

Enon and Adaiz stood silently, taking in the words of the Triad, trying to hide their own excitement.

"Considering this information, we now have two objectives to accomplish before our deadline arrives and we rid this universe of the Plaguers. First, if the technology behind the Eschless Funnel is valid, we must possess it for ourselves. Such technology would secure our future forever. It would open the door to Lucien rule of not just our star system but of the universe itself.

"Second, we must prevent the Plaguers from ever regaining this technology. With it, they could surely build weapons and ships that would allow them to defeat us, even in the limited time they have left.

"To achieve both of these objectives, we have selected you, Leader Enon-Amet and Officer Adaiz-Ari, for the honorable mission of following the Plaguer ship to its destination."

Adaiz felt his heart leap. What honor they would bring to their family, to their clan, and to their race. If this technology was real and they succeeded in capturing it, they would secure a future for the Lucien greater than any he had ever dreamed possible.

Three Years Ago

That audience with the Triad was now a decade and a half gone.

Now, removed from that day by both time and enormous spans of distance, Mission Officer Adaiz-Ari stood in the semidarkness of the cramped Lucien ship and watched the winking lights of the main control panel. All was well with the ship's systems, and beautiful Galea was light-years away.

He picked his way carefully around the perimeter of the tiny one-room craft, glancing at other control panels set into the smooth, curved metal walls. The controls were beautiful in their industrial simplicity: banks of readouts and small indicator lights, cased in metal plates, which were in turn cased in the metal of the walls.

He ran a hand over the bank that controlled the sleepboxes. The skin of his hand, he noticed, was now light brown, with a yellow undertone. So long away from sunlight, even if the time were spent in a sleepbox, was unhealthy. He ran his hand over his bare chest, noting that the skin there was faded and his ribs were beginning to show.

The air smelled stale. Adaiz rechecked the air filters and found them functioning properly. The ship air was reading in a normal, healthy range. He mused that a computer, however, could not appreciate the subtleties of taste inherent in a living organism. Simply because the air was breathable, one could not assume that the air was pleasant. Ah well, few missions were intended for this long a period.

He moved to the sleepboxes and looked in through the thick plastic at his older brother and crewmate Enon. The two of them woke by turns, twice a year. Six months ago it had been Enon who was awake, checking on the ship and on the sleeping form of Adaiz.

Adaiz was concerned with Enon's pallor as he watched his sleeping body within the box. His skin had become a dull gray, no longer reflective at all. He wondered about the long-term health effects of this journey on both of them. Certainly so many years spent in deepsleep were not beneficial. But it did not matter. The mission was their duty, and they were honored to carry it out, whatever the personal cost. Their own lives amounted to little. Their physical bodies and the decades of this mission were merely the passing of dust in space. There would be other lifetimes.

Ahead of them in the cold blackness of space, the Plaguer ship was barreling on toward its destination, and they were following. It would be only a few more years until they both arrived.

In a few hours Adaiz would return to his own sleepbox. Now, however, it was time to clear his mind and reaffirm his place in the scheme of the universe. He sat on the floor and crossed his legs.

From a pocket in his trousers, he pulled out a small book with a braided leather cover and filament-thin pages written upon in calligraphy. This was his copy of the Katalla-Oman, the Lucien book of self-knowledge. The Katalla-Oman had been handed down to their race in the distant past, it was said, by Omani himself, the god of wisdom and unity.

Adaiz gently flipped it open and read aloud his favorite chant. He had known it by heart since childhood, but the feel of the book in his hands and the timbre of his voice when he was reading aloud were pleasing.

I, Adaiz-Ari, of Warrior Clan and Clan Providence

Am awareness

Am light

Am a point of knowing

With closed eyes, I can yet see
Apart from body
Apart from the asteroids which are my home
Apart from sun and stars

The universe
It surrounds me
It passes through me
But still I am

Awareness

Light

A point of knowing

As he spoke the final words, he could feel their meaning. His body faded. The ship faded. He could feel himself as a point of awareness. Time did not matter, space did not matter. The whole of the universe was his. He existed. He knew. He was.

Chapter 4

One Year Ago

Harris Edward DeLacy III, or Eddie as he was known to everyone except lawyers, was doing sun salutations on a yoga mat in his bedroom. He relished the feeling of his muscles as he exercised. He worked hard to keep himself lean and strong with yoga, jogging, and occasional classes in martial arts. It was the only thing he worked hard at. It was the middle of the afternoon in Los Angeles, and there was bright sunlight streaming in from outside.

He could hear Callen in the bathroom, just getting out of the shower.

"Where are the extra towels?" she called, her voice carrying through the closed bathroom door.

Eddie was holding downward dog, the final position of the exercise. "In the cupboard under the sink!" he called back.

He held the position for five breaths, then came out of the stretch and sat down on the mat. Callen appeared with a towel wrapped around her. They had spent an hour together in bed, and she always took a shower after making love. Eddie would soon shower too, but for the moment he was savoring the feeling of his body after being with her. She slept with him so little these days. It was no longer like it had been in college, or even in high school, when they had drawn each other into brief, passionate affairs between other relationships. Eddie was afraid that she was finally outgrowing him.

"Come here," he said, taking her hand.

She complied willingly, settling into his lap and kissing him. He kissed her back for longer than she was expecting. She put her hands on his shoulders and withdrew from him.

"What are you doing?" she asked.

"What does it look like?"

"I have to go, Eddie." She stood up and started collecting her clothes. "We really should stop doing this."

"Why?"

"Because it's too easy to fall back into being together." She was pulling on her underwear. She was quite pretty. Though her body was perpetually ten pounds overweight, the weight did not look bad on her; it added to the curves of her chest and waist. Eddie had always loved her body and loved making love to her. "We both know we're not going to spend the rest of our lives together."

"We do?" But he knew it was true.

Eddie's father, Harris Edward DeLacy, Jr., was the chief executive of Bannon-DeLacy, the aerospace firm founded in 1912 by Harris Edward DeLacy, Sr., prescient engineer and businessman. Callen was Callen St. John, whose father was the chairman of Bannon-DeLacy. She and Eddie had grown up together, had shared each other's amazement that the families they had been born into were so different from the ones they would have imagined for themselves.

She pulled on her jeans and her shirt and looked around for her socks.

"They're on the chair," he said, smiling, because she always forgot where she left her clothes.

She didn't move to get them. Instead, she came back over to him and took a seat on the mat. "I do love you, Eddie."

"I love you too. You know that."

"Yeah." She slid her arms over his shoulders. "But it's not *that* kind of love, is it? You could be my brother."

He hugged her and shifted her body so she was lying down across his legs. She looked up at him. He had shaved that morning and his face was smooth. He had brown hair that was slightly curly, and it was unkempt just now, as it often was. He was good-looking, but she knew that he was careless about such things. He said, "Then I think what we did this afternoon is illegal in most states."

"You know what I mean. We're thirty-two now. I have to figure out what I'm doing with my life."

"You're outgrowing me," he said quietly, running a hand through her hair.

"Maybe," she agreed. She took hold of his chin between her thumb and forefinger and lightly shook his face. "It's just—I can never find the center of you, you know?"

"Yeah," he said. "I have that problem too."

She used his arm to pull herself up to a sitting position. "I really have to go. I have a meeting in twenty minutes." She worked for an advertising agency. Her brilliance as a writer went into ad campaigns to sell cars and soft drinks and feminine hygiene products. But she didn't seem to mind. She didn't need the money, but enjoyed her job and enjoyed Los Angeles. He admired that without understanding it.

He watched her get up and put her socks and shoes on. "Okay," he said, after a long pause.

"Okay, what?"

He put his hands on the mat behind him and leaned back into them. "Just okay."

She smiled at him, understanding. It was okay with him that she didn't want to sleep with him anymore. He was still her friend and would always be her friend. She nodded.

"I think I'll go back to Egypt," he said after a few moments. He said it just as though he were proposing a trip down the block to get a cup of coffee. It was his way. Everything was casual.

"Did your father reinstate your allowance?" she asked with a hint of mischievousness.

"I don't have to depend on him," Eddie said with mock pride. "My mother takes pity on me from time to time. Behind his back, she sends me money when she worries I might be starving. If she won't pay for a trip, I could always sell my car."

"Right. Who needs a car in L.A. anyway?"

He smiled at this, but he was already daydreaming about his trip. "I've always thought the center of me was somewhere over there."

"If there is a center of you." She was dressed now. She came over and kissed him on the forehead.

"That's all I get?" he said petulantly.

She patted him affectionately on the cheek. "Might as well start now." She glanced at her watch. "Good-bye, Eddie. Love you."

"Me too."

She walked out of the room and a moment later he heard the front door open and shut behind her. Then there was the engine of her car as it pulled out of his driveway and slowly faded away.

He sat where he was for a few moments, then he moved onto his knees and started his yoga routine again. He was thinking of Egypt.

Chapter 5

> In my vision I saw a storm-wind coming from the north,
> a vast cloud with flashes of fire and brilliant light about
> it; and within was a radiance like brass, glowing in the
> heart of the flames.
>
> —Ezekiel 1:4

The Engineer walked the brightly lit catwalk that encircled the
engine room below. He could look from this raised height
down into the central control space for the ship's great drives.
Down there were eight stations, each one manned at this moment, for the ship was preparing to shift phases.

He carried an opaque clipboard propped between his chest
and hand. He was marking on it with a stylus. This catwalk
was one of the observation points on his comprehensive
checklist. He wore a one-piece uniform of white material, with
a name tag on the breast which read simply "Engineer." It had
been their pact, on embarking, to give up the names of their
old life, and take new ones for this historic trip. Thus, each
member of the crew was called by whatever job he or she did.

On his chest, next to his name, was a stylized representation
of the ship's famous engine. The Engineer loved that picture.

Below were his junior engineers, each doing their own
checklists to ensure their areas of supervision were in perfect
operating order. The Second Engineer, or "Second" as he was

known, was busy disassembling a set of flow pipes. The Engineer watched Second's actions and smiled. The man was good.

He made a full circuit of the catwalk and then stepped over the side, into a heavy air chute that floated him down to the main floor. Here he examined the work in more detail. He stood over Second as the man carefully catalogued the state of each piece he removed, then set them all down into neat rows of crystalline parts on a sticky pad on the floor behind him, safely waiting to be reassembled.

"How's it going, Second?" the Engineer asked.

The man looked up only after noting down the piece in his hand and ensuring it was secured on the floor pad. "Very well, sir," the man replied. "Slight wear on a few parts, but well within our projections. You'll have my report within the hour."

"Excellent." He moved to the Third Engineer, and then the Regulator and the Powerhouse Controller, and the other four men. All reported the status of their areas. The Engineer made the proper notations on his clipboard, then launched himself back up onto the catwalk. From there, he stepped into a corridor beyond, leading him deeper into the ship.

He wore thin boots which made very little noise, even while walking over the slip-proof ridged surface of the hallway. He loved the silence of his tread. It allowed him to listen only to the ship. The noises of the ship itself were faint, but the Engineer's ear was tuned to every nuance. There was a steady hum, just below audible range, a hum he could feel in his teeth and bones. It was not jarring, only soothing. There was no rhythm to it, for its hum was too consistent. It was the sound, the Engineer thought, of pure power.

The ship was called the *Champion,* and she was his child. He did not invent the principles of her engine drives, that leap of engineering known as the Eschless Funnel. No, that incredible feat had been accomplished by another, by a man named Eschless, who had lived two generations before the Engineer's birth. But Eschless had only written the theory of such an engine. Not until now, not until this ship, had man ever put the theory into true application.

Before Eschless, the Kinley had believed that nothing could move faster than particles of light. Indeed, it had been proved again and again over centuries, that it was not possible to accelerate an object to light speed. Yet Eschless, like a few men before him in the history of their race, had unwound what was known, unraveled the universe, then tied it up again in a new shape. Of course, the beauty of it was that the shape was not new at all. It was the old shape, the shape the universe had always had, but none before Eschless had ever been able to see it that way.

And now, mere decades later, the Engineer was walking the corridors of the first Eschless Funnel ship, a ship he had designed and built. The secret lay in the probability drives, which sat at the ship's core. There was no more difficult field of mathematics to master than probabilities at the quantum level. It was a chaotic realm, where nothing was stationary and you could never know the specifics of anything with total precision. But that did not matter, it turned out. You did not have to know the exact location of an electron at a particular moment, nor its energy, nor its speed. You only had to know that all of these things fluctuated wildly and could be anywhere within an almost infinite range of numbers at any one time.

Such fluctuations could lead individual particles to hold vast amounts of energy for brief periods. Under ordinary circumstances, this energy was quickly relinquished, but this did not take away from the fact that, for a moment, the vast amount of energy was there.

This had been understood for centuries. But not until Eschless had anyone found a way to directly stimulate subatomic particles to high-energy states. Eschless's breakthrough was this: you excited the particles in a small region of space into achieving, simultaneously, quantum fluctuations toward the highest levels of energy. You then stole this energy and directed it—to an engine. Thus you reaped the moments of highest energy and let the universe itself worry about keeping the energy balance sheets in order. Behind this engine, as it moved through space, was a permanent eruption of new particles, forced into existence by the huge energy deficit left in the ship's wake. The new particles were "brought to life" to counteract the actions of the ship's drive. The engine that accomplished this was called the Eschless Funnel. It stimulated the fluctuations, funneled away the highest moments of energy, and then moved along its way.

That was where things got tricky, because the amount of energy created by such a system turned out to be nearly infinite, and infinity was an odd thing. When you built a ship based on the Eschless Funnel, it had a theoretically infinite capacity for motion. The universe, however, did not allow for infinites. So the ship, technically, was not moving through space in the classic fashion. It was moving in a parallel stream, the stream of the infinite, where traditional physical barriers did not apply. This stream was still within the physical universe, but it was like a small enclave, with a different government and different statutes. The speeds they could reach in this stream, while not infinite, were far greater than the speed of light.

All of this knowledge had gone into the *Champion,* the first such ship to carry people. The *Champion* was operating perfectly. They had been traveling at super-light speeds for three months. They were now close to their point of arrival, and the Engineer was preparing the *Champion* to shift phases and move back into the normal stream of space, back through the light barrier into relatively slow speeds.

The Engineer ducked down a side passage, which led at a downward slope to the machine room. The hum of the engines was louder here. Around him on all sides, just beyond the walls, were the guts of the ship's drive, the complicated city of coils and pipes and crystalline throughways, all working in harmony.

My ship is the naughty child who steals the cream off the top of the milk, the Engineer thought, *taking the very best for herself.* He couldn't have been more proud.

He emerged into the machine room. This room was like a great switchboard. Here many of the systems met and made energy exchanges. This was the transfer hub between the raw energy that propelled the engines and the tamer energy that was directed to various internal areas of the ship.

The man who tended this area was called the Mechanic, and he stood in front of the bank of readouts and manual override switches which were arrayed along the far wall of the room. The Mechanic had the gray skin and hair of Herrod's eastern provinces.

"Hello, Mechanic," the Engineer said as he moved into the room.

"Hello, sir," the Mechanic replied, not glancing at him, but keeping his eyes fixed on the readouts.

"Is your checklist complete?"

"Yes, sir. Here."

The Engineer examined the Mechanic's list, which clearly displayed that every item in the machine room had been carefully examined and tested. "Excellent," he said, a bit surprised the man had finished so quickly. He walked over to the bank of switches and began a spot check. It was just a matter of protocol, but after a few minutes he found something wrong. A set of valve switches were tight, indicating lack of use. He quickly checked the automated computer log and discovered that these switches had not been cycled for nearly three weeks. Any standard check would require cycling them several times to ensure they were functioning correctly.

"Mechanic, you marked these switches as complete. But they haven't been examined for weeks."

"Sir, I'm sure I did examine them. The fault must be with the computer."

"Mechanic, there is no fault with the computer. How could there be?" The Engineer was feeling bewildered. Why would this man falsely claim to have examined something when he hadn't? The safety of the entire crew depended on everything working perfectly. Was it merely laziness?

"Sir, I'm sure the switches are in working order."

"That's hardly the point, Mechanic." The Engineer unclipped a portable communicator from his belt and called into the engine room. "Engine Supervisor," he said into the device,

"I need you in the machine room. You're going to walk the Mechanic through his checklist from beginning to end."

"Sir, that's hardly—"

"Mechanic, wait here for the Engine Supervisor to arrive. I've got the rest of the ship to examine."

The Captain sat in a chair in his private ward room, scanning through the Engineer's reports.

The Engineer was leaning against the opposite wall, looking perturbed. His clipboard hung down by his side, clipped to his belt.

"Captain, he's just sloppy," the Engineer said.

"I'm sure it wasn't intentional," the Captain replied, his face still turned to his lap, where the reports were spread out, leaving the Engineer with a view of his short blond hair. That hair and his blue eyes had been famous back home. The Captain had earned the right to his current position after being decorated by the Combined Leaders of Herrod for establishing a self-sufficient scientific base in the asteroid belt around Herrod. He had been the perfect choice to head this historic mission, the first manned mission in an Eschless Funnel ship, the first interstellar voyage. They were heading for a planet called Earth, which was eight light-years distant from Herrod.

The Kinley had been studying their neighboring stars for a few generations. Their closest neighbor star was home to a planet named Rheat, on which they had discovered a race of tall, silver creatures called Lucien. The Lucien were, at the time the Kinley's probe arrived in orbit around their planet, engaged in all-out clan warfare. Considering them a dangerous race, the Kinley had left their probe in orbit to keep an eye on them but had decided emphatically against a manned trip to Rheat.

Instead, Herrod had sent small unmanned observation ships to Earth, the next-closest livable planet. To the amazement of the Kinley, they had discovered that Earth was home to humans. From pictures brought back by their probes, it appeared the Earth humans were nearly identical to the Kinley. This seemed to indicate that there had been a great, galaxy-wide seeding of the human race at some distant point in history. It was only natural to want to examine these humans and the cultures they had developed. They had immediately begun plans for a manned mission to Earth.

The crew of the *Champion* were scientists for the most part, and their goal was simply to study this new planet and its life-forms. It was a peaceful mission, and they planned for more to follow within four years. It was hoped that Earth would enable scientists of all disciplines to learn more about Herrod by comparing it to a smaller planet.

"It doesn't matter if it was intentional or not, Captain," the Engineer said. "The Mechanic's job is vital to the ship. Sloppiness can be fatal. He did a better job when the mission first started, but lately . . ."

"Aren't you blowing this a little out of proportion? It was a few switches. And as you said, they were in working order, even if he hadn't tested them."

"Captain, I don't want him on post."

The Captain could see that the Engineer was seriously annoyed. That was not good. The Engineer was possibly the single most valuable member of the crew, aside from the Captain himself. The Captain had recruited him for this mission because he was considered by many to be the most brilliant living scientist on Herrod. Aside from his understanding of the Eschless Funnel and related physics, he held over two hundred patents on other scientific techniques. The Engineer was a wealthy man back home, but he had been excited enough to cast his lot with this mission, even bringing along his wife, a renowned doctor.

The Captain knew the Mechanic had a way of irritating people, and he frequently found himself smoothing over such difficulties. The Mechanic was not a bad man, however, merely hard to deal with sometimes.

"He's been with me for years, Engineer. I'll talk to him. Don't worry. I'll make sure he understands and is more careful."

*   *   *

It was sometime later that the Captain called the Mechanic to his wardroom.

The man showed up within minutes, his gray face looking tired, his coveralls smeared here and there with grease.

"Mechanic." The Captain greeted him warmly and gestured for him to have a seat. There was tea in a pot and the Mechanic poured the Captain and himself a cup each.

The Captain had known the Mechanic since his earliest years in the space services on Herrod. The Mechanic had been in charge of the shuttle that ferried the Captain from Herrod to the asteroid belt during his years establishing a colony there, and he had served with the Captain on a dozen other missions. They were not exactly friends, for the Captain was certainly the senior of the two, but the Captain felt they were as close to being friends as two men in their relative positions could be.

"Oh, that's very good tea, Captain," the Mechanic said, leaning back in his chair and smiling as he sipped the hot, sweet liquid.

The Captain had brewed the drink himself. Making the perfect pot of tea was one of his special talents, something he never relegated to an assistant, and the Mechanic's compliment pleased him.

"Tell me about the crew, Mechanic," the Captain said after he had breathed in the aroma of the tea and taken several sips from his own cup. "What's the general tone as we approach deceleration?"

"Good, I think, Captain. There is nervousness, of course, for who really knows what it will be like when we land? But they will follow your lead. They look to you to learn what their own reactions should be. They trust you."

"Good, because I'm nothing but excited."

"Then they'll be excited," the Mechanic said. "Especially when these damned checklists are done and we are allowed to get on with our jobs."

"I heard you had a bit of an incident with the Engineer."

"We're all chafing a bit under his minute examinations, Captain. What can you expect?"

"Was there some problem with your station?"

"No, no. Everything's in working order. But the Engineer has to find something he can order to be fixed. Otherwise he wouldn't feel it was his mission."

The Captain smiled slightly at this. It was true, the Engineer had a proprietary—some might even say arrogant—attitude toward both the ship and the mission. "At any rate, the inspections will be done soon."

"May the mother be blessed for that," the Mechanic said, raising his glass and downing the remainder of his tea.

"Until then, you should be more careful."

"Atmosphere entry in five minutes, twenty-four seconds," the Engineer called out to the bridge at large. "Captain, I am taking the pilot chair."

"Yes," the Captain said, watching the projections in front of him on a foldout screen. He could see their approach line through Earth's atmosphere.

The Engineer slipped into the low booth positioned at the front end of the *Champion*'s bridge. The booth had sat unused, except for weekly inspections, since initial takeoff months earlier. Inside was a chair and an array of controls that differed from others in the surrounding room. This was the chair for piloting the ship through atmosphere.

They had made the shift back into sub-light speeds without incident. For the past two weeks they had been decelerating as they neared their target. They had now been circling Earth for a full day, and had chosen their landing site, within easy reach of the first civilization they would study. There was nothing left to do but land.

The Engineer strapped himself into the chair, and slid his arms into the control mechanisms, which wrapped around his forearms and had a lever for each of his fingers.

"Atmosphere shields, Engineer," the Captain said.

"Yes, sir." The Engineer's left arm moved, sliding the shield lock into place. There was a faint vibration as the shields closed over the entire front portion of the ship, making it aerodynamic for its descent to the planet below.

In a moment, the whole ship began to vibrate. It was a shock after months of perfectly smooth motion, but the crew was prepared; on the bridge and throughout they were strapped into landing chairs.

The Engineer's fingers and arms were manipulating the controls, guiding the ship through the window he saw projected before him, guiding it to a safe trajectory through the upper layers of atmosphere and then onto a dwindling heading that would take them to their target landing area.

"Stratosphere cleared," the Engineer said softly, his quiet voice being carried directly to the Captain's ear, just as the Captain's was to his.

"Stratosphere cleared," the Captain repeated.

The shaking abated as the ship adjusted to its new medium and began to brake.

"Course set and locked, Captain," the Engineer said.

The ship made a long, long, falling arc through the atmosphere for several hours, until, as they approached their destination, they were only a few miles from the surface.

As the ship entered the final stage of flight, its engines released a great blast of heat and light, diffusing the excess energy still left over from the Eschless Funnel drives.

On the ground below, city dwellers, farmers, artisans, noblemen, and servants living along the Nile River turned their eyes to the sky and caught a glimpse of a large metallic bird with a tail like fire and a cry like thunder splitting the heavens.

The survey crew had arrived.

Chapter 6

One Year Ago

The last curtain of gray rolled back, and Pruit opened her eyes in the biofluid of her crib. She was awake again. And this was year seventeen.

She brought her eyes into focus as the biofluid began to drain. Niks was not sitting over the crib. This should have been surprising, but in her barely conscious state all Pruit felt was a sense of relief. He had reverted to regulation waking protocol, she assumed. He was lying in his own crib and waking simultaneously with her. The life systems monitoring computer was controlling the cribs automatically, just as it should. But why now? she wondered, as full consciousness began to return. Why now after seventeen wakes?

The plantglass slid back and the colder air of the ship washed over her. The crib's arms withdrew into the wombwalls.

Pruit grasped the top of the crib with her hands and pulled herself to a sitting position. She expected to find Niks emerging from his crib at the same moment, his hair dark and wet from the biofluid, his face weak but smiling. Instead, she found herself staring at the closed top of his crib.

No. She saw after a few moments that it was not completely closed. The plantglass was slightly ajar.

She felt a surge of panic. Her mind cleared of sleep and her eyes whipped to the manual controls above Niks's crib. There were four blue lights glowing on the panel. Blue meant danger. Or malfunction.

Pruit hauled herself to her feet. The final bloodarms, snaking out of the veins of her legs, snapped out of her skin and recoiled against the wombwall with her sudden motion. She steadied herself against light-headedness, then swung out of the crib and reached for the controls.

She hit the button to retract his glass. The glass did not move. She pushed the button again, holding it in to reset its function. Slowly the plantglass slid back.

Pruit stared into the crib. Inside was a shell, a husk. Where Niks's body should have been lying, encased in biofluid and nurtured by the crib's arms, there was a dry crib, and resting within it a desiccated human form.

Pruit's legs gave out beneath her, and she fell onto the edge of his crib.

"Blessed Life!" she breathed. "Niks . . ."

For it was Niks, without doubt. She touched him. His face, despite its contorted appearance, was recognizable. His body was as dry as a reed, thin and tiny, all fluid gone, all life gone. One arm was out of place, as though Niks had reached up toward the plantglass, tried to pry it open.

Before Pruit could control her body, she was turning her head aside, and a wave of nausea hit. She retched and threw up the biofluid left in her stomach.

"Central, wake!" she yelled.

"I'm here."

"Central, Niks is . . . Review his crib data!"

"The life systems computer has not given the data to Central yet."

Pruit clenched her teeth in frustration. The life systems computer was an autonomous subsection of the Central computer system. It had been designed that way so a malfunction in the overall ship would not necessarily impact the health of the crew.

"Central, override! Tell me what happened."

There was a brief pause, and then Central spoke. The computer's voice, usually blandly pleasant, had dropped to a quiet, firm tone. The voice programming would only do that in situations where the data it had to impart, based on the instructions of its programmers, was judged to have potential emotional impact on the crew.

"Pruit, Niks's crib reports that Niks is no longer alive."

Pruit's head was in her hands, and she was looking down at the dried body in the crib. Her eyes were burning.

"I know that, Central," she said quietly. "Tell me why."

"It happened ten months and fifteen days ago," Central said, reviewing the data. "It was not a malfunction in the crib."

"Then what?"

"It appears Niks left his skinsuit on when he entered stasis."

"Saving Father . . . ," she whispered.

She and Niks were both fitted with skinsuits, a web of cells that lived in the upper layers of their skin and could retreat back into their bodies, or rise to the surface to provide an additional layer of "skin" as needed to protect them from microorganisms in strange environments.

They activated their skinsuits as a matter of course upon waking, to protect themselves from any radiation or stray organisms in the ship. They had to be deactivated prior to stasis, however, for they would, by their very nature, repel the advances of the crib and treat the bioarms as a threat. Since their earliest training for this mission, they had drilled the simple procedure for deactivating the suit before stasis. It should have been second nature to Niks.

She could imagine what had happened. The crib had tried to activate. Niks's skinsuit had repelled it. The crib had continued its standard functions and begun to assume control of Niks's body. This would have caused the skinsuit to draw more heavily on the resources in his body to put up greater resistance, acting on the erroneous assumption that his body was under heavy attack. Ultimately, the skinsuit would have drained him in a misguided effort to save him. As the scenario played out in her head, Pruit felt a great surge of impotent frustration. After all their worries about the hazards of the stasis cribs, Niks had been killed not by his crib at all, but by his skinsuit, a mechanism designed solely to enhance his life.

Niks must have realized that something was wrong as he was falling into sleep. He had tried to pry open the plantglass, but by then he must have been half in stasis, with his body half-dead. It had been too late. Those who had designed the ship could not have anticipated every possible crew error.

Pruit pushed the heels of her hands into her eyes, trying to wipe out the thought of Niks struggling in the biofluid. She couldn't avoid the image. She pushed herself away from the crib and stood up.

"Central, take control of the life systems computer," she ordered. "Fill Niks's crib with biofluid."

"May I ask why?" Central said, still using the quiet tone.

"I want all ship life systems resources used. We are going to regenerate him."

There was a long pause as Central scanned through its vast databanks of programming instructions, looking for an appropriate response to this irrational request. After several long moments, the computer spoke:

"Pruit, that is not possible."

"It is possible!" she yelled, looking down at the remains of Niks. "Fill the crib!"

At her command, biofluid poured into the crib. Niks's body was so light it began to float. Pruit's stomach turned again and she averted her eyes. That was Niks in there, that was him, hollow and dry . . .

"Pruit, what you ask is not possible," Central said slowly and clearly. "We have no such resources on this ship. It is doubtful such resources exist even on Herrod."

Pruit did not respond. If only she could shut his crib, go back to sleep and wake in a year to find that none of this had happened. She stared at a corner of the tank, watching it fill, avoiding the sight of the floating husk within.

She knew that Central was right. Niks was gone. He had died ten months ago, from a stupid mistake, a mistake that was easily avoidable. And it was her fault. If she had insisted on following their sleep protocol, they would have caught his error before it was too late. She had been flattered by his code breaks, and that had cost him his life. She sank down to the floor and began to cry.

Several hours later, Pruit had dressed herself. She was not wearing her coveralls. She had put on her dress uniform, a slim red jacket and tan pants, silver braid twisted around either arm as a sign of her rank, and several medals ranged on a vertical band along her upper sleeve.

Niks was wrapped in a blanket in her arms. He weighed almost nothing. She stood in front of the sentient tank, the large dark box situated at one end of the ship that had sat unused until now.

"Central," she said, "fill the tank so the ship can reclaim the body."

The door of the tank sat at waist level, and it slid open to reveal a long, flat tray, large enough to hold two adult humans lying side by side, and about nine inches deep. The tray was filling with biofluid.

Pruit pulled out the tray and carefully set Niks's blanketed body upon it. Then she touched the panel and watched the tray retract and the door slide shut. The tank would break down the body and reclaim the chemicals into the ship's life system.

"Central, open log."

"The log is ready for your entry." The voice was still gentle and Pruit hated the computer for knowing she was vulnerable.

She stared at the tank. That was not Niks inside. Niks, the spirit, the man, had left his body here ten months ago. Where was he now? Had he returned to their home on Herrod? Was he already a child in his next life, thinking of her, wondering about her?

"I, Sentinel Defender Pruit Pax of Senetian, report the death of my shipmate, Sentinel Defender Niks Arras of Telivein. I am assuming command of this mission. Central, please post time and date. Close log," she said quietly.

Her hand was touching the tank, and she imagined that she was touching him. Clasped within her hand was the small crystal that had hung around his neck. She wore an identical crystal around her own. The crystals were ancient. They had been a parting gift from the commanders of the Sentinel. They were small, no longer than her little finger, and of similar girth. They were of a clear orange cast, with two blue data bands. They were both partially damaged, with cracks here and there from being crushed at some point in their history. But with an ancient crystal reader, parts of the data they held were still decipherable. They contained several poems.

Her favorite ran thus:

> *Yea for we are the conquerors*
> *And all that is lies before us*
> *A black domain of stars*
> *And we the brightest lights within it*

She loved that poem. It expressed the naive, exuberant sense of destiny of those ancient Kinley who were reaching for the stars. It was a simple, beautiful, and proud view of the universe and the Kinley place within it. Such childlike certainty of place could have only occurred before the Great War, before they were pounded to near oblivion. She and Niks had shared that poem with each other, had taken it as their personal mantra. It reminded them both of what their race could be, and tied Pruit even more strongly to the heart of herself that said to the Lucien, "You won't win."

Now the meaning of the poem seemed hollow without him by her side to share it. She crushed the hard surface of the crystal into her palm as she leaned against the tank.

Niks. She remembered their first kiss, years before. They had been standing in the park with the light of late afternoon trickling in through the city dome. Their lips had touched, and it had been right. She had loved him immediately. She had always loved him. Her mate. Her partner for life.

She knew she should say good-bye. She should open her mouth and tell Niks good-bye. But she could not. She was thinking of the way he liked to kiss her belly button, of his hands when they touched her, of his face. She was thinking of the intimate moments they had shared in their years together.

She found that her head was against the tank and she was crying. His body was probably dissolved by now. There would be no trace of him, just a blanket floating in the biofluid. After another year of sleep she would be at their destination. Their whole mission lay ahead, and she was alone.

She moved to a putty control pad and found herself accessing Central's speech controls. Almost in a trance she commanded the computer to assume Niks's voice. Central had hundreds of hours of records of them speaking and it was a simple matter to execute her command.

"Central?" she asked tentatively after withdrawing her hand from the controls.

"Yes?"

Pruit's heart jumped, because it was Niks's voice coming from the walls. Some objective part within her recognized that she was not thinking rationally. It did not matter to her at this moment; she wanted to hear him, to speak with him, to know that she was not by herself.

"Niks," she said, "I don't know how I'm going to do this without you."

"I—"

"Just let me talk, Central," she said quietly.

Central fell silent.

Pruit took a deep breath. "I'm not sure I know how to live if you're gone," she whispered, embarrassed that she was speaking to the computer, but somehow still comforted. Even as she spoke the words aloud, she knew that they weren't true. Without Niks she could not see herself being happy, for he was the one who had taught her happiness. But that did not alter the purpose of her life. There had been a core of steel in her since she joined the Sentinel.

Her hand strayed to her arm and her fingers moved over the medals pinned there. There were several for space missions she had flown prior to this one, most with the purpose of locating precious metals from asteroids. One medal was for finding a potential breach of the main city dome before a leak could occur. Her vigilance had saved thousands from radiation exposure. Her fingers moved to the topmost medal. This was a Star of Valor, for tracking down that Lucien spy.

She felt the grief of Niks's death, but she knew this would not incapacitate her. The grief was real, but her determination was stronger. She would give her whole life to fight for her people's survival. She thought of the words of their poem, and she knew her own heart.

"Pruit . . ." It was Central, with Niks's voice.

"I know," she said. "I don't mean it. I can live. There is a chance for us, and I will take it. Even alone."

Chapter 7

Present Day

"Africa. Egypt, Libya, Tunisia, Algeria, Morocco, Mauritania . . ." Pruit recited the names as she jogged. The treadmill faced a large screen which displayed a map of the planet Earth.

Her ship was in orbit around the fifth planet of the system, a gas giant named Jupiter by the inhabitants of the third planet, Earth, her target.

She had reached her target star system and come out of stasis six months ago. Her mission was now in its second phase. From one of the control stations at the middle of the ship she could hear the alternate crackle and blare of the frequencies Central was monitoring. Earth had fared reasonably well in the last five millennia. The planet was in a slightly more developed state than would have been ideal for Pruit's mission, but the availability of fast transportation technology would be helpful.

She was allowed to make no transmission to Earth until her body was in shape and she had learned the languages she would need for the remainder of her mission. She had selected two languages: English because it was the dominant language of the planet as a whole, and Arabic, because it was the dominant language of her target area.

With the help of Central's language-learning facilities, she had achieved a good fluency in both over the past months. The languages had no common root and entirely different alpha-

bets, so this had been no easy task. But Pruit had honed her
language skills on Herrod, where the soldiers in the Sentinel
learned up to five ancient Kinley languages as training. These
languages, dead for thousands of years, with odd syntax and
varied pronunciation, were used by Kinley to speak in codes
that the Lucien who barricaded had difficulty breaking.

English and Arabic had unique personalities; though Arabic
struck Pruit as the more sensitive and civilized of the two,
English was the more expressive.

She checked her heart rate and distance, and saw that it was
time to cool down.

"Screen off," she said, and the screen went blank, the fibers
that made up its surface returning to their neutral smoothness
and light tan color. The screen retracted into the wall at her
side.

She grabbed a towel, sat on the exercise mats nearby, and
began the cooling stretch routine.

There was a jump in volume from the control station. Central was scanning up and down on Earth's broadcast frequencies, looking for an ancient beacon that did not seem to exist
any longer or, if it did, was drowned out by the cacophony of
transmissions from the rest of the planet.

She waited to see if Central would comment on the abrupt
noise, but the computer remained silent. Nothing new to report. Probably an entertainment program starting its broadcast.
This world Earth was inundated with entertainment programs.
Having few real worries of their own, in Pruit's view, the natives delighted in make-believe ones.

Earth was an interesting world in terms of natural resources.
In addition to huge bodies of water, it appeared to have an almost unlimited supply of metals. Herrod was the opposite. It
had almost no naturally occurring metal ores. Metals existed
on the atomic level, bound up with other substances, but copper, gold, silver, tin, aluminum, and their ilk were virtually
nonexistent in their naturally extractable forms. As a result, the
Kinley civilization had matured without metals to mark their
development. There was no iron age or bronze age in their his-

tory. The result of this was a science based almost exclusively in organic compounds and biological material.

As Pruit spread her legs out to either side and laid her chest on the floor, she was aware of the pleasure of having her body fit again. She had been so drained upon waking the final time, that it had taken her a full six months to regain muscle tone and strength. She had achieved them at last and her muscles were now long and lean, her skin healthy and less ashen. Her hair had even regained much of its former shine. She was physically ready to begin the next phase of the mission.

When her stretches were finished, she performed a brief fight routine, landing kicks and punches into a heavy target dummy. Then she showered and changed into her coveralls. She took a seat at the medical station, and slipped the medical reader around her wrist.

"Central, please confirm my medical check. I'm ready to move the mission into the third phase."

There was a pause as the computer examined her readings.

"You're ready, Pru," the computer agreed. It was still using Niks's voice, and it had developed his patterns of speech more and more since her final waking. Pruit supposed the computer was continually drawing on recorded conversations between Niks and her. Central even altered its voice tone based on Pruit's attitude, much the way Niks would have done.

"Good," she answered, peeling the reader off her wrist. She felt the glow of anticipation pushing out the sadness that had lately occupied her mind. "Let's get to work."

She slid into a chair in front of the primary control station and pulled down three books from a shelf on her left. The first was her mission Master Book of contingencies. She opened it and flipped to the current page. It read:

> Using reference material 20.-c, transmit to beacon location.

She opened her reference book and confirmed the transmission frequency and target location. She had rehearsed this a dozen times in the last six months, and already knew that she would be targeting an area on the Nile River, but she went through the motions of confirmation nonetheless.

She opened the third book, the book of background materials, and flipped to the page marked "Final Transmission from Survey Crew." On this page was a copy of that final ancient transmission. Written in the script of a long-dead language was the information she needed: the frequency and code words she must use: "Rescue has arrived." In addition, there were several entry combinations she would need later.

She sank her hand in the putty control pad and entered the frequency and the code words into the ship's computer.

"Central, I'm ready to send transmission."

"Acknowledged, Pruit."

She moved her hand and executed the transmission. She was sending her message in a single, compressed nanosecond to avoid detection by anyone on Earth. If the beacon set up by those long dead members of the Kinley survey team was still there, was still operable, her message should provoke a reply.

The chances were slim, but she had her contingencies. If this did not work, she would move to the next plan on her list and begin a search for the beacon on the ground. She wondered how long they had lasted, those survey crew members who had entered stasis. Had they slept fifty years? A hundred? Two hundred? Did they die quickly in the first few years, or did they live a long time and eventually give up hope and rejoin the world around them? Could a beacon survive so long? Doubtful.

An hour passed, ample time for the signal to reach Earth and a reply to be sent. None came.

"Central, re-send every hour and continue monitoring all traffic."

"I will," the computer responded in Niks's voice. But the response was far more patient than Niks ever would have been.

Pruit looked again at the final transmission from the survey crew. It was a last desperate plea from six people who wanted to return home:

... in stasis we await your return. Do not forget us ...

There was no way they could have known how little of their home was left when they sent that message. They had planned to go to sleep for a few years, but Herrod itself had almost gone to sleep forever.

Chapter 8

2606 B.C.
Year 1 of Kinley Earth Survey

> Then the earth shook and quaked; and the foundations of
> the mountains were trembling and were shaken, because
> He was angry.
>
> —Psalms 18:7

"Mother's Love, it's murderously hot today," the Captain
breathed as he wiped his forehead with a handkerchief.

He sat on a litter which swayed rhythmically as the litter
bearers beneath it jogged across the low, rolling hills of sand
and dirt which separated the survey team camp from the cities
along the great Nile River. There was a canopy stretched over
the litter, so he was sitting in shade, but the heat of the air itself was stifling.

The litter bearers were all lean young men, their bodies perfectly muscled. They wore only a small strip of material
around their waists, which was tied in front. The two ends of
the material hung down over their genitals, providing only the
slightest amount of covering. They did not mind. Nudity was
not something the natives here found embarrassing. In such a
warm climate, clothes were often a hindrance to work, and
many in the worker class did without them entirely.

The litter bearers were sweating profusely, but they were
used to their task and kept up their steady pace.

The Captain's wife, the Archaeologist, sat in a litter to his left. She too was mopping her brow. He glanced at her pro-file—fine features with long blond hair tied up behind her head. He had always thought she was beautiful, but now as he looked at her he thought perhaps stately was a better word.

On the other side of the Captain, the Mechanic sat in his own litter. The Captain could tell that the man secretly reveled in being carried by others. He was fanning himself with a palm leaf.

Behind the litters ran ten workers, each carrying a small sack full of the medicinals they would be using to tend to the citizens of Memphis. Behind them were three water bearers who periodically brought ladles of water to the others.

The Archaeologist had many qualifications for being on this mission, aside from being the Captain's wife. She had spent her professional career in digs all over Herrod, where she had studied dozens of ancient cultures. Her specialty was the evo-lution of government in society and its relationship to religion.

The Captain had always been proud of finding a wife so comparable to himself. They had been together for over twenty years. Their one child, a son, was with them on this mission.

This was to be their first visit to Memphis, capital city of the Egyptian empire. The Archaeologist had been studying the culture from afar to prepare them for this day. They had many local workers at their camp, which sat in the desert between the Nile and the Red Sea. By carefully questioning these workers over the past three months, she had developed a very good idea about how Egypt was organized. She was briefing her traveling companions a final time as they approached the city.

"Egypt is an interesting place," she said. "The kingdom stretches over hundreds of miles along the banks of the river. Because of the great distances between the cities, there is a tight-knit bureaucracy in place to ensure things are run prop-erly.

"The king is the intermediary between his people and their many gods. And there are many gods. Every town or village has its own, and these are lorded over by the higher, more powerful deities. It's pretty typical, as societies progress, for the local gods to be subsumed within the personalities of the larger gods, until ultimately there are only a few left, each with dozens of aspects. Egypt is in the early stages of this.

"The people are quite superstitious, which is normal for this stage of development. Their science is rather crude. They still have not figured out the wheel, for example. Nature is unexplainable in many ways, so they create gods to explain it.

"Because the kingdom is so large, it will be important for the king to categorize us. We must strike just the right tone. We want to show that we are powerful, so he does not threaten us, but we don't want to appear too powerful, or we might soon be deified, and then we will have entirely disrupted their religion."

The litter bearers slowed now. They had come up over a rise and were passing through the villages that lay outside the walls of Memphis. These villages were groupings of small houses, lined along the sides of the canals that ran out from the river. The houses were all of mud bricks, made from a mixture of riverbank mud and straw which was left to bake in the sun. The mortar to hold the bricks together was a combination of mud, straw, and sand which was usually smeared over the entire surface of the walls to make them smooth and weather-resistant.

There were windows facing north, to let in the cool breezes that came from that direction. There were gardens behind walls, where the tops of trees were visible. Trees were considered highly valuable in this desert land.

Men, women, and children walked along the dirt streets, which were packed as hard as rock on the main throughways. The Captain could see women and men washing clothes and gathering water in the canals. They were a dark-skinned people, with dark hair, most naked from the waist up.

Children stopped and pointed as the three litters passed through. They chattered wildly to each other as they watched the fair-complexioned people being borne past. News of their ship's arrival in Egypt had spread quickly through these villages and through the cities, and it was known, or at least rumored, that these golden-haired people were the ones who had come from the sky. This was impressive, but within the context of the Egyptian worldview, not outrageous or unbelievable.

Upon the survey team's arrival in the desert, King Snefru, ruler of all Egypt, had sent an emissary with armed escort to their camp. The Captain had explained to the emissary that their mission was entirely peaceful, and they wished only to observe local culture. In exchange he had offered to share his team's medical knowledge with the king and his people. As a token of friendship, the Captain had asked the Doctor to prepare a small medicinal kit for use by the king's own physicians, and he had invited the physicians to come to camp and be trained in the use of the kit.

The king had sent back a reply indicating that the visitors were welcome to stay in his kingdom as long as their intentions remained peaceful and as long as they attempted no influence of a political nature. He thanked the Captain for his gift, but did not send his physicians for the training.

He's waiting to be convinced of our competence, the Captain mused. *And, as my wife says, he wants to categorize us. Are we a threat?*

With the king's approval, they had begun to treat the locals in a minor way, first gaining the trust of those who made the twenty-mile trek to the camp in hope of being healed. Many of those had stayed to work in the camp, finding the survey team both friendly and generous.

Today would be their first foray into the city to treat the population there. The Captain had now fully realized the value of their medical knowledge. Every human had ailments. By curing them, the survey team immediately became treasured friends. The king, by messenger, had given his permission for this day's outing, and the Captain was determined to make the best of it. It was his hope to be granted free access to all Egyptian cities for his entire team. This would allow them to quickly catalog Egyptian society, and then they would be free to move on to one of the other Earth cultures.

The Doctor herself should have been on this expedition, but two of the local women working at camp had gone into labor that morning, and with the high infant mortality rate in this land, she had preferred to stay and deliver the babies. The Captain and the Archaeologist had sufficient medical training to address the local ills, and the Captain had brought along the Mechanic as a helper.

"How do we strike the right tone?" he asked his wife.

"We do a good job, we cure people, and we show deference toward the king and his family. To other high officials we adopt an attitude of friend. Thus we make the king feel important, but establish ourselves a senior to any of his underlings."

"Very good. Look there."

The three of them looked up and saw the encircling wall of Memphis coming into view. It was a tall mud-brick structure, and even from this distance, they could see the great open doors leading into the city.

They were now joining other traffic heading for Memphis. There were men driving donkeys laden with produce, teams of oxen pulling sledges loaded with bags of seed or flax or small cages full of geese. A few young men with military bearing, dressed in the short linen skirts of the upper classes, walked briskly toward Memphis, perhaps heading back to their army battalion at the end of a furlough.

The Captain found his eyes wandering to the shapes of the young women. Most wore thin, snug dresses which left their breasts bare. With their hardworking lives, they stayed trim and healthy, and the Captain found them beautiful.

Within half an hour, they had reached the city. The gates, which were twenty feet high and thirty feet wide, were flung open for the day, but would be closed at sunset. Ten guards were posted at the sides of the gateway. They were tall young men, with short linen skirts bordered in green, the color of their army division. They carried long spears and small oblong shields made of tough leather. Their dark hair was shoulder length, and combed back from the forehead.

They saluted by bringing their fists to their chests as the Captain's entourage passed through the gates. It was a sign that the king welcomed them.

They passed into the city, and the change in atmosphere was immediate. Here was a cultural center. There were buildings and private houses lining the street, many in tight rows of abutting structures. Wood was in use as well as mud brick. In the more well-to-do houses, there was a wide gap between the roof and the top of the walls. Through this gap came breezes to keep the interior cool.

There was a smell of human waste, for there was no sewage system in Egypt. Instead, families were forced to collect their waste and carry it outside the city walls, where it was dumped into an ever-increasing pile. Much waste was dumped into the river as well. Thus infection was rampant among the lower classes, for though the Egyptians were a clean people, and fond of bathing, their water supply was polluted.

As they made their way down wide streets, the Captain caught a glimpse of the king's palace atop a hill at the very center of the city. It too was mud brick and wood, for the Egyptians only used stone for temples or tombs. The palace was an impressive complex of structures nonetheless. From the Captain's vantage, he could see several graceful buildings of three stories set in an enormous garden of flowering trees.

"Look there, darling," he said to his wife, and she followed his gaze.

"It's beautiful."

There were crowds forming around them, people pointing and gossiping. It was clear their reputation had preceded them. The people here were more sophisticated. Most wore wigs of false hair, elaborately coifed into tiny curls or long, straight tresses with decorative hairpins. The children wore their hair in a sidelock, a single long lock on the right side of their heads, with the rest of the head shaved. Many of the women had fine linen dresses, some with rich dyed colors. There was jewelry on almost everyone who could afford it, much of it featuring designs in colored stone.

As the Captain's entourage made its way to the market square, it pulled a crowd of city folk with it. They would have an enormous audience today.

At last they reached the square, and their litter bearers deposited them on a stone dais in the corner. Here the workers who had followed the litters from camp carefully unloaded their burdens. The Captain instructed his three water bearers to ladle out generous portions to the men.

The Archaeologist busied herself setting up the jars of medicinals on wooden crates along the front end of the dais, and she began instructing the Mechanic in how to prepare some of the more common poultices they would use. Inside the city walls, the heat was even more oppressive, and the Captain took a long drink of water as he surveyed the market square.

Mud-brick market stalls covered an area of over two acres, the proprietors within selling everything from produce to wool to cosmetics to livestock. The square had four ornate wooden gates leading into it and on all sides was bordered by large, well-kept houses. This was a desirable neighborhood.

The morning market rush was over, but there were still a few hundred customers browsing the stalls and haggling over goods. These customers were now being overwhelmed by the hundreds of people who had followed the Captain through the streets. A long line of prospective patients was already forming in the midst of the crowd.

"Are you ready, dear?" he asked his wife as she set up the last of the medicinal pots.

"Yes, we're set."

The Captain turned and spoke to his workers, addressing them through a translator that enabled him to carry on natural conversations in the local tongue. The translator was a small, flat strip that wrapped around the user's ear and down along the jawline to his chin. Inside was a computer with advanced language programming. If the translator was exposed to a language for a sufficient amount of time, it would begin to translate from Haight, the language he and the rest of the survey team spoke, into the local language. It drew power from the kinetic energy of its user. "Organize the line, and show people up to us one at a time."

The chief worker nodded, not in the least bit fazed by the fact that the Captain's voice and mouth motions were out of synch. After all, he had been working at the camp of the sky visitors for over a month. Miracles were commonplace.

Under the direction of the Captain's men, the crowds stood back, and the line of patients was left with a clear path to the dais. The first patient was ushered up the three stone steps to the top of the platform. He was a middle-aged man, his natural gray hair sticking out beneath his dark black wig of tight curls. His face was lined and he had lost several teeth. He gestured to his shoulder. On inspection, the Archaeologist found that there was a sharp splinter of wood lodged deep under the skin. There was an angry wound around the splinter. The Archaeologist tended to him herself, numbing the area with a poultice that combined some of the medical supplies from their ship with local herbs, then carefully cutting in and removing the splinter.

The Captain moved on to the next patient. This was a grandmother, and her complaint was indigestion. The Captain asked her to catalog her symptoms very carefully, then he looked through a set of medical crystals laid out on a table behind them. He slipped one into a crystal reader and scanned through the data bands. Using the search index on the crystal, he made a diagnosis, and concocted the woman a small vial of medicine to be taken over the next week. She took it from him and bowed gratefully.

It continued this way for some hours. The Mechanic helped them with the mixtures, and occasionally supplemented the Captain's strength when they had to set bones. Many of the complaints were dental. The Doctor had explained to them that tooth decay was one of the banes of this society. The stones they used in their mills left hard particles in the flour, which eventually wore down the teeth of even the most healthy citizens.

They had no resources to replace teeth, so they had to settle for removing infected ones and giving their patients hard balls of painkiller and disinfectant which they could chew to ease the ache and promote healing.

It was tending to one of these toothache cases that the Captain found himself pressed up against a young woman with bare breasts, as he peered into her jaw. Despite her troublesome tooth, her breath was sweet, as though she'd been chewing mint leaves, and her body was pleasantly curved. He was forced to stand close to her to reach the infected tooth, and one of her breasts was pressed up against his chest. He felt his body's response to this touch, and he looked up for a moment, to find the Mechanic looking at him.

When at last they had removed the tooth and sent the girl on her way, sucking on her painkiller, the Mechanic whispered, "You're such a loyal old dog, I bet you didn't even remember what a young breast felt like." The Captain smiled without commenting.

Some time later, when the sun had already begun to go down in the west, there was a commotion near one gate of the square. Looking up from the tasks at hand, the Captain, Archaeologist, and Mechanic saw a large procession entering the marketplace. A way was being cleared through the onlookers near the north gate. A murmur was running through the crowds. The Captain caught some of it: "It is He? Truly?" "The Blessed One comes . . ." ". . . the king himself is here . . ."

The Captain covered his translator so he could speak in privacy, and said to his wife, "The king. That's what they're saying. He's coming."

"Remember what I said. We'll show him deference, but make it clear that we are powerful and unafraid."

The Captain nodded and glanced around. He had a gun at his waist, and so did his two companions. There were additional sidearms in one of the crates they had brought from camp. Against spears and arrows they would have a distinct advantage. But the important thing was not to need weapons. Surely the king was only coming to observe the miracles of healing.

They quickly finished the patients they were tending to, then watched as the royal procession made its way through the crowds. At the front were twenty soldiers, whose kilts were trimmed in gold, and who wore matching gold necklaces. These wielded long switches, which they used to force people out of the way.

Behind them came three dignitaries of the court, men who wore short linen skirts, over which their burgeoning paunches hung slightly, and heavily jeweled necklaces. Each wore a light cloak over his upper body, into which were stitched designs indicating his rank. They were bracketed by servants who held up parasols and fanned them.

Behind these figures were the litter bearers. There were two litters, both of finely carved, heavy wood, painted in blues and greens. Linen hung down on all sides, and servants ran along beside them, carrying parasols and fans in case they were needed.

Each litter was carried by eight men, and these chanted as they walked to keep the time. The words were translated for the Captain as "Joyous is our work, joyous is our service to the king."

Between the litters was a man with two dogs and a tame monkey on leashes, apparently the pets of the king.

Behind the litters were twenty more soldiers, an honor guard. They wore skirts of brown linen, and no jewelry save for a single bracelet on either arm, which was set with jade beads. The leader of this group wore a cheetah pelt like a cape over his back. The tail hung down between his legs and the head was perched on his left shoulder. The front claws hung down his chest.

The Mechanic let out a low whistle. The royal train was an awe-inspiring sight.

Slowly, the procession came up to the dais, close enough

that the litters were a mere fifty feet away. The bearers finished their chant and were silent. The crowds stood well back.
The line of patients remained where it was, but no one approached the dais. With some signal from within the litter, the
servants drew back the linen hangings and revealed the form
of King Snefru within. He was a modest looking man, with a
folded kerchief over his natural hair. Rising up from his forehead was a jeweled cobra, clearly a sign of his rank. On his
chin was the false beard which the Captain had heard was
worn by all Egyptian kings during important or ceremonial
events.

A moment later, the linen on the second litter was removed.
Within was a woman in her late twenties, apparently the
queen. She was slender and beautiful, with long black hair,
natural hair, that hung about her shoulders and over her
breasts. Her large eyes were outlined with kohl which made
them enormous and dark. She wore a band of colored stones
around her forehead which set off the honey brown of her
skin.

As a body, the people in the square went down on hands and
knees and touched their heads to the ground. The king made a
small gesture indicating that he accepted their prostration.
Then his eyes turned to the Captain. The Captain met his gaze,
then bowed, bending at the waist and lowering his head. His
wife and the Mechanic followed suit. Their bows were re-
spectful, but not prostrating.

One of the three official figures standing in front of the litters stepped forward and addressed the crowd with a well-
trained voice.

"His Majesty acknowledges your presence. You may stand."

Carefully, the crowds got back to their feet, and the three on
the dais unbent. The official turned to his king, and the king
signaled again. The man turned to the dais and approached.
When he was within easy speaking distance, he addressed the
Captain.

"His Glorious Majesty wishes you to continue your work
here. He will watch."

"We are most honored by his presence," the Captain said, bowing again. The official did not bother to repeat this. Perhaps the Captain's sentiment was too obvious to be committed to words.

"Let's continue," the Archaeologist said.

The Captain gestured calmly to his workers and they continued their ministrations with good success. The third patient to be brought up, however, was someone the Captain recognized. It was a young man with dirty hair and a childish face who had been out to see them at the camp.

"We've seen this one before," he said to his wife, shielding the translator. "Twice." He remembered him well. The boy had been out to the camp to seek help for a swollen foot that had threatened to become gangrenous. The Doctor herself had tended to the boy and told him to bathe the foot three times a day in the herbs she had given him. On the boy's next visit, the Captain had seen him and had reiterated the order. Now the boy was back, and it was clear he had not been taking care of the foot. The swelling was worse, and there were several black veins running along the inside of his arch. The flesh had begun to smell putrid.

With their limited supplies, there was little they could do for gangrene. And with the king's eye upon him, the Captain was irritated. He could not cure this boy.

"You've seen us before," the Captain said to the boy as he examined the foot.

"Yes," the boy responded. He was leaning heavily on a cane. He wore a loose light robe, in the fashion of old men, that had been cut short so it would not touch his foot.

"You haven't followed our orders." The Captain's voice was a little bit sharp. He did not want this boy's carelessness to be attributed to the survey team's lack of skill. Down below, he saw the conversation being relayed to the king.

The boy looked sheepish and shrugged his shoulders.

"You fix it," he said.

The boy's attitude annoyed the Captain further. As he looked closely, he could see that gangrene had indeed settled in the foot, and amputation would be needed. The boy was crippling himself for life with such carelessness, wasting the limited time of the crew, and most important at this very moment, making the Captain look bad.

"You could die from that foot very soon," he said, his voice rising slightly. "We will have to cut it off to save you."

Grimly, the Archaeologist nodded her agreement.

The diagnosis shocked the boy, and he shook his head, whispering, "No . . ."

"What do you expect when you don't keep it clean?" the Captain continued. "It would have been simple to fix it a month ago."

"You can fix it," the boy muttered. The Captain was omnipotent, was he not?

"We are not here to perform magic on your body! We offer help, but only if you will follow our orders and tend to the wound."

"You can fix it," the boy muttered again, somewhat petulantly, as though the Captain were refusing to heal the foot on principle.

"I can't fix it now!" the Captain said, provoked to raising his voice. He saw the king listening; he saw the crowd staring up at him. "Do you understand? We will amputate the foot, or you will die. It's too late!"

"You fix it!" the boy said desperately.

"It's too late!" the Captain said, almost yelling. "Too late!" And then, as his voice rose in anger, it happened.

There was a deep, loud rumbling beneath his feet. As he watched, the far end of the plaza heaved upward impossibly, the earth itself rising. The paving bricks surged up, carrying people with them in a great, rolling wave. All around the square, the market stalls began to crumble, falling on top of people who were stumbling to hold their balance. The earth roared. The Captain watched as one of the gates into the square collapsed in upon itself and fell to the ground, crushing dozens of people beneath it.

The jars of medicinals rattled on their crate and jumped off

of it, shattering on the bricks below, spattering onto the soldiers and the official who stood by the dais. The king was
gripping his litter. The bearers were tottering, but somehow,
through force of numbers, holding on. The queen's litter fell,
and she landed roughly on the ground.

Behind the dais hung the upper story of a nobleman's house.
The Captain turned to see several large clumps of brick work
themselves free of the structure and come flying down toward
his wife. He grabbed the sleeve of her shirt and pulled her
aside, as they passed inches from her head. The blocks hit the
dais with a crash that was drowned in the general thunder of
the ground. The Mechanic had fallen to his knees.

And then, as suddenly as it had begun, the wave stopped.
There were several moments of minor tremor, but these
calmed quickly, leaving the earth still. The Captain and his
wife stood holding each other on what was left of the dais. The
marketplace was a shambles. Stalls had collapsed on their
owners; wares had fallen and scattered. People were crawling
from the rubble, searching for children, or staring numbly at
the destruction. Many had been trampled beneath frantic feet.

The crowd in the square was now milling about, helping the
injured or crying out for the dead. All around the perimeter
buildings had crumbled, setting off avalanches of bricks and
wood. From where he stood, the Captain could see scores of
bodies beneath rubble.

It was a miracle he and his wife had been unscathed. Down
below, servants and soldiers were scrambling to help the
queen off of the ground. She stood shakily, but was not seriously injured.

"Look," the Archaeologist said.

The Captain followed her eyes and saw that the masonry
that had so narrowly missed her had found another target. The
boy with the gangrenous foot lay crushed beneath a pile of
bricks, only one arm and one leg visible. His cane had been
knocked free and lay a few feet off.

"Sweet Mother," the Captain cursed. And then he saw that

the natives were looking at him. They had stopped their movements and stood with eyes fixed in his direction.

An older man in the long yellow robe of a priest said loudly, "Attend, the god is angry!"

All eyes were on the Captain now. Even the king and the queen were staring at him.

The priest slowly sank to his knees, placing his hands on the ground in a sign of worship. The Captain watched as one by one the others in the square did the same. Only the king and queen and their attendants did not bow, though some of the servants looked as though they felt they should.

The Captain's eyes were drawn to the queen. She was standing near her broken litter, looking up at him. Slowly, the corners of her mouth twitched up into a smile.

Chapter 9

Twenty miles away, long past the last mud huts in the outlying towns and beyond the border of fertile land, in the desert that lay between the Nile and the Red Sea, was the survey team camp. The camp was a small town of its own. Its buildings were varicolored fabric tents with crystalline ribs holding them up, a cheerful arrangement against the stark desert. Each member of the team had a small tent as living quarters, and each scientific discipline, such as geology, mineralogy, medicine, zoology, etc., had a work tent.

The living tents, arranged in concentric rings, were quite pleasant inside. The walls provided excellent insulation from heat and cold, while allowing in fresh air and plenty of light during the daytime. At night, built-in lamps filled the tents with a mellow glow. Each was equipped with a refrigerator and a sanitary latrine. They were almost luxurious, considering their setting.

A few hundred feet from the edge of the camp were the tents and crude mud huts of the workers, which had been thrown up haphazardly by their occupants. These were men and women who had come to see the magic ones and had stayed to work. The huts were built of mud bricks, like all dwellings in Egypt, and a typical hut contained a small court of paved stones with a few rooms behind it, including a small bedroom and a tiny kitchen. A canopy was usually thrown up over the court to provide shade. Others had tents of coarse linen which they had brought with them from the towns and cities. These too had awnings propped up in front of them. In the early evening, when all work had been done and dinner was over, the workers would sit under their canopies and chat, drinking beer or tea and enjoying the evening breezes.

On the other side of the camp was the shuttle, a sleek vehicle with a pearlescent hide which stood upright on its back thrusters, ready to leap into the sky. It was a simple fusion-drive craft, which had been nestled into the hull of the mother ship during the journey to Earth. Upon arrival, it had been used to ferry the team from the *Champion*'s landing site to the campsite. They would ultimately use it to travel all over the world, when their research in Egypt was done. But it was a precious vehicle, with few replacement parts, and they did not use it unless absolutely necessary. It was an object of some awe to the locals, some of whom had been caught making offerings to it late at night.

On this afternoon, the Lion, son of the Captain and the Archaeologist, sat at a large wooden folding table in front of the shuttle, eating cold soup, flatbread, and local beans, and making notes in his log. He had lately been studying a herd of antelope that were migrating south.

His name had not always been the Lion. Originally he had been the Zoologist, for this was his profession. The Lion was a name given to him by the natives. He was over six feet tall, with broad shoulders and incredibly strong arms, built from years of studying and handling animals. His blond hair fell to his shoulders and framed a wide handsome face, darkened by the sun, but free of wrinkles, for he was still in his early twenties. The dark-haired natives had seen an obvious resemblance to a lion, and the name stuck. Soon the crew and even his parents had begun to call him Lion as well.

Near the table was the Engineer, who had set up an outdoor testing station for one of his current projects. On the table near the Lion were several dozen data crystals, ranged neatly according to some system the Lion could not decipher. Next to them was a large crystal reader, the Engineer's special reader, which was, he often bragged, at least three times as fast at finding information as any of the other readers in camp.

At the moment, the Engineer was assembling a box of some sort, using crystal sheets for the sides and soldering them together with a hand tool. He took frequent breaks to run back to the table and study something else in the reader. The Lion finished his lunch while watching the Engineer's frenetic motions with some amusement.

"What are you doing after lunch?" the Engineer asked, as he jotted something down, while his eyes were pressed to the eyepieces of the crystal reader.

"I have a feeling I'm going to be helping you," the Lion said.

"How very right you are." The Engineer laughed. "Hand me that blue crystal, will you?"

The Lion stood up, pushing his dishes safely to the center of the table, and examined the crystals. "Engineer, there are at least twenty blue ones here."

The Engineer made a sound of mock exasperation and removed his eyes from the reader, then grabbed the correct crystal without even appearing to look at his choices. "Really, Lion, if you're going to help me you'll have to be quicker than that."

The Lion laughed. "I'll keep it in mind."

"Ah, that's it. Right there." He scribbled a formula down then moved back to the box he was making. The Lion moved over with him. Near the box was a small cauldron with some kind of liquid within it. Around the cauldron were several stacks of mineral powders of different colors and a large piece of rock.

"What exactly are you doing?" the Lion asked.

The Engineer smiled. "I'm being very clever." He was mixing several of the mineral powders into the liquid, measuring each.

As he worked, a woman approached them from the workers' huts. She was covered in blood, and her short, curly hair was disheveled.

"Your wife, Engineer," the Lion said softly.

The Engineer looked up immediately, and caught sight of his wife, the Doctor.

"Stir this for me, would you, Lion?" he said, handing him a spatula and making a stirring gesture. "Keep adding the red stuff slowly until the measuring cup is empty."

The Lion complied, and the Engineer met his wife as she approached. She was pulling skin-tight surgical gloves off of her hands and she looked exhausted.

"Two deliveries," she said, wadding up the gloves, and tucking them into the blue smock she wore, which was purple with blood. She pulled the smock off as well. She was petite, with olive skin, dark brown hair, and green eyes. She was thirty-nine years old, and though her face was not especially beautiful, something about the whole of her was intelligent and attractive.

"How are the babies?"

She ran a hand through her hair and smiled. "They're fine. One was breach, but I got him out all right. Had to open the mother, but she's fine as well. They named the baby 'N-Genir,' after you."

He hugged her. "Well done, darling girl. Would you like to watch your brilliant husband at his latest work?"

"Sure." She let him guide her into a sitting position at the table, and sank down gratefully.

"Hello, Doctor," the Lion said.

"Hello, Lion, king of beasts." It was her pet name for him because he was in truth gentle and thoughtful and not at all ferocious unless he had good cause. She watched as her husband added more powders and the Lion continued to stir. "Whatever are you doing, darling?"

"I'm making stone."

"What?" both the Lion and the Doctor asked it at once.

"We grow crystal sheets at home to build our buildings, don't we?" He added a final dash of something grainy and green. "Well, rocks are nothing but crystals, different kinds mixed together. Even metals are actually crystals, on the molecular level. But rocks are much more interesting to look at—marble, diorite, granite. Of course, you can't build a hundred-story building with rock, it's not flexible enough. You need special flexi-blends for that. But you could build something smaller.

"So I'm going to grow rock. These are the ingredients—hornblende, feldspar, quartz, mica." He gestured to the sacks of mineral powder. "They go into an emulsion, and I'm copying this." He held up the rock that sat near the cauldron. It was a rough chunk of granite. "When I add the catalyst, each mineral crystal will begin to grow, and when they fill up the mold, I'll have rock. Help me with this, will you, Lion?"

Together they lifted the cauldron and carefully poured its contents into the crystalline box.

"Now for the catalyst." He took a small vial from his pocket and poured it into the mold, then stirred it briskly for a few strokes. Then he placed a top onto the box and bound the whole thing with a strip of flexible plastic, which he secured with a lynchpin. The Lion and Doctor watched raptly.

"What are you going to build?" his wife asked, never doubting that he would succeed. There had been too much precedent for any doubt.

"Whatever we want. Better labs, better houses. Isn't it too bad that the natives only use stone for their graves? Maybe give them something nicer. Grow them houses, really."

They waited, the Engineer studying a timepiece that dangled from his belt. The Lion and the Doctor both realized that they were holding their breath in anticipation. Soon, the plastic around the mold began to strain. When the Engineer judged the time was right, he picked up a mallet from the table and placed a chisel on the lynchpin. He lifted the mallet and swung it down. As it struck the chisel and the chisel struck the pin, the desert groaned. The groan deepened, became a rumble, and then the ground shook. It was as though some great motion were taking place deep within the earth.

The Lion watched as the table leapt up from the desert floor. Behind it the shuttle itself was moving, vibrating on its support struts. The table jumped and twisted and landed on its side.

The Engineer watched as the mold, freed of its lynchpin, fell apart. The substance within had expanded, forcing the sides to separate from each other. A hard block fell out onto the desert floor. Even at this moment he noticed that the resulting cube looked more like cement than natural rock and would have to be reworked. Then the cement block bounced toward him and he jumped to one side, pulling his wife safely away.

After several seconds the ground quieted. There were a few residual waves of motion, but these soon dissipated. The disturbance had been brief but intense. The three of them looked back at the camp. The domed tents still stood, relatively unaffected by the motion. But beyond them, at the workers' camp, most of the huts had collapsed.

"Mother save us!" the Doctor breathed, and then she was running toward the huts to tend to the injured.

"What in the name of Her Wrath was that?" the Lion asked, moving to follow the Doctor.

"Unstable land mass, I think," the Engineer replied. "Shifting to relieve pressure."

"That was pretty violent! How big an area do you think was affected?"

The Engineer and the Lion looked at each other and a thought passed between them.

"The *Champion*!" they said in unison.

In minutes they had climbed up into the shuttle, strapped themselves into the pilot seats, and had the engines revving up. The Engineer waited only till power reached minimum safe levels, then he gunned the throttle and sent them skyward. At ten thousand feet he leveled off and pointed them north to the Mediterranean Sea. Below them the camp had disappeared and towns along the Nile flashed by. It was difficult to see damage from their altitude, but the Lion thought he could see larger buildings in other cities collapsed into rubble.

The river was the only clear feature from this height, its canals cutting through the narrow strips of fertile land on either side. Heavy boat traffic moved up and down the water. Then they were over the delta, where the great Nile branched into a dozen arms on the final leg before returning to the sea. Then they were over the ocean. Below them, along the coast, Egyptian ships sailed east and west on trade routes, their sails augmented by slave rowers. The sea looked blue-black today, against a sky of pale blue.

As they flew, the Lion glanced down at the ocean and noticed something strange. He saw a long dark line far out in the water. It was not a straight line, but a slight arc, and it was moving—very fast, he realized. He did not recognize what it was, but he knew there was something wrong about it. It was moving toward the coast.

"Engineer, look at that."

The Engineer glanced down, then he and the Lion knew what it was. Like a three-dimensional drawing on a flat piece of paper, its shape suddenly made sense, and they stared in horror as the line defined itself into a wall of water. No wave could ever be that high. Just as they realized what it was, it swept into a caravan of ships and engulfed them entirely. They were too high up to see the encounter in much detail, but it was clear the ships and their crews were destroyed. And the wall of water was heading for the coast.

"Saintly Mother's curse!" the Engineer breathed. The shaking of the earth had covered an enormous area and his urgency to find their own ship doubled.

He arrowed the shuttle north and west, and soon they were approaching their landing site. They flew above a chain of tiny islands, and the Engineer let the shuttle lose altitude. Theirs was the second-to-last island in the chain. In a few moments they could see it, its steep cliff walls rising high above the ocean surface.

"Weren't there seven islands?" the Lion asked.

"Yes, seven."

"I only count five."

The sea was in turmoil. The Engineer reached the landing island and put the shuttle into hover mode above it. The island was very small, no more than three acres of surface area. It was rocky and well guarded, for it was all cliffs, with no beachfront where someone might land by sea. It had been the ideal resting spot for their ship: safe from natives, and, they had thought, high enough above the water to be safe from the sea.

But there was no ship on the island below them, only scrub plants and rocks. The Engineer circled the island twice, and they both scanned and scanned again the barren rocks beneath them, as if the ship might appear if they were to look hard enough.

"It's not the right island," the Lion said at last.

"What do you mean? We're looking at the coordinates. That's it."

"No, it's not the right shape. And it's too small. Somehow this is the wrong chain. The coordinates are off."

"No," the Engineer said slowly, as understanding dawned. His voice lost all emotion. "The coordinates are correct. It isn't the right shape. And you counted right, there are only five islands. But we're in the right place."

He moved the shuttle down for a closer look at the north side of the island. "Look, Lion, it's gone. That whole cliff face is new. Half the island sheared away into the sea."

It took the Lion a moment to believe it, but he saw that the Engineer was right. The cliff face was clearly new. The rock was lighter and unweathered. And the sea below was churning.

Somewhere down there, under the tossing whitecaps and millions of tons of stone, was their ship. Destroyed. The *Champion*, the first manned ship using an Eschless Funnel, the first interstellar transport. Gone.

"We're stranded," the Lion said slowly. He did not say it fearfully, merely as a fact they would now have to examine.

"Yes," the Engineer agreed. "But not for long, Lion. The next team will be here in a few years. We'll send the courier tomorrow." He was referring to the tiny unmanned Eschless

Funnel ship they used to send messages back and forth from home. "Maybe they can outfit the new ship to accommodate a double crew. We'll be all right."

He swooped the shuttle down close to the water, but the churning ocean was too wild for them to see below the surface.

"Mother of All," the Engineer said quietly, "I loved that ship."

Chapter 10

Present Day

It was past midnight in Egypt, and the desert air was chilly. In Cairo, that city known as Mother of the World, where old mosques and Roman fortresses and modern high-rises elbowed each other for room, most of the population was sleeping. Twenty miles away, on the Giza plateau, stood the last of the Seven Wonders of the World. The Great Pyramid, which had once been covered with white limestone, now stood shorn of its fine casing. It was a dingy brown color that faded into the night.

The troop of white-clad guards with machine guns over their shoulders had long since left for the day, and the plateau was watched over by a handful of sleepy night guards who were kept company by the stray dogs who prowled the plateau hoping for food from the tourists.

Near the Great Pyramid were its two successors, pyramids of the same proportions, though smaller than their great brother. All three had been built by kings of the Fourth Dynasty, nearly five thousand years before. The Great Pyramid, however, had something the other two did not. It housed a large, empty chamber situated almost in the very middle of its bulk, and above this room were five smaller chambers, stacked on top of each other, which performed a function loosely analogous to organ pipes. The design of the pyramid was such that it would transmit and enhance any sound that passed through it.

For hundreds of years, since an entrance had been hacked into the pyramid by Al Mamum, Caliph of Cairo, in the ninth century, visitors to the pyramid had noticed that speech inside the great chamber was almost impossible. Echoes in the room were so loud and of such great length as to interrupt all subsequent speech. The granite walls themselves seemed designed to amplify sound. What visitors and scholars did not realize was that the granite and the pyramid were equally receptive to vibrations of other kinds.

That night, at two o'clock in the morning, the Great Pyramid was hit by such a vibration. Pruit's brief transmission fell squarely upon it. The wave of this transmission hit the outer stone of the structure and was passed inward to the great chamber. Here it was amplified, enhanced, and sent back out through the walls. The entire transaction took no more than a single second, but during that second, it was as though a shiver had passed through the pyramid.

Out on the plateau and a little way off, two guards paused in a game of cards by flashlight and turned to look at the pyramid. Whatever had happened had passed, though, and there was nothing to look at but the profile of the massive structure against the night sky.

The shiver that passed through the Great Pyramid was redirected by mechanisms built into the stone itself and was emitted with a new destination in mind. Forty-five miles away, an underground receiver caught the shiver and passed it on.

In a dark room that lay below the desert, encased in natural rock, something very old began to wake up.

Chapter 11

The Mechanic felt, rather than saw, the lid of his stasis chamber withdraw. Its motion made a low rumble, almost below his audible range of sound. *Which wake is this?* he wondered. *Forty-four? Forty-five? Forty-three?* He could not remember and would have to look it up on the computer. Anyway, what did it really matter? What were two hundred years here or there?

He sat up, and his head and torso came out of the thick grease that encased his naked body. It was not grease exactly, for it was organic in composition, but it felt like grease, machine grease that had been exposed to cold weather and was partially congealed. It was called "gunk" in the casual language of his one-time peers. The gunk was not cold, despite its texture, and it smelled awful, like compost that had just begun to decay. It was brown with an undertone of green.

As he sat up, the lights of the cave came on, dim yellow glows around the walls. The Mechanic carefully pulled a long plastic tube out of his throat and unhooked his nose plug. The smell of the gunk assailed him, but he had grown accustomed to it. He unhooked the various other tubes that were attached to his body and let them fall back into the soup. He looked like a troll who had just risen from a swamp, his dark gray hair and the gray of his skin matted with the gunk. He grasped the sides of his tank and stood up. The tank was raised several feet above floor level, and when he stood, his head reached nearly to the ceiling of the low room. Inches above was the artificial rock that enclosed them, and beyond that was the natural rock into which their room had been inserted.

The stasis tanks themselves were made of the same artificial rock that formed the floor, walls, and ceiling. It was a substance created from a combination of metal and stone, an ingenious invention of the Engineer that had proved ideal in keeping out the elements. There were eight tanks sitting in a row across the floor of the room, each resting on a stone pedestal that concealed the inner workings of machinery that kept the occupants of the tanks alive.

The Mechanic wiped as much of the gunk as he could off of his skin, then carefully stepped out of the tank and onto the rock floor. There were slight brown markings on the ground where he had dripped gunk on previous wakes and not bothered to wipe it up. In the closed system of the cave, it did not disintegrate.

As he walked toward the tiny latrine and shower alcove, something caught his eye. He turned to the computer, embedded in the rock wall to his right, and saw that the crystal screen had come to life. Typically the computer did not rejuvenate itself automatically; it was up to the Mechanic to tell it to wake. But there it was, already on.

He took a seat on the stone bench before it, stray pieces of gunk sliding off of his skin as he did so. There were words on the crystal of the screen, a log of recent communications to the computer. They read:

Transmission received:
"Rescue has arrived" (frequency) (time stamp)
Execute command—Wake Tank #5
Repeat transmission (time stamp)
Repeat transmission (time stamp)
Repeat transmission (time stamp)

The "Repeat transmission" lines continued, dozens of them. The Mechanic stared at the top three printed lines for several moments, unable to believe what he was reading. Someone had come for them. Five thousand years late, someone had come for them. And the computer, unaware that vast reaches of time had come and gone, had simply executed its standard program: wake tank number five—the Mechanic's tank.

He checked the computer's internal clock and found that this was not a standard two-hundred-year increment. He had been woken early, at least twenty years early.

He stared at the message awhile longer. Rescue. Why? After such a time period it no longer made sense. Could it be a chance transmission? But the transmission had been repeated at regular intervals throughout the past three days, while the Mechanic woke.

He could trace the transmission, he realized. Shakily he slid his hand along the right edge of the screen, manipulating a control panel and requesting that the computer find the origin of the message. The computer sent a tiny signal from the cave to the beacon pyramid. The signal bounced directly back, modified by the infinitesimal remnant vibrations of the last transmission. This modification, when analyzed, would yield the origin point of the transmission.

He waited as the computer parsed the information. It was successful, and in a moment he was looking at a map of the star system. The signal had originated from an orbit around the fifth planet.

Could the Earth locals have achieved the capability of making such a transmission? In his previous wakes he had detected no indication of advanced cultures on the planet above. Civilizations must have risen and fallen scores of times in the outside world, but there had never been much technological advancement as far as the Mechanic could tell. Never a hint of radio communications. But still, it was a possibility.

He instructed the computer to monitor communication frequencies in the local area. The computer hummed for several moments, rejuvenating the portion of itself that would be necessary to carry out this task, for much of the computer was kept in a stasislike state to survive the long years in the cave. After a few minutes, the computer complied.

The noise almost blew the Mechanic's ears out. There was an avalanche of transmission traffic. As the computer scanned up and down standard frequencies, the Mechanic heard voices, data, static, and more voices in languages that were totally unfamiliar, pouring over each other. A mere one hundred and eighty years had passed since the Mechanic had last awakened, but in that short space of time the world had come alive.

Could the locals have sent the transmission? he asked himself.

No, unlikely, he answered. *It was sent on the beacon frequency and with the code words.* He was dividing himself into two parts, his standard procedure when debating a course of action. One part was sure of his abilities and his needs and was willing to do any action necessary to guard his own interests. The other part, while aware of these things, was primarily concerned with the actions others might take if they disagreed with the Mechanic's intentions. The second part of him was his cautious adviser.

What does it mean, then?

It means the Kinley have returned, he thought.

They cannot possibly believe that we are still alive. That was his cautious side. *Five thousand years is beyond the realm of credibility. It's only because the Engineer, may the Mother curse him, was so careful in designing this cave that we have survived.*

That's true, that's true. And we haven't all survived, have we? The Mechanic smiled.

So why? his cautious side asked. *They are transmitting to the beacon, which means they are aware of our final message to home. They know the code words. They are definitely looking for the survey crew. If I hadn't changed the computer program, the beacon would already have sent them our location.*

Maybe they're looking for something the survey crew had. Or something the survey crew left here. What?

Some physical thing of permanence, perhaps? Maybe the

beacon itself. But this didn't ring true. The beacon was an impressive structure, but other than its inherent purpose to transmit messages, it held nothing of real value. *What else is there? What else would be valuable enough to make this trip after so long?*

Neither side of the Mechanic was able to answer that. He sat in front of the screen for several more minutes, but he could not yet puzzle it out. He noticed his body then, still naked, with gunk drying to his skin in several places. He took one last glance at the message on the monitor, then stood and headed for the shower.

The shower and latrine were built together in a small alcove at one end of the cave. The fixtures were of the same metalrock that was used everywhere in the room. They looked, felt, and operated just as they had when they were first installed. If it weren't for the computer date log, there would be little reason to believe more than a few months had passed over the last five thousand years.

When he had cleaned himself, the Mechanic put on a suit of brown cotton work clothes from one of the sealed drawers embedded in the cave walls and sat down at the computer again. Another repeat transmission had arrived while he was bathing, but he ignored this. It worried him that the Kinley were arriving—for if they found him, he might have to explain those empty stasis tanks. But he had come to the conclusion that anxiety was premature. He had too little data and must research present-day Earth. The more he knew of his actual circumstances, the better he could judge his choices.

With a few adjustments to the crystal display, he was able to tune in television broadcasts and soon found himself looking at Earth in vivid color. He was assaulted with images of people, buildings, automobiles, airplanes, wars, food, entertainment programs, heads of state giving addresses, and a hundred thousand other views of a technological civilization.

The Mechanic watched for hours, unable to understand the languages, but nonetheless able to discern the level of the civilization. Earth had finally reached the very beginning of a technological curve that would vault its natives from quaint tribal loyalties to space-faring masters of their planet and their sun. Herrod, too, had gone through this stage, though the specific trappings had been different.

It was clear that the people of Earth, or at least the people of the richer nations, had mastered planetwide transportation and had achieved a high standard of living. They were, perhaps, about seven hundred years behind the Kinley civilization to which the Mechanic had once belonged, the civilization that had gone to war just before the Mechanic and the others had gone to sleep:

Suddenly the Mechanic had an inkling of why this new Kinley ship might be coming. If he was right, it would make his own circumstances very interesting indeed. He felt a jolt of excitement in his stomach.

Could they really be looking for—

No, he told himself. *Don't even think it. Not yet.*

He manipulated the screen to turn off the Earth transmissions. He had seen enough. It was time to ask questions.

He locked the computer into the frequency of the last transmission. He responded with his own message, aimed through the great beacon at the ship circling the fifth planet. His response was three words:

Who are you?

Chapter 12

"I need two tickets to San Francisco," said Pruit in English. "I want to see the Golden Gate Bridge."

"Which airline would you prefer?" Niks asked.

Pruit was in the sentient tank, in her blue one-piece undergarment. Her body was horizontal, lying in the tank's long tray. The tray was nine inches deep and filled about seven inches full with a highly cohesive biofluid called sentient fluid. She could lie there in clothing, but the fluid would not penetrate cloth. It touched her skin but would not stick to it. It filled her ears, but would drain out easily and completely when she sat up.

Above her was the curved dome of the tank ceiling, fashioned of brown solid-reed. The tank door, which sat at waist level when viewed from outside, was shut. This was a tiny world of its own. It had been three days since she sent the first transmission to Earth. Central repeated the transmission hourly, but there had been no response yet.

It was not Niks who spoke to her, of course, but Central. They were using a free-form discussion program that allowed Pruit to speak new languages naturally and learn to explore their limits. If she made an egregious error, Central would stop the conversation and repeat what she said, comparing it to how others would say it. These examples were drawn from conversations they had observed on Earth broadcast channels. Some of Pruit's early lessons had come, conveniently, from local education programs broadcast to students studying English. Pruit was now so fluent that she almost never made mistakes.

The thick fluid of the tank was infused, during these sessions, with sentient receptors. These molecule-size receptors were designed to recognize and transmit infinitesimal variations in sound, and thus could teach Pruit proper pronunciation. With Pruit lying in the tank and the receptor-laced fluid filling her ears, Central spoke to her directly from the receptors at her eardrum. The voice of the computer was adjusted to sound as though Central were lying next to her in the tank.

"I don't care which airline," Pruit said, enjoying English very much now that she was fluent enough to understand it conceptually as it was spoken. "Just get me the best deal."

"For two, you said?" Niks asked. "Who's your companion?"

"Who do you think?"

"Evit, that guy in the class ahead of us in Sentinel training?" His tone was teasing and intimate.

Pruit smiled. How often he liked to tease her about Evit, with whom she had had a brief relationship when she was fifteen. Before that kiss in the park, before Niks had touched her and made her his own.

"Not Evit, Niks," she said, refusing to be baited. "You."

"Good." Niks sighed. "A few days alone together outside of this ship."

"With a queen-size bed."

"I'll make love to you on fresh white sheets, and then we'll sit outside and look at the ocean."

"The ocean," Pruit breathed, thinking of the vast reaches of water she had seen in the transmissions from Earth. "Can you imagine?"

"Not really. Not until I see it."

They were both silent for a moment, thinking of the ocean, trying to grasp what it would be like.

"Great Life, I've missed you, Niks," she said quietly.

"I've missed you too."

Pruit sat up onto one elbow and turned her head, expecting

to see Niks lying in the sentient fluid beside her, just where his voice had told her he'd be.

But there was no one there. She was alone in the tank, and Niks was dead. The sentient fluid dripped from her ears, and her eyes welled. Even after all these months, she had been fooled, for a moment, into believing the fantasy.

She sat there, feeling that the wind had been knocked out of her. She opened her mouth to tell Central to drop Niks's voice, but before she could, Central spoke.

"Incoming transmission, Pruit," the computer said, still in Niks's voice, this time coming from the walls, since the fluid had drained from her ears. "Survey frequency."

Excitement pushed away her other emotions. "Open the tank!"

The hatch door slid up, and the tray rolled out. Pruit stood, letting the thick fluid slide off her body and clothes, then jumped down to the ship floor.

She slid in front of one of the control stations and sank her hand into the putty pad.

"Central, message on screen."

In response to her command, the filaments of the screen grew themselves into a short pattern of words. They were Haight, an ancient Kinley tongue, the same she had used to transmit her original message.

They read:

Who are you?

"Central, it's written in Haight. I assume it's an automated response, though my reference book indicates that we would be sent coordinates, not a text message. Can you identify the exact source of the transmission?"

"It's coming from the beacon coordinates and is directed squarely at us. The transmission is not especially strong, but it's well targeted and came in over other noise."

"Have we heard Haight from anywhere else on Earth? Do you have recordings of it from the traffic you monitor?"

Central ran a double-check of all transmissions recorded in the last six months. "Nothing."

"Automated then," Pruit concluded.

She entered into the computer, in Haight, her response:

> Sentinel Defender Pruit Pax of Senetian. Destination: Kinley survey team stasis cave. With what am I communicating?

The Mechanic sat in the dimly lit cave, his shoulders hunched slightly and his eyes closed in half-sleep. He was leaning against a wall, his legs sticking out along the cool floor. He had little energy at the beginning of a wake, and he already felt himself fading.

Then the computer let out a chime. He stood quickly, ignoring the protests of his body, and slid back onto the stone bench. There was Pruit's transmission, spelled out across the screen.

"Sentinel Defender Pruit Pax of Senetian," the Mechanic said slowly out loud. The title meant nothing to him, but why should it? Herrod had aged five thousand years, time for civilizations to rise and fall and rise again. But this person was communicating to him in Haight. They had preserved some things of the previous world.

He must find out why they were here. He could assume that the sleepers were not part of their equation—they would be thought long dead. He doubted whoever was up there communicating would give him more information without a knowledge of who he was. And would that be safe to reveal?

It would be safe, he decided. He would not reveal his location, nor anything about his current circumstances. The shock of hearing from him, a living man, when they clearly believed themselves to be speaking to a machine, might elicit useful information that would not otherwise be offered.

Having placated himself, he entered his next message:

> Survey team member. Stasis sleeper. Woken by your transmission. What is the purpose of your mission?

He sent this message, then retired back to the floor, where he allowed his eyes to drift closed. It would be nearly an hour before the signal made its way to the Kinley ship and the ship responded.

Pruit stared at the new transmission, and found that she had an odd sensation in her stomach. It was a feeling of mixed dread and excitement—dread at the possibility that the unfortunate survey crew had been waiting all these years forgotten, excitement that they might be alive, for this would make her mission much easier. Lying over both of these, however, was incredulity.

"Central," she said slowly, "did you read this?"

"Yes."

"Is it possible? Could they be alive?"

"You are as well educated as I in any information that would answer that question. Perhaps we should ask whether it's *im*possible."

"How can we answer that?"

"Exactly. We can't."

"But five thousand years, Central! It's at least improbable."

"I agree."

Pruit grabbed the mission Master Book of contingencies and scanned through it. Far down the list of possible situations, she found her current set of circumstances:

> 74.-yi Transmission to beacon provokes response
> from original survey team stasis sleepers.

She remembered drilling this contingency during mission training, but she and Niks, and their instructor as well, had always viewed that contingency and its neighbors at the bottom of the list as drills done more for principle than for actual need. She was now thankful for the thoroughness of the planners who had compiled the Master Book. She refreshed her memory of this contingency and saw that she was not forbidden, in the present circumstances, from revealing the target of her mission.

Pruit double-checked the transmission protocol, ensuring that the data she sent would be compressed into a nanosecond and undetectable as anything of value by Earth monitoring stations. Then she transmitted a reply:

> Purpose of missions to find transportation
> technology used to reach Earth.

When the message arrived, the Mechanic sat in front of his screen and began to smile. His smile broke through to laughter, the pained, mirthless laughter of a man unused to the emotion. That first inkling he had had upon seeing the incoming message had been correct.

"I'm right," he said aloud. "I'm right." *The war back home must have been devastating. They've lost the Eschless Funnel. And I've got the Eschless Funnel.*"

Yes, he, of all the people that existed at this moment in time, possessed the secrets of faster-than-light travel. He possessed those secrets right here in this cave. The Kinley had clearly lost them, and the people of Earth outside had no clue that such a technology could exist. Only he, the Mechanic, long-time lackey and second-class citizen, owned the most valuable knowledge in existence.

But they arrived here, the cautious half of him argued. *And if their ship is traveling below the speed of light, they've been on this mission a long time.* Herrod was approximately eight light-years from Earth. In a ship with an ordinary drive, this would take at least ten years, likely longer. *Fifteen years,* he thought, *or twenty. They must be desperate. And that means they won't be brushed off easily.*

No, they won't be brushed off easily, he answered himself, *but they also do not know where I am, or who I am, not exactly. And they are strangers to the world out there. I have the advantage of surprise and a degree of invisibility.*

His stomach was churning with anxious elation. It was time to stop being the secret plotter. He could move into the open now, become the man he had always dreamed of being.

After several long minutes of staring at the screen and fantasizing about the future, he switched off the computer and turned away. It was time to prepare.

Pruit waited, but she did not receive a response. She re-sent the message twice, but could not raise the elusive sleeper.

"Central, we'll continue to monitor. But it looks like we've lost whoever or whatever it was down there. Possibly an automated response after all. I'll continue with the standard plan."

"Agreed."

Chapter 13

Eddie DeLacy was crouched down in the midday sun, working gently at the sandy dirt in front of him with his small pick. He was covered in dust, and sweat had drawn runnels through the dun-colored powder on his face. He took his hat off for a moment and wiped his forehead on a sleeve. He stood up and stretched and surveyed the dig site.

There were twelve mounds being worked, and they formed a loose rectangle, hitting at various points the outside walls of the temple they were exhuming. They were in Egypt, in the desert west of the Nile. To the north, through the haze that hung over the dirty-gold sand, Eddie could make out the Red Pyramid of Dashur. To the south were smaller pyramid structures around Maidum. Around the edges of the dig were the green and brown tents of the archaeologists and the hired workers. Parked beyond the tents were two beat-up Land Rovers from some era near the Second World War. Between these vehicles was the camp cook, who was grilling fish for lunch. From a camp oven came the smell of baking pita bread.

One of the local workers saw Eddie standing, and ambled over with a fresh canteen of water.

"God's blessing," Eddie said in Arabic, and immediately drank away half the canteen. He restrained himself from pouring the rest over his face. They had ample water, hauled in every few days from the nearest town, often by him, but there was no extra to waste.

"Get back to work, you lazy bum!" a voice called over at him.

Eddie turned and saw Emmet Smith, the archaeologist in charge of the dig. Emmet smiled at him good-naturedly, and Eddie said, "It's like a desert out here!" They laughed at the familiar camp joke, and Eddie crouched down again and resumed his work with the pick.

They had only been at the site for four weeks, and already the dig was proving unusual. This was a temple to Osiris, built in the Fourth Dynasty. It was a fairly small structure, only about two thousand square feet, but from what they had uncovered of the walls, it was unique. Many of the rooms appeared to be carved from enormous solid blocks of dark gray marble. The ceilings and walls and floors were all formed of a continuous run of stone, which smoothly made right angles and continued on. Though the rooms lay crumbled into pieces now, they had uncovered enough large sections to get a good idea of the overall structure.

In the solid, unbroken rooms, there were no discernible joints. The only explanation was that the builders had quarried out giant blocks, some weighing hundreds of tons, and then carved out the rooms. It seemed an unimaginable amount of effort. In addition, their chiseling had been so expert that the walls were perfectly smooth from one end to the other. There were no ripples of uneven carving. The stone had been shaved as exactly as if modern builders had verified the work with a laser.

Eddie was working on the contents of one of these remarkable rooms. It was a chamber where sacred objects had been stored. In the chalky soil, he had already unearthed several stone vessels for anointing oils and a chest that might once have held medicinal herbs. He was now uncovering some kind of heavy box. One corner of it stuck out from the soil, a dull black stone that he thought might shine up nicely once it was exposed and properly wiped off.

Emmett and two other archaeologists had put together this dig a month before, with Eddie's help. Emmett, though he had tenure at Brown University's Egyptology Department, had not been able to get funding for this particular dig, despite numerous grant proposals. Fourth Dynasty temples were simply not of academic interest at the moment. Egyptology, like most disciplines, followed trends and fads, and certain ideas went into and out of fashion. Presently, the Fourth Dynasty was out, and much later dynasties were in. Eventually the pendulum would shift the other way, but for the moment Emmett had been out of luck.

Eddie had met him at a conference in Massachusetts just eight weeks previously, and immediately been intrigued by this dig. Though he could not ask his parents for money, he felt no qualms about hitting up other relatives and business acquaintances of his father to fund this bit of exploration. Though most of the DeLacy clan and cohorts agreed with Eddie's father that Eddie was a bit of a deadbeat and dilettante, most still liked him greatly, and were willing to help him out, provided his demands were not too frequent or excessive. So he had cobbled together the money in fairly short order, and soon Emmett and his colleagues found themselves in Egypt, working long weeks to unearth this particular temple.

Though others might consider the Fourth Dynasty passé, it was Eddie's primary interest in Egyptology. This dynasty, which was generally considered to span from 2613 B.C. to 2498 B.C., was a time when the Egyptians rose almost overnight, in a historical sense, to the height of their considerable talents as architects. During this dynasty was the construction of the Great Pyramid of Khufu, that monument to human endeavor which was now the last remaining of the fabled Seven Wonders of the World.

It was odd that their architecture excelled at such a rate during that time. Many other facets of Egyptian society, such as the arts and fabrication of their intricate jewelry, would not peak until nearly a thousand years after those architectural achievements. And furthermore, their architectural acumen seemed to fade as quickly as it bloomed. Only two successors to the Great Pyramid were built, both standing near it on the

Giza plateau. All three pyramids were built within about fifty years of each other, within the lifetimes of just a few of the pharaohs of the Fourth Dynasty.

After those monuments, the Egyptians lost their ability to create anything quite so grand. All later pyramids were but poor copies that quickly began to crumble.

In addition, the Egyptian religion went through substantial changes in the Fourth Dynasty. During this era, the god Osiris emerged from a position of relative obscurity to become one of the central figures of the Egyptian pantheon. He took on his role as the lord of the land of the dead. He became the great god who presides over the weighing of the heart of the newly deceased. After the Fourth Dynasty, it was only with his approval that the spirit of a dead man or woman might be blessed and enter the land of the gods.

The pharaohs also took a more direct role in religion at this time. It was in the Fourth Dynasty that kings began to add the title "Son of Ra" to their names, thus stating their divine parentage outright.

Even here, in the ruins of this temple, the workmanship of that dynasty was evident. Even in this simple stone box Eddie was working out of the sand he could see the quality of the stonework. The corner of the box was so perfect as to be sharp. The plane of the box's upper surface met at perfect right angles with the planes of its sides. There was not the faintest trace of a chisel mark anywhere. He continued to work at it, now with his pick, now with his brush, gently pulling away the layers of history that had buried it.

Eddie wished his father could see him here and feel the excitement he felt with this work. His father had never quite recovered from the disappointment of discovering that his son had neither the skill nor inclination to go into the family business. Worse, he had come to realize that Eddie had too little discipline to be good at much of anything.

Eddie recalled the defining argument with his father. Harris DeLacy had yelled at him, "What are you waiting for? Life to find you?" Eddie had replied, "Inspiration! I don't want to waste my life doing things I don't care about." At this, Harris had laughed with exasperation, and said, "Life doesn't always supply inspiration, son. Eventually you have to *do* something with yourself."

Eddie knew his father was right. He loved Egypt and had amassed enough university credit to have a master's degree in Egyptology, but he had been too careless to keep track of his courses or follow up with his universities, and so he was left with no degree, not even a basic bachelor's.

The truth, which Eddie was forced to acknowledge to himself, was that he would not make a good archaeologist, even if he had succeeded in getting a degree. He was interested only in the brilliant moments when an archaeologist discovers something that changes the way the entire profession approaches Egypt. The more mundane drudgery which made up 99 percent of any scientific endeavor was something for which he had no patience. He knew this was a failing in his personality, but he had no way of remedying it.

In light of this, Emmett had made a deal with Eddie in exchange for the funding. Eddie was allowed to participate in the dig in any way he wished. If he found himself bored, he could move his attentions to something else. If an area became interesting to him, he was free to devote all of his time to it. The arrangement was perfect for Eddie.

He had now freed the whole front of the box from its encasing sand. It was about eighteen inches wide and twelve inches high. There was a faint line running along the sides of it, razor thin.

In another half an hour, Eddie had freed the box entirely. It was perfect, smooth and unblemished. He dusted it well, then lifted it and examined all sides. As he did so, he felt part of it move. The faint line he had seen was in fact the joint between a lid and the bottom of the box. The joint had been so perfect as to be almost invisible.

He was holding the box upside down, and now righted it and set it on the ground. The lid was now ajar. On some instinct he glanced around to ensure no one was looking at him. He wanted to savor this discovery alone for a few minutes.

He removed the top, and found himself looking in at a box full of sand. Gingerly he reached in and began to scoop it out. In a moment, he felt something hard within the sand, and he gently brought it to the surface. He caught his breath as he looked at his find. There in his hand was a perfect crystal of a most unusual design. It was pale orange and clear, but there were bands of dark green running through it at regular intervals. The green formed neat planes through the lighter crystal. And yet the crystal itself was perfect. There were no cracks where the orange and green met. In fact, on closer inspection, the green seemed a part of the orange, grown into it, but in a perfectly geometrical way. He had never seen anything like it.

He quickly scooped out the remainder of the sand and was thrilled to find seven crystals in all. They were of different sizes, but all were clear orange with bands of green. They were beautiful. He counted them again, and then, on an impulse, took the two smallest ones and slipped them into his pocket.

Then he called out: "Emmett! Come here, you've got to see these."

When the three archaeologists and the workers had all had their fill of staring at the crystals and holding them up to the sun, Emmett carried them away to the main tent, to study them in more detail.

Eddie went back to his own tent, a small affair of army green, that was just large enough for his sleeping bag, camp light, and a few personal items. He buttoned the flap open to let in sunlight and lay back on top of his sleeping bag. He drew the two crystals out of his pocket and held them up in front of him, turning them slowly around. He watched the green rings catch the light of the sun.

Chapter 14

The Mechanic stood before the cave's largest wall vault. At the touch of his fingers on the coded lock, the metalrock door slid away, hissing slightly. The vault had been airtight. That was the Engineer's workmanship. The door had not been used for five thousand years, and yet it worked perfectly and had perfectly protected the contents of the vault. The Mechanic felt a small surge of annoyance at another reminder of the Engineer's genius.

Behind the door was a space ten feet wide and two feet deep, as high as a man's head. It was the repository of Kinley wisdom. Hanging from the wall at eye level were rows of soft leather cases containing data crystals. Below these, stacked to chest height, were manuals, paper copies of the most relevant information contained in the crystals. These manuals were large books of filament-thin pages bound loosely between strips of plastic. They were manuals of geological science, animal biology, archaeology, and dozens of other disciplines. They had been used for quick reference by members of the survey team, and they contained all needed information for maintaining and even rebuilding their ship, as well as running their camp day to day.

The Mechanic ran his hand along the stacks of books until he found it: the manual to their spaceship. Within its pages were instructions for building an Eschless Funnel–driven ship from the ground up. He pulled them from the stack. He continued to scan the books and found a manual of general physics that also discussed the Eschless Funnel. He took that as well.

Then he pulled out a manual of human biological science and flipped through it. From what he had observed of modern Earth on his computer screen, local medicine was in a barbaric state. The Earth natives may have built ships to take them into space, but they were dying of things the Kinley had been able to cure for centuries.

He scanned the stacks of books to ensure he was leaving nothing that would mention the Eschless Funnel. Then he began on the crystals. Each leather case was clearly labeled, one for geology, one for atmospherics, etc. Every case of crystals contained a library's worth of information. The Mechanic pulled down three cases, one labeled "General Physics," one labeled "Advanced Physics," and one labeled "All Ship Systems." Those three were the only sets that made reference to the Eschless Funnel.

He carefully opened the cases and removed the crystals, setting them in neat rows on the floor. They were clear or pale orange or yellow, with data bands of darker colors cutting through them. In all, there were about a hundred of them on the floor.

He returned to the closet. On one side were tools and small pieces of machinery. With a little searching he found a first aid kit, a jawline translator, and something of real value—a stunner knife.

He hefted the stunner knife and fiddled with a dial at the base of the grip. He fiddled with it, changing the intensity of the electricity it generated. Then he returned to the rows of crystals on the floor. He stared at them for a few moments, a smile pulling at his lips. He, the Mechanic, had power over all of that knowledge. He was the one who would decide what would survive and what would be destroyed. Those Kinley may have been traveling for decades to get to Earth to recover this technology, but it was his to dispense or withhold. And he would withhold it from them, for the Kinley would consider it was theirs and take it from him without compensation. He could not have that. Compensation in great amounts was exactly what he needed. There was a whole world outside, a brand new technological Earth, and someone out there would pay dearly to have an exclusive right to those manuals. When they did, the Mechanic would finally have what he had always wanted. He would live a life as blessed as the Captain's. He would be a god among men. He would not have the divine trappings, but the pleasures of modern Earth might prove to be superior.

He sat cross-legged on the floor and picked up one of the crystals. He flicked on the stunner knife and touched it to the crystal's base. Immediately, the crystal changed texture and seemed to expand. On closer examination the Mechanic could see thousands of cracks which had grown within milliseconds like infinitely branching tiny trees. The crystal was compromised at the microscopic level and the data bands were ruined.

The Mechanic smiled again and picked up the next crystal. It took nearly two hours, but he destroyed every one. Now the only record of the Eschless Funnel existed in those delicate paper manuals. His manuals. His monopoly.

He loaded the ruined crystals back into their cases. He would bring them up to the surface and scatter them. He turned to the stasis tanks. It was time to consider the others.

He walked along the row of tanks. All but three were empty now, their lids drawn back, their interiors dry. The Mechanic recalled their occupants. The first tank had held the Engine Supervisor. He was the one who should have been woken by the computer at regular intervals. He was the one who was supposed to maintain the cave, the tanks, and the sleepers. But the Mechanic had bested him. Secretly he had changed the programming, and it was tank five, the Mechanic's tank, that the computer had been called upon to wake. It had only been a small change, a simple alteration that had gone undetected by the Engineer, but it had made all the difference.

"I never regretted you," the Mechanic said.

He had turned off the Engine Supervisor's tank on his first wake. They had only been sleeping for five years then. The

Engineer had suggested a five-year interval, for they had all been certain that rescue was on its way, and they did not want to risk missing the arrival of help. The logic of the kill had been simple: kill the Supervisor and take his job as maintainer of the sleepers. This put him in control of their tiny crew. He had planned an explanation of how the Supervisor's tank had failed, but that had never been necessary. Rescue had never arrived and so there had never been any need to wake the others.

And he did not regret it, for the Engine Supervisor had been the Mechanic's senior officer on the ship, though he was ten years his junior. Their relationship had never been pleasant.

The next tank had held the Surveyor, one of the scientists in the crew. The Surveyor had caught the Mechanic in a lie once, when they were at camp. The Mechanic claimed that he had double-checked the safety of their drinking water. The Surveyor, who had been secretly watching the Mechanic, claimed that he had not. And the Surveyor had been right. The reprimand still rankled. That had been the final straw in a long list of grievances against the man. The Mechanic had cherished fantasies of revenge for years.

He had not killed the Surveyor right away, however. Instead, he had relished the knowledge that he could end the man's life at any time, on any whim. Finally, on his twentieth wake, one hundred years had passed and he surmised that rescue would never come. He had taken a long drink of wine from the cave's stores and switched off the Surveyor's tank. If only he had been able to see inside as the man died! But the sense of vindication was still pleasurable.

After that, he had set his sleep interval to two hundred years to put as much distance as possible between himself and the legacy of the survey team outside. But every time he woke it seemed easier to go back to sleep than to venture out into the world above. And he had certainly never felt the urge to wake the other sleepers. So here he was now, five thousand years later.

The next two tanks were empty and had never been occupied. They had been intended for two members of the survey crew who had disappeared before the sleepers left for the cave.

The fifth tank was the Mechanic's own. The sixth belonged to the First Mate. It was working perfectly, as it had all these years, and inside of it was the First Mate, one of the senior ship's officers on their mission. The Mate was not an engineer, but he had known the ship inside and out.

"I think you could build an Eschless Funnel if you had to," the Mechanic said quietly. "And you could certainly explain the principles of one." He let a hand slide along the tank top. "That makes you a threat to my monopoly, friend. I have nothing else against you. I'm sorry."

He moved his hand to the control panel, punched in his override code, and turned the tank off. The tank began to beep, asking him to verify his command. There were several levels of safeguards, and the Mechanic patiently navigated them all. Within minutes, the lifesystems of the tank had ceased to function, and the Mate was dying. It would take a few hours, at the slow metabolic rate within the tank, but the Mate would soon be dead.

The final tanks belonged to the Engineer and the Doctor. Husband and wife sleeping side by side though millennia.

The Mechanic stood by tank eight. The Doctor, the Engineer's pretty wife. His faithful wife. The woman he loved and who loved him. The Mechanic put both hands on the surface of her tank and breathed deeply. He had loved the Doctor himself, had been smitten with her when he first saw her back on Herrod, as they prepared the ship. She had never known this, had never paid enough attention to the Mechanic to notice, perhaps. She was pleasant to him, friendly to him, occasionally showed him some sympathy, but the Mechanic knew that she had never once, not ever, thought of him romantically.

She was not a danger to his monopoly, for she did not understand the physics of the Eschless Funnel. He did not have to kill her. But what would it be like for her to wake from her deep sleep and find that her beloved husband was no longer beside her? That would be wonderful.

He moved to the Engineer's tank. The Engineer was a brilliant man, as the Mechanic had been reminded many times daily over the course of knowing him. The Engineer had designed the ship. The Engineer understood the Eschless Funnel as well as Eschless himself had once understood it. Perhaps even better.

"And like the Mate, sir, that means you must go." He laughed quietly. "You've ordered me about for years. This decision is really too easy."

He moved his hands to the tank's control panel. Then he stopped himself.

Quietly, he thought, *And is it too easy for you?* He thought for a moment of what it would be like to have the upper hand on the Engineer. Something worse than murder began to form in the Mechanic's mind.

I have the upper hand right now, his more cautious side pointed out. *The smart thing is to kill him.*

But what would it really be like to see him helpless? he wondered. *Surely that would be worse than death to him. And the Doctor—the Engineer would see her and know her, and know that he could no longer take care of her . . .*

Killing is safer.

But not as satisfying! I haven't had much satisfaction in my life.

He debated silently for a moment, then found that he was convinced. *Just do it right,* his cautious side conceded. *Make sure he's crippled permanently.*

He reached for the control panel and entered his override code. He quickly starved the tank of oxygen. Silently he counted the seconds. They slid by and became minutes—one, two, three, four, five, six, seven, eight, nine, ten, twenty, thirty. . . . Thirty minutes without oxygen. The tank was sounding an alarm. The body within was dying.

The Mechanic slowly turned the oxygen back on, and the alarm quieted then eventually extinguished. Three flashing lights continued on the panel, indicating that the life within was alive, but grievously damaged. The Engineer would never again be able to understand the complicated, delicate equations which described faster-than-light travel. He would be lucky if he remembered his name.

He checked the readout on the Mate's tank and found the man dead. His body would be slowly dissolved, and then the contents of the tank would drain, to be recycled and used for the remaining tanks.

The Mechanic turned away from the tanks and gathered his things.

Chapter 15

If God did not exist, it would be necessary to invent him.
—Voltaire

It was Emergence, the season when the Nile floods receded, and the dark, rich earth emerged from beneath the waters, fertile and ready for planting. At the survey camp, the desert was hot, but there was a breeze and even a faint hint of water in the air. Rainfall was rare, but not unheard of at this date, and there was a chance for moisture from the heavens.

The Captain stood at the edge of camp with the Archaeologist and Doctor, who were filling a small case with medical supplies for him. Some way off the Mechanic stood waiting by two litters and their litter bearers. A few servants from camp also waited patiently.

After the earthquake and the loss of the *Champion,* they had sent the tiny, unmanned courier ship home explaining their situation, and asking for modified plans for the next ship coming to Earth, which had originally been scheduled to arrive four years after the *Champion.* This courier would take three months to arrive at Herrod, and a return message would take another three months. They had at least two more months of waiting before they heard from home. There was nothing to do but continue with their work.

The camp had grown. Small stone buildings were going up,

designed and built by the Engineer, with stone he grew himself, which perfectly matched the natural local stone. The workers' huts had all been rebuilt, and the small township of locals had grown.

"I think this is everything you might need," the Doctor said as she quickly examined the items she had packed for the Captain. "No matter what the cause of the queen's stomach trouble, you should be able to help her. But I really would feel better if I were going with you."

Queen Hetep-heres, wife of King Snefru, had sent a messenger to camp that morning, asking that the Captain, leader of the healing visitors, attend to her at once in the palace at Memphis. She had briefly described a mild stomachache.

"I'd like you to go with me, but she specifically asked that I alone go and bring only a few servants," he said. "I'll pass the Mechanic off as one so I can have some protection, but I can't pretend you're anything other than our chief doctor. If she's pleased with things, perhaps I can bring you next time."

"All right. But call if you need a consultation," she said, tapping the communicator clipped to the Captain's waist.

"I will." He shouldered the pack, and the Doctor walked back to her camp medical station, where a line of patients was already waiting for her.

The Archaeologist waited until the Doctor was well out of earshot, then looked up at her husband and spoke seriously: "Knowing about the hierarchy of government here, there could be several reasons they're calling for you alone. Remember, they will want to categorize you, and they haven't been able to do this yet. The workers at camp are whispering to each other that you're a god. This could be a threat to the palace. Or a boon, for there is nothing better as a king than clearly having a god on your side."

"Perhaps she really just wants medical treatment," he ventured.

"Yes, perhaps. But if they perceive you as a threat, this is an easy way to get you there alone, on their terms."

He took her words seriously, though he was distracted by

thoughts of the queen. There was another possibility his wife hadn't mentioned . . .

"If it comes to physical danger," she continued, "you should use the idea of godhood to its full advantage."

"What do you mean?"

"Claim it outright."

"Darling, I can hardly—"

"Only if you have to." She put her hands on his shoulders and leaned close to him. "Only if you have to. I don't want you getting killed up there."

The Captain was moved by the concern in her voice. Their mission charter forbade them from disturbing local religions and customs, but he could see his wife did not care at the moment. He brushed a hand across her cheek. "All right, then. In this unlikely case, which god should I be?"

"Osiris," she said without hesitating. It was evidently a matter she had considered extensively.

"Osiris," he repeated. He knew very little about Egyptian religion.

"He's a strange god," she said, "without a clear-cut job in the Egyptian pantheon. But the stories about him make it clear that he's a martyr. He is married to Isis and has a son called Horus—fits well for us. And he has blond hair."

"Really?"

"It may just be the sun's rays shining behind his head, but it's close enough." She smiled and tugged at his hair. "He was, the story goes, murdered by Seth, his brother. His death, through many bloody battles, was ultimately avenged by his son Horus. A martyr is the most sympathetic and thus the most powerful figure in any religion."

"If he's already murdered, how can I be him?"

She smiled as a teacher might at a naive student. "Your death doesn't matter. The god is ever-living. If you have already died, then you are now incarnated again. It will not matter to them, for the god is timeless. Perpetually living out his destiny."

The Captain looked down at her, the fine bones of her face,

her blue eyes with traces of lines around them. "You really do love me, don't you?"

"Always," she said tenderly, taking his hands in hers. "This is only a last recourse. As you say, maybe she only has a stomachache." She glanced over at the Mechanic, who was still staring at them with impatience. "The Mechanic says I'm a trusting wife to let you go off alone to tend to that beautiful queen."

The Captain pulled her close and kissed her forehead. "As if I could ever look at another," he said. They smiled at each other, then he released her and walked to the litters. The Archaeologist watched as the litter bearers took up their positions and the Captain and Mechanic climbed in. Then she walked back to camp.

"It takes a patient man to have a wife," the Mechanic observed as he settled into the cushions of his litter. "I couldn't do it myself."

"It has the occasional reward," the Captain said, glancing back at her.

It took three hours to thread through the outlying villages and then the city proper, making their way to the hill at the very center of Memphis, where they were ushered out of the packed streets and through the palace gates. The Captain threw back the curtains of his litter as they passed through the king's gardens. There were orchards of fig and olive and date and plum trees, groves of neat vines, clear pools of water where birds bathed themselves, and a thousand species of flowers which bobbed their colored heads in the afternoon breeze. Gardeners, naked except for small strips of cloth tied around their waists, tended to each plant by hand, watering them from clay pots. Members of the royal family took their leisure in the gardens, picnicking or lying in shade.

Turning his head, the Captain could see out over Memphis and down to the Nile itself, wide and brown, carrying ships back and forth and up and down, enabling the trade of the entire nation.

The palace itself was not one building, but many. There was

a residence for the king, a residence for the queen, a harem building for the king's many consorts, concubines, and lesser ladies, and endless rooms for servants. The buildings were of mud brick and wood, whitewashed and decorated with murals.

Since entering the palace gates, the litters had been escorted by a squad of house guards, strong young men with short black wigs and dark chests. The escort led the Captain and Mechanic to the queen's house, stopping them in a great pillared forecourt, shaded by high, leafy palm trees growing from pots along the perimeter.

Here they dismounted their litters and, with the small cadre of servants they'd brought from camp, were shown to an entrance hall. They were met by a chubby eunuch with dark, oiled hair and heavy jewelry. He conducted them through shady halls, past rooms of women servants and children, up two flights of wooden stairs, and at last to the chamber of Queen Hetep-Heres.

"Your men servants must wait outside," the eunuch said to the Captain in effeminate tones.

The Captain had not thought of this. He had brought the Mechanic and three male workers to provide him some protection and also to make him look important for the queen. He had not thought to bring women, preferring to save them the long, hot journey to the palace. But of course men would not be allowed in the queen's chamber unless absolutely necessary.

He gestured at the Mechanic. Reluctantly, the Mechanic nodded and took up a position at one side of the door and the men followed suit.

The Captain and the eunuch entered the room. The Captain's first impression was of light and space. It was a very large chamber. Unglazed windows along the ceiling let in fresh air and streams of sunlight. There were soft carpets on the floor and finely carved wooden furniture, colored in gold and black and green.

The queen lay on a narrow green couch with wooden legs carved like lions' paws. She wore a long wig of tiny braids

which hung about her shoulders. Her dress was pale blue
linen, with a V neck, and strips that covered her breasts and
tied behind her neck. The Captain found himself breathless for
a moment. Her beauty had dulled in his memory since that day
in the market square and it was now reinstated in its full flush.

He bowed slightly. "Your Highness, it is an honor."

She returned the bow with a nod of her head. He moved forward with his pack and knelt by her, smelling the honey scent
of her perfume. He began his examinations with questions
about where she felt pain, what she had eaten, and if anything
of late had been upsetting to her. He spoke through his translator but used whole sentences of the local language, for he had
been dedicating himself to learning it.

He was surprised when she broke off, after answering several of his questions, and turned to the eunuch, who was hov-
ering nearby.

"Ptah," she commanded. "I wish you to stand in the corner,
with your back to me."

The eunuch hesitated for the briefest of seconds, then
dipped his head and obeyed. His new position put him out of
earshot.

"Cap-tan," the queen said, looking at him. "I fear my ailment has solved itself since the morning. My stomach is quite
well. But there are other reasons for you to be here."

Her voice was low and intimate as she said this and he
knew immediately that there was no danger to him here, at
least none of the kind his wife had prepared him for. He kept
his face blank, but he was very aware of the positions of his
hands, which were resting on the couch next to her stomach
and breast.

"There is magic in you," she whispered. "That much we all
agree." She touched his translator. "And you have the color of
the sun." She touched his hair. "But I want to know. Are you a
god? The workers in the fields murmur that you are. Some of
the merchants seem to agree. But we in the palace do not
know."

The Captain guessed then that her husband the king did not

know of this visit. She had called him on her own and it seemed she felt the same attraction for him that he was experiencing for her, an overpowering sense of their bodies and their closeness.

There was no need to make the claim of his own godhood. It was a last recourse and he was in no danger. No, there was no need, except his own need to be great in the eyes of this woman, to have power over her. Before he allowed himself to think, the words were forming on his lips. "Do you not know me, lady? Do you not see the god Osiris kneeled before you?"

She drew in her breath slowly, staring up at him with a look that was a mixture of fear and desire. "It is as I thought . . . ," she whispered, and she touched his hair again. "Your rage was great in the market that day. Will you bring destruction upon my husband's land?"

"No," he said softly, already feeling the weight of his deification. "Not destruction. Only peace and longer life."

She smiled and he smiled back, a superior smile now, the smile of a god at a mortal. He would not touch her today. He would not kiss her or caress her, though it was clear to him that she would welcome such an advance. All of that would come later. No, a god has patience. And he was now a god.

Chapter 16

"There's no reason to take this as anything other than what it says," the Doctor argued. "It says rescue must wait, not rescue won't be sent."

"But there is no way to judge the magnitude of what's happened." The Archaeologist's voice sounded calmer than she felt. "We're operating off too little data."

"That could be said of either course of action," the Doctor pointed out. She wore a look of numbed shock, poorly concealed by an attempt to speak rationally.

The entire crew was present. They were sitting in the meeting tent, around a large table of heavy, dark plastic that the Engineer had designed some months before. It was nighttime outside, but the tent was well lit with yellow lamps. A few of them were already beginning to wonder how long they would continue to have such luxuries. Though everyone was there, only the chief officers of the mission were involved in this argument. The others were waiting to see what their leaders would say.

The courier ship had finally returned from Herrod, bringing their response. The crystal computer cell on which the response had been coded was sitting in the center of the table. Beneath it was a sheet of paper onto which the message had been transcribed:

War. We hold tenuously. Rescue must wait.

That was all. No explanation of who was at war, no detailing of the extent of damage. Just seven words.

"I don't understand who could be at war," the Engineer said quietly, and not for the first time. "Things have been very stable."

"That's exactly the point," the Captain replied. "We don't know who's at war, we don't know who's holding tenuously. What we do know is that rescue will not be coming as scheduled."

"It could be," said the Engine Supervisor, piping up for the first time, "that only the station receiving our last message was under attack. Perhaps there's been a governmental coup and the space agencies have been shut down."

"There could be additional messages on their way here." This from someone else.

The faces of the crew sitting around the table were an interesting study in human stress. Each wondered what had happened back home, and each had a different reaction to the uncertainty. Most were in mild shock at the least. Some were running, for the moment, on automatic, as their minds tried to envision the fate of loved people and places.

The Lion did not contribute to the debate. He was sitting quietly, watching the faces of the others.

"Could be, could be, could be," the Captain said dismissively, standing up to capture their attention completely. "Everything we conjecture could be. It could be that the message is a hoax. It could be that Herrod has been destroyed entirely. And any scenario between those two extremes could be. There is no way to know. Perhaps we will never know. I am holding this meeting because we must change the way we think about this mission. Nothing about our return is certain." He looked at the faces in front of him. "Therefore we must operate as though we won't be going home. We should think about making a life here."

That caused an uproar; there were shouts of "No" and "You can't be serious." Seated next to the Doctor and the Engineer, the Mechanic whispered pointedly, "That's easy for *him* to say."

"Yes," the Doctor muttered under her breath. "Exactly." Then she raised her voice and aimed it at the Captain. "That might be convenient for you, Captain, but the rest of us don't find life here quite as appealing."

The room quieted. The Doctor had expressed feelings many of them shared. The Captain turned to her, knowing he should ignore the comment but out of pride unable to do so. "What do you mean by that?"

"What do you think I mean?" she asked, holding his gaze. "You haven't done much to dispel the natives' image of you as a god."

"What choice has he had?" This from the Archaeologist, who rose from her chair to defend her husband. "As long as they look to him for wisdom, we, the crew, are safe. He didn't conjure up the earthquake, but it's served us well."

"Served us well?" the Doctor said incredulously. "Thousands of people were killed! We spent months tending to the injured."

"Unfortunate," the Archaeologist responded, modifying her tone somewhat, "but it has also been useful. Don't think the king would have continued to tolerate us in his land if we were ordinary mortals."

"Again, convenient reasoning," the Doctor said. The Engineer tried to soothe her by patting her hand, but she ignored him. "But I didn't see us in any danger before he was a god." She turned back to the Captain. "Doesn't it bother you that you're violating our mission charter and the code of a scientist?"

"I didn't ask them to worship me," the Captain said.

"You haven't asked them not to." It was the Lion who said this, entering the conversation for the first time. His voice was quiet as he looked over at his father and mother.

The Captain looked back at his son. "It is an expedient I've made use of, nothing more."

"There are surely other ways of befriending and appeasing

the king," the Lion said, still quietly. "We've all sworn oaths as scientists and observers. You are disrupting their religion."

The Captain sighed, irritated at himself for being drawn into argument. It was none of their business what he did. "I acknowledge that I have not always made perfect choices," he said in a tone that was almost contrite, "but this is not the time for a philosophical debate. There are other matters at hand."

This small admission of responsibility served its purpose. The Lion fell silent and attention came back to the reason for the meeting.

The Archaeologist resumed her seat, and the Captain slowly sat down as well. "What concerns us now," he continued, "is how this message alters our mission. And our lives. I believe we should prepare for the worst. First of all, we should confine ourselves to the local area. I don't think it's wise to use the shuttle unless absolutely necessary. We must assume that we can't count on rescue at all and act accordingly, conserving our resources and supplies."

"With all due respect, Captain," said the Engineer, "they will come for us. How long it takes is another matter, but they will come."

"How can you know that?"

"Because I put myself in their place," the Engineer explained. He, of the group, seemed the least emotionally affected by the news from home. This was not actually the case, but he had trained himself over the years to attack problems without emotion. Emotion could follow later but if surrendered to up front would cloud the issue. "If the war was not overly destructive," he continued, "Herrod will still have all or most of its space-faring capability. Facilities may take some time to return to normal operation, but they will eventually be up and running, and there will be no reason not to complete the full course of surveys on Earth. In fact, the war will likely increase interest in locating other livable planets. No one wants to have all their eggs in one basket, so to speak.

"If, on the other hand, the war has caused significant destruction, space-faring capabilities may be severely affected.

Even so, I believe they will come here, for the same reason. With the exception of the planet inhabited by the Lucien, Earth is the closest livable world. And we, the survey team, have already established a base here. In addition, we are a team of scientists in all the major disciplines one would need to help build a civilization. A destructive war will remind everyone of the importance of having colonies elsewhere, and Earth is the natural choice. I can imagine some of the more militant religionist groups already planning a trip here.

"If it's the first scenario, I would guess a maximum of ten years for rescue to arrive," the Engineer said. "This would allow time for the space agencies to regroup and get back up to speed. And we should receive further communication as things on Herrod return to normal. If it's the second scenario, however, it could be quite a while before others arrive here. Maybe as many as a hundred years for society to recover and a mission to be mounted."

"In essence, then, you're agreeing with me," the Captain said. "We need to prepare ourselves. We need ways of living here indefinitely. As several of you point out, there may still be further communication from Herrod. The next few years will show us, one way or another. Is there anyone here who disagrees that we should take precautions against the possibility that we are stranded—at least for the foreseeable future?"

He looked around the table. The faces of the others were motionless. He no longer had their undivided loyalty, but they agreed with him because there was nothing to do but agree.

"Very well then. It's late. We'll adjourn for the evening. In the morning we'll begin realistic planning."

The others nodded, everyone feeling tired now, tired and numb. Nothing was certain any longer.

Chapter 17

Pruit was strapped to the control chair of the landing pod, studying the screens and dials that lined the circular chamber. She was hurtling through space on a trajectory that had sent her from Jupiter to Earth in a single week. The pod had launched itself off from orbit around Jupiter and achieved full acceleration within an hour. Pruit and Central had devised the vector so the pod would appear as a meteorite thrown off by Jupiter and traveling at a steady speed in the direction of Earth.

The pod was oddly shaped. The bottom, or front half of the ship, was spherical. To this sphere was appended a cylinder on which were mounted the fusion propulsion jets. Pruit's seat and control panels were inside the sphere. The space was just large enough for her to stand up, though there was nowhere to stand, for the chair took up almost all available space. If she stretched her arms out in either direction, the walls were just beyond her reach. The only light came from the screens, which gave off green and red glows.

The pod had originally been fitted with two chairs that sat back to back. She had modified it, during her six months in orbit, to accommodate a single chair that rotated in a full circle and provided her access to all controls.

She was wearing her red fullsuit, an outfit of thick material designed to monitor her body and repair it if that were necessary. Inside the suit were dozens of bioarms working in symbiotic relationship with her body's organs. The gloves of the fullsuit hung at the edges of her cuffs and could be flipped up with a touch on the suit's control flap at her chest. There was a hood behind her neck that could also be flipped into place. The suit was connected to the pod's biosystem and took care of Pruit's body waste and nutrition needs during the week-long trip.

Pruit had closed live radio contact with Central when she launched the pod. The increasing time delay of transmissions from the pod to the ship made communication irrelevant, and radio silence helped her avoid detection from Earth stations. She was keeping a voice log for Central, however, in accordance with mission procedure, and this was periodically compressed and sent back to the ship in short, nearly undetectable bursts.

"Central, I am in Earth's gravitational field," Pruit reported, as she watched the screens.

Her only views of the outside were through the monitors spread out around her. She watched the visual approach screen, where, in schematic, she could see the pod approaching Earth at an angle that would send her skimming across the upper atmosphere and gradually bleeding off speed, just as a meteorite might do.

"Central, approaching point of contact with atmosphere," she said. She rotated in the chair and checked another monitor. Central had carefully mapped all known pieces of debris in orbit around Earth. This information had been freely broadcast and was not difficult to come by, but Pruit was concerned. The volume of space junk was high and there could easily be items that were unrecorded. So far, however, the pod had not picked up any unaccounted for motions.

She watched the approach and checked the monitors that oversaw the exterior skin of the ship. The pod began to vibrate as it pierced the thin layers of the upper atmosphere and the skin heated up. But the monitors reported that all factors were within expected limits.

"Atmosphere entered. I am beginning my descent."

She looked again at the map of her approach. The pod would make one long curve through the atmosphere, blazing from friction, then drop straight down the last five miles in a braking maneuver that would land her in the open desert to the west of Cairo.

The pod shook more violently as it began to lose altitude. Far below on Earth, she was passing over Asia, then the Pacific. The shaking lessened, became rhythmic. The ocean was down there, but Pruit could not see it, only a somewhat geometrical representation of it on one of her screens.

She crossed over the coastline of North America, crossed over the border of night and day, and suddenly there was an alarm. She swiveled in her chair to look at a proximity monitor. There was a low-orbit satellite moving from its projected course. It was being repositioned, perhaps, and it was moving very quickly. Pruit's careful approach line had skimmed very close to the satellite, and now there was almost no room to maneuver. She pounded her hands into the putty controls, forcing the pod to skip to one side. It was too late. There was a grazing impact, a crash of metal against the hull, and the ship began to spin.

She was knocked sideways in the chair and felt her body strain against the straps. The chair spun to one side, and she tried to right it as the pod heaved. She grabbed the control panel with both hands to steady her position.

"Central, impact with pod!"

She scanned the monitors. The satellite had hit the back thrusters. And what about the fusion pile? She scrambled to get data, clutching the control panel as the pod spun and lurched unpredictably. Then there was a rending screech in the cylinder at the back of the ship. It was followed immediately by an explosion.

Pruit was thrown forward onto the panel, the wind knocked out of her by the straps. She felt blood in her mouth and saw red splashed across the monitor. The pod had begun a crazy spiral motion. It was not keeping course. It jerked and spun, and Pruit lost her grip and was thrown back into the chair, which twisted away.

She caught herself with one leg and forced the chair back into position. She kicked down on a lever and locked it into place. She found the propulsion screen and studied it. The impact had compromised the casing on the fusion pile, weakening it. And then the pile had blown.

She punched at the putty control pad and brought up a schematic. On it she could see that the whole left side of the propulsion system had been knocked loose. The pod was out of control. She would have to disengage that bracket and make do with the two remaining firing systems. Gripping the panel with one hand, she punched the orders to release the propulsion bracket.

Blue warning lights sprang up across the panel indicating that the pod could not comply with her request.

"Disengage, by all that lives!" Pruit yelled in frustration. She hit the sequence again and still the pod would not comply.

She was wildly off course. The pod continued to buck and spiral, and now Pruit felt heat seeping into the ship. The pile had melted the outer layer of skin and the heat was penetrating the pod. She felt the fullsuit kick into action to protect her.

"Disengage!" she yelled again, pounding the sequence. Nothing. The bracket must have fused to the ship. She could imagine the back end of the pod. The skin was scorched and attempting to regrow, but the heat of the exploded pile was too great. The new skin was burned even as it was formed.

She would have to disengage it manually. Pruit detached her fullsuit from the ship then pressed the release on her harness and was immediately thrown out of the chair. She hit a set of panels and was thrown again. The fullsuit was too bulky for movement within the tiny pod; she could not get purchase to hold herself still.

She ripped open the flaps of the suit and kicked it off, falling sideways as she did so. The bioarms were yanked from her body as the suit slid off. She was thrown again, hitting her head against the ceiling. But her hands found one of the hand-

grips along the upper part of the chamber. Above her was the
cylinder. At the end of the cylinder was the manual lever for
the propulsion bracket.

It took a moment for Pruit to realize that her hand was burning. The handgrip was far too hot to touch. The whole cylinder
was billowing with heat, and now her fullsuit was off. She
pulled her undershirt down over her hands and gripped two
handgrips, one on either side of the cylinder opening.

The ship bucked and she lost grip with one hand. She
swung through the air to hit the wall above the main control
panel. She kicked out from the wall and grabbed hold again.
Her hand was bare now and the metal scorched her. It no
longer mattered. The pod was plummeting off course. In minutes she might be plunging into the ocean. She grabbed tightly
onto both handgrips and swung her feet up into the cylinder.
She could feel the heat on her skin, burning her.

Her legs landed against the cylinder wall.

"Great Life!" she screamed in pain, as the whole side of her
left leg was burned. She pushed harder with her arms, forcing
more of her body up into the cylinder. She could see the lever,
though the air around it was shimmering with heat. Her skin
was burning. She kicked at the lever. And missed. She pushed
herself up further with her arms and kicked again. Her foot hit
the lever but it did not budge.

She screamed and kicked it again and again, forcing the
lever into motion. It was partially fused, but her foot connected with it over and over, and finally she could hear it
creak.

"Ten lifetimes cursed, you will disengage!"

She kicked it a final time and felt it give. There was a long,
low, moaning sound as the bracket, freed of its hold on the
ship, ripped itself away.

Pruit let go of the handgrips and fell six feet back down into
the sphere. She landed half on the chair and half on the control
panel. Her body was crying with pain, but she could feel that
the pod had steadied.

Her hands and legs were blistering as she pulled herself upright. It felt as though her right foot were broken. Probably it was.

She scanned the monitors, feeling her body starting to give out. She thought of her mother and father and Makus back home on Herrod, and the domed cities, and the wasteland that stretched around them. And she thought of the Lucien, efficiently putting their plan of annihilation into action, the years clicking by, heading inexorably toward their attack.

"I will see this through," she said aloud, and the sound of her own voice gave her strength. "I will see this through."

She was off course, but the two remaining propulsion systems were still operable. She sank her hand into the putty, ignoring the pain of this action, and quickly computed a new course. She would not make her original target. She requested that the pod computer get her as close as it could.

She turned to check the other systems. The outer skin of the pod was badly damaged. It appeared the whole cylinder was stripped. The navigational capabilities, however, were still functioning. Then she saw another cluster of warning lights. The braking system. She swiveled in the chair, feeling pain shoot up her legs, and looked at another screen.

The brakes were gone.

"No . . . No!"

She reset the control panel and two of the lights were extinguished, indicating that the brakes were not completely inoperable. There was still some minimum function. If she programmed the pod correctly, there might be enough brakes to land her within the limits of physical tolerance.

She glanced back at the approach monitor and saw that the pod was over the Atlantic Ocean. She was losing altitude quickly. The new approach vector showed her arriving in Africa. It was impossible to compute exactly where.

She set the new braking function. There were only a few minutes left before the pod entered final stage and she plummeted down to land.

The pod began to fill with biofluid. It quickly pooled on the floor and began to rise. The landing would be so rough, she would need the fluid to act as a buffer on impact. Pruit hauled herself out of the chair and grabbed at her fullsuit. She would need it to survive this landing. She pulled the suit toward her, feeling the burned skin on her hands lacerate as she did so.

She lifted a foot and pushed it into the suit. The pain was excruciating, but the bioarms were already growing out to repair her. She lifted her other leg but was thrown from the chair before she could complete the motion.

With a jolt, the pod had switched to final landing phase. She was beginning a freefall to the ground below. The biofluid was up to her knees now. She clutched at the fullsuit and forced her other leg inside. She could feel the bioarms gently penetrating her skin, and there was immediate relief. But the pod had begun to rock. The brakes were uneven, firing out of synch, and the ship bounced erratically. She could not steady herself to pull the suit on.

The biofluid passed her waist level and began to crawl up her chest. Without the suit on she would not be able to breathe. She managed to get her left arm inside the sleeve. Then she was thrown out of the chair and against the wall.

The biofluid was around her neck now. She was floating to the top of the pod. Her right arm flailed, trying to find the other sleeve. The fluid reached the top of the sphere. Pruit was being floated up toward the cylinder, where waves of heat were boiling down at her. She could not go up there. She took a deep breath of hot air and dove under the biofluid. She got hold of the loose side of the suit. Above her the biofluid filled the cylinder. There was no more free air in the pod.

I will not die here! she screamed in her mind. *I will not die here! I will find the Eschless Funnel and I will see my home again!*

She felt the final reverse thrust of the brakes. There were only moments left. Her right arm was still loose. Her head was uncovered. She could not breathe.

Impact. The pod hit the ground hard, and Pruit felt the shock wave of the sudden stop pass through the fluid and through her body. But the brakes had worked well enough to save her. She felt a stab of pain in her left leg and realized that it had been slammed hard into the edge of a control panel. It felt like it was broken. She was swimming in biofluid and her lungs cried for air.

She grabbed at the hatchway below the cylinder. The wheel mechanism would not turn. Her chest was burning. She would have to take a breath. Even if it meant she would die, she would have to take a breath.

I will not die here!

She tugged harder, using the last ounce of strength left in her body, and she felt the wheel give. Slowly the hatch opened a crack and she could see the biofluid pouring out. She kicked the hatch with her right knee, the only part of her legs that remained functional, and forced it all the way open.

The biofluid poured out of the pod, carrying her with it. She felt another impact as her body hit the ground outside. Pain rushed over her again, hot and electric. Her lungs gasped for air. It seemed as though she had no control of them. The biofluid poured onto her as it drained from the ship, and she inhaled it along with the air. She crawled forward, out of the deluge, gasping and coughing.

"I'm alive," she breathed. Her hands gripped the grass and soil below her. Then her vision clouded and blackness swept over her.

She had arrived on Earth.

Chapter 18

The boy was tall, with broad shoulders and dark brown skin. His face might have been beautiful if it hadn't been warped into affectation by his current profession. He wore loose pants that reached down to mid-calf and a tank top that showed off his admirable shoulders and arms. A small gold cross hung around his neck. He shaved his head regularly and there was now black, quarter-inch stubble sticking up from his scalp. His features were classic African, beautiful and a little bit wild. But he had not been born in Africa. He had grown up in poverty in Paris, and had come to Cairo three years before, when he was fifteen.

The Mechanic noticed none of these things as he followed the boy up the narrow, curving staircase that led into the depths of a tenement building in a decaying slum section of Cairo. He did not care where the boy was from nor how he had come here. He had chosen him for his strong, young build and nothing more.

"This way," the boy said, as they reached a tiny landing. He led the Mechanic into a low hallway that smelled of urine and had garbage strewn about in the corners. It was nighttime, and there were no lights in the hall, but a streetlamp outside partially illuminated the space through an open window frame. The building was like every other on its street, a five- or six-story pile of brick and mortar and cracking plaster, that had never been fully finished, for the government taxed real estate owners only when their buildings were complete. From its upper story raw steel bars poked upward between a forest of makeshift television antennas.

The Mechanic felt nauseated as the smells from inside and outside washed over him. "It doesn't matter, it doesn't matter," he muttered. "This won't take long."

"What did you say?" the boy asked, turning his head and looking at the Mechanic flirtatiously.

The translation of the boy's words was not immediate, but the Mechanic did not care what he had said. He nodded brusquely that they should keep moving.

The boy made his way to the final door in the hallway, which he carefully unlocked and pushed open. The Mechanic followed him inside.

The boy busied himself lighting several hurricane lanterns. As they began to fill the room with soft orange light, the Mechanic saw that this was an apartment of several small rooms, each separated from the others by hanging curtains. The space was clean, or at least cleaner than the rest of the building. There were large, soft pillows lying around the floor, and blankets and shawls folded near them. An ornate hookah stood in one corner, and there were several gummy cubes of hashish laid out neatly on a small side table. The Mechanic's eyes flicked over these without registering.

"Please sit," the boy said, gesturing to the pillows.

The Mechanic paused for a moment as the translator decoded these words and conveyed them to his ear. He had roamed the streets for three days listening to conversations, giving the translator enough exposure to learn the local languages. There were several tongues being spoken in this city, but Arabic and English were the primary two, and the translator could now handle both of these with little hesitation. This boy, however, was speaking an English heavily influenced by some other language, and the translation came on a slight delay.

When the Mechanic understood the boy's words, he took a seat, letting his backpack drop to the floor. He wore a *gal-*

labiya, the loose white cotton robe of the natives, with an over-robe of thicker wool that hung on him like a cape. His gray skin made him look sickly. He seated himself so his stunner knife, strapped to his ankle, was easily accessible. He had adjusted its dial and set it to human tolerances.

The boy gestured to the hookah and the cubes of hashish. "May I offer you the pipe?" he asked.

The Mechanic shook his head dismissively. The boy was used to his clients experiencing some embarrassment. To save the Mechanic the trouble of making the first move, he smiled and pulled off his tank top, then knelt in front of him. He brushed a hand across one of the Mechanic's shoulders and whispered, "What would you like, then?"

The Mechanic was disgusted by the boy's proximity. He smelled of some kind of oil, too perfumed and mingled with the smell of sweat.

The boy gently took the Mechanic's left hand and kissed the palm. The Mechanic forced his lips into a smile and ran his hand behind the boy's neck. The boy looked pleased. Then the Mechanic shifted his weight. In one motion he unseated the boy and sent him falling backward onto the floor. With his right hand he grabbed the stunner knife from its ankle sheath and flicked it on.

The boy was confused. He could not see the knife yet and he was unsure whether the attack was foreplay or a serious threat. Then the Mechanic brought the knife up and lightly pierced the skin at the intersection of his jawline and cheek. The boy's expression changed to fear as he felt pain shoot upward into his head. The fear melted into anger as he realized that he could easily overpower this man. He moved his arms to throw the Mechanic off of him, but his arms would not respond to his command.

The tip of the Mechanic's knife had found the nerves of the boy's jaw, and it had begun to overload them with small electrical signals directed at the central nervous system and the brain. The signals told the boy's body to shut down his motor controls, to render him motionless.

The boy's shoulders and hips twitched as he tried to move his limbs, but they were increasingly unresponsive. In moments, his body relaxed into limpness on the floor. His eyes stayed open, staring up at the Mechanic, but they were fading out of focus.

The Mechanic pulled his arm from under the boy and got to his feet. His heart was beating quickly, and he felt adrenaline fear in his veins. He had never been good at physical confrontation—how many times had he suffered in silence rather than face up to his tormentors? But the boy was immobilized and the most dangerous part of this deed was over. He sheathed his knife and straightened his robes.

He looked down at the boy, lying awkwardly with one of his legs twisted and one arm tucked under his body. Seeing him helpless, the Mechanic became annoyed and kicked him in the side, just between his hips and ribs. "You won't touch me like that again," he said in disgust. He wiped his left hand on his outer robe to remove the boy's smell from his skin.

Then he settled himself cross-legged on the floor and pulled his ancient first aid kit from the backpack. Inside were several dozen vials of ancient medicinals, and next to these were two new vials containing mixtures the Mechanic had compounded earlier that day. He took one of the new vials and poured it into a hypodermic syringe.

He turned to look at the boy as he screwed a large needle into place atop the syringe. He held the hypodermic up teasingly. "I have your future in here," he said, squeezing the bubbles from the mixture. The boy's expression did not change, of course, but the Mechanic imagined that he was silently terrified.

He knelt on the floor and inserted the needle into one of the arteries in the boy's neck. Slowly, he injected all of the mixture. The boy did not move, could not move; his blank eyes stared up at the ceiling. But the Mechanic knew that the boy's circulatory system was carrying the injection throughout his body. Through his capillaries it would reach the cells of his muscles and his organs, and when it did, it would create a great want in him, a want that only the Mechanic could fulfill.

The Mechanic removed the syringe and stood back. The stun of the knife would be wearing off soon and the boy's reactions would be unpredictable.

After several minutes, there was a twitch in the boy's hand. Then his dark eyes blinked. Soon his arms and legs began to move. His motions were erratic as his body tried to regain control of itself. Then the boy let out a wail of agony, rolled onto his stomach, and curled himself into a ball.

The Mechanic's mouth twitched. *First stage of addiction,* he thought. *The body is drained.*

The boy began to writhe, clutching at his stomach, his arms, his feet, his head. "Dear God!" he cried out in French, biting his hand to stop himself from screaming. "Dear God!" He turned his head to look at the Mechanic. "What have you done to me?" he cried.

"I have given you a disease, of sorts," the Mechanic said, standing well away from the boy and holding his stunner knife at ready.

"Why?" the boy cried. "Why . . ."

"I need your help."

The boy convulsed in another wave of pain. Then he forced himself up onto hands and knees. He tried to lunge, to rush the Mechanic, but he found that he could not. His muscles did not obey; they were cramped, weak, drained.

"What have you done to me?" he cried again, and his arms went to his abdomen, clutching it tightly. He rolled himself into a ball again and retched violently, but there was nothing in his stomach. A continuous low moan issued from his mouth.

After a few moments, the Mechanic said calmly, "I have the cure to what you're feeling. I can fix you." Despite the pain, the boy turned to him and gave him his full attention, and he noticed now that the Mechanic was speaking through a strange device on his jaw. On the street, it had been too dark to see his face clearly. "What do you call yourself?" the Mechanic asked.

"Jean-Claude." This between clenched teeth.

"Jean-Claude," the Mechanic repeated, pronouncing the name awkwardly. "You must pay close attention." He knelt in front of Jean-Claude and then, with the deactivated stunner knife, prodded gently at the bottom of the boy's chin, forcing him to turn up his face and look at the Mechanic. He held up another vial for him to see.

"In this vial I have the antidote to the craving your body feels. I have what it wants." He shook it in front of the boy's eyes. "I have only enough for one dose. When I give it to you, you will feel much better. It is possible you will feel better than you have ever felt. But this will not last. Within the space of one day, the want will be upon you again, just as strong, perhaps stronger. Only I can mix you another dose of antidote. If you harm me in any way, you will never have that dose. Do you understand?"

The boy stared at the Mechanic through eyes that were bright with pain. "What do you want?"

"I want your help. Your service."

The boy gestured at his body. "You can do whatever you want with me. I would have done it anyway."

The Mechanic shook the boy's chin hard. "Not your body, gutter rat! You will protect me. You will make sure that I am always safe. For if something happens to me, you will die a long death that will be unimaginably painful. What you feel now is only a small taste of the pain in store for you. Do you understand?"

The boy did not understand, not really, but he wanted what was in that vial. He wanted it with every fiber of his body.

"Tell me you understand," the Mechanic said.

"I understand," the boy answered.

"Good. Then lie back and hold yourself still."

Jean-Claude did. The Mechanic poured the second vial into the syringe. He injected the antidote into Jean-Claude's neck, nearly missing the artery in the boy's jerking body.

As the mixture entered his veins, Jean-Claude felt instant relief. It was as though every cell within him had cried out for water, and then a river had drenched him. No, not a river, a mountain stream, running with the purest water of early ice melts. A substance so clear, so perfect, that every cell cried out in relief. And after relief they sang to him in ecstasy. The injection vaulted him from pain to comfort to physical exhilaration within the space of a few moments. He felt his body filling with energy.

He looked up at the Mechanic, who now stood above him holding the stunner knife.

"Very good . . ." Jean-Claude whispered. And it was.

The Mechanic smiled. He had acquired his first slave. This one was to be his guard, his muscle. He would need one more. Someone skilled in the politics of this planet, someone to guide him through the negotiations ahead.

Three days later, Nate Douglas, a young consular aide at the American Embassy in Cairo, sat in Jean-Claude's room with his hands tied behind his back, staring at the Mechanic. Jean-Claude stood patiently behind the Mechanic, watching the proceedings with detachment.

"The United States, England, France, Germany, China," Nate was saying, his hands twisting against the rope, his body jerking in small spasms he could not control. "Any of the major industrial nations—"

"Which are . . . ?" the Mechanic prompted.

"There are quite a few!" He stared at his tormentor. The man was wearing local clothing, but he did not look like a local. His skin had gray tones that Nate had never seen before. The cast of the man's skin reminded him of an albino, but it was truly gray, not white. The man spoke to Nate through some sort of translation device mounted along his jaw. It was a technology the American had never before encountered.

He was asking questions that had obvious answers, questions that marked him as completely unfamiliar with the political structure of Earth, marked him almost as . . . a newcomer. This was a train of thought Nate could not follow at the moment. His body was experiencing a gnawing pain that consumed most of his attention.

He had known it was a mistake to follow the boy back to his room. There were easier and safer ways to indulge his urges, but he had been swept up in a momentary sense of adventure when he saw Jean-Claude standing on the corner. The boy was very fine looking, and Nate had given in to temptation. He tried to keep his homosexual encounters few and far between, but he could not always stop himself. Now here he was, a prisoner of a man whose business Nate wanted no part of.

"You will write down the names for me," the Mechanic said.

"Yes, sure, I'll write them down. . . . Can I have some water please?"

"Not yet," the Mechanic said with infinite patience. "What other countries?"

"Japan. Russia, maybe, but they have enough internal problems that I don't think the government would be overly interested. You could sell whatever this is to them, but they would probably sell it again to someone else."

"On what would a sale to one of these countries depend?" the Mechanic asked.

Nate sighed, twisting in his ropes. "Several factors. They would want to verify that the technology works, of course. That would come first. Then they would want to know that it will give them something others don't have. If several countries are interested, that would increase the value, just as it would in any bargaining—a little water, please!" The words seemed ripped out of him. His throat was burning. He swallowed convulsively.

"No, not yet."

Nate shut his eyes as a wave of nausea and pain washed over him. He would try to tell this man whatever he could. Anything to be untied and have a glass of water. "Of course, you should be careful," he explained. "If you reveal what your technology is, there's always the chance that they will be able to duplicate it on their own."

"That won't be a problem in this case," the Mechanic said. "Even if they know this technology exists, it would take several centuries to approximate it—if ever."

Nate's heart sank. He should have been intrigued by this revelation, but all he could think was that he was in far over his head. This man was an unknown quantity. Possibly not even from Earth. Could that be? Could he be alien? A day ago, an hour ago, Nate would have scoffed at such a suggestion, but now? The translator at his jaw, the skin, the injection—all things Nate had never encountered before. And here he was, caught in this man's web.

He pushed this from his mind. All that mattered was their present conversation. He must make himself useful to this man, and then maybe he would get something to drink. "Will you tell me what this technology is specifically?" he asked. "Why it's so valuable? Perhaps I can help you strategize."

The Mechanic was filling the syringe again. "I will tell you soon," he replied, leaning forward with the needle.

Nate began to struggle. "What is that? Please don't!"

"Jean-Claude!" the Mechanic called. Jean-Claude moved forward and used his big arms to hold Nate in place. Somewhere in his mind, Jean-Claude perhaps felt the horror of what he was doing. He was making another slave for the Mechanic. But he was caught in the wonderful grip of his antidote, and he would not let such thoughts bother him.

"No!" Nate yelled, as the needle pierced his throat. He tried to kick the Mechanic, but his legs weren't working properly now. The pain was great and it was becoming greater. He felt the energy draining from his muscles, and a terrible craving invaded him.

Chapter 19

Adaiz-Ari bent over the stream and brought up a handful of water. He could see the reflection of his face, copper-colored skin, and reddish hair. He had cut off his two long queues and now all his hair was cropped close to the scalp. He doused his head, then dipped and doused again. He ran wet hands over his face and stood up.

His chest was bare and he wore loose trousers that tied at his waist. On his feet were simple sandals with foam and rubber soles. This was the typical outfit of a Lucien civilian. Nearby was the loose, hooded robe he wore over his clothes. His body was beginning to recover from the deprivations of the ship.

They were taking a brief rest in a small depression between two low hills. There were sparse trees here, and grazing antelope who fed on the short grass. In the trees were dozens of small monkeys who chattered incessantly to each other.

Enon-Amet was also kneeling at the stream. His silver hands lifted the water and poured it over the top of his head. Then his head and neck twisted in a quick motion, allowing the water to spill evenly in all directions. The movement reminded Adaiz of a bird, and he envied Enon for its fluidity.

Enon stretched his long arms, then stood up from the water, reveling in the sun on his bare chest. His skin was regaining some of its silver reflectiveness and was beginning to fill out over the articulated sheaf of bone that extended from his waist

to his shoulders and made him, like all Lucien, difficult to
wound. This sheaf was crowned by a high collarbone that pro-
truded upward several inches in a distinctive wide ring. A Lucien could lay his head down along one shoulder within the
protection of this collar.

Enon had also been wearing a full-body hooded robe since
landing on earth, to cover his alien shape from human eyes. At
the moment, however, they were concealed in the depression
where they stood, and it was safe to be robeless for a little
while. They had, in fact, encountered no humans yet.

"Here," Adaiz said to his brother, holding out a canteen of
water that he had treated to make potable. The canteen had a
nozzle to fit the Lucien mouth.

Enon took the canteen and drank several gulps of it. "So
good," he sighed. "I had almost forgotten what a difference
freshness makes."

"This rivals the freshest water on Galea," Adaiz said, "or
perhaps it is simply my human taste buds."

"No, it is wonderful."

They spoke Avani to each other, but Adaiz had prepared for
this part of their mission by learning English, the most widely
used of Earth languages. He had become fluent while still on
the ship, during the months when they were orbiting Saturn,
watching Pruit's ship as it orbited Jupiter. How easy human
languages were for him after speaking a language designed for
other mouths! His Lucien brother had learned some rudimentary phrases in English, but Enon found the speech quite difficult.

A monkey screeched nearby, his voice rising above the general cacophony of his cohorts. Adaiz and Enon turned to watch
the creature's incoherent diatribe as he swung about the tree.
Enon flexed his antlers in the Lucien equivalent of a smile.
There was wildlife in fascinating abundance here.

Lucien had little truck with animals in the current incarnation of their society. There were only a few tame species that
lived as pets, and of course fish in their growth tanks. It had
not always been so. In the ancient times, when the Lucien still

lived on their home planet Rheat, there had been oceans and forests and wildlife, and a Lucien population reaching into the billions.

Then had come the Plague, the ancient war with the Kinley. Though the Lucien had rained bombs down upon those Kinley humans, and had admittedly been the first to strike, the humans had not retaliated in kind. Instead, they had devised a biological weapon against which the Lucien had no defense. They had released a Plague upon Rheat, and it had, within a matter of weeks, killed every man, woman, and child upon the planet. None had survived. Only the few Lucien living in their asteroid colonies had escaped death, and the Kinley had ever afterward been known as Plaguers.

But Adaiz would not dwell on thoughts of those times. His mission was here and now and, when successful, would prevent such devastation from ever recurring.

"Elder Brother, shall we have an Opening?" Adaiz asked.

"Yes," Enon replied, cocking his head to one side in agreement. "It will be good to relax our minds that they may better absorb this environment."

The two of them sat down facing each other, their legs crossed in front of them.

They began with three deep breaths. Though Adaiz was the younger brother, he had passed Enon in understanding and application of the Katalla-Oman, the book of self-knowledge, and Enon now respectfully deferred to him in matters of meditation. As they began their breathing, Enon was following Adaiz's lead. When they expelled their third breath, they allowed their eyes to float closed.

"First is awareness of body," Adaiz said softly.

They relaxed themselves by feeling every muscle. Slowly, as Adaiz became aware of his muscles, they released their hidden energy and became neutral. He could sense his organs and his skin; he could feel his whole body.

"I am aware of it," Enon whispered, echoing Adaiz's own mind.

"Very good. Second is awareness of environment," Adaiz intoned quietly.

Adaiz let his awareness travel beyond his skin, beyond his body. He perceived the grass beneath him and felt a slight breeze on his forehead. Being in open air on a planet was an awe-inspiring experience. The blue of the sky seemed to go on forever, and the horizon appeared to him impossibly far away.

Adaiz reached out for Enon's mind. When he touched it, instead of peaceful relaxation he could feel the thoughts churning in his brother's head.

"Older Brother," Adaiz said softly, "your mind is loud."

"Yes," Enon whispered, "you are right. It is difficult today, in this new place."

"For me also. Shall we try again?"

"Yes."

Adaiz started the ritual over, and this time, as he expanded his awareness, he felt his mind floating through the past hours of their journey. They had landed on earth the night before, hiding their small shuttle ship in the lush cloud forest to the north. They had been working their way south ever since, out of the forest and into gentle hills at the edge of wide grasslands. Adaiz found himself both dreading and longing for his first encounter with the native humans, though he could not understand this emotion. After all, he was Lucien, and there was no reason to believe he would feel anything special for the foreign creatures who made this world their home.

Adaiz caught himself. His own mind was becoming loud. He dissolved these contemplations and concentrated instead on perception of the world around him. His body sat on grass; his face was brushed by a breeze; there were scents of water and animals and vegetation in the air. Slowly, he knew these things, he felt these things, he became these things.

Ten minutes later, when they surfaced and became aware of their bodies again, Adaiz felt powerful and relaxed. His mind was his to control.

*   *   *

In predawn of the following day, they came up over a long, low rise and saw, nestled in a clearing between bushes and trees, the object of their search. Enon, whose eyesight was somewhat better than Adaiz's, spotted it first. The sky was still dark. Only the east was yet light, but when Adaiz squinted his eyes, he could see the Plaguer pod, a dark brown shape that was too regular in this wild land.

The two of them worked their way toward the landing site as the sky grew lighter. In half an hour they were approaching the pod across its clearing. From this proximity, Adaiz saw that it had been a very hard landing indeed.

The pod appeared to have skidded before settling. There were several long grooves where it had torn away vegetation. The bottom, spherical half of the ship had dug itself three feet into the soil. The top, cylindrical half pointed out from the ship at an awkward angle.

They signaled to each other, and each of them pulled his hood up over his head and checked to ensure his weapons were ready. Adaiz approached first. As he neared, he was hit by the smell of the ship. It was a sickly chemical burning, which he guessed must be coming from the propulsion system. Even three days after landing, the odor was acrid and strong.

He reached the pod and glanced around it. He could see no one. He touched the outer skin of the sphere and felt that it was tough and slightly warm, almost . . . alive. The Lucien were aware that the Plaguers' technology was heavily based in biology. It seemed biology extended even to the outer layer of their ships. Near the upper cylinder, where there had clearly been an explosion, the skin was scarred and scabbed like real skin would be, and in many places he could see that it had attempted to regrow.

He located the hatchway, which stood ajar, and gestured to Enon that he was going to look inside. Enon tilted his head in assent.

Adaiz peered into the pod. The controls had all gone dead. The interior was hot, too hot for human comfort. There was no one in the sphere. He pulled himself in and glanced up into the cylinder, where the air was even warmer. It too was empty. He quickly dropped back down and out, already sweating.

He found the human occupant of the pod outside, lying close up against the craft, in the shadow of the cylinder which hung above the man's body at a thirty-degree angle from the ground. In this early light it was almost impossible to make him out. All Adaiz could tell was that the figure was human.

"Come," Adaiz said quietly to his brother.

Enon joined him and together they peered down at the crumpled shape.

"Is it alive?" his brother asked.

"I don't know," Adaiz said. He removed his robe and got down on hands and knees in his trousers. He crawled up to the man, feeling the heat radiating from the cylinder. The man's back was to him, with his stomach hugging the skin of the pod. He was not moving. He appeared badly wounded and was tangled in a suit of red clothing. Adaiz pulled gently on the man's undershirt and rolled him onto his back.

Something was odd about his shape, but the man still lay in shadows and was difficult to see. He seemed fairly small.

"He's breathing," Adaiz said softly. The man's chest was moving, but shallowly. He put a hand to his neck and felt a faint pulse. The skin was cold and moist, as though he'd been through a fever and his body was now running at a subnormal temperature.

The red fullsuit was over the man's legs and half tucked under his body. Adaiz took hold of it and pulled the man out of the shadow and into the blue light of dawn.

He could see him clearly then. And in a surprised flash of understanding, Adaiz realized that it was not a man at all. It was a woman. The knowledge was shocking somehow. It was a girl. Not him, but her. She.

"It's a woman," Adaiz said slowly.

"Interesting. I've never seen one."

"Neither have I."

Indeed, she was the first human woman Adaiz had ever seen in person. The few humans who had been bred by the Lucien were all male, for the male gender was slightly less prone to infection and disease, and the Lucien had not wished to breed both sexes. He had seen pictures of women in books of anatomy, but never in the flesh. Looking at Pruit, Adaiz noticed immediately the differences in her appearance, differences he had not imagined from looking at mere pictures. Her coloring was just like his, but her build was slighter, more curved, more delicate.

His eyes moved to her hands and legs. Her ankles were in the suit, but above the suit line her legs had blisters and dark singes of black. Her hands were also purple with burns. One of her ankles looked broken.

"Omani's Heart," he breathed, "that was a rough landing."

Enon studied her with him, but his eyes could not as easily discern the magnitude of her wounds. "Do you think she will heal?" he asked.

Adaiz knelt and studied the red suit. Its surface was very tough and finely woven. It was thick and quite heavy, and he could feel unknown mechanisms within it.

"I'm not well enough trained in human physiology to answer that," he said. "But I think her suit is intended to repair her. I'll try to attach it to her properly."

"Mark her first."

Adaiz tilted his head in agreement. Marking her was needed, for they wished to follow this woman, if she recovered, and find the technology she sought. He withdrew a small marker from his pack and gently eased Pruit onto her side. He pulled up her shirt and ran a hand along her spine. It was different, he noticed, from his own. The arch was more pronounced and her waist curved down into it. Her lines were nicer than his, he thought.

He placed the marker tab against her mid back and jiggled it. He felt the tiny metal mole within the tab release and slide under her skin. Then he studied her back. The marker made a tiny additional bump along one of her vertebrae, almost unnoticeable.

"I'd prefer two for safety," he said.

"It seems sensible," Enon replied.

Adaiz marked her again, lower on her back. His placing of the second mole was better. Only his knowledge that it was there allowed him to see its location.

"While you tend to her, I want to examine the pod," Enon said. Adaiz could tell the girl was of little interest to his brother.

"All right," he replied.

Enon moved off, leaving Adaiz alone with her. He rolled her onto her back again and sat looking at her for several moments. Her face was covered with bruises, but despite them he was intrigued by her features. They were gentler and narrower than his own and, he thought, more pleasing to the eye.

He found that he wanted very much to touch her, to let his hands run over her body. Even now he felt himself reaching for her. It was something about the difference between her and him. The difference made him long to bridge the gap and be close to her.

He stopped himself and studied these feelings. They were urges of his own body, he quickly realized. *Is this what humans feel?* he wondered. He did not like the sensation of being at the mercy of his flesh.

He brought his attention back to the work at hand. She was hurt and would die without his help. He busied himself untangling the red suit and pulling it up flat beneath her. His chest came into contact with hers as he did so, and he was surprised by the electric sensation this produced in his own body. He looked down at her breasts beneath her shirt. In his studies of human anatomy, he had wondered many times about breasts. They seemed unwieldy features, but now that he saw them up close, he realized how well they complemented the female form. Gently he lifted up her shirt and looked at them more closely. They were each about the size of a fruit that could fit neatly into his cupped hand. Her copper skin was lighter beneath her shirt and her breasts were light tan. The nipples were much darker, a reddish brown. They were beautiful somehow.

The urge to touch her—not to touch, he realized, but to caress—was great, and it could not be justified as professional curiosity. This in itself made him recoil. Growing up without human women around, Adaiz had prided himself on living without the urges of the flesh. He had always felt superior to his Lucien friends, who seemed to lose the ability to fully control themselves when an attractive female was near. He would not give in to such a physical demand. He took a deep breath and quieted his mind.

The sun was nearing the horizon now and Adaiz could already feel the air warming up. He pulled her shirt down to cover her and tucked her arms into the sleeves of the suit. He flipped the suit gloves into place over her hands.

He watched in fascination as the bioarms of the suit grew out and reached for the girl's skin. Plaguer science was truly impressive. Adaiz would recommend, upon returning home, that the Lucien spend more time studying it.

He gripped the sealing fob of Pruit's suit, which was down by her hip. He slid it up toward her neck, pulling the suit closed as he did. Near the top, he stopped. There was writing inside the suit up by her chest. He studied it. It was her name, written in Soulene, the modern Plaguer tongue, which he could both read and speak. "Proo-it," he sounded it out. "Pruit." Her name. He pulled the fob the rest of the way up and found that he was relieved to have her body out of view.

Only her face remained uncovered, and he pulled the hood out from underneath her head. "Pruit," he whispered again, not knowing why the name intrigued him so. At the sound of his voice, her eyes twitched. He paused, watching her. They twitched again, then slowly came open, blue human eyes staring upward.

He watched as partial consciousness returned to her. She moved her head slightly. Adaiz felt a quickening in his heart as he realized that she was looking up at him. Her eyes came into focus. Her lips moved, as though she would speak, but no sound came out.

Her eyes fell shut. Adaiz paused for a moment, then reached

again for her hood. Before he could move it, her eyes opened again.

"Who are you?" she asked in a voice scratchy with thirst and pain.

Before Adaiz could decide whether or not he should answer, her eyes closed again. This time they did not open. Exhaustion had reclaimed her.

Adaiz sealed her hood into place. She was now completely enveloped in the fullsuit, and as he watched, it shifted itself into an active mode. There was motion in the layers of the suit. It was beginning to minister to her wounds. It would take care of her.

He turned away. Enon was now inside the pod, studying the controls. Adaiz felt no urge to join him.

She. She. She had spoken to him. She had looked at him. She had seen him.

His body was chattering to him all on its own. *She.*

His mind was loud.

Through clouds of pain and unconsciousness, Pruit saw the face of a young Kinley man leaning over her. She knew he was Kinley by his coloring and features, but behind him was a great dome of blue. She was conscious for only a moment before her eyes fell shut again. This time, however, she was not falling back into agony. She was swathed in her fullsuit, and her body seemed to float in its care. The bioarms had entered her skin and taken over her physical functions.

In long pockets between layers of the suit was biofluid and everything her body would need to make it well. She was hurt badly enough to strain the suit's resources, but it would find a way to heal her nonetheless.

Chapter 20

Eddie stood at the only public phone, and perhaps one of the few phones of any kind, in the town of Dashur, seven miles from the dig site. Dashur sat near the distinct border of fertile land and desert, that almost sharp line where foliage ended and sand began. A small canal off the Nile ran parallel to Dashur's central street, which was a wide path of dirt and stone, trod to almost cement hardness by generations of feet. There were date palms across the narrow canal, towering over mud-brick huts and small farms that were tended by dark men driving donkeys.

The phone stood outside a small restaurant that served pigeon and fresh pita bread and an assortment of pickled vegetables. Along the street were market vendors, selling fresh produce. Several donkeys pulling carts of tomatoes passed as Eddie consolidated an enormous pile of coins from his pockets and prepared to dial. A young boy driving one of the donkeys turned to him and smiled at the sound of the coins, a sprig of grain grass clenched between his teeth. Eddie smiled and flipped a coin at him. The boy caught it neatly and slipped it into his pocket.

The phone was mounted in an open stand, shielded from the sun by a yellow metal box which bore the word "telephone" in Arabic. The box was covered in dust, but other than that it had not been defaced in any way. The phone was an object of some importance to the town and was respected. Eddie leaned in under the lip of the box to shield his head from the midday sun.

A waft of fresh bread from the restaurant hit his nose as he picked up the receiver. He was long since over the typical bout of dysentery, known as the Pharaoh's Revenge, that a traveler endures in the first few weeks in Egypt, and he was now free to enjoy local foods without fear of the consequences.

He dialed a long series of numbers, and then plugged the phone with a seemingly endless stream of change until at last he heard the clicks of the call going through. He glanced at his watch and calculated the time difference, realizing it would be the middle of the night in Los Angeles. He decided she would forgive him. The phone began to ring.

"Hello?" The voice on the other end had clearly just woken up.

"Callen?"

"Eddie?"

"Did I wake you up?"

"It doesn't matter." She sounded fully awake all of a sudden, as though she had been eagerly awaiting his call.

"Can you hear me okay?"

"Yeah, yeah. It's a good connection."

"Did you—" he started.

"Listen, Eddie," she said, interrupting him excitedly. "I have news!"

"What?" he asked, excitement gripping him as well, for he assumed she was talking about the same subject on his mind.

"I'm engaged!" She sprang the words on him without further warning.

"What?" He was truly stunned.

"I'm engaged, can you believe it?"

"I've only been gone for two months. How could this happen?"

Callen took his tone as humorous, and continued, describing the man who had won this commitment from her. Eddie took only parts of it in. He fed another meal of coins into the phone as she spoke. It was hard to believe she was serious.

"He sounds great," Eddie commented halfheartedly as she wrapped up the panegyric to her betrothed.

"What's the matter?" she asked, only now realizing that he wasn't quite as thrilled as she had expected him to be.

"I don't know, it just sounds so . . . final."

"Of course it's final," she said, coming down from her excitement. "I'm not making marriage plans on a whim. I thought you'd be happy."

Eddie wiped his forehead. "I know we decided not to see each other anymore. I just didn't know that you meant really and not ever."

"I have to get on with my life," she said gently. "Teenage affairs aren't supposed to last into your thirties."

"It seems so . . . I don't know—adult."

"You say that like it's a bad thing."

"I'm just surprised," he said. He took a breath and looked around the village, suddenly less enchanted with his surroundings. Then he forced himself to lighten up. He wasn't being fair. "I'm sorry. I am happy for you." He said it with difficulty. "I'm sure he's a great person and you'll have a wonderful life together."

"That was amazingly lukewarm."

"Well, give me a second! I'm getting used to the idea." Why was he surprised? It was bound to happen sometime. Callen was going on without him, as she had always threatened to do. She had left him back in childhood where he probably belonged. Unless . . . unless he could change somehow. "I am happy," he said again, and this time he almost meant it.

"Good." She didn't sound convinced.

"Really. Next time we talk, I swear I'll be happy."

"Okay, okay." He could tell she was smiling now. "I have other news."

"Don't tell me you're pregnant!"

"No," she laughed. "About your crystal."

His initial excitement returned immediately. The crystal was the reason for the phone call. He glanced around him, feeling guilty. There were men sitting outside the restaurant, drinking sugared tea, and a few children playing on the bank of the river. No eyes were turned to him. "You heard back from the crystallographer?" Eddie had sent her one of the two pilfered crystals, mailing it from a hotel in Cairo so it would look like a tourist trinket to customs. With its industrial manufacturing divisions, Bannon-DeLacy employed dozens of experts on crystals, many varieties of which were used in building heavy machinery. Callen had agreed to pull a few strings and find someone to help him.

"Yes," she said, her tone also becoming excited again. "I even went to see him. He's enthralled."

"What did he say?"

"He said it's a diamond, though it's an odd shape for a diamond, with something else suspended within it to create the orange coloring, probably iron combined with another element. He'd have to chip off a piece if we wanted to know the component parts with certainty, but he didn't want to damage it unless he had to."

"What about the green bands?"

"He doesn't know what they are. Says he's never seen anything like them. They were definitely grown in at the time the crystal was formed. Even though they're a foreign substance, they don't weaken the structure of the crystal as a whole. He tested it."

"How does he think it was formed?"

"He's stumped, Eddie. And that doesn't happen to this fellow very often. He wants to find out who has the patent on the technique. He's already thought of a dozen possible applications. So where did you get it?"

Eddie chuckled, drawing out his own delicious feeling of suspense. "I didn't exactly get it."

"What do you mean?"

"I stole it."

"Eddie!"

"Actually I found it, and six others like it. They were inside a stone box that was buried in a temple of Osiris that's been underground for about five thousand years."

There was a long pause on the other end of the line, then: "Eddie, it's not a natural crystal. He said it would be impossible for something like this to occur naturally. It's an industrial-grade diamond, extremely pure, not something that can form outside of a lab."

"I know, Cal," he said simply. He had already guessed that the crystals could not be natural. Though Emmett Smith had not yet had time to send the other crystals to experts, he felt certain they would eventually meet with the same conclusion. "That's why I sent it to you. It's man-made, by a process that isn't even in use yet, but it's been buried in the Egyptian desert for several thousand years."

Again the pause, as though all of Eddie's wild theories over the years were flooding back through her mind. "Are . . . are you sure?"

"The dirt and sand around the temple have not been touched. And we've dated it from an inscription on the temple door. I'm very sure."

"Jesus!"

"Not Jesus, Callen," he smiled into the phone. "Someone long before him."

"What are you going to do?"

"I'm going to keep digging."

Chapter 21

The gods were respected for their magical rather than
their moral powers.

—J. E. Manchip White
Ancient Egypt: Its Culture and History

The Mechanic sat by a clear pool of water. He was leaning
over the surface and studying the reflection of his face. His
dark gray hair was long, and he wore it in a loose tail at the
back of his neck. His face was shaved, and his skin was deeply
lined from years in the hot Egyptian sun. His features were
plain, that much he knew, and he wondered vaguely what it
would be like to be beautiful. His mouth twisted into a wry
grimace at this thought, and he slapped the water, disrupting
his image. *Beauty can't win love,* he thought. *Or loyalty. Not
really.*

He was sitting in the royal gardens, leaning out over an artificial pool that had been designed in the shape of a lily.
Nearby, an ancient gardener was bent over a plot of vegetables, carefully watering each one. The man was all but naked,
and though his skin was beginning to droop, his muscles were
still clear and strong from a lifetime of physical labor. The
Mechanic watched him for a moment, wondering if he could
order the man to go get him something to drink. He did not

want to try this, for if the man refused, the Mechanic would be shamed. *Cursed locals,* he thought. *Dirty cursed old man.*

He was waiting in the garden for the Captain, who was now ensconced in one of the royal garden lodges with none other than Queen Hetep-heres. In the last months the Captain had become her lover, and they met in secret in that lodge, hidden at a remote corner of the palace grounds. None but the queen's closest servants were privy to their meetings, but the rumors were already spreading.

Every time the Captain met her, he brought along the Mechanic to stand outside the door as a guard. *As a servant,* the Mechanic thought. *That's what I am now. Maybe that's what I've always been.* Today, however, he had wandered away. Let the Captain hire a local guard if he wanted protection. The Mechanic was tired of that job.

"What are you doing here?"

The Mechanic was startled. He turned toward the voice and saw a soldier below a stand of fig trees. It was Seka, one of the king's personal honor guard, a man with muscles like thick ropes beneath his dark skin. He wore a brown linen kilt, and a cheetah skin over his back. The Mechanic could see the hilt of a long knife sticking up from his waistline, and he carried a ceremonial spear as a sign of his rank.

"Waiting," the Mechanic replied.

"Who gave you permission?"

The Mechanic studied the man for a moment, scared of him. Then he smiled. He saw the right course of action. The Captain could fend for himself. "I am here with my master."

"Your master," Seka scoffed. "Who has given him permission?"

"Surely you have heard," the Mechanic said sweetly. He spoke without need of a translator. Like the Captain, he had learned the local tongue. "His permission is from the queen. They meet regularly. They are meeting right now." He could see the shock on Seka's face as his words sank in.

"They . . . He . . . he is alone with the queen?"

The Mechanic laughed. "Come, come, Seka. Don't play the innocent. You have heard the rumors, surely."

"I do not listen to rumors."

"Then you will always be the last to know."

"Wait here!" He was flustered. He stared at the Mechanic for a moment, then turned and jogged back toward the palace.

The Mechanic smiled. It was time to stop being the Captain's lackey. Slowly, he made his way back to the lodge.

The interior of the lodge was beautiful. It was one large spacious room, with a vaulted ceiling and several windows set high in the walls. A breeze came through these, just strong enough to ruffle the draped fabric around the bed.

The Captain stood behind a carved folding screen, changing out of his survey team standard-issue work clothes and into the light robe that had been laid out for him. He had bathed before coming, and his hair, which had grown long over the past years, was oiled slightly and tied in a thick braided loop at the base of his neck. It was a hairstyle unique to him, something that set him apart from the wigged men of the upper class. He would never have hidden his blond hair beneath a wig.

Changed into the robe, he stepped out from behind the screen and beheld Hetep-heres, sitting on the edge of the bed. She wore a loose white gown though which the brown skin of her body was easily visible. Her eyes were dark with kohl, and they had been painted with a hint of green beneath them.

"Revered Queen," he said, allowing himself a slight smile so she would know that the sight of her pleased him. "It is good to see you."

Hetep-heres bowed her head slightly and also allowed herself a smile. "Honored Lord, it has been too long."

"For that I am sorry," he replied, "but my time has been consumed in many things." It had been too long. But he did not trust himself to see her often; his desire for her could too easily overwhelm him. He was playing with fire in more ways than one. Though Hetep-heres, her servants, and the women she called her friends all secretly avowed their belief that the

Captain was Osiris, he still did not know the king's view. He had asked Hetep-heres several times, in a roundabout way, what her husband's beliefs were on this matter, but the queen did not know for sure. Thus the Captain was risking his own life every time he came to her. Far from keeping him away, this knowledge was part of her allure.

Slowly he walked over and took a seat on the bed. Everything in his attitude spoke of the favor he was granting her by appearing in her presence. Their speech to each other was always formal.

Hetep-heres took one of his hands and brought it to her lips. "Am I in your mind when you do not see me in the flesh?" she asked.

Gently he put a hand under her chin and lifted her face. He kissed her slowly and deliberately. "You are in my mind," he said. She smiled and touched his hair. Though some of it had given way to gray in recent years, it was still a sign of his status.

He pulled the tie of her gown, and it fell away from her shoulders, revealing her arms and chest. He kissed her neck very gently. Slowly his passion grew and they moved farther back onto the bed. She let her gown slip off of her entirely and reached for the Captain's robe.

Then the mood ended abruptly. There was a loud bang at the door. There was no warning, no sound of men outside, no hint of anything wrong, just a bang of a foot on the door, and then it was open and four men were inside the room, each of them holding spears and knives. The Captain sprang up to his knees and saw that they were men from the king's personal bodyguard, led by Seka, that viper who jealously guarded his master's house. The head of the cheetah on Seka's back stared at the Captain from his left shoulder, and its dangling paws looked ready to pounce.

"Seize him!" Seka yelled. Two men grabbed the Captain, whose robe hung off one shoulder. He did not struggle with them, though rage and fear were vying for control of his emotions. Through the doorway, he could see the Mechanic, standing in fear to one side.

The men dragged the Captain from the bed roughly. It was their intent to kill him, that much was certain by their attitudes. The Captain felt a surge of terror, but he knew his demeanor in the next few moments would be critical.

"You lay hands on the god!" Hetep-heres shouted. She was sitting up on the bed, still naked.

The Captain blessed her in his mind. The force of her words gave him the strength to play his role.

"You profane me with your touch!" he said in anger. He still did not struggle, for if he were to do so, it might be said that the guards had overpowered him. By holding himself still, it appeared that he simply did not deign to use force against them. "I am here on a duty of love but I will smite you if I am provoked to anger."

The two men holding him took his words to heart, and he felt their grip on him relax slightly. That was good. It meant they feared him. They were here at Seka's orders, not out of personal outrage. The Captain tore his arms away from them in a single quick motion.

The cheetah-clad Seka, however, was not cowed. He grabbed the Captain's shoulder, pushed him up against the wall, and leveled his spear at the Captain's heart.

"We shall see who smites whom," he said slowly. "If you are a god, you have nothing to fear from my spear." He raised it, preparing to strike.

"Hold!" a voice called from behind them. The Captain's assailant turned and saw the king himself standing in the doorway. King Snefru was out of breath, and he held the door frame as he looked in at them. Behind him were ten other guards. Snefru wore the short, white royal skirt, tied with a golden sash. His head was covered by the royal kerchief, the *nemes*, striped red and white. On his chest was an enormous pectoral of an eagle made from semiprecious stones and gold. It was out of place from his run.

The king was small in stature, but his face was angry, and the power of his anger could be felt by all present. Hetep-heres shrank back toward the head of the bed, quietly drawing the covers up over her body.

"Sire," Seka said, "I wished to keep this knowledge from you. I am ridding you of this presumptuous foreigner who has taken the queen as his woman. His death is my duty, but the queen herself is yours to punish."

Snefru walked up to the guard and grabbed the spear from his hand. "Are you stupid, or are you disloyal to my throne?" he asked. "Or is it both at once?"

"Sire?" He was shocked to find his master's anger directed at him.

Snefru slapped Seka's cheek with the spear, hard enough to leave a mark. "Take him to his barracks," he commanded the other guards. The men outside took hold of Seka and drew him out of the room. The Captain could see the Mechanic move closer to the doorway to watch, while still maintaining a safe distance.

Snefru turned to the Captain, who was straightening his robe. "Your worship," the king said, "I offer my humble apology for this interruption." He bowed his head low. "I am honored that you see fit to enrich my bloodline with your divinity, Lord Osiris."

The Captain heard the name, and it washed over him like cool water. Osiris. The king was a believer. The king had spoken his name aloud. Osiris. By that simple fact, the Captain truly became Osiris.

"There is no need to hide your love in this chamber, my lord. The palace is at your disposal."

"I thank you, honored king," the Captain said, assuming the proper tone and keeping in abeyance the shaking that threatened to overwhelm his voice.

"The chief guard will be adequately disciplined."

The Captain knew that Seka might well be executed, but he was still angry at the forced entry and felt no urge to intercede on the man's behalf. It was only the luck of timing that had saved him from the man's sword. "I leave that to your judgment," he said.

Snefru bowed his head in acknowledgment. Then he turned
to Hetep-heres, his wife and queen. "Revered wife, I understand your desire to lie with our divine visitor." He moved to
the bed, where she sat with the covers drawn up over her body.
He kissed her forehead, and the Captain saw that Snefru truly
held no rancor toward her. "Do not fear my anger. I am
pleased. He will enrich my line."

The Captain watched as Hetep-heres accepted her husband's
kiss. He could read her mind, for he had learned much about
her over the past years. She was honored by the god's interest
in her, but she had never once thought of the benefits to Snefru's line, of that much the Captain was sure. It had been a personal triumph for her, bedding a deity. But Snefru, the Captain
knew, was lucky to have her. Snefru had been the son of a very
minor wife of the previous king, Huni. Hetep-heres had been
the daughter of Huni's queen. Her half brother would never
have been able to secure the throne without his marriage to
her.

She smiled at her husband, saying, "Thank you, sire."

Snefru bowed once again to the Captain, and then withdrew
from the room, taking the last of the guards with him.

The Captain stared after the king a moment, then crossed
the room and closed the door, not even glancing at the Mechanic, who stood looking in at him. His mind was churning.
He was happy that the king had acknowledged him, but the incident had left him shaken.

Hetep-heres threw back the covers, beckoning him back to
the bed, but lovemaking was now the last thing on his mind.
He must figure out a way to cement his position. Without a
word to her, he changed back into his trousers and shirt. She
watched the screen in silence, nervous at his manner.

Dressed again, he said, "This must wait for another time."
He kissed her lips gently, then turned and walked out of the
room.

Outside, he found the Mechanic sitting with his back against
the wall. "Let's get back to camp," the Captain said brusquely.

The Mechanic got to his feet and joined him. They walked down a flight of garden steps toward their litters.

"I think it was the Lion," the Mechanic said quietly.

The Captain turned to him. "What?"

"You don't think the king just showed up, do you? I think it was the Lion who got the guards riled."

"I don't know what you're talking about!" the Lion said, his voice edging with anger.

"You've spoken against me to the king's guards," the Captain repeated. He, the Archaeologist, and the Lion were in the Captain's work tent. He had never bothered to upgrade the tent to a more permanent structure, for the camp was not where his primary interest lay. The Lion and his father were standing, and the Archaeologist was sitting in a chair behind the Captain's desk, watching their faces. "If things hadn't gone the way they did, I might be dead now."

"Believe me, Father, I say as little about you as I can."

"I'm not interested in having that argument now," the Captain said, goaded by his son's tone and its intimations of disapproval.

Ignoring this comment, the Lion pressed on. "What do you expect? You are making love to the queen! That will hardly promote domestic tranquillity."

"Actually," the Archaeologist said softly, "I believe the king now approves."

"How proud you must be!" the Lion said, turning on his mother. "Now your husband has everyone's permission to carry out this affair."

"The agreements between your mother and me are our own concern."

The Lion turned again to his father. He saw a man with features very similar to his own; they shared the same hair, the same skin, and faces that were as alike as brothers', excluding the difference in their ages. But the Lion could find little else they had in common anymore.

"I know my mother has taken to sleeping with her guards,"

he said, somewhat more calmly. He was resigned to these facts, though they didn't please him. "I could understand if you two were no longer happy with each other, but that doesn't seem to be the root of it. You're becoming strangers to me."

"This place is different," his mother said quietly. "We've agreed to live by different rules."

"I suppose that is your right," her son said after a pause. He was tired of this conversation. His parents now spoke a language that did not ring true to him, and he saw no reason to continue arguing. "You accused me of speaking against you to the guards, Father. I'm telling you I did not. My wager is that the Mechanic was the source of that information."

He looked at his father, but the Captain's face betrayed nothing. "At any rate," the Lion continued, "you shouldn't believe everything you hear. I know I don't. If I did, I might not speak to you at all."

With that, he strode out of the tent and into the afternoon sun, leaving his parents behind.

A little way off was his new wife, Ipwet, sitting with the Doctor and tending to several of the local children. The Lion pushed his parents from his mind and admired his wife as he walked over to her. She was a native girl, several years his junior, with dark, perfect skin, and a smile that made him weak.

"What's the matter?" she asked as he arrived at the table. His face held residual anger.

"It's not important," the Lion said, giving her a hug and burying his face in her neck.

"Are you sure?" Ipwet asked. "Something with your parents?"

"No, no, my heart," the Lion insisted, "it's not important."

"It was a near thing," the Captain said, sinking into a chair next to his wife. "But, as it turned out, a watershed moment."

"You seem to have navigated it quite well," the Archaeologist replied. Her tone was devoid of emotion.

The Captain studied her. "It hurts you when I'm with her."

She leaned back in her chair and looked up at the tent ceiling. Her blond hair, graying somewhat now, was pulled back from her face into a braided bun. "No," she said slowly. "Not anymore. You've at least been good enough to inform me of your intentions, and I've taken . . . comfort as well."

"Yes, so I've heard." He smiled at her in a somewhat prurient fashion, but she did not return the smile or even look at him.

"And I think there will be other consolations for me."

The Captain grew serious then and turned toward her. "There will be many consolations. For both of us. As long as we are in agreement."

She looked at him. "In agreement how?"

"The king named me as Osiris. The deed is done. In his eyes I have become the god incarnate."

"Congratulations."

"Now I must live up to it. *We* must live up to it."

She said nothing for a moment, thinking of what this might mean. Then, "Osiris has a wife. You want me to assume her role."

"I need you as my Isis. Together we can truly live like gods here. Apart we are vulnerable. They know you are my wife. A god may please himself with humans, but he would only marry another god. If you are human, then I am not who I claim to be."

"And aren't we human?" She said it not as a practical question, but as a philosophical one. "I told you to be a god. But underneath that, aren't we human?"

"What is a god but a man or woman who inspires those around him?"

It was a new thought for her, which took a few moments to digest. Perhaps he was right. Slowly, she said, "What about the son? What about Osiris's and Isis's son Horus? I don't think the Lion will willingly take on the role."

"He already has the role, like it or not," the Captain said. "He'll have to learn to behave himself."

Chapter 22

Present Day

Pruit stared up at the face of a tall black man. He wore a loose skirt of fabric that had been twined around his legs and groin, and a wide, flat, disclike necklace of joined beads. His dark skin looked unhealthy; his eyes were rheumy and the skin beneath them sagged, though he could not have been more than twenty years old. He had several open sores on his ankles and around his mouth. He stood at the edge of a village of mud-brick huts, a guard, holding a long spear with buzzard feathers tied beneath the spearhead.

The village behind him was nearly still. A single cow wandered listlessly through the mud between the huts, its ribs sticking out beneath its dirty hide. There was a cooking fire somewhere, but there was little else to mark this place as a living town.

The man spoke English, after a fashion, and he seemed much impressed with Pruit's clothing. She was wearing her red fullsuit, had been walking with it on for several days. Though she did not know it, her suit was much like the orange biohazard suits worn by a disease team that had passed through this village during the previous week. This made her a figure of authority and some awe to the young man.

She had rolled up the legs of the suit and her feet were in her traveling boots. Her right foot was still quite stiff, but the suit had repaired it enough for her to walk. Her left ankle, which had also been broken, was usable only because she kept the suit over it day and night.

She did not know how long she had lain in the shadow of the pod. Weeks certainly. She could not remember sealing her fullsuit, but apparently she had managed to do so.

The burns on her hands and arms were gone. All that remained were a few trace scars, dark against the copper brown of her skin, and even these were fading. The suit's gloves hung loose, but her hands were still protected by a thin layer of webbing from the suit. Her head was uncovered during the day. At night she sealed the suit fully and let it continue its repair work.

"I need to find an airport," Pruit said again, speaking as clearly as she could.

"Aer-port," the man repeated, still not understanding.

She realized that he would have little need of that word here, in one of the more underdeveloped areas on the planet. She mimed an airplane's wings. "Airplane."

Understanding dawned quickly with this visual demonstration. "Aeroplane," the man said, smiling and showing her a row of yellowing teeth.

"Yes!"

"No aeroplane," he said gravely, shaking his head. "Maybe Shinyanga."

"Shinyanga?" The word meant nothing to her.

"Aeroplane in Shinyanga," the man repeated.

"Oh," she said, understanding now. She pulled out her map and located the town he was referring to. Pointing to it and holding the map up for him, she asked, "Shinyanga?"

The man made a gesture of dismissal. Pruit understood. He did not read, and maps were of no consequence to him. But it did not matter, she could see Shinyanga. It was twenty-five miles away and could be reached, she estimated, with another day's walk.

She smiled at him. "Thank you." She put out a hand to shake his. The man clasped her hand, smiling at the city custom he had seen only once or twice in his village.

As Pruit's hand met his, she felt something in her fullsuit change. The webbing over her hand began to thicken, concentrating the suit's energy there. Her eyes turned to the small readout mounted in the fabric on her right shoulder. It was flashing a warning. Her hand was in contact with a threatening virus.

The man looked at her a bit apprehensively when she did not release him. Not wanting to offend her, however, he did not pull his hand away.

Pruit watched as the webbing achieved maximum thickness and her suit kicked into action. The webbing had grown partially over the skin of the man's hand as well, though she held it at an angle that would prevent him from seeing this.

After a few moments, the readout displayed a calmer message. The suit had analyzed the virus and could now neutralize it.

Pruit smiled at the man, trying to put him at ease so he would not pull his hand away. In another moment, the suit relaxed. The webbing on their hands faded back to its usual level. She released her hold on him.

"Thank you," she said again.

The man looked down at his hand. There was an odd sensation in the fingers and palm where the suit webbing had gently penetrated his skin. He rubbed at his fingers and stared at Pruit. She had powers he did not understand, but for him this was normal—he had not understood the workings of those others in biohazard suits either.

"It's all right," she said. She could see that he already looked better. Nothing obvious had changed, but there was a glow of life about him that had not been present before. His body now had the cure to the virus within it.

She turned and began to walk away. The man looked after her for a few minutes, then ran back into the village. Pruit smiled. Through touch and breath and saliva he would spread his cure to his family and then to his town.

After several minutes she had passed out of sight from the village and back into open land. She was crossing an area of low hills and open plains. There were animals everywhere. She should have been enthralled with the environment. Instead she felt unprotected.

She glanced up at the sky. It made her nervous, those endless reaches of blue, hanging above her from such a height. Even after days of walking in the open, she was uncomfortable, constantly reaching for the face mask that should have been there but wasn't. Outside had never meant anything pleasant to her, but it would be a constant feature of this mission. She would have to teach herself to relax.

Chapter 23

Jean-Claude stood behind the Mechanic's chair, giving the conversation just enough attention to know when the Mechanic would need something from him. They were in a café, sitting at a small table in one of the establishment's shady corners. Cairo was a city of cafés, for they were the place where men could meet and discuss the events of the neighborhood or the world, while smoking and playing cards or dominos or backgammon. Every street had at least one, whether it was simply a few tables and chairs set up in an alley, or a large, open saloon with fine wooden tables and attentive waiters, like the one where the Mechanic and his slaves now sat.

The Mechanic had a small cup of Turkish coffee in front of him which he did not deign to drink. Nate occupied the neighboring seat. Across from them were two Frenchmen whose casual clothing belied their actual stature. Nate was doing the talking for the Mechanic, and he wore, as he often did in recent days, a slightly dazed look. His tan silk suit, which had been crisp and fresh when he had first laid eyes on the Mechanic, was now wrinkled and frayed. That was also a fair description of Nate himself. Weeks as the Mechanic's slave, meeting with such men as these, sleeping only little and with difficulty, had taken their toll on him.

"What guarantee do we have of the technology's validity?" the more senior of the two Frenchmen asked, his educated English softened with a slight accent.

"You have this," Nate said. He drew out several sheets of paper from his briefcase and slid them across the table. The men glanced at the papers briefly, their eyes traveling over rows of mathematical equations and diagrams, then the more senior man folded the papers carefully and slipped them into the pocket of his loose linen jacket.

"Those formulas do not offer the key to the technology itself," Nate explained, "but they will prove to you that this level of technology does exist, and that it is in the possession of my friend."

Jean-Claude noted that Nate said the word "friend" easily. Nate had given up hating the Mechanic and now moved through the days in a semi-trance, simply praying for his own release. Jean-Claude was thankful that he himself was not so far gone.

He thought about his situation. He was addicted to a drug that could be supplied only by the Mechanic. While in the grip of that drug, he experienced heights of awareness and energy he had never before, except perhaps in childhood, reached. When the drug wore off, he was transformed into a husk of a man begging for an injection. When the Mechanic chose to withhold the drug for a few hours to punish him—which happened quite frequently—Jean-Claude would experience wrenching convulsions as he lost control of his muscles and felt the craving envelope him. Still, in the in-between times, when the drug was wearing off but still there, he maintained some semblance of his old self. Nate had lost even this.

Jean-Claude's right hand moved up to his neck, where his small gold cross hung. "Give me strength, dear God," he breathed.

"Satisfy yourselves regarding the technology," Nate was saying. "He will expect your offer within seven days. By the fifteenth of the month he will decide which offer to accept."

Jean-Claude watched the impassive faces of the Frenchmen. He was sure they would soon be convinced of the verity of the Mechanic's claims. Everyone was. In front of him the Mechanic sat silently. He did not speak in these meetings. His head was only inches away from Jean-Claude's hands. It would be so easy to reach around the man's neck and squeeze the life out of him.

Jean-Claude released his cross and gripped the back of the Mechanic's chair. But his hands would go no farther. The Mechanic's death would mean Jean-Claude's death as well. He was not that desperate yet. He would find a way, somehow, to take out his revenge. When he did, the Mechanic would learn what it meant to cower.

Chapter 24

Pruit stood in a bathroom at the Cairo airport, examining her left ankle. She was seated inside one of the convenient changing stalls ranged at one end of the large room, which were lit with yellowish fluorescent lights. Outside the stall, dozens of women passed in and out, speaking to each other or to their children in Arabic and English and several other languages.

Pruit was in her underwear, Earth-style underwear now, which she had bought in Nairobi along with two outfits of Western clothing. She ran a hand up and down her ankle. The bone was healing nicely; she could walk without a limp now. The leg was still stiff when she stretched, but even the stiffness was fading. As long as she continued to sleep in the fullsuit at night, she would soon be completely repaired.

She had waited three days in the tiny town of Shinyanga, sleeping on the covered cement platform at the edge of the small paved strip that served as an airport. It had rained constantly and heavily, a great downpour lit at night by streaks of lightning. On the third day the sky had cleared and an airplane had landed. She had managed to barter with small items from her pack for a seat, and had taken the twin-engine propeller to Nairobi.

In Nairobi she had entered real Earth civilization. She had taken off the fullsuit, for she found immediately that it attracted attention. She had not been able to take another flight to Cairo that day because she lacked a passport. People spoke

English there, but the local accent was difficult for her to understand. She had spent two confusing days in Nairobi until she had managed, at last, to acquire a forged British passport bearing her picture.

She had now arrived in Cairo, which had been sprawled below the plane like an enormous brown blight upon the Nile and its fertile land. This was a much larger and more metropolitan city, and she was anxious about her ability to pass as an Earth native here.

She examined the contents of the small backpack she carried. She had collapsed her fullsuit, and it was now stowed neatly in the bag. With it were her weapons: two knives and two small firearms. She had disassembled her weapons to make them less noticeable, and their odd shapes and essentially biological construction had allowed them to escape detection.

She slipped her knife blades onto the hafts, clicking them into place. The knives were made of white solid-reed with a tensile strength greater than many metals. The blades honed themselves, shedding layers of reed cells as needed to keep the edges fine. The hafts were of the same material, and when she joined them to the blades, the seam grew together, making a single piece. She strapped one knife at her right ankle, and the other to her ribs, below her right arm.

The firearms were also of solid-reed. They were worn on the underside of her palm, with the flat butts extending up her arm a few inches and locking gently around her wrist. The barrel of the weapons rested along the underside of her middle finger and was held in place by tabs that wrapped around her index and ring fingers.

One gun was designed to shoot laser light of varying intensity. The other shot small deadly bullets of the toughest solid-reed Herrod could produce. Pruit was less comfortable with the second gun. Growing up under city domes, she thought of projectile weapons as extremely dangerous. Every Kinley child had nightmares of throwing something at the dome too hard and seeing a crack form, then hearing the hiss as radioactive air began to seep in.

But either weapon might be appropriate here, she reminded herself. She strapped on the guns, one on her left ankle and one on her left ribs, in the opposite positions to the knives.

She checked her skinsuit. It was fully active now that she had taken off the fullsuit. There was no sign of it on her at the moment, for it was retracted into the upper layer of her skin, waiting for a biological menace in her environment to kick itself into action.

Pruit slid a finger along the underside of her left forearm and activated the skinsuit control panel. Skinsuit cells pulled themselves out of her arm and formed a small readout in shades of blue and red. With her right hand, she manipulated the readout, checking the suit's functions. Everything was operable.

She dressed herself in cotton pants and a cotton blouse and running shoes. The clothes were loose enough to cover her weapons and she found them quite comfortable.

She pulled out a stack of paper money from Kenya. She had traded several pieces of gold and silver, items that had been stocked in the pod survival kit, to get the cash, and she would now trade it in for the local Egyptian money. She tucked the bills into one pants pocket and slid her passport into the other.

Leaving the changing booth, she studied herself in the bathroom mirror, standing next to several other women who were washing their hands or touching up their faces. Her brown-red hair was drawn back tamely into two small braids that reached her shoulders at the back of her neck. Her copper skin was not the rule here, but it did not stand out. Only her blue eyes seemed unusual, when taken with the rest of her coloring, but she did not believe they were odd enough to mark her as alien.

Eddie stood outside the customs area at the Cairo airport, looking across the small barriers at the crowd emerging from baggage claim from a London flight. As third-world airports went, this one was fairly nice. Built in the 1960s, it featured gray and beige linoleum tiles and recessed fluorescent lighting along walls of an abstract honeycomb design. It was reasonably clean and was kept secure by hundreds of military guards in jaunty dark-blue uniforms with machine guns over their shoulders. Over loudspeakers, a pleasant female voice announced arriving and departing flights in Arabic and English and French.

Eddie had driven from the dig to the city the night before and had stayed at the Semiramis Hilton, a tall modern hotel perched in gaudy self-complacency at the edge of the Nile. He had reveled in the hot shower, and now wore pressed cotton slacks and a white jersey and a baseball cap, everything feeling wonderfully clean after weeks at camp. He was tan from his time in the desert, and his good-looking face stood out against the white of his shirt. He knew he looked attractive, and he was glad of it. He was here at the airport to meet two archaeologists who were joining the dig. One of them was Gary Brewer, a well-known British Egyptologist specializing in the Old Kingdom, which encompassed the Third through Sixth Dynasties. The other was Julianne Malcosky, an American expert in the evolution of Egyptian religion. Julianne was the reason Eddie had volunteered to make the airport run. He had met her at several Egyptology conferences over the last few years. She was unattached, or so he had gleaned, and he had notions of a brief fling while sharing the dig site together. He was not a woman chaser, though his good looks provided him with opportunities for intimate encounters. He admired beautiful women, would sleep with them if the occasion arose, but he soon tired of them if there was no intellectual substance behind the skin. Julianne, he knew from his few conversations with her, was bright and driven, and it seemed only natural to him that they should be drawn to each other.

Julianne had connected onto this flight from New York. Gary had boarded in London. As Eddie watched the passengers slowly making their way through customs, he saw the two of them emerge together from the baggage claim doorway, pulling their extensive luggage behind them. Gary, Eddie now noticed with some annoyance, was an attractive man in his forties. Irritatingly, the two were deeply engaged in conversation. From their attitudes it appeared they had been talking for hours, had perhaps managed to sit together on the flight. There was even, Eddie had to admit to himself, a visible spark between them.

He waved to them, and they smiled as they reached him. There were introductions, then Eddie signaled for a porter to bring their bags outside for them.

"You have three meetings in Giza tomorrow, Gary," Eddie said, "so I thought it best if we stay in Giza tonight and tomorrow night, then head out for the dig together the day after."

"Sounds fine," Gary replied, emitting a world-weary sigh and smiling in what Eddie considered an obnoxious, self-obsessed fashion. Julianne rubbed Gary's arm lightly as a gesture of comfort.

Eddie turned away, leading them out into the late afternoon sunlight and hot air blowing in from the desert. They waited at the curb, and Eddie scanned the packed cars for the van he had hired to bring them to their hotel. It appeared the driver had been forced to make another circuit of the airport.

The new arrivals chatted with him about the dig, and then fell back into conversation with each other, continuing a friendly debate. Vexed that he had been so thoroughly pre-empted, Eddie put his hands in his pockets and sighed his own world-weary sigh, searching for the van. As his eyes traveled over the honking cars and pedestrians pushing baggage and the guards idling along the walls, he noticed a girl crouched down on the sidewalk, studying a map spread out in front of her. There was a backpack slung over her shoulder.

There was nothing particularly unusual about her, but he found his eye staying with her for a moment, and he caught sight of something shiny around her neck. It was a pendant hanging off a leather thong, and because of the way she was crouched over, it had come out from underneath her shirt and was hanging in the air below her chin. Without thinking, he took a few steps toward her. There was something oddly familiar about the necklace. It was a few more moments before he realized what was holding his attention: she was wearing one of his crystals. The shiny object on her necklace was none other than one of the crystals he had stolen from the dig. He moved nearer to her and now he was certain of it. There, on a leather strap, was a small orangish crystal with two dark bands of color crossing it. He caught his breath. He was standing only two steps away from her now, and she heard him and turned her head.

When she turned, he could see the crystal very clearly, resting against the white of her blouse. It was not exactly like his, he now saw. The bands on hers were dark blue, not dark green, and her crystal had cracks running up from one end, as though it had been partially crushed at some time. Other than these small differences, however, they were identical in form.

It took a moment for him to realize that she was staring at him. His eyes moved from the crystal to her face.

"Yes?" the girl said.

She was rather exotic-looking, with brown skin, blue eyes, and reddish-brown hair, a rare combination. Her face was pretty or, more accurately, Eddie thought, striking.

"Sorry," Eddie said, flustered for a moment. To cover for his presence next to her, he glanced down at her map and said, "Can I help you with directions?"

"I'm going here, to Giza." She pointed to the location on her map. Looking more closely, he saw that she was studying a large, topographic map of Egypt, with elevations marked clearly and small X's the only indication of towns and cities, though she had written city names in small letters by some of the X's. It was not at all the kind of map a tourist would have. "Is a taxi the best way to get there?" She gave her words an unusual intonation, but Eddie could not immediately recognize her accent.

"Uh . . ." He was trying to get his mind around her, with her strange map and the crystal. "Yes—yes. A taxi is fine."

"Good." She stood. She was perhaps five feet, eight inches

tall, with the slight, wiry frame of a dancer. She was already looking around for the nearest taxi.

To stall her, Eddie blurted, "You're going to see the pyramids?"

"Pyramids?" She began walking toward a cab, shouldering her backpack more firmly.

"At Giza," he said, walking after her. "The Great Pyramid."

She hesitated for the briefest of moments, then she said, "Yes, of course."

"Eddie!" he turned and saw Julianne and Gary calling to him. The van had pulled up and they were already loading in their bags.

"Be right there!" He turned back to the girl. She was opening the door to a cab.

"We're going to Giza," he said quickly, not wanting her to leave. "You're welcome to ride with us. There's plenty of room."

She paused and studied him for a moment, then smiled and shook her head. "Thanks, but no." He noticed that her speech was already becoming more natural, more like his own. "I'd prefer to go by myself."

"All right. I understand. You don't know me." He took a step back so she could close the taxi door. "But you should stay at the Mena House. It's the only nice hotel in town and the Great Pyramid is right across the street."

"Thanks."

"Really, you should stay there. It's very convenient."

She nodded slightly, dismissing him, then leaned forward to speak to the driver. One of her hands gently tucked the crystal back under her shirt.

"Where did you get that necklace?" Eddie asked, before she could give the order to go.

She paused and looked at him. "It was a gift."

"Is it very old?"

"Yes, very." Then she leaned forward and told the driver, in Arabic, to head for Giza. But Eddie could see that he had

caught her attention now. As the taxi pulled away, she looked
back at him and they held each other's eyes for a moment.

Eddie stared after the taxi until it was out of sight. He was
thinking there was something serious and strange and both
wrong and right about her.

He was brought back to himself as the others called his
name again, and he joined them in the van. As the vehicle
pulled out of the airport, Julianne and Gary were still talking
to each other and they were sitting quite close together despite
the car's roomy interior. Eddie no longer noticed.

Chapter 25

Pruit sat at an outdoor breakfast table in the restaurant of the Mena House, under an awning of striped red and white. It was early and she was the first diner. From where she sat, she had a view up the cement walkway that followed a winding route back to the hotel proper. Beyond the walkway she could see the hotel building, framed by tall palm trees and green lawns. Behind the building, looming huge against the sky, was the Great Pyramid.

On the table in front of her was a plate of fruit and fuul, an Egyptian fava-bean breakfast dish which she was enjoying very much. All fresh food was delicious after living so long on the ship. Spread out in the center of the table were her maps. As she ate, she studied her smallest-scale map of the target area. The beacon was very close to her present location, probably in the proximity of the pyramid.

When that young man had spoken to her at the airport and mentioned the Great Pyramid, she had only vaguely remembered reading something about it when she researched her target area. The pyramids were monuments of some kind. She had not assigned them particular importance, however, for they were just one more item among hundreds of thousands of items related to Earth.

The evening before, however, she had read about the pyramid in a hotel brochure. It was estimated to be nearly five thousand years old and so might have been constructed during the survey crew's tenure. It took on new relevance to her mission.

She glanced around to ensure she was still alone on the patio. Seeing that she was, she pulled up the sleeve on her left arm and activated the skinsuit control panel. The cells seeped up from her skin and formed themselves into the display. She manipulated it and in a moment it presented her with the precise Earth coordinates of her location, bouncing its signals off various earth satellites to determine this with exactitude.

She compared these to the coordinates of the beacon site on her map. Then she looked back up at the pyramid and calculated the distance. Something occurred to her.

She reached up under her blouse and pulled out her laser gun, fitting it to her right hand. With her thumb she tapped the amplitude control, setting it at its lowest value—infrared radiation. The gun used this for range finding and was capable of bouncing beams off objects, then receiving them back and measuring the distance. With her little finger she tapped on the receiving function of the weapon.

She sighted down her hand and aimed it at the top of the pyramid. She fired. A weak, invisible beam shot out from the gun, hit the pyramid, and bounced back to her, all in the space of an eyeblink. She glanced at the receiver. It gave her the exact distance to the pyramid and the direction the laser had traveled. She plotted these on the map in front of her. The line she drew led straight to the target mark.

The beacon wasn't close to the Great Pyramid. The beacon *was* the Great Pyramid. She smiled, thinking of an old adage that warned against things too obvious to see. Despite the accident with the pod, her mission was moving along very well.

She looked up the stone walkway and saw a man approaching from the hotel, so she slipped the gun back into its holster on her ribs. After a moment she recognized the man as the one who had spoken to her at the airport yesterday. She had hoped to see him again. After his comment about her crystal, she had wondered if he might know something of the ancient Kinley technology left on Earth. She surreptitiously slipped off her crystal necklace and tucked it into one of her deep pants pockets. She would wait to see if he asked about it again.

In a few moments, he had arrived, and he was smiling at her.

"I hoped you took my advice and stayed here," he said. "Would you mind company for breakfast?"

"Not at all." She gestured to one of the other chairs at her table.

He put out a hand and said, "I'm Eddie."

"I'm Pruit," she said. They shook hands.

Eddie went inside to get breakfast, then joined her. She saw him looking at her neck, but the crystal was no longer there. She could not tell if he was suspicious of her or merely curious. In either case, his interest in her was not flirtatious in the least. She did not know quite what to make of him.

After exchanging a few pleasantries, Eddie said, "I'm free until this afternoon. Would you like a tour of the Great Pyramid? I'm an excellent guide."

She almost said no but stopped herself. A guide familiar with the pyramid could be helpful, and she wanted to see if he had anything else to say about her crystal. If she decided later she did not want him around, she did not think it would be difficult to lose him.

"All right."

An hour later, she and Eddie were up on the Giza plateau, that desert prominence that held three enormous pyramids and a city's worth of other burial structures. They stood directly beneath the Great Pyramid, squinting in the bright morning light. It rose above them, tier upon tier of brown weathered blocks falling gently up and away until the four sides reached each other at the very top.

It was still early, and there were only a few locals in worn cotton gallabiyas standing near the pyramid to hawk postcards and other trinkets to the tourists. Some way off were men on camel- and horseback waiting to sell rides on their animals. A camel-mounted police squad passed by the pyramid, patrolling the plateau.

The Giza guards wore white military uniforms and carried machine guns. Three of these men were gesturing them away.

"Closed," one of the guard said.

"Why?" Eddie asked.

"Closed," the man said again, unable to explain in English.

"Why closed?" Eddie asked in his broken Arabic.

The man answered with a short sentence of which Eddie understood only a few words. Pruit saw his confusion and translated. "He says it's closed pending a seismic study."

"You speak Arabic?"

"Yes." She turned to the man. "Why seismic?"

"I have heard that it was shaking slightly a few weeks ago," the man told her, quite pleased that a foreigner spoke his native tongue, and with only a slight accent. So few tourists bothered to learn local ways. With her good Arabic, he was even willing to forgive her for walking around with her head uncovered. "Nothing was damaged. But Mr. Hawass, who runs the plateau, is only thinking of safety."

Pruit felt a surge of excitement. If the pyramid had been shaking a few weeks ago, the motion had probably been caused by her own transmission. This was verification that it was indeed the beacon. She explained to Eddie what the man had said.

"Shaking?" Eddie asked. "It's been standing for five thousand years. What are they worried about?"

She shrugged. "Safety, he says. But I'm not personally worried. I'd still like to go inside. Can we bargain?"

"Always." Eddie sized up the man. Despite the guards' formal uniforms and considerable firepower, they were generally a lax lot. Their training was minimal, as was their pay, and they were open to bargaining if it was perceived as harmless in intent. "Tell him that we would be very thankful if he could find a way to let us in," Eddie said, as Pruit translated. "We have come so far that it would be worth a great deal to us . . ."

He walked Pruit through the ritual of baksheesh. Though Westerners often mistook baksheesh for a bribe, Eddie understood that its meaning was quite different. Baksheesh was simply money given as charity or in recognition of a service rendered. It was the grease of all human affairs in Egypt and most of the Middle East. After many polite rejections by the guard, the deal was sealed for four hundred Egyptian pounds, and they were invited to return during the lunch hour, when the other employees of the plateau would be less attentive.

Accordingly, at noon, Pruit and Eddie were quickly ushered up the steps carved into the bottom tiers of the pyramid's face and into the doorway that had been hacked through the outer walls by Al Mamun, Caliph of Cairo, in the ninth century. They passed two other guards sitting on either side of the small, low door. These stared at them without comment for they were, of course, getting a cut of the baksheesh.

Then Eddie and Pruit stepped into the pyramid, and they were alone. He could see the glow of anticipation on her face. He felt it himself, though he had been there many times before. Inside they were forced to stoop, for the ceiling was low. After a few steps they were out of the sun and into the artificial yellow lights that ran along the walls.

"This isn't the original entrance," Eddie explained, as they made their way down the narrow entry corridor toward the intersection of the ascending and descending passageways. Though the tourist authority kept the pyramid clean, there was gritty dust and sand on the floor where they walked, blown in daily from the plateau, but it dwindled as they progressed further inside. "The original entrance is the one you could see farther up the outer wall. Until Muslim times the pyramid was completely covered with white casing stones and no one knew the entrance was there." They walked a few minutes in silence, and then he said, "That crystal you were wearing yesterday, where did you say it was from?"

"It was a gift."

"From family?" he asked.

"Yes, from family. Why?" Did he know something of Kinley technology? Or was he simply interested in the crystal because it looked unusual? It was difficult to tell.

"I'm just curious. Do you know where it's from?"

"I didn't ask." With that, Eddie seemed to drop the subject.

They reached the intersection of the passages, and could almost stand up. "When it had its casing stones, the pyramid was perfectly smooth on the outside and bright white," Eddie said. "Can you imagine how beautiful it must have been?"

"Precisely geometrical."

"Even aligned to the Earth's axis and the points of the compass."

Pruit smiled and nodded. As a beacon, it was a bit more impressive than she had expected. It appeared the survey crew did nothing halfway.

"Of course the casing stones were pillaged to build Muslim Cairo, but it kept its original form for almost four thousand years."

He ducked into the ascending passage, which led up into the pyramid at an angle. The ceiling here was under four feet high, and they stooped low again, being careful of their heads. They walked on a wooden ramp with cross-strips of wood nailed on as footholds. There was nothing to see here but the bare walls and their feet moving steadily beneath them. This passage continued upward for quite a long distance, uncomfortable to traverse stooped over as they were, and at last let them out onto a landing. From there Eddie took her up a short flight of metal stairs, installed by the tourist authority, and into the Grand Gallery.

"Wow." The word fell from Pruit's lips as she emerged into the gallery and gazed up at the corbeled walls rising above them. It was the first time she had found use for that slang word, and she thought it fit the situation quite well. On either side of them were courses of limestone monoliths. Each course overhung the course beneath it, so the walls steadily grew together as they reached toward the ceiling, nearly thirty feet above. In front of them the floor led up toward the very center of the pyramid. The ramp here had been placed over stone that was smooth to the point of being shiny. "How heavy are the stones?" she asked, studying the walls.

"Some of them as much as two hundred tons."

They began to climb the ramp.

"Do you know how they did it?" she asked after a while. She was forming some theories of her own. It could be done with solid-reed, she mused, but solid-reed would not look so much like natural rock.

"There are many theories: thousands of slaves moving the blocks on wooden rollers, floating the blocks downstream, even using enormous kites to lift the blocks from the quarries to the building site. But there's an increasing consensus in the scientific community that we really don't know how it was done."

After several minutes of slow progress as they both stared upward, they reached the top of the gallery and stood looking back down at it. It was an impressive structure by anyone's reckoning, a feat of engineering that remained unrivaled, in many ways, even by modern Earth. And, Pruit thought, it was a missing link in the histories of both Earth and Herrod. Was that sleeper really alive? Or had she been talking to some ancient computer program? Did someone still exist who would know what had happened almost five thousand years before?

Eddie let her take in the view, then he stooped down again and led her through the short passage into the King's Chamber. When they stood up again, they were in a large hall constructed of smooth monoliths, empty except for a stone sarcophagus at the opposite end of the room. The walls were of pinkish granite, colored by the yellow of the lights. The ceiling was formed of nine immense blocks. Pruit and Eddie were now in the very center of the pyramid.

"Welcome to the Hall of Echoes," he said. As he spoke, his voice reverberated, the sounds falling into each other, the earlier words interrupting those that came later. Pruit looked up and let her eyes run over the walls that she realized had been designed particularly to treat sound in that way. Even now, shorn of the casing stones that had made it perfect, and defaced by the forced entry of recent peoples, this beacon performed the functions for which it had been created.

"It's amazing," she said softly, and the quiet tones of her voice began to echo through the chamber.

Eddie walked toward the sarcophagus. When his back was to her, Pruit turned toward the wall and quickly pulled a small device from her pocket. It was circular and flat, about three inches in diameter. It was a tiny transmitter. She had programmed it, back on the ship, with the survey team beacon frequency, and she had given it instructions, the night before, to request certain things from the beacon.

She glanced at the transmitter and tapped through its various displays, double-checking that everything was correct.

"Pruit."

She turned around, the transmitter hidden in the palm of her left hand, to find Eddie looking at her. He was sitting in the sarcophagus.

"You're in the tomb?"

"I don't think it is a tomb," he said. "No one ever found a body. Listen." He lay down in the sarcophagus and waited for the echo of his last word to slowly fade out. Then he sang a long and low om, letting the note roll off his tongue and into the room. Pruit listened as the note hit the walls and the room began to vibrate with the sound. The om carried for many seconds after his voice had stopped.

Eddie sat up in the tomb. "They don't let you do that on the usual tour. Would you like to try?"

She paused, then nodded. "All right."

He stepped back out onto the floor and she climbed into the sarcophagus, still clutching the transmitter in her hand. She lay down on cool ancient stone, feeling the dust on her clothes and the enchantment of the pyramid. She waited for the room to quiet. Eddie moved a few feet away and closed his eyes to listen. He was out of sight from her current position.

"Ommmmm," she sang, pitching her voice low, as he had done. She heard the sound reach out and come back, reach out and come back, again and again. The pyramid was taking her voice and repeating it, letting it echo up and down through the five stacked chambers above, then back into the hall around them. She listened, and as the waves of sound began to fade, she pressed her thumb into the transmitter, giving it the order to send.

The transmitter released its commands to the pyramid, and the pyramid, receiving orders on the proper frequency, took those commands within its walls, within its very structure, amplified them, then sent them on.

Pruit could feel the building shake. No, it was not a shaking exactly, it was a vibrating, a shivering, and the structure seemed to let out a great sigh as the shiver passed through it, a sigh of every stone block contributing to the message.

"Jesus!" she heard Eddie say.

Pruit looked at the transmitter. It had asked a question and it had received an answer. On its small display she saw a new set of coordinates. She had the location of the sleepers' cave.

She sat up in the sarcophagus and looked at Eddie. He was standing in the middle of the room, his arms held out by his hips as though he were preparing to balance should the pyramid come tumbling down around him.

"Jesus . . . ," he said again, looking at her. "What was that?"

"I don't know." She tried to look concerned. "Should we leave?"

It was after their hasty retreat from the Great Pyramid that Eddie found his way into Pruit's hotel room. He watched her head for the hotel pool to take a quick swim, and then bribed a hall maid to let him into her room. He had hoped to spend no more than five minutes inside, but it was closer to a half an hour before he emerged.

Chapter 26

> He is my very good friend, and an honorable gentleman.
> —*Timon of Athens*, William Shakespeare

"You can still change your mind, Lion," the Engineer said.

He and his wife and the Lion stood in the bright, cool hall that was the Engineer's workshop at camp. The building was made of green-black diorite, a beautiful stone that glowed when the sun hit it. The walls and roof had been grown in place by the Engineer, the crystals of diorite forming in days what would have taken nature a hundred thousand years to accomplish. The ceiling was suspended from four stone posts which stood as outcroppings at each corner of the walls, leaving the upper portion of the hall open to the outside. The sun brought in sufficient light to work by, and the dark stone kept the space cool.

"No, I can't," the Lion said, checking over the packed wooden crates that were lined along the walls. "I have a wife. We plan to have children soon."

"There will be room for her." The Engineer was packing sets of data crystals into soft leather cases. "The Biologist and the Jack have yet to confirm that they're coming with us. There will be extra tanks."

"Take her home with you and raise your children on Herrod," the Doctor said.

The Lion studied his friends. The Engineer looked stronger and healthier than he had on his arrival on earth. He had filled the last seven years with projects to improve their life in Egypt. He had supervised the construction, or perhaps growth was a better word, of a dozen beautiful buildings at the camp. His brown hair had grown out, and his skin was deeply tanned, as was the Doctor's. The two of them nearly looked like natives.

It had been five years since the last message from home, the message informing them that rescue must wait. The Engineer's conviction that rescue would eventually come had not flagged in the intervening years, but he had become convinced that it might be a long time before it arrived.

"My wife and I have a life here," the Lion told them. "My children will be natives. It no longer bothers me that I might never see Herrod again. This is my home."

The Engineer looked at the Lion, his closest friend on this long mission. "I admire that. It would be easier if I felt the same way, but I am somehow compelled to go back." He put an arm around the Doctor. "We want to stand together on Beacon Hill when the sun rises. That's where I proposed to her. Even if we return to find a generation gone and things greatly changed, we want to be home. The First Mate left his wife and son on Herrod. How can we not go back?"

"I understand your reasons. If I had no wife, perhaps I would be coming along."

"Will you at least pilot the shuttle with me on our way to the cave? A last project together?"

"I don't think that would be wise."

"Why not?"

"I think it's better if I don't know the location of the cave. I think it's better if no one does."

"Lion, we would trust you with our lives without hesitating," the Doctor said.

"Yes, I know," the Lion said. "And I would do my best to deserve that trust. But I am not the only one to think of." The

Lion held the Engineer's gaze, willing him to understand him without being forced to explain.

The Engineer nodded. "Oh. Your parents," he said slowly. "They would never take actions to put us in danger, Lion. I'm sure of it. The Captain is very serious about his promise to erect the transponder tower. I have already helped him select the design. He won't fail me. I know him well enough to know that."

"I wish I felt confidence in that statement, Engineer, but I don't. I don't even know how to evaluate his actions anymore. Or hers. It's as though the center of their personalities has moved and they no longer follow logical patterns of motion."

The Engineer and Doctor smiled. "It is a little like that," the Doctor agreed. "Is it true the queen's son is your half-brother?" The Captain had grown less and less attached to the others at the camp. Most of the time, the only news the crew had of him was through rumors.

"It's true," the Lion said. "He's called Khufu. I was worried that he would be attacked by the other princes, but instead they have welcomed him as a divine addition to the house-hold." He said the words with a sense of bewildered disagreement.

The Engineer shook his head. "When we were still on Herrod, planning this trip, could you have imagined your father in his present circumstances? He was such a serious and upright hero then. The physical world is something I understand, Lion. Human behavior is another matter."

"Apparently so."

"But I have faith in the promise the Captain gave me," the Engineer said.

"Good," the Lion replied, "and I will be around to ensure your faith is justified."

The Engineer smiled. "I appreciate that." He scanned the room. The crystals and tools were packed now and so were all the things he would need to outfit the cave. "I'll get the Mechanic to start moving these things to the shuttle."

That brought up the other subject the Lion had on his mind.

"Engineer," he said slowly, "how much do you trust the Mechanic?"

"What do you mean?"

"Do you think he's a good person?"

"I don't know," the Engineer said after a moment. "He's sloppy in a way that's dangerous. But if you push him hard enough he gets his work done."

"I think he's a little worse than that," the Lion said.

"He's very quiet," the Doctor reflected. "He doesn't say much and people mistake that for being sullen."

"Are you sure it's a mistake?"

"He's shy, Lion. He's always been in the Captain's shadow."

"The Captain's shadow," the Lion repeated softly. "That's a good way of putting it. Standing in the shadows, whispering things."

"What are you talking about?" the Engineer asked.

The Lion ran a hand through his long blond hair and expelled his breath. "I don't trust him," he said flatly. "And it's not just sloppiness or incompetence or shyness. He's always . . . lurking. Listening to other people's conversations. I feel like his intentions aren't honest. Like he wants trouble between people. And power for himself."

"You sound like a bitter old gossip!" the Doctor said.

"That's what my wife told me," the Lion said, smiling because he knew he did sound like a gossip. Beneath the smile, however, was frustration, for it was difficult to give reasons for what he felt, but at the same time it was important he make them understand. "Think about our time here. When there were disputes, wasn't the Mechanic usually involved somehow?"

The Engineer considered this. Then slowly he said, "You may be right. He was often involved in trouble."

"It's a small crew," the Doctor argued. "We're all involved with each other in one way or another. I know he's not very likable, but are you sure you're basing your feelings on fact?"

The Lion's face lost its humor and so did his voice. "I don't trust him, Doctor. And I don't think you should. There will only be a few of you in the cave, close quarters. In a very real way, all of your lives will depend on each other. The crystals you're taking with you are extremely valuable in a primitive world like this. Maybe tempting. I'll be around to make sure my father is never tempted to take them, but I don't think the Mechanic deserves to be in your group."

They both stared at him. The Doctor was shaken by his words. "We can't— We can't leave him out," she said softly. "We've already told him there was a tank for him."

"Does it matter?" the Lion asked. "It's up to you who you bring. I don't think any of the others will object to leaving him out."

The Engineer shook his head after a few moments of contemplation. "I don't think he's quite as bad as you make out, Lion. I can watch him. He won't have a chance to hurt us."

The Lion studied their faces for several moments, wishing he had more concrete evidence to give them. But there was almost nothing, just a feeling. "All right," he said at length. "Then I have something to give you." From a deep pocket in his pants he withdrew a small rectangle. He handed it to the Engineer.

It was a little crystalline display. On it was a glowing dot, which was moving slightly. It was a monitor for a homing device. The dot was moving on a map of the local area. The Engineer fiddled with the tabs at the sides, and the scale changed, showing a map of a much larger area, and then all of Egypt.

"A homing device?" he asked.

"It's in the Mechanic's neck," the Lion said. "I drugged him a few years ago and placed it there myself." He saw the Engineer and Doctor exchange a look and continued quickly, "I just— I thought it was a good idea to keep track of him. But now there are only a few weeks left until he goes with you. You should have it. Watch it. Make sure he doesn't do anything strange."

"What would he do?" They were both looking at the Lion as if he had gone a bit crazy.

"Just don't trust him all the way. Please." His voice had an edge of desperation.

"All right, Lion," the Engineer said, pocketing the display. "If that's what you advise, I'll take it to heart."

The Lion smiled then and clapped the Engineer on the shoulder, relieved. "Good."

Chapter 27

There were four-foot waves, fairly mild. The sun was partially obscured by high, thin clouds, but the day was warm. The Biologist was aft, in the small private cabin she shared with the Jack.

The Jack was up by the rowers, picking out landmarks on the coast as they sailed by. He specialized in numerous disciplines, including the study of atmosphere and the interaction of humans with their environment, and he had been known to members of the survey crew as a "Jack of all trades."

This was their second week aboard ship. Balancing in the aisle between rowers, the Jack let his eyes sweep over the coastline. He had several maps, all of them generated by the *Champion* as they made their approach to Earth. His primary map at the moment was of the Mediterranean Sea. They were sailing west along the south shore, heading for the strait that would let them out into the great ocean beyond.

The ship was extremely well designed. The Egyptians were excellent shipwrights, and the Jack, a hobby sailor since childhood, had made only a few minor design improvements. Their ship employed both rowers and sails, and the combination allowed them constant mobility.

The Jack found his landmark and marked it on the map. He would look again in a few hours. He oversaw a change in shift of the rowers, then moved aft and entered the cabin where the Biologist lay sleeping on their tiny bed. He pinned the map back into its place above their small desk and studied it for a moment more, making mental estimates about travel times over the next months. They were making good progress.

He and the Biologist had lost faith in the Captain years ago. Recently, as the others prepared to go into hibernation, they had decided to make the best of their life on Earth and to do it as far away from the Captain as possible. The ship had been the Biologist's idea, and the Jack had readily agreed. It was dangerous, of course, but who cared anymore? They were in the unique situation of being able to live solely for the thrill of new adventures. With the Biologist's considerable medical ability, honed over the past seven years to a fine skill even with primitive supplies, and the Jack's knowledge of engineering and ecology, they felt themselves adequately matched to the elements.

Their plan was to sail to the two great continents that lay west, beyond the ocean. Exploring those lands would be their lives' work. They had hired, without difficulty, young Egyptian men who wished to accompany them on this journey. They were a small group, everyone participating voluntarily, and there was a general air of excitement about the ship.

The Jack sat on the edge of the bed and kissed the Biologist's forehead. Her eyes came open.

"We'll reach the strait by tomorrow afternoon," he said.

She smiled up at him. "And then the wide world beyond?"

"And then the wide world," he agreed.

Chapter 28

Present Day

Jean-Claude lay on his cot with the covers thrown off of him. It was late at night, but he was not tired. He was staring at the ceiling. It was decorated with repeating patterns of red and green, an Arabic design. It was a beautiful room in a beautiful suite. The countries courting the Mechanic had given him money to live like a prince while he made up his mind to whom he would give his precious technology.

There were long gauzy curtains on windows that stretched nearly from floor to ceiling. Through these came moonlight, bright, for the moon was nearing full. It threw the furniture of the room into sharp relief. Jean-Claude held a dark hand up in front of his face, examining its silhouette. *It is not my hand anymore,* he thought. *I have no control over how it is used.*

The Mechanic slept in a bedroom mere yards away, but the heavy door between the rooms was firmly locked. The Mechanic took no chance that his slaves would mutiny against him in the night. Jean-Claude could imagine him in there, resting peacefully on white sheets, a gun under one pillow, his evil electric knife still strapped to his ankle.

Nate had warned the Mechanic that their rooms might be monitored, so they moved to new rooms each night, and every stop in the past several days had been nicer than the last. A few feet away, Nate lay in his own cot, the covers pulled up to his head, his body curled on its side.

Jean-Claude put his hands together on his chest in a gesture of prayer, but found that he could not pray. It seemed inappropriate coming from him, as though God would smirk down at him and wag a finger in his face to tell him his prayers were not welcome. Even as a prostitute he had not felt as degraded as he did now.

Tears came to his eyes. *Heavenly Father . . . !* he cried in his mind, but that was all that would come. There was nothing to say and there would be nothing to say until something inside of him broke.

He was still in the grip of his antidote, which the Mechanic had given him an hour before, still felt its ecstatic embrace, but this ecstasy no longer blotted out all thoughts as it once had. Through his high, his mind buzzed with hatred and half-formed plans. Both were useless. He drove a hand into the bed beneath him in frustration.

He noticed a motion by his side then. Nate was there. He had slipped quietly out of his cot and was now kneeling by the side of Jean-Claude's bed. Crouched there he looked like a troll out of a childhood nightmare. Nate reached out a hand and gently touched the dark skin of Jean-Claude's thigh.

Jean-Claude batted his hand away. "What are you doing?" he asked, raising himself up on his elbows.

"We'll never get out of this," Nate whispered. "Never." He had large dark circles around his eyes, visible in the moonlight, and Jean-Claude could see the drawn lines of his mouth. He looked ten years older after his weeks in captivity. Nate reached his hand out again and gently stroked Jean-Claude's stomach. "We'll never get away from him alive."

Impatiently, Jean-Claude batted his hand away again. "There is no we," he said with his heavy French accent. "There is you. There is me."

Nate looked up at him with tortured eyes. Suddenly, he lifted his other hand from beneath the cot and brought up a hunting knife. Jean-Claude had no idea where he had found it. Its blade was bright in the moonlight. He caught Nate's hand by the wrist, and Nate struggled against his grip.

"What are you doing?" Jean-Claude hissed.

"Kill me!" Nate said. He dropped the knife and it fell onto the bed next to Jean-Claude. "Kill me. Please!"

Jean-Claude released his arm and pushed him away. "Go back to your bed."

But Nate took up the knife and tried to put it in Jean-Claude's hands. "Please, Jean-Claude. You helped him trap me. I don't want to be here anymore. End it for me."

"End it yourself!"

"I can't . . ." He crumpled onto the floor, clutching his knees to his chest and sobbing into his arms. "I can't . . ."

Jean-Claude studied Nate's pathetic figure. He felt rage return at the sight of him, rage at what the Mechanic had done to this man. It was a good sensation; it made him feel strong, though he was powerless to direct this strength. "Do not give in yet," Jean-Claude said, his voice now soft. "We will find a way out."

Nate shook his head, but his sobs slowly died. Jean-Claude lay back down, and he heard Nate crawl back to his own cot.

"I'm sorry," Nate whispered after a few moments.

"I too," Jean-Claude replied. The rage was dying. He stared at the ceiling and fingered his cross.

Chapter 29

Eddie, Julianne, and Gary were outside the lobby of the Mena House, loading their luggage and other supplies into the back of an ancient Toyota Land Cruiser that looked as sturdy as a battle tank. Eddie saw Pruit emerge from the hotel and he walked over to her.

"Are you leaving?" she asked him.

"Yes, we're heading back to the dig."

"Where did you get that car?"

"I rented it from an outfit in Cairo. We could use an extra one at camp."

She studied the car for a moment, then said, "I think I'll get one too."

"A Land Cruiser?" he asked. "What for?"

"To drive."

He studied her skeptically for a moment. "To drive where?"

"I haven't decided yet."

His tone became serious then, and he was happy to have a valid reason for proposing what he wanted to propose. "Pruit, you seem a bit naive for someone who speaks fluent Arabic. Aren't you familiar with the Muslim culture?"

"What do you mean?"

"I mean that driving around in the cities by yourself is all right, but heading out into the country—or into the desert—as a woman by herself is just silly."

"Who said anything about the desert?"

"What else is there to visit in Egypt?"

"You don't think I can take care of myself?"

"Actually, you probably can. But there's no reason to court trouble or to flaunt your liberated femininity to Arab men. They find it annoying, and they're not always a pleasant bunch when annoyed. Now, where are you planning to go?"

She hesitated for a moment, then seemed to make up her mind. "I want to visit a dig my parents participated in when they were in college. It was their one big academic adventure and I thought they'd like to see pictures of me there." Eddie thought he must have been mistaken the other day when he found her accent unusual. She sounded like she had grown up in California, as he had.

"Where was this dig?" he asked.

She took out her map and pointed to the location. "Somewhere around here."

Eddie studied the map. He had never heard of a dig out that far. It was not impossible, but it was unlikely.

"How about this: you ride with us, until I drop these two at camp." He glanced over his shoulder, and caught the archaeologists in a fairly intimate moment as they sat together inside the truck. "I could use the company anyway," he said wryly. "And then I'll take you there. Fair enough?"

"Isn't it a bit out of your way?"

"They're dying to get me away from the dig. There will hardly be room for me with the new arrivals." This was not exactly true, but Pruit wouldn't know.

"All right. Suit yourself," she said.

He smiled and headed to the truck. Pruit went inside to gather up her backpack.

Chapter 30

Adaiz watched Pruit and her male companion as they spoke to each other outside the hotel. The hotel stood in the shadows of the ancient pyramids which Pruit had seemed fascinated by the day before. There were two others in their party, another man and woman, who were now sitting in the back of the car together. The man's arm was around the woman's shoulders, and as Adaiz watched, he leaned forward and let his lips touch hers. Adaiz turned away, disliking the sensation that kiss provoked in him.

Pruit was speaking to the tall young man who had accompanied her into the pyramid. The way they spoke to each other was different from the way they spoke to others. Pruit seemed happier, somehow, when she was addressing him. There was a subtle change in the way she stood and the set of her face.

Adaiz was irritated at a feeling of jealous. He found himself wondering if she was drawn to that man, if she wanted to be near him the way those two in the car were near each other. She was the first human woman he had ever seen, the first who had ever spoken to him, and he felt a proprietary urge toward her.

Adaiz was concealed in an old green Jeep, army surplus from decades before, with a battered soft top and plastic side windows which were yellow with age and therefore concealed him well. He wore dark sunglasses and a baseball cap to further cover his face, should Pruit happen to look his way. But she had never shown any signs of concern that she might be followed. How could she suspect, after all, that the Lucien had tracked her across light-years, aware from the beginning of her desperate mission?

At length, Pruit joined the other three in their car and drove off. Adaiz followed them for a long way through city streets and onto a busy highway, but when they turned from the main road an hour later, entering a deserted village, he could not follow them without being noticed.

He pulled the car to the side of the road and watched the monitor that tracked the two tracers in Pruit's back. They were heading out to open desert. It would be impossible to follow her there. It did not matter, however. Her ship was disabled and thousands of miles away. If she found what she sought in the desert, he would be able to intercept her before she got the information off-planet.

Slowly, Adaiz started up the Jeep and turned around, heading back into the city. He would follow her again when she returned to the anonymous crowds of Cairo or Giza.

He left the Jeep at the hotel where he and Enon-Amet had been staying since Pruit's arrival in Egypt. Enon seldom left the room. Both of them were terrified of what might happen if he were to be exposed in public. In this Arab country, however, Adaiz felt Enon was fairly safe walking the streets as long as Adaiz was with him and Enon kept his hood drawn and his pace short, like a human's. Still, they would not risk him outdoors unless it was absolutely necessary.

Instead of returning upstairs to his brother, Adaiz let his feet carry him away from the hotel. This was a market day, and the streets were thronged with locals. The traffic in this city was always heavy, but today it was almost at a standstill on the main streets. A dirty brown miasma hung over the cars, pumped into the air by their inefficient engines.

Adaiz breathed in the exhaust, tasting the chemical components and wondering at the deleterious effect it must have on the human natives. He was walking down a street of small stores and clothing shops. Nearby a group of young girls stood in front of a window, looking in at the dresses displayed on mannequins. Next door several heavyset older women in black robes and white shawls picked through produce on an open stand, complaining loudly to the proprietor about imagined and real blemishes on the fruit. Men in business suits walked in groups, speaking in animated tones to one another.

Adaiz took it all in, as he had each day since coming to human civilization. Information about this human society—a different society from the Plaguers—would be of use to the Lucien, and it was his duty to take in as much as he could. In truth he did not much like these walks he forced himself to take. The sight of so much humanity crowded in upon itself, in societies grown out of human experience and human nature, brought on a barrage of emotions he could not easily categorize or control.

Nearby a young couple held hands, the woman's belly swollen with pregnancy. A group of small boys were kicking rocks along the sidewalk and singing a wailing Arab song. Adaiz was overcome for a moment and he stopped, leaning his body against a lamppost as people moved by him.

His mind was loud, almost screaming. But with what? He took a series of deep breaths and forced himself to calm. He studied the emotion that was sweeping over him, analyzed it. It was not surprise, or anger, or happiness, or disgust, or any of the feelings he had thought at first glance it might be. Instead, he realized it was longing.

But longing for what? He was not human, though his body might think otherwise. He was Lucien, every inch of him. He knew where his heart lay, and that was eight light-years from this alien world, at home on lovely, sacred Galea.

Chapter 31

The Toyota bounced along at a slow but steady pace, carrying them across a series of shallow, rolling dunes, as they traveled north and west in the thousand-mile stretch of desert that separated Egypt from Libya. They had dropped the other archaeologists off at camp the day before, and early that morning had set out to Pruit's destination. The other members of the camp had not even questioned Eddie's desire to go off with her. He had struck a deal to be as flighty as he wished without comment from them, and they had every intention of honoring their end of it.

Eddie was in the driver's seat. Pruit had been happy enough to let him drive while she navigated. They had let some of the air out of the truck's tires to give it a better grip on the sand, and they were making a good five miles an hour average as they worked toward the invisible point in the distance which Pruit had marked on their map.

Pruit sat in the front passenger's seat, looking out the open side window. They both wore T-shirts and shorts. All around them sand stretched away to the horizon. Behind them, she could just make out the Red Pyramid of Dashur, tiny at this distance, almost lost in the haze above the desert. It was the only remaining sign of civilization.

The sand was ugly, almost as though it had been mixed with dirt. Here and there dunes of loose shale stood over buried ancient structures, for perhaps only a tenth of the secrets of Egypt had yet been uncovered.

This landscape fit Pruit's idea of "outside" better than any she had yet seen. This was a killing land. Without their truck and the jugs of water they had stacked in it, neither of them would survive here for long. Her urge to pull on a face mask was great, but she forced herself into an attitude of relaxation.

She wondered what she would tell Eddie when they arrived at their destination. There would, of course, be no abandoned dig site waiting for them. There might be no sign at all of what she sought.

Why had she allowed him to come with her? There were various answers to that question, but most of all, it was because she liked him. Eddie was a new breed of creature to her, a man who had never been anything but happy or bored in his life. He had an air about him that spoke of long afternoons lounging in the sun, despite his intelligence and the fitness of his body. This seemed frivolous in a way, but it was also pleasant to be around. She was not worried about handling Eddie. There was nothing threatening about him.

"Look at the map," Eddie said. "See that ridge to the left? Check our course."

She studied the map and penciled in their current path.

"We're doing fine. This is the right direction."

He took a long drink of water from the plastic bottle next to his seat. "You didn't tell me—what was this dig exactly?"

She didn't turn her head from the view. "Some tomb. What else?"

"What dynasty, do you know?"

"I can't even remember. Five thousand years ago, something like that."

"Fourth Dynasty then, probably. My favorite. What did they find? I didn't know there were any mortuary structures out this far. We're going a long way past the usual border of ancient civilization."

"They didn't find much." She sat back into her seat and looked over at him. "Just a few artifacts, nothing major." After several days talking to Eddie, the American idiom had become quite natural for her. "I'm embarrassed to say I don't know much about it." She would have to come up with something more convincing than that before they arrived.

Eddie looked at her. He was smiling slightly. Slowly, he said, "You're wondering what you're going to tell me when we get there, aren't you?"

Her eyes met his, but she kept her face casual. "What do you mean?"

"Pruit, you aren't a bad liar," he said. "It's just not possible to appear completely normal when you're new somewhere and you're spending a lot of time with someone who's not new."

She felt a jolt in her stomach. "What do you mean?" she asked again.

"There are too many little things. I wouldn't have noticed if I'd seen you for an hour, but it's been three days. The way you spoke when we first met. The way you tasted my omelet yesterday morning—like you had no idea what you were in for. But mostly it was the pyramid. And the crystal."

"The crystal," Pruit said quietly. "What do you know about that?"

Eddie stuck a hand in one of his pockets, pulled something out, and handed it to her. It was a crystal, orange with green bands, much like her own. It was undoubtedly of ancient Kinley origin, and her heart sped up. She would have to get it into her crystal reader as soon as possible.

"I know I found this one and six just like it buried in a temple that's been under the ground for five thousand years," Eddie said. "I know we don't have the ability to make a crystal like this now. I know it's not natural."

"You found this at your dig?" she asked, and now she felt a pang of panic. Had she overlooked something? Was Eddie's dig site in some way relevant to her mission?

"Tell me who you are, Pruit."

"You tell me," she said.

"At first I thought you were an archaeologist, someone who had been to Egypt before. But it was obvious after a few minutes that that couldn't be the case. Then I thought you had stolen your crystal from another dig site, or someone had stolen it and given it to you. Then you and I went into the pyramid and it shook, and you didn't seem the least bit surprised."

"Why should I have been surprised? The guard told us it had been shaking for several weeks."

"So now," he continued, ignoring her, "I've started to think that you're not from here at all."

"What are you saying?"

"I'm saying Earth isn't your home."

She smiled somewhat condescendingly at his earnest look. "That's a fairly drastic conclusion from pretty flimsy evidence."

"Yes, I know," he said, his voice now betraying excitement. "It sounds crazy, and truthfully it never would have occurred to me. But yesterday afternoon I went into your room."

She stared at him and her smile evaporated. Her supplies and her tools were essential to her mission, and there was no excuse for leaving them unguarded. "You went into my room?" she asked quietly.

"I was looking for the crystal. But I found your backpack, and inside it was that red suit of yours. It took twenty minutes for me to figure out how to unroll it, but eventually I did. I put my hand in one of the sleeves and I watched those arms grow out. Grow out! Into my skin! Are you going to tell me that was made somewhere on Earth?"

She held his gaze then looked away, back out at the desert.

"Tell me who you are, Pruit."

"I'm not sure you'd want me to tell you," she said quietly. "It would change things for you."

"Good!" Eddie looked away, saying nothing for several moments. Then, almost whispering, he said, "I've been coming to Egypt since I was a teenager, and wandering and meeting strangers and hoping for . . . something. My whole life I've wanted to believe that you exist."

"Me?"

"Someone like you."

She looked at him skeptically.

"There are huge holes in the history of our race," he said. "Maybe you can explain some of those dark areas."

Pruit smiled at him, with some pity. It was up to her whom she took into her confidence. If Eddie ever proved to be trouble, she could easily make sure he never had the chance to betray her. But he seemed to think her mission would solve some personal dilemma for him. "I am here to shed light on ancient mysteries. But not yours so much as my own."

"So I'm right?"

"Yes. I am new to Earth."

She did not elaborate, though she could see he had an avalanche of questions waiting.

"Just tell me this," he said. "Are you bringing changes to Earth?"

"Eddie, your world is no concern of mine. I only hope to find what I need and then leave this place behind."

Slowly, he nodded. "I'm happy to be the one helping you," he said seriously. "No," he corrected himself. "I'm ecstatic to be the one helping you."

"I appreciate your help." She sighed, then activated the skinsuit control panel on her left forearm. Eddie watched intently, but did not comment. She marked their current precise coordinates on the map. "This is so much easier than trying to estimate with your compass."

The sight of the skinsuit was a final piece of proof, and he began to laugh quietly. "Will you tell me what we're going to find?"

"Something very old, and, I hope, very valuable," she said. "At least to me." She said no more, partly because she did not want to explain the entirety of her life and mission just yet, partly because she enjoyed keeping Eddie in suspense. It would be a tiring conversation anyway, and she needed to keep herself fresh as they closed in on their destination. "Now, let's see what this crystal of yours holds."

She reached for her backpack and drew out an odd contraption that looked something like a microscope, with a large, irregularly shaped body. It was made out of a crystalline substance with a metallic luster. At the top of it was a double eye-piece.

"What is that?" he asked. "I couldn't figure it out yester-day."

She cast him an annoyed glance. "It's a crystal reader," she said. "The ancients of my world used crystals for data storage. They hold an incredible amount of information. I want to see if yours is relevant to me."

She took Eddie's small crystal and inserted it into the side of the reader. The machine made a soft whirring sound and the crystal disappeared within it. Pruit peered through the eye-piece. The reader scanned for the first line of data and dis-played it, the words spelled out before her in Haight. She scanned through pages and pages, and at last lifted her head.

"What does it say?" Eddie asked her.

"It's a medical handbook, describing how to use local plants to make medicines for various ills. Very interesting, but not relevant to me, unfortunately." She handed it back to Eddie.

It was nearly evening when a long, low ridge of rocks came into sight in the distance ahead of them, standing out clearly against the sun in the west. By then, they had been driving for nearly ten hours, and both were exhausted. Pruit continued to watch the coordinates as they read out on her arm. It became evident that the rocks were their target.

They drove up to the base of the ridge, then got out of the car, shouldering two large backpacks Eddie had prepared for them, which contained water and food and camping necessi-ties.

"It's not far," Pruit said, as they reached the rocks and began to pick their way up toward the top of the ridge. "Maybe two hundred feet in a straight line."

They slowly made their way over dusty, shale-covered rock to the crest of the low ridge and found themselves looking down at several other tiers of ridges stretching away for half a mile. The sun was low in the sky, shining in their eyes and casting long shadows between the rocks. They worked their way through the trough between the first ridge and the next, then to the top of the second rise. Pruit's eyes were on her suit readout. They were now only thirty feet away. She scanned the rocks, but could see nothing.

"Thirty feet that way," she told Eddie, pointing. "Can you see anything?"

"No."

All that was visible was rocks and sand. They continued down and in a few minutes arrived in the trough between the second and third ridges. Pruit held her left arm in front of her, watching the coordinates as she moved. Her skinsuit locating device was accurate to about ten feet. In a few moments, her suit informed her that she had arrived.

"Apparently, I'm here."

Eddie came up next to her and they scanned the sand.

"There!" he said, pointing to a small depression near the foot of the ridge.

They moved closer and could see that rocks had recently been moved or thrown from the depression—there were several dozen large stones that had been pushed outward from a common center. A few of them were perched precariously on top of each other, in positions that would certainly change over time.

He was here, Pruit thought. *It was not a computer. It was a person. I woke him and he left the cave, just days ago.*

"Something happened here recently?" Eddie asked, studying the stones.

"Yes, I think so," she said. "Let's dig." They let their packs drop to the ground and they began to scoop away sand from the bottom of the depression. The sun was dipping below the horizon now, and the sand around them was in darkness. In moments their hands touched something hard. They pulled more sand away and saw a dark surface, hard like rock, but too smooth to be natural. Pruit cleared away more sand until she had uncovered a circular hatchway. Its position in the trough between two ridges protected it from wind and weather, and its isolation in the desert kept it far from prying eyes. If the covering rocks had still been in place, it would have been almost impossible to find.

Eddie stared at the hatch, trying to contain himself. "I assume this is it," he said.

Pruit was too intent at her task to catch the thrilled humor in his voice. Her fingers felt along the edges of the circle, and a small flap of the stone-like material flipped up, revealing a hand pad and a dial of Haight letters. She pulled a folded piece of paper from her pants pocket and read the instructions she had copied out of her mission Master Book. She knew them by heart, but read them carefully anyway. Then she placed her hand in the pad and quickly rotated it in a specific sequence to point at various of the letters. When she reached the final one, the hatch activated.

A screening force field sprang up, ejecting her hand from the pad and sending her sprawling back onto the sand. The grains of sand that had remained on top of the hatch sprang away. Then the hatch began to move. Silently, it rose up, pulling with it the telescoping vertical tunnel beneath. It rose a foot, clearing the surface level of the sand, then stopped.

"In case the trough had filled with sand," Eddie said quietly, marveling at the engineering. "The hatch could always rise above it."

Pruit nodded, but she was searching for far greater feats of engineering. She watched as the hatch silently slid open. As it did, dim yellow lights came on in a room beneath it.

She and Eddie looked at each other.

"Holy Christ," he breathed.

They looked down through the hatch and saw a stone ladder leading through a narrow chute to a passageway below.

"Let's go," she said, her calm voice belying the excitement she felt. Through her clothes she made a quick check of her weapons. Then she swung her legs down through the hatch, grabbed hold of the ladder, and climbed out of sight. The ladder was about twenty feet long, leading through a chute of the same substance as the hatch, ending three feet above the floor. She dropped down and looked into the passage before her. It was high enough to stand in, with an arched ceiling and perfectly smooth walls. Its floor sloped gently downward, leading farther underground. The lights were thin recessed strips that she guessed were using a chemical reaction to generate the yellow glow. They were quite adequate to see by.

"Toss the packs down and come in!" she called up to Eddie.

He did, and she caught them, setting them to one side. Then she could see Eddie against the evening sky and he was making his way down the ladder.

"Shut the hatch if you can."

He examined the underside of the hatch rim and found a simple tab. He pushed it and the hatch slid shut above him. He started down the ladder. As he did, the telescoping hatch retracted back to its original level. He smiled at the workmanship. There was no other possible reaction to something so old that worked so well.

They passed down the hallway and came to a full-size door set in the side wall at the end of the passage. Pruit flipped up the stone cover to the hand pad and, referring again to her paper, entered the combination. Three doors retracted in quick succession, disappearing into the walls on either side. Beyond them was a ten-foot passage and another set of doors. She entered her third combination, and watched as the final doors drew away. They found themselves looking in at the sleepers' cave.

It was a large, rectangular room that appeared, like the tunnel, to be carved from dark rock. The ceiling was low, perhaps nine feet above the floor. Immediately in front of them were the stasis tanks, large, dark, coffin-shaped boxes on bases that held them three feet above the floor. The tanks stretched in a line of eight along the far wall.

They stepped into the cave and saw that there was little else inside. To the immediate right of the door was a shower alcove. On the far left wall a computer of some sort was embedded into the rock. There were several outlines on the walls indicating where sealed storage space would be found. Nothing else.

Eddie let out a low whistle. This was his every archaeological fantasy come true.

Pruit scanned the stasis tanks. The last two, the two just in front of them, had lights on their control panels. There were two sleepers yet alive.

Chapter 32

They camped that night in the tunnel outside the stasis chamber, unrolling their sleeping bags and eating a light dinner of peanut butter and jelly sandwiches prepared by Eddie.

Before going to bed, Pruit had entered the commands into the stasis tanks to wake the occupants, and she had discovered that the waking process was lengthy, perhaps as long as three days. She had turned her attention to the computer, and had eventually succeeded in waking it up. Its operations were completely unfamiliar to her, however, and she preferred to wait for the two sleeping strangers to join her before she attempted to use it. If they could not help, she would try it again.

She and Eddie had found the large storage closet filled with leather cases of data crystals and paper manuals. Her first urge had been to scan all of the crystals immediately, but she had stopped herself. They had been driving and walking for over twelve hours, and she knew that she was tired. It would be better to examine them with a fresh mind.

So they had each showered, giving each other privacy while doing so, and then put on their lightest set of clothes and climbed into their sleeping bags in the hallway.

They spent the next day in the cave, with Pruit studying every crystal in the crystal reader, while periodically checking on the waking stasis tanks. She was concerned that there seemed to be some malfunction with one of the tanks, but the occupant appeared to be waking nonetheless.

Pruit let Eddie look through the reader eyepiece from time to time, but the script was totally alien to him, and he soon occupied himself studying the interior of the cave.

"We don't know much about the Eschless Funnel," Pruit explained as she inserted a new crystal and focused the reader. This one was on botany, a library's worth of information. It would one day prove quite interesting, she was sure, for it addressed the subject from an entirely different perspective than its current orientation on Herrod. But for the moment it did not concern her. She set it aside and took up the next crystal. "If we did, perhaps I wouldn't need to be here. We know it was named for its inventor, Eschless. But beyond that we're in mystery."

"Why Funnel?"

"Your guess is as good as mine. The current thinking is that the engine funneled the ambient energy of the universe into something usable, but really who knows? Maybe the engine was just shaped like a funnel."

"But you know that it was invented," Eddie said, inspecting the empty stasis tanks. "Wouldn't that make it possible to duplicate the invention? This isn't rock, by the way."

"I think it's some mixture of rock and metal. Probably much stronger than either on its own. Remind me to take a sample of it. To answer your question, no. It hasn't been possible to duplicate the Funnel, because we have no record at all of the technology itself. The Funnel was what we call a technological flash, a sudden breakthrough that sends the technology of a whole culture leaping forward instantly. I'm sure Earth has had such flashes."

"The telephone," he agreed. "Or the microchip."

"How can you generate a flash? By its very nature it is the brilliant inspiration that changes the way people think." She began on a new case of crystals. These took up the subject of atmosphere. Again quite interesting, but not relevant to her search. "We estimate that we are about five hundred years behind our ancestors, technologically. Maybe more. And we can't wait that long for inspiration." She expected him to ask why, but his attention had moved to other things.

"What do you think happened to the occupants of the other tanks?" Eddie asked, looking at the six empty chambers. "If some of the tanks had malfunctioned, wouldn't they all have malfunctioned eventually?"

"One would think so," she agreed. "We'll have to ask those two for answers." She nodded toward the two waking tanks.

"Pruit, look at this!" Eddie picked up something between two of the tanks and handed it to her.

It was a data crystal, yellow-orange with red bands and five inches long. She took it in her hands and saw that there was something wrong with it. It was broken, cracked inside into a hundred thousand tiny pieces. Pruit gently slipped it into the reader, but the device could make no sense of it. She removed it and turned it around in her hands. With slight pressure from her fingers, part of it broke off, disintegrating into grainy dust.

"Odd. It's been ruined somehow." Eddie looked for more around the tanks and in the corners of the room, but that seemed to be the only one.

Pruit continued her examination of the healthy crystals. It took several hours to scan all of them and wade through every paper manual, and Pruit was entirely disappointed. Not one made mention of the Eschless Funnel. Not one.

They ate dinner outside, up on top of the closest ridge, watching the sun set. There were high, sparse clouds over the desert that day, lit in brilliant red and purple by the setting sun. The sand was darkening to brown, and the view was beautiful.

"Do you know what the survey team did here?" Eddie asked. "Did they interact with the Egyptians?"

"They were supposed to study Earth objectively. But they must have interacted. They built the Great Pyramid. It was the beacon to call us to their resting place. They were responsible for the crystals you found and for who knows how many other parts of ancient Egypt. But I don't know any specifics of their interaction."

He had already guessed as much about the pyramid, but it gave him the greatest satisfaction to hear her say it. After all the opposing theories about its purpose and origin, the pyramid could now occupy a position of some certainty in his mind.

"But why are you and I both human?" he asked. "If that was the first contact between our worlds, why are we the same?"

"Answering that question was one of the reasons for their trip here. We still don't know why. But our current theory is that civilizations come in long cycles. We think there are dozens of earlier incarnations of our own world, and in one of them, perhaps, we colonized your world, or you colonized ours. Or some other civilization brought humans to both. Anything is possible."

As they watched, the sun slipped below the horizon. There were already stars visible in the east.

"How far away is home?" he asked her.

"Eight light-years, give or take." Even though she had traveled it, this distance seemed unreal to her. It was only a number.

"How long did it take you?" For Eddie, travel measured in light-years was beyond the scope of anything but science fiction.

She leaned back onto the rock beneath her and looked up at the sky. "Eighteen years."

"God," he said quietly, not knowing how else to respond. "But your age . . ."

"Sleep cribs, like the ones in the cave. Different technology, but with the same purpose. I was only awake for a few days each year."

"Is it so important for you to find this?"

She turned so her elbow was resting on the ground and her head was in her hand, facing him. "Yes, it is. There are only a few livable locations on our planet. We have no unpolluted bodies of water. And there are . . . other complications." Still, she did not want to explain about the Lucien, or the deadline that was hanging over her people. For once she was enjoying the landscape of this world, felt almost comfortable outside. She did not want to ruin the moment with her own anger. "We need a way to build fast ships and fast weapons, and perhaps even a way to bring a large portion of our population off Herrod. The Eschless Funnel would make it possible."

"And why you?"

"Why not?" she asked. "It would be someone. Why not me? There might be other missions following mine. There was talk before I left of at least one mission to come later. But resources are scarce and I must assume that I'm the only one. It was an honor to accept this assignment. It means my peers thought me one of the best."

"But your family."

"I miss them, of course." She said it quickly, as though she hoped to avoid the emotional impact of her words by not hesitating. "But I hope to see them again. And when I return it will make all the difference to their lives." She wondered for the thousandth time what her parents thought had happened to her. *Am I dead to them?* She paused, not entirely successful in eluding emotion. "I trained for this mission a long time, Eddie. I knew what it would be like before I left."

"I'm sorry." He could think of no other response.

"There will be other lifetimes," she said quietly, knowing that there would not be other lifetimes on Herrod unless she was successful. She settled onto her back and looked up at the sky again. "Happier ones I hope."

"Is that what you believe? That you'll live again?"

"Of course."

When Eddie did not respond, she turned to face him again. "You don't believe in your own immortality? I thought all civilized peoples would understand that."

"I want to believe in it."

"Then believe." Slowly she reached over and took his hand in her own. She shook it as though it were an inanimate object. "This isn't all there is to you."

He smiled.

"Think of how lucky we are. We can experience art and

love and beauty. We are infinite, just as those things are infinite."

"Infinite . . . ," he repeated softly, looking up at the stars.

"Why can we persevere even when life is painful?" she asked, her voice dropping because her words had become more personal. "Because we are greater than obstacles or pain. The world around us may exist. But we live. We *are*."

The last word fell between them and left them quiet. Eddie was watching the deep blue of the sky, moved by what she said. But Pruit found that she had become sad. She was reminded of the reasons her life was painful, and in particular of Niks, who still existed somewhere, she knew, but no longer with her. He had gone ahead into his own future, leaving her alone in the present.

"*You* are," Eddie said quietly, after a few moments, echoing her words.

"We're not so very different, Eddie," she whispered. She felt rising within her sadness for Niks, mixed with the grief she bore for her family and her entire race, and she knew if she continued sitting there it would engulf her. She sat up and ran her hands through her hair.

Eddie studied her. At a cursory glance she was just a girl with an interesting face, of average height, with nothing much else about her to classify her as unusual. But she had willingly given up everything she knew and loved to be here.

"We are different," he said.

She didn't answer. She was losing the battle to retain her composure and knew her voice would break if she spoke.

"I can see the way you look at me," he continued, aware that something in her tone had changed but not aware of the depth of the change. "I'm a frivolous man in a world where it's all right to be frivolous. You think I've never known hardship. You think I'm lazy." He paused and smiled, for he was also describing how he thought of himself. "And you're right. I am." He laughed. "My father's been telling me that for years. But somehow it matters more to me now. I'd like to be . . . useful to you."

She was looking away from him to hide the twitching at the edge of her mouth and the tightness around her eyes. After a few seconds she managed to fight down the sorrow, at least for the moment. She had heard Eddie and appreciated his words. After a long pause, she said quietly, with a hint of humor in her voice, "Thank you, Eddie. I didn't think frivolous. But lazy did enter my mind."

Eddie laughed. Pruit did not, though she managed a smile. It was not a happy expression, however, merely an indication that she was glad of Eddie's companionship. Eddie had not yet seen her happy.

When the smile faded, Pruit could feel sadness returning. She got to her feet. "I think I'd like to walk a little bit alone."

Eddie looked up at her, but her face was turned away. "All right," he said.

She walked off, moving along the top of the ridge, leaving Eddie sitting by himself. He leaned back and looked up at the stars, hoping that she was right, hoping that there was more to him than a hand, or an arm, or any part of his physical body. Hoping that he was infinite.

Pruit was reaching into the crib. She could feel Niks, she was grabbing his shoulder. She could see him through the biofluid, though it was hard to make out his face. She was trying to hold him, but he was slipping away from her. The crib was far too deep. It seemed to go on forever below her, miles of biofluid, stretching down into blackness. She had to pull him out, she had to get a hold on his body, drag him up into the air, drag him into safety.

She felt his arms moving, struggling. He was trying to grasp her, but as they touched, he was already sliding and falling. She was holding his arm, trying to grip it harder, but she could not hold him.

"Niks, hold on!" she yelled. "Grab my hand!"

She felt his elbow, his wrist, his hand, and then his fingertips. They touched her and then they were gone, and she could see him sinking in the biofluid, being drawn away. He was still struggling.

"Niks!" she yelled. "Niks!"

"Pruit . . ." He was calling her name, but his voice was wrong.

"Niks!"

"Pruit! Pruit!"

Pruit woke and found herself in darkness. She discovered that she was sobbing, her body weak and spent. She tried to orient herself. She was in the tunnel. She remembered that. Someone was holding her, someone had hands on her shoulders.

"Pruit." It was Eddie. She remembered now that Eddie was with her.

Eddie reached into his pack and turned on a small camping light. It looked as though he had been asleep and she realized that she too had been sleeping.

Pruit got ahold of herself. It had been a dream.

"You were yelling," Eddie said gently. In the light he could see her face, red from tears and exhausted.

"I'm sorry." She said it in Soulene, and Eddie stared at her blankly. "I'm sorry," she said again, switching, with effort, to English, "I was . . . dreaming."

She had herself under control now. It was a relief to be awake.

Eddie slowly released her shoulders. "Not a very good one?"

She shook her head, "No," and buried her face between her knees, which were now drawn up to her chest. "No."

"Do you want to talk about it?"

She did not want to talk about it, but she felt herself running from the dream and did not like that either. Grief would not decide for her what she would or would not say. "Niks . . ." She said the name quietly, and Eddie could see how much it cost her. "Niks was someone I . . . lost along the way." A new tear rolled down her cheek. "My partner," she whispered.

The word "partner" carried such weight that Eddie could

guess at their relationship. It was obvious she did not want to say any more, and he had no desire to push her. "I'm very sorry."

Pruit nodded and took a deep breath. "Yes, me too." She pulled her sleeping bag up around her legs. Eddie saw a hollowness in her eyes as she looked down the tunnel. "It doesn't matter," she said at last.

"It does matter," he whispered.

Pruit looked at him. "It does matter," she agreed. "But it doesn't change why I'm here. It doesn't . . . it doesn't change the Lucien or the bombs or the deadline, or the future of my people." Her voice was breaking again.

"What are you talking about?" He asked it softly, not sure he was ready for her answer. But her answer came, pouring out of her in a rush, borne on tears that she had never let to the surface until now. She told him of the Lucien and their history with the Kinley. Of the spies and the meteors and the plan to wipe Herrod clean. She told him about the poem in the crystal around her neck, and she told him the Lucien would never win, could never win. She would never let them win.

He was helpless against the avalanche, could do nothing but listen and try to understand the magnitude of what she lived with every day. After long minutes, the tide gradually subsided, and she was left wordless, gasping through the tears.

Gently, he put his arms around her and hugged her. He did not dare say anything. What could he say? Slowly, she began to calm. Her breathing became less ragged. Her muscles relaxed somewhat in his arms, and her chest stopped shaking with grief.

Eddie helped her back into her sleeping bag, pulling it up around her. He slipped into his own bag, and put his arm around her again, holding her body to his, his chest on her back.

After a few moments he felt her take a deep breath, and then her breathing became almost normal again, slow and deep. She took his hand in one of her own and held him to her.

"Thank you for being here with me," she whispered.

"You're welcome."

Then, safe in the warmth of that friendly embrace, the dream of Niks and the horror of the future faded for a moment and she drifted back to sleep.

Chapter 33

Adaiz-Ari's eyes were closed. He was standing on both feet, balanced on his toes, and his arms were held in front of him. Between his human hands was his dirk, a short, straight dagger, still in its sheath. He could not see the knife with his eyes, but he could feel it, its weight, its position, the curves of its handle.

Facing him was Enon, also with eyes closed, also leaning forward to balance on his front toes, both knees of each leg held slightly bent.

They breathed in unison, a short inhale, a long exhale, each feeling the muscles of his body, each slowly gaining awareness.

This was the egani-tah, a form of Opening, an ancient pre-battle ceremony that had been handed down since generations long before the Plague. The two participants in an egani-tah first became aware of themselves, then aware of their surroundings, then aware of each other, then they confronted each other in a rite of battle.

Adaiz could now feel every muscle. He could feel the blood begin to flow more freely, could feel his heart beating slowly and deeply. He continued the ceremonial breathing, short in, long out. Still holding his position with eyes closed, he moved his awareness to the room. He was now using the fundamental part of himself, the immortal spirit which was him, shorn of all physical trappings. The Lord Omani described the spirit as "that which is"; all else might pass, but the spirit remained.

Adaiz could feel the rug beneath his body, every piece of furniture in this open hotel room, could feel the heat outside, trying to get in through the closed windows and thick curtains. When he had encompassed the whole room within himself, Adaiz let his attention turn to his partner.

There. There was Enon-Amet. He saw his body, silver skin, long legs held perfectly still, eyes closed. Adaiz moved his awareness beyond the physical. He saw Enon-Amet himself, the spirit, and at that precise moment, Enon reached out and found the spirit of Adaiz.

Their awareness met and became joined to each other in the common purpose of the egani-tah. Together they opened their eyes.

They were looking at each other across the room, holding their positions, holding their knives. Each kept his mind empty of thoughts. Together they were aware only of themselves and of their surroundings. They drew in the final breath of the first position, then released it from their lungs slowly.

Then they pounced. Adaiz leapt forward, his hands gripping the dirk and whipping it from its sheath. Enon leapt at him in precise unison, each acting with full knowledge of the other. Enon's own dirk was unsheathed in his hand. They closed the distance between them and landed facing each other. Adaiz struck out at Enon with his right hand. Enon-Amet neatly parried the thrust, then returned it and was blocked swiftly and perfectly by Adaiz. Their motions were not choreographed, but they were delivered with full knowledge of both participants. Their minds held each other and the instincts of the fight passed freely in between. Thus each was safe from the other's blows as long as their connection remained perfect. High masters of the egani-tah could perform the ritual fight for hours, each partner working in precise harmony to parry and thrust at the other. Such masters could also, at certain times, achieve the egani-tah in real battles, encompassing their opponent and taking control of the fight.

Enon and Adaiz circled each other, holding their knives ready. Enon passed his knife to his right hand and stabbed for-

ward in a fluid motion, aiming for Adaiz's stomach. Adaiz
jumped back gracefully, turned, and brought his knife down in
an arc toward his brother's neck. Enon brought his left arm up
and blocked the motion.

We are perfect, Adaiz and Enon thought together. It was the
first discreet thought they had shared. Until those words ran
through their minds, there had been nothing but sense of motion and the half-conscious knowledge of the fight.

This is the beginning of the end, they thought, and neither
knew with which the thought originated. *We are thinking now,
instead of being. But thinking is unavoidable.*

Adaiz struck out with his leg, and Enon skipped aside. Their
motions were still coordinated, but there was already something less graceful in the ceremony.

Are we losing each other? they thought. And then the
thoughts came in a rush, issuing from each of them and both
of them, things they had never spoken aloud, things they had
hoped were deeply buried. *We may be losing each other we
are not one we are different we are here on this strange world
and this has shown us our differences we are still Lucien we
are brothers . . .*

They struck at each other, and parried, and turned and
struck again, slightly off, though still managing to work together. And then there was a rending sensation as they felt
themselves peel away from each other and become distinct beings again, separate. Their thoughts ran together but they were
out of synch and pulling apart. *We are brothers— but there is a
world out there I have never imagined— we are Lucien— am I
Lucien?— there is confusion— what is this confusion?— is it
mine?— is it mine?*

Enon kicked out at Adaiz and he moved aside a moment too
late. The foot grazed his thigh. It did not hurt much, but it
marked the fading of their union.

Their minds were apart now. They could feel each other's
thoughts, but their origin was clear. *Yes, I am confused and my
mind is loud.* That was Adaiz-Ari. *There are humans here by*

the millions, and they have mates and children and speak in my range and their urges and customs are natural . . .

There was also Enon; *My brother is distant, can he really hold himself objective in this world, would it be so wrong for him to long for the society he sees here, I think I would if I were in his place . . .*

Adaiz struck forward with his knife and Enon did not block the blow in time. The dirk moved forward to the thin seam between the sheaf of bone covering Enon's chest and the sheaf that protected his lower abdomen and pelvis. Adaiz stopped the knife just as its tip touched Enon-Amet's skin. It would have been a deadly blow.

The brothers looked at each other, the knife between them. Their breathing was heavy and unsynchronized.

"We have lost it," Enon said aloud, and with those verbal words they both felt themselves returning to their separate identities. They were Enon-Amet and Adaiz-Ari and they were standing together in a hotel room in Heliopolis, a section of the city Cairo on the planet called Earth, years and years from home.

Adaiz tilted his head in agreement and let his knife arm drop back to his side. They held each other's gaze, both feeling the weight of the separate thoughts that had passed between them, each unsure now how to respond to the other.

At last, Enon said slowly, "I would never doubt you, Younger Brother."

Enon flexed his antlers in a gesture akin to a human smile. Adaiz pulled on the muscles of his face, making his ears move slightly and his forehead rise, in his human version of the same expression.

"And I would never doubt your trust, Older Brother," Adaiz replied.

Chapter 34

The two stasis tanks began to sound an alert, and a yellow light on each started to blink at regular intervals. The meaning was clear: the occupants of the tanks were about to wake. Pruit and Eddie stood a few feet back, watching as the lights began to blink faster. They were, perhaps, analogous to the rate of bodily functions of the people within.

At last the yellow lights switched to white and there was a long, soft chime. With the faintest of rumbles, the tops of the two tanks withdrew. Pruit caught her breath, and she could feel Eddie's anxious excitement as he stood beside her. Instinctively, they took a few more steps back.

Within the tanks, they could see a greenish-brown substance, like thick grease. In a moment they could smell it as well, organic and a bit unpleasant.

Then there was a hand. It reached up from the congealed substance, wet clumps of the brown stuff stuck to it, and grasped the side of the tank. Then another hand, grasping the other side. The fingers of the hands tightened their grip, and with a pull, a woman's naked upper body came up from the grease.

The stuff was on her face and plastered in her short hair. Slowly, she used a hand to wipe her eyes. She opened them. Disoriented, she looked around the room, shakily taking in the tanks, the lights, and then Pruit and Eddie. She found the tube in her mouth and pulled it out, gagging as she did so. She let it drop back into the grease.

"Hello?" the woman said in Haight, her voice faint and scratchy. She began to remove the other feeds and tubes attached to her body.

"Hello," Pruit said gently. She knew firsthand the disorientation that came from stasis. The most she had ever slept at once had been a single year, however. She could not imagine waking to find that millennia had come and gone. She would have to be very careful about the way she informed them.

"Who are you?" the woman asked.

Before Pruit could answer, a man's form lunged up from the other tank and into a sitting position. His eyes shot open, despite the grease, and he tried to draw in a breath. He gagged on the tube in his mouth. Frantically, his hands came up to his throat and he tried to breathe again. He could not, and he started to choke.

The woman saw his distress, and tore the remaining tubes from herself, then leapt from her tank. Her naked body dripped grease as she stepped across and took hold of the man.

"Darling, darling, relax," she said. The man continued to convulse, trying to cough out the tube in his throat while simultaneously trying to draw a breath.

Quickly, and with great skill, the woman took hold of the back of his head with one hand, holding him by his hair, and pulled the tube out of his mouth with the other.

The man gasped in great gulps of air. The woman unhooked the remainder of his tubes. After several moments, the man calmed a bit, and she put a steadying hand on his shoulder. He turned to her with an unsettled look.

"Ay-ah-ah . . . ," he said. "Geh-geh-gra . . ."

The woman stared at him. "Darling, what's the matter?"

"Ah-ah-ah-ah," he said again, his mouth and throat clearly straining with effort. "Ay-geh-ge-ah . . ."

"What's he saying?" Eddie whispered.

"Nothing," Pruit replied quietly. "Nonsense words. Something's wrong."

"What's the matter?" the woman asked. "What's wrong?"

*   *   *

The Engineer turned toward the sound of her voice. She was standing by the side of his tank, and she was naked. He knew her, he recognized her, was somehow familiar with every part of her and every gesture of her hands and face, but beyond that he was sure of nothing. He moved his hands and felt them moving through the gunk. *Gunk,* he thought, not knowing how he knew the word. His eyes flitted around the room. The yellow lights seemed too bright, and he squinted. There were two other people present, standing a few feet off. They were strangers. He was confused.

"Ay . . . ay . . . eh-kree . . . ," he said, not knowing what he meant to say, but aware that neither his thoughts nor his body were responding to him.

He felt the touch of her hand on his shoulder. "What is it, darling? What are you trying to say?" His eyes focused on her. She was precious to him, that much he knew. She was his for some reason.

"Kre-guh . . ." He could not make his vocal chords respond to him. His hands reached for his throat, but there was nothing to feel but his own skin. He wanted to speak, but why? What was the purpose of speech?

"Look at me, darling," she said slowly. "Look at me."

The Engineer understood her, though he had no specific knowledge of the words she used. He turned his head to face her.

"Do you know me?" she asked.

He put a hand on her shoulder in an effort to prove to her that he did know her. Then his eyes filled with tears.

"Help me get him out of the tank," the woman said, turning to Pruit and Eddie.

They moved forward and, under her instruction, took hold of the man and helped him down onto the floor.

"Lie down," the woman ordered him gently, pushing him to the floor when he didn't respond to her command. She began to check his body, looking in his eyes, feeling at various pressure points. She was careless of her own lack of clothes.

She turned to Pruit. "There. In that drawer," she said, pointing. "There is a large medical kit. Bring it to me."

Pruit complied instantly, finding a large, light kit tucked into one of the wall drawers. The woman unrolled the kit and picked out a V-shaped device. She checked the dials, then began to shake it, apparently recharging it through this motion. After several moments, she adjusted the dials again, then slipped it onto the man's neck. The device lay along either side of the neck and sat on the man's breastbone.

"Ah-ah-gre-ga . . . ," the man said, trying to move.

"No, no, darling," the woman said softly, putting a hand on his forehead. "Lie still for a few moments."

He was soothed by her and lay back, shutting his eyes. The woman studied the neck device and fiddled with it for several minutes. Then, when it had told her all it could, she sat back onto the ground and swallowed hard.

"What is it?" Pruit asked.

The woman looked up at her. "Massive damage to his brain. He seems to have motor control, but even that has been impaired."

"I'm very sorry."

She did not seem to hear Pruit. "I can fix him. Maybe. When we get home." She ran a hand through the man's grease-caked hair. He opened his eyes and looked up at her.

Pruit was silent. How could she tell this woman that there was no home, not the one she remembered?

The woman's mind came back to her present circumstances. She looked around the room, at the other tanks, which stood empty.

"Who are you?" she asked Pruit. "Where are the others? How long have we been sleeping?"

"I think . . . I think you should get washed up and dressed. Then I'll tell you what I know." They should at least be comfortable.

Slowly, the woman nodded. She helped the man to his feet. Pruit gestured to Eddie and he brought them the light robes and suits of clothing they had found in some of the cave storage drawers.

The woman took the clothes and guided the man to the shower alcove, her arm across his back. His gait was unsteady. He was trying to speak again, but words would not form.

Pruit nodded toward the door of the cave, and she and Eddie slipped outside to give them privacy.

A half an hour later the woman and man were seated on the floor of the cave, dressed in brown suits of work clothes. Pruit sat in front of them. Eddie stood, leaning against the wall.

"First of all, I'm Pruit Pax," Pruit said.

"I'm the one called the Doctor," the woman said. "This is my husband, the Engineer."

"It is a pleasure to meet you."

The Doctor smiled politely, but it did not look like the moment was particularly pleasurable for her. Now that the woman was clean and dressed, Pruit saw that she was quite pleasant looking. Pruit recalled her genotype—olive skin, green eyes, and curly dark brown hair—from an ancient picture book she had had in school. She would have been from the Southern hemisphere, where now was only radioactive glass, stretching forever. Looking at her, Pruit experienced the uneasy sensation of staring deep into the past.

"Back on my ship I thought I was communicating with someone inside the cave," Pruit continued. "But contact ended. I arrived at the cave three days ago. Your tanks were the only ones still occupied. Outside, it looks like someone might have left the cave in recent months, but I don't know for sure. I do know that there were warning lights on your husband's tank."

"It doesn't make sense," the Doctor said quietly, trying to think things through. "The computer is programmed to wake one of us up at the first sign of trouble . . ."

Pruit waited for this thought to run its course and the Doctor's attention to return to her. Then she continued: "Now, as to who I am. I am Kinley. I'm from Herrod, but it is not the same Herrod you know. You've been asleep for five thousand years."

"What?" The Doctor almost laughed. Then she stopped herself and tried to imagine that unimaginable span of time. "Are . . . are you sure?"

"Yes, very sure," Pruit said.

Eddie, who could not understand Haight, could nevertheless clearly follow the gist of the conversation by the woman's expressions.

"The truth is," Pruit continued, her voice soft, "I didn't come here for you at all. We never imagined you'd be alive after so much time."

"You don't know the way my husband designs things." The Doctor tenderly put a hand on the leg of her damaged husband.

"I have to be blunt," Pruit said. "I'm here because I need the Eschless Funnel."

The Doctor stared at her for a moment, nonplussed. "The Eschless Funnel? What do you mean? Haven't you traveled here with it?"

"No, quite the opposite," Pruit said. Then she gave the woman a history lesson, telling her about the war with the Lucien and briefly outlining the following five millennia and the current threat. The Doctor was very curious about the Lucien. At the time of the survey mission, the Kinley had known that the Lucien existed and had even sent a probe to monitor Rheat, the Lucien homeworld. But they had decided against contact with the Lucien race, for they were considered extremely volatile. Pruit explained that that very probe had been one of the causes of the war. The Lucien had seen it as a territorial infringement and had been galvanized to strike back at the Kinley.

The Doctor was left in shock by Pruit's explanations, thinking of her family and friends and the great cities of Herrod. "All gone . . . ," she whispered.

"You can see the urgency for me to get records of the Eschless Funnel."

"Yes—yes, of course," the Doctor said, forcing herself to regain composure. "In the closet. Crystals and paper manuals."

"They're not there. We've checked the closet and the entire cave."

"But they must be." The Doctor got up and went to the closet. With a cursory examination of the leather cases of data crystals, she saw that all of the ones relating to the ship itself and physics in general were missing. Then, with Pruit's help, she went through every paper manual. Again, there was nothing.

"I know they were here," the Doctor said. "I put them here myself."

"We did find this." Pruit handed the Doctor the broken crystal. The woman studied it and pressed at it with her fingers. The crystal disintegrated under her touch, whole chunks of it falling off.

"I've seen this before," the Doctor said. "It's been destroyed by very heavy electricity. Deliberately, I would imagine." She surveyed the stasis tanks and the entirety of the cave. "We need to open the computer log and find out what happened to the others."

She slid onto the stone bench in front of the computer and with some manipulation of the controls along the edge of the screen brought up the log of the stasis tanks. There were hundreds of pages of log entries, most of them standard reports of "no change," which had been taken weekly. Here and there, however, she found anomalies.

"This doesn't make any sense," she said, picking out the anomalies and asking the computer for details. "The Engine Supervisor died almost immediately, after only five years. Then the Surveyor died after one hundred years. Then nearly five thousand years passed with no change, no one dying, no problems. Then, three weeks ago, the First Mate died." Her voice did not betray emotion at the loss of these people. There were too many sudden changes in her awareness for real grief yet. Her attitude was professional. "Their tanks malfunctioned all of a sudden. I know he built safeguards against that." On reflex, she turned to her husband for confirmation, forgetting already that he would be able to assure her of nothing. "But, look! The Mechanic has been waking. Every two hundred years. Look! He woke again." She queried one of the log entries and brought up a new page. "Several weeks ago. He woke without incident."

"The Mechanic," Pruit repeated. "Then I spoke to him. I must have. He told me he was a stasis sleeper. But why would he leave?"

"A better question would be why was he woken by your transmission at all. That job belonged to the Engine Supervisor, and in his . . . ," she didn't want to say death, ". . . in his absence should have fallen to the Engineer. There's no reason for the Mechanic to wake. In fact, we programmed the computer to make sure he didn't . . ." She trailed off and fell silent at a sudden thought. Then her face lost color and she seemed paralyzed for a moment.

"What is it?" Pruit asked urgently.

"Oh no," the woman said softly. She turned to the computer and quickly entered in a series of commands. Pruit watched her navigate several screens of information and begin scrolling through what looked like a long list of programmed instructions. Then the Doctor stopped and stared at the screen.

"What's wrong?" Pruit asked.

"He changed the program," the Doctor said quietly, her voice dead. "He changed it so he would be the one to wake." She stood up from the bench and started to pace, looking at the tanks and her husband. She dug the heels of her hands into her temples.

"Who?" Pruit and Eddie were both staring at her.

The Doctor turned to them. "The Lion warned us. We thought he'd gone a little crazy, what with his parents becoming gods and his friends leaving him. But he warned us, and I didn't believe him. I said it was all right and the Mechanic should come with us."

"I don't follow you . . ."

"He did it. That's the explanation. For their deaths," she

gestured at the empty tanks, "for the missing books, for the ruined crystals. He did it."

"Who?"

"The Mechanic."

"Why would he do that?"

"Because the Lion was right." Tears sprang up in the Doctor's eyes. "And my poor husband, my poor husband . . ."

"What is it?" Eddie asked Pruit. She translated for him quickly.

The Doctor leaned against the wall and slowly slid down to the floor, letting her face fall into her hands.

"But why would he destroy the crystals?" Pruit asked. "And the manuals—what would he do with them? Would he destroy them too?" She felt herself beginning to panic. What if the records had all been destroyed? What if she had gotten so close, only to find every evidence gone?

The Doctor was rubbing her forehead, then she stopped, as another flash of understanding came over her. "Sweet Mother," she breathed. "I see it very clearly. Now—now that his damage is done—I see his mind perfectly." She turned to Pruit. "He has destroyed my husband's mind. He has killed the First Mate. Both of them knew the Eschless Funnel. He ruined the crystals. And the manuals—the manuals he took."

"Why would he do that?"

"Because you were looking for them and they're valuable!" she said. "They're worth something. A lot. Perhaps an infinite amount. And now he is the only one with control of them."

Pruit translated for Eddie, and they both stood still, watching the Doctor. Even the Engineer was staring at his wife, a look of uncoordinated worry on his face.

Suddenly, the Doctor's expression changed. She jumped to her feet. "We can find him. We can find that cursed bastard." She began to open the drawers in one of the walls and violently searched the contents. In a few minutes, she found what she was looking for. It was a small translucent rectangle. She unzipped the top of her coveralls and slid the rectangle against her stomach, using the heat of her body to wake it up. In a moment she held it out for Pruit.

"A tracing device," she said. "In the Mechanic's neck."

Pruit took the screen from her. She and Eddie examined it. They were looking at a topographic map of Egypt, with a small glowing dot representing the Mechanic's location.

"That's Cairo," Eddie said.

The Doctor zoomed in the view. The glow was now moving, though very slowly. Then, as they watched it, it disappeared.

"What happened?" Pruit asked.

"Is that a modern city? If it is, other electromagnetic transmissions will disrupt the signal. It was designed for a primitive world."

Pruit translated for Eddie. They watched several more minutes and the glow returned once, for a few moments, then blurred and disappeared again.

"We know he's in Cairo," Eddie said. "We can find him, Pru."

Chapter 35

Year 12 of Kinley Earth Survey

> Enter with him
> These legends, Love;
> For him assume
> Each diverse form . . .
> Be, Love, like him
> To legend true.
>
> —W. H. Auden

The Lion and his wife Ipwet were shown quickly into his mother's receiving chamber by a lady's maid who nearly prostrated herself before the Lion. In Ipwet's arms was Isha, their three-month-old son. The Lion's wife was still somewhat weak from childbirth, and she leaned heavily on her husband's arm. It had been a difficult labor and birth, and as there were few medicinal remedies left from the survey crew stock, she had had a slow recovery.

The receiving room was large, with a high ceiling and a mural on the walls, depicting a stylized portrait of his mother as Isis, advising men from her great throne. There were no windows. Despite the bright midday sun outside, the only light here came from candles and oil lamps. The chamber sat on the ground floor of his mother's sanctuary, a building of fine marble which had been constructed, or perhaps grown was a better word, the year before. The Lion had not yet been inside. It had been nearly two years since he had seen his mother. He and his wife had moved from Memphis, taking a small country estate. He had almost convinced himself that he left the city because he wanted to farm the land, but in truth he was putting distance between himself and his parents.

In the center of the room was a throne-like chair on a high dais. Bracketing it were smaller chairs which the Lion could only assume were to be occupied by the priestesses of his mother's Isis cult. The remainder of the room was open and daunting space. Visitors, he surmised, were required to stand.

Despite his efforts to ignore all news of his mother, he had heard that her following was growing. Both his mother and his father could do nothing wrong. Every action of theirs simply became incorporated into the myths of their existence, and every old myth was warped and twisted to fit them. It was cowardice in him, he realized, that allowed him to hope his parents would return to rationality if only he gave them enough time.

Now he was back in Memphis at last, with his wife and their new son. It was only right that the boy's grandmother was introduced to him.

"Did you know it was like this?" he asked Ipwet, nodding to the room.

"I have heard . . . ," she said quietly.

There were footsteps and a doorway in the far wall opened. It was not his mother. Instead, it was a richly dressed native woman of middle age, with thin strands of gold braided into her graying black hair. When she saw the Lion, she touched both palms to her forehead and then to her thighs in a gesture of worship.

"That's not necessary," he said.

The woman smiled, acknowledging his words but not agreeing with them. "The Revered One has spoken many times of your modesty. Please," she said, gesturing to the door. "Your mother awaits you in her private chamber."

She threw the door wide and the Lion and Ipwet passed through. They followed her down a short passageway with

walls and ceiling painted in an underwater scene of fish and
hippopotami and crocodiles and tall papyrus. They could not
help but admire the artistry. It appeared that no expense had
been spared. At the end of the passage they came to a set of
doors cast from copper and decorated all over with images of
the goddess at work. In one panel was Isis bringing health to
the sick. In another was Isis supporting her husband, the god
Osiris. In yet another was Isis striking one of the unfaithful
with a terrible bolt of lightning. Her face was recognizable as
his mother's and Osiris's as his father's. Despite what he had
already seen so far, the Lion was shocked at the self-love evident in those doors.

Noting the Lion's attention, the woman said, "Have you not
seen these yet? The likenesses are very good. Look here and
you will see a familiar face." The Lion looked where she indicated and saw the image of Isis giving birth. The face of the
boy child issuing from her had unmistakably been based on
his own.

"Your birth, Lord Horus."

The Lion was barely able to contain his anger at hearing
that name, but he felt his wife's hand on his arm and maintained his calm.

"Please take me to my mother," he said, keeping his voice
under control. He was here to present his son and did not want
to argue the question of his own divinity. He wanted a pleasant
visit with his mother, some part of him hoping that a reminder
of her family would draw her back to her old self.

"Of course." She pulled the copper doors, which swung
open slowly on their great hinges. They found themselves
looking in on an enormous bedchamber. As in the receiving
room, there were no windows here, only yellow lamplight.
The floor was of alabaster, with thick woven carpets laid over
it. There were tapestries on the walls, and these featured
scenes of Isis the lover, embracing her husband Osiris. The
Lion almost laughed at these, so far were they from the present state of affairs.

The bed itself was the key feature of the room. A down mattress sat on a huge wooden base of fine light wood stained to a honey glow. Carved animals chased each other across the wood, painted in red and gold. There were posts at each of the four corners, carved like a woman's arms reaching upward, and a canopy arched above. Loose white linen hung down on every side, though it was pulled back at the foot of the bed to allow a view inside.

At the edge of the bed sat his mother, her legs folded beneath her, a blue and crimson robe hanging around her body. She had lost weight, he saw, though she had never been heavy. Her hair was tied up behind her head in a fashion that accentuated the shape of her face and her high cheekbones, now quite prominent. Her eyes had been darkened with kohl in the local fashion. She had achieved, the Lion thought, the image of a priestess. Or even, he conceded warily to himself, a goddess.

"Mother," he said, pushing aside other thoughts and greeting her with warmth.

As he approached, she turned her face to him, but did not move. When he reached her, he could see that her eyes were clouded and red. She moved her head slightly to look at him.

"My son," she said after a moment.

He leaned over and embraced her. She returned the gesture, but unsteadily. He pulled back, aware now that something about her was not right.

"It has been too long," she said perfunctorily, slurring her words. She spoke to him in the native tongue. She no longer used her own language.

"Are you sick, mother?"

She did not answer him immediately, for her attention was drawn away from him by the sound of slow laughter. The Lion turned to see three young women lying together amid blankets and cushions in one corner of the room. They were giggling in the same sloppy way his mother was speaking. One kissed another's neck as her hair was stroked by a third. Their easy manner spoke of long nights together with his mother in this room.

The Lion watched them for a moment, then turned back. "Your tastes have changed," he remarked without emotion.

She smiled absently at the girls. "They are beautiful, are they not?"

"Have you taken something?"

She opened her mouth and displayed a small bread wafer dissolving on her tongue. "A pleasant opiate," she said. "To let the consciousness wander." She paused, perhaps unsure what she had or had not said to him. "It has been too long, my son," she said again.

"I have brought my son Isha." He gestured Ipwet over to the bed and gently took Isha from her arms. He held the baby close to his mother, one time called the Archaeologist, and before that, far back on Herrod, known as Elena. Now he was not sure how to address her. "Your grandson."

With difficulty, she brought her eyes into focus on the boy. She stared at him for a long moment, taking in his dark hair and tan skin, seeing her son's features in his face and also those of his wife. Slowly, she turned back to the Lion.

"A half-breed," she said.

"What?" The Lion was sure he had misheard her.

"You dilute yourself, son."

Ipwet felt her face coloring. The Lion felt dread, then shocked anger as the import of her words sank in. Carefully he handed his small son back to his wife. He stared down at his mother. "I dilute myself?" His voice was soft but carried rage.

His mother merely looked up at him and smiled a condescending drugged smile.

His patience at last snapped. "I dilute myself!" He yelled the words at her. "Look how you are living! Look at your life! Are you even alive?"

Despite the drug, his mother was roused by his words. "You do not raise your voice to me!"

"You insult my wife to her face while you sit here in your den, with your lovers and your opiates! You're not even worthy of my visit!"

The Archaeologist's eyes cleared a little as anger washed

over her. She picked herself up onto her knees and slapped the Lion hard.

"You will never raise your voice to me! You owe me your life and your station!"

"My station? I am not Horus, mother! I am your human son. Human. Like you!"

She slapped him again, and screamed. "Shut your mouth!"

Two guards entered, hearing her yell. The girls across the room had stopped giggling and were now aware that their mistress was in a fury. "Out! All of you!" the Archaeologist raged.

The girls got up onto shaky feet and disappeared through a side door. The guards ducked back out, terrified of her.

The Lion stood before his mother, thinking how fitting and proper it would be for him to slap her, then carry her from this room and this sanctuary and back into the world outside. But he saw that she was too far gone. She had lost herself completely in the fantasy of godhood.

She was pointing her finger at him now, sitting up on her knees at the end of the bed. "Do not ever challenge me again," she said, her voice low and her finger shaking. "If you care for the life of that half-breed son of yours, you will take this to heart. Play the role that is given to you, or there may be no role left for you to occupy. Stay away from Memphis."

The Lion felt tears come to his eyes, not at her threat, but at the sight of her so transformed. "I comfort myself," he whispered, "in the knowledge that you are no longer you."

He turned from her and left, taking his family with him.

Chapter 36

Present Day

Pruit was a block behind the Mechanic, following him through a walking district near the Cairo Museum. She had spotted him half an hour before, guided to his location by Eddie, who spoke to her through a cellular phone from their hotel room. The Engineer and the Doctor were with him, and Eddie was monitoring the Mechanic's location on the screen they had brought from the cave.

Eddie had wanted to come with her, but Pruit had preferred that he stay at the hotel. She found that Eddie had had training as a fighter, but it was of a rather informal kind. The task of finding the Mechanic might well lead to physical confrontation, and Pruit felt she was better suited to handle it alone. She was teaching Eddie her stretching and fighting routines, however, and they were exercising together each morning.

So Eddie had remained in the hotel and had guided her to the Mechanic. The signal of the Mechanic's tracing device was sporadic, and it had taken Pruit most of the day to at last catch up with him.

She had found him as he walked along city streets. He was bracketed by a tall, young black man and a short American sweating in a dark blue suit. The Mechanic himself had been easy to spot once he was within eyesight. The Doctor had described him well. His skin was gray, for he belonged to one of the ancient Herrod genotypes. His pigmentation no longer existed on Herrod; it had been absorbed into the homogenous body type that was salvaged after the Great War.

Other than his skin color, he was an ordinary-looking man with a homely, almost unnoticeable face. He wore a loose cotton robe of native dress and was generally unremarkable.

The day was pleasantly warm and the sidewalks were full, for it was the time of the midday meal, and men and women thronged the streets. The street she walked now was lined with apartment buildings, the bottom floors of which held restaurants or other small businesses.

Pruit followed from a distance as the Mechanic turned a corner, walked down another block, and arrived at the patio of a small restaurant. The black man leaned down to the Mechanic and whispered something. The Mechanic turned and spoke to the American next to him, then back to the black man for several moments. Then the black man disappeared into the restaurant. Three Asian men approached and the group took seats around a table.

Pruit turned off her phone and slowly worked her way closer.

"The girl is still following you," Jean-Claude whispered to the Mechanic as they arrived at the restaurant. The Chinese men were already approaching.

"Who is she, Nate?" the Mechanic asked.

"I couldn't tell," Nate said.

"She is not alone," Jean-Claude said. "There is a young man following her. I believe he is with her. They have the same look." He was coming down off the high of his antidote. He still felt exhilaration, but there was a hint of the low to come.

"I want to know who they are," the Mechanic said. "We are near your apartment, Jean-Claude, yes?"

"Yes."

"You get them for me. I will meet you there when this is finished."

Jean-Claude nodded, then slipped into the restaurant. He passed through and out the back door. He should have been nervous about the encounter ahead, for the two following the Mechanic could be anyone, could be killers, but he felt nothing but his own need—the need to do this task for the Mechanic so he would be granted the next dose of his private heaven. He found his way through an alley, heading in the direction where he last saw the young man following Pruit.

Pruit had reached the restaurant. She stood concealed behind potted trees at the edge of the patio fence. Around her, foot traffic brushed past, upwardly mobile businessmen, office girls, and older people in more native dress, going about their daily business. She edged down a narrow passage between the patio and the neighboring building. Through the plants she could see the Asian men and the back of the Mechanic's head. She moved closer, bringing herself within earshot.

"We will need more time than that to satisfy our scientists. With a technology this complex, we will need room to breathe." This from one of the Asian men.

"You do not have more time," Nate said. "You may have what he has granted. If it's not sufficient, perhaps this deal isn't for you."

Pruit felt her stomach turn. The Doctor was right. The Mechanic had taken those manuals because they were valuable. He was bargaining with the Eschless Funnel. That she had traveled eighteen years to find that manual, that it was the key to the survival of his own home planet, these things did not matter. He was hawking it like a ware at a local market. She felt righteous rage well up inside her.

Before she had time to consider her possibilities for action, something heavy hit the back of her head. The impact was hard, sending her forward onto her knees. Pruit felt the pain of her knees on pavement, then there was another impact and the world around her faded to black.

Chapter 37

Adaiz-Ari woke to find himself groaning. The pain in his head was so great, he felt it might burst. He could feel his forehead pushing against something rough, and there was a constriction in the blood flow to his feet and hands.

He groaned again and forced his eyes open. He was looking at a rug which lay an inch away from his eyes. He was on the floor somewhere. He had been stripped of his shirt, and with it the gun that had been holstered to his side, but he still wore his loose trousers. He tried to move his hands to bring himself up off of his head, but he discovered that his hands were tied tightly behind his back. As he pulled at them, his feet moved and there was greater pain. He realized he was on his stomach and his feet were bent up toward his back, tied to his hands. Struggling would only make the rope tighter.

He slowly worked his body around until he was lying on his side. A few feet away was the young black man, one of the men Pruit had been following. This black man was sitting on a large cushion on the floor. His hands were twitching slightly as he watched Adaiz, but otherwise he was still. Next to this man, lying on the floor, were several weapons. Adaiz saw his own dirk and gun and four others. He turned his head more, and Pruit came into view.

She was lying on the rug facing him, tied just as he was. She had been stripped down to an undershirt and underwear. Her loose clothing, which had concealed the other weapons he saw, lay a few feet away. Her head was turned to one side, her cheek pressed against the floor, and she was still unconscious. This was the first time he had been so close to her since that morning by her pod. Now that he had been in human cities and seen the different shapes and colors of humanity, he could better appreciate how much he and Pruit resembled each other.

Adaiz stopped this train of thought. He had been thinking of her as an inanimate object. But in a few minutes Pruit would be waking up to the painful realization of her location. She would see Adaiz, and she would question him. He did not want that. Until he had the Eschless Funnel in hand, he would prefer she did not know of his presence.

He looked over at the black man again. The man glanced at Adaiz, then away, and Adaiz could see that there was something making the man uneasy. Adaiz tested the ropes on his hands again. They were tied tightly and wound around his wrists several times. He glanced at the pile of weapons, and a new resource occurred to him. On the left hip of his trousers was a clip to hold his dirk. This clip was sewn into a thick band that ran around the waistline of his pants. He was facing the black man and his left hip was up. Slowly he moved his hands and felt for the clip. It was still in place. He worked it backward so it would be out of the man's sight. Then, with his fingers, he carefully pried off the clip's rubber covering. The black man was now biting his fingernails with some nervousness and he paid no attention to Adaiz.

With the rubber off, Adaiz could feel the corrugated edges of the clip. Gently he began to rub his ties against them.

Lying a few feet away, Pruit slowly became aware of pain. She could feel her cheek pushing into something rough and hard. At the back of her neck was a throbbing ache that seemed to course up into her head with hot bolts of electricity. She moaned as she came awake.

Her eyes opened and she found herself looking across a floor at black legs folded beneath someone sitting nearby. She tried to concentrate, remembered then that she had been watching the Mechanic at a restaurant and had felt an impact from behind. Just as Adaiz had done, she tried to push herself up from the floor, only to find that she was bound tightly. She moved her eyes to survey what she could of the room. This small motion provoked a new burst of pain and she let her eyes fall shut.

When she opened them again, she found the black man studying her.

"When is he getting back?" she asked.

The man shrugged and looked away. She could see that he was edgy. She ignored the pain and scanned the room. It was small and underfurnished, cushions and blankets on the floor, a few chairs here and there. There was a smell of garbage and decay coming from outside. There was dust on the shelves as though no one had been here in weeks.

She turned her head to the other side, and found herself looking into the face of a young Kinley man, tied like she was and lying on the rug a few feet off.

He was awake and looked as though he had been conscious for some time. It shocked her for a moment, seeing a familiar face. It was like looking into a part of her life that was long past. Then she realized his face was not familiar, at least not in its particulars. It was only his coloring that she recognized.

Adaiz stared back at her, still working his hands gently and imperceptibly on the clip.

"Who . . . who are you?" she asked him in Soulene.

Adaiz pretended he didn't understand.

"Who are you?" she asked again, her voice now clearer and more coherent.

Still he did not answer her. With his wrists he felt a slight lessening in the tension of the ropes as he managed to cut through a single strand.

"Who are you?" she asked again, this time in English. Why wouldn't he answer? Was it possible he wasn't Kinley? But he must be. Except for his shorter hair, she could have pulled him from the ranks of her Sentinel class.

Adaiz turned his head from her.

"Why won't you answer me?" She had returned to Soulene. It was impossible that he did not understand. "Are you from a second mission? When did you arrive?"

Jean-Claude glanced at her as she began to speak in an unrecognizable tongue, but she was doing nothing of a threatening nature, and he soon let his eyes wander. His antidote had almost completely run its course and he could feel the jumpiness that preceded deep craving. He stood from his cushion and began to pace.

Pruit glanced at the black man, then back to Adaiz.

"Answer me!" she said, her voice rising. Who was this man?

"You don't know me," Adaiz mumbled, his face still turned away. He said it in English.

"You're Kinley," she said in Soulene. "I know you are. Please . . . Tell me who you are."

He turned to look at her and saw that her face was taking on a strained expression that must indicate frustration.

As he turned his head, Pruit noticed something odd in the way he moved. His motions were quick and smooth, and they seemed to start and stop very suddenly.

"You don't know me," he whispered to her in Soulene. He did not know why he switched to her language. It made no logic tactically, but something in him wanted to let her know that her senses did not deceive her.

Pruit recognized something in his face then, something almost out of a dream, his face leaning over her and the blue dome of Earth sky behind. "Yes I do," she said. "I've seen you before."

He did not answer.

"Talk to me!" she yelled.

"Keep quiet!" the black man hissed, stopping in his pacing to look over at her. He was biting his knuckles.

Pruit lowered her voice. "Please . . ."

"There is nothing to speak of," he said softly. "We do not know each other."

His Soulene was very good but not quite perfect, as though he had a slight speech impediment. *No,* she thought. *That's not it. Soulene is not his native language.* Then who was he?

He turned his head away from her, and again she noticed the way he moved, the sudden stopping and starting with no tapering off. He was either in motion or still, and there seemed to be no gradient between. It was unusual.

"Why won't you talk?" she asked, her voice sounding desperate.

Still turned away from her, Adaiz said, "There is nothing to say."

She heard it then. There was a lisp in his speech. He had tried to disguise it by whispering, but at last she had caught it. His motions, his lisp; they fit together. She felt a sick sensation in her stomach as understanding came to her. He was Kinley, but he was not Kinley. He was Lucien. He was one of their spies, trained in Kinley ways, but here, under the stress of captivity, his natural body language had given him away.

She looked at him, an odd mixture of rage and terror welling up within her. Her first thought was, *This is a traitor, a human they have raised and who has willingly become one of them.* Then her second thought was worse: *The Lucien are here. They have followed me. They know that we know. And they know the purpose of this mission.*

"I know what you are," she breathed.

Adaiz caught the tone of her voice and turned to look at her.

"You're one of them," she said slowly. "You're Lucien."

Adaiz could see the look on her face, and he could feel the emotion it represented. She hated him, and the knowledge of that hate affected him deeply. She was the first human woman he had ever seen. He had carefully tucked her into her fullsuit so she would live; he had experienced pleasure at touching her. He did not want her to know that he was her enemy.

He stared back at her and did not deny her accusation.

"Saving Father!" Pruit said, the rage coming to the surface. "You work for the destruction of your own race!"

He did not want to argue, for what could that accomplish? But Adaiz felt himself provoked to answer.

"The Lucien are my race," he said. "They are my brothers and my family." Why did he feel the urge to justify himself?

"Is that what they tell you so you will do their dirty work?"

"There is no 'they'!" Adaiz said, his voice rising in anger and his lisp becoming stronger. "I am 'they.'"

Pruit laughed unpleasantly. "How do they manage it? How do they make you such a loyal slave?"

"By Omani!" he yelled in Avani, then switched to Soulene. "I am Adaiz-Ari, of Warrior Clan and Clan Providence! I am a member of a race that seeks knowledge and brotherhood. There can be no slaves where there is enlightenment!"

"Enlightenment? For hundreds of years you've choked us! Blockaded us so we remain at your mercy!" In her anger, she moved her arms and legs and felt her ropes tighten.

"It is not a blockade," Adaiz said slowly, anger now burning within him. "It is a quarantine." He was still working on his ropes. He did not let emotion distract him from that track. He felt a second thread unravel in his bonds. "What kind of a race would kill every man and woman and child on a planet? What kind of a race would design a plague to do this and then re-lease it? By the merest luck we had our asteroid colonies and some of us were able to survive."

"What harm could we do you now? But still you are unsat-isfied and you want us gone—from your universe, from life it-self!" Pruit's eyes were burning and she was yelling.

"Be quiet!" Jean-Claude yelled back at her. He was now searching through a cupboard, looking for the cubes of hashish he had left in the room. He did not know what effect they would have on him, but he hoped they would do something, anything, to allay the growing craving within him. Outside, it was twilight already, and still the Mechanic had not returned. What if he had forgotten? What if Jean-Claude would be left all night without his drug?

"How can you even claim to be harmless?" Adaiz demanded, more quietly. "You have shown us what harm you can do. Infinite!"

"What would you expect us to do? You bombed our cities," Pruit said. "You bombed us without discretion!"

"We never sought to annihilate your race! A planet can survive a bombing. Your plague wiped us clean!"

Pruit's voice dropped to a deadly low tone. "Do you know how many of us survived your attack? Do you know how many healthy humans remained on Herrod after the bombing stopped?"

Adaiz did not answer her. He did not know.

"Fewer than one thousand."

He said nothing, showed nothing on his face. But the number shocked him.

"Less than one thousand!" she hissed. "Did you ever wonder why we all look the same? Did you ever wonder why it took so very long for us to recover? Do you know what radiation does to the human body?"

Adaiz did not know the answer to these things. He was still recovering from the shock of her first revelation. Whatever he had imagined, it was a far greater number. Less than one thousand? Could that really be true? The Lucien had not known this. After the Plague it had been a thousand years before they had any news of the Kinley. And they had always assumed that the humans were far less affected by the war than the Lucien had been.

"Ninety percent of survivors of the bombing died within the year," she said. "Ninety percent! And ninety percent of those died in the next two years. And so on."

Adaiz could not stop himself from asking, "How . . . how did you recover?"

"One doctor and a few others spent their lives taking genetic samples of five hundred survivors, the healthiest. Reproductive cells where possible, other cells if that was all they could obtain. He mapped out the recovery of the race by careful screening and incubated fetuses. It took more generations than we can count. So don't preach to me about annihilation."

Adaiz was shaken by her words. He had not known the extent of the damage on Herrod. "We have evolved to become a very different race than we were," Adaiz said quietly. "We are more than warriors now."

"And now, because you emerged first," she continued, ignoring him, "you decide the future for us."

"We must make our judgments," Adaiz said. "Your population is growing faster than you can make room for it to live. This can only lead to a desire to colonize. In the near future you will emerge as a space power—a colonizing space power. We cannot allow that, because we are your closest neighbors."

"So you'll wipe us clean."

"You chose your path ages ago."

"Do you know why our population continues to grow?" she asked, her voice soft. "Do you know what the half-life of plutonium is? Ten thousand years. We have no room, but we must grow. You know nothing of what we face. We have mutations, even now. They happen less and less frequently, but they happen. We still do not reproduce naturally. If you want a child, you will be impregnated by a healthy egg that has been fertilized with healthy sperm. It might be several hundred years old. Everything is screened, and still there are mutations, even without leaks from the dome. That is how insidious radiation is. We have to expand our numbers until we have enough people with healthy genes to maintain the population naturally. We are still several generations from this, and until we achieve it, we are a race in name only."

Adaiz suddenly saw the Plaguers as a race performing an elaborate balancing act, with the scales below them ready to tip one way or the other at any time. He struggled to regain the view of them he had held since childhood—a race barbaric enough to effect the destruction of another sentient race. The Lucien taught that their own ancestors bore much of the blame for the war and the Plague, but there was always the caveat that they, as a race, had changed, become more civilized, found religion in Omani and his gentler ways. For the first time Adaiz thought that such a change might be possible for the Plaguers as well. Still, he clung to the wisdom of destroying Herrod. Lucien civilization was in a state of unprecedented prosperity, and it was in the best interests of the race to maintain full control over their home system. One's own survival must come first.

"Just think," Pruit continued, her words holding all the hatred that language could transmit, "if you had been born on Herrod, you might know these things and even feel concern for the future of your kind."

Whatever sympathy Adaiz might have felt for her was killed by those words. "You are not my kind," he said. "You will never leave here with the technology you seek. And your race will die." He held her gaze for a moment, then turned his head away. Their discussion was over. A third strand of rope came loose and he felt the whole grouping start to give.

Pruit let her head rest against the floor again. She felt spent. It took several moments for the anger to release her, but the pain finally brought her back to her current situation. She had not noticed her head as she argued with Adaiz, but now that they were quiet, the throbbing returned. She moved her attention to the black man. He was pacing by the window, something clutched tightly in his right hand. As she watched, he paused and opened his hand, looking at a small gummy cube of an amber shade. His other hand was clutching at his stomach. He appeared to be in pain.

Jean-Claude hesitated, then carefully set the cube of hashish in his mouth. He leaned back against the wall and closed his eyes, savoring the taste. How many times had that flavor meant the coming of a beautiful drug fantasy? But now, as the cube began to dissolve, Jean-Claude only felt the craving within him growing stronger. He spat out the hashish, and his arms hugged his abdomen. Nothing would satisfy or even soothe him anymore, nothing but his own antidote. He let out a low moan.

Both of his captives were looking at him now, but he didn't

care. Yes, he did care, he reminded himself, for he must watch them, he must watch them for the Mechanic. The Mechanic would be mad if something went wrong, and if he was mad, this craving would never stop, it would only grow stronger, and then would come the convulsions and they would eat him up and if there was still no antidote he would cramp up into a ball and the pain would slowly kill him.

Watching the black man, Pruit saw his mounting panic. She had planned to wait without struggle for the Mechanic's return. Surely he would question her and she would find a way to free herself and learn of his plans as well. But there was something wrong with the man. She watched him with her medically trained eye and realized he was experiencing withdrawal from something his body required. He had grown increasingly agitated, and now his digestive tract appeared to be cramping. There was, perhaps, opportunity here.

"He gives you something, doesn't he?" she asked, intuitively deducing the Mechanic's method of encouraging loyalty.

The young man's head turned to her. His breathing was ragged, and now his fingernails were driving into his palm.

"He gives you something that keeps you with him."

Slowly, he nodded. "Yes," he whispered.

"How often do you need it?"

"Every day." He paused. "More often would be better." He was biting the inside of his bottom lip now. His throat was dry and beginning to feel sore.

"Is that how he trapped you?"

"Yes . . ." He twisted his neck in a gesture of pain.

Adaiz watched this conversation warily and continued his quiet escape plan. His hands were losing sensation and the muscles of his forearms were aching, but he steadily rubbed the rope on the clasp. With the other two now occupied, he began to edge very slowly toward the pile of weapons.

Pruit was beginning to see the Mechanic in the proper light. He had been a quiet, unassuming member of the crew, but he was an individual who festered on the inside and waited for a chance at revenge. He was someone who had no consideration or even thought for other people.

She saw her path to the upper hand with this young black man, and if it worked, she would be able to surprise the Mechanic when he arrived. "I can free you," she said.

"Only he can do that," he replied without emotion. The thought existed like a mantra in his head. *Only he can do that* . . . "He has it with him always and only he can mix it."

"Do you know who he is? What he is?" she asked.

"I am beginning to know."

"I have come from the same place he has," she said, "but my medical knowledge is better. I can free you."

Warily, he allowed a small spark of hope to flare up in his mind. "Why should I believe you?"

"Where is the risk in believing me? If I can't do what I say, you are no worse off. Let me free you. You have no loyalty to him, that much is easy to see."

"You know nothing of me."

She could see that he was almost beyond hope. He had nearly given up the idea that he would ever again have control of himself. "Untie my hands and I will show you," she said softly.

He laughed derisively.

"You have disarmed me," she pointed out. "Your master is coming soon. You can take my offer or not."

Jean-Claude paced. The leg cramps were starting. Soon he would not be able to walk. What if she was tricking him? Did it matter? Surely he could defend himself. As long as she was still here when the Mechanic arrived, he would be safe. He rubbed his face with his hands, then made up his mind.

He moved to a wall cabinet and pulled out a slender silver thread with small handles on each end. Both prisoners recognized it. It was a garrote. Jean-Claude carefully wrapped it around the girl's neck, then gripped it tightly in his left hand. He put a foot in the center of her back, pressing her down into the floor. With his right hand he carefully untied her hands, leaving the ropes on her feet intact.

Adaiz continued to move toward the weapons. In all, he had moved no more than a foot or so, but this put him in close range of his knife and gun. He could feel the ropes on his hands beginning to fray.

As Pruit pulled her hands free, the black man tightened his hold on the garrote. His grip was unsteady. He was losing motor control. The razor wire pulled at Pruit's skin. Any more pressure and it would cut her. Slowly, she pulled herself to a sitting position, feeling pins and needles in her hands as blood rushed back into them.

Pruit looked at him and spoke very gently. "What's your name?"

"Jean-Claude."

"Jean-Claude, I will have to touch my arm and then touch you." Jean-Claude managed a nod.

She activated her skinsuit control panel and it grew into view on the underside of her forearm. Jean-Claude seemed to relax at the sight of this alien technology. It gave her credibility.

For several minutes, Pruit manipulated the panel, preparing it for the examination she wanted it to make. This would be somewhat beyond the usual functions of the suit, but within its potential capabilities.

"I have to touch you now. Your ankle would be a good place."

"Do it," he said.

Gently, Pruit laid her hand on his dark ankle, with her fingers touching the large artery there. Her skinsuit kicked into action. Its cells congregated around her hand, growing out of her skin into a whitish layer that became thicker and thicker until it spread to Jean-Claude's skin as well. He stared at her hand on his ankle and gasped slightly at the sensation of the suit penetrating his skin. It was more electric than painful, as the cells of her skinsuit grew into his artery.

Pruit watched the readout as the tiny suit cells made a tour of Jean-Claude's body to determine what ailed him. Several minutes passed and then she had her answer. The suit had found what he was addicted to and, by analyzing the addictive need, could now reverse it.

Pruit smiled at Jean-Claude. "He has taken away your body's ability to assimilate certain essential vitamins," she explained. "The withdrawal must be very painful. But I can fix it."

She manipulated the control panel and the suit began to work on a cure for Jean-Claude. The layer around her left hand and his ankle grew thicker. Pruit began to feel a draining sensation. The suit was drawing heavily on the resources of her own body to perform this task. She felt herself becoming thirsty and then dizzy.

Jean-Claude's muscles began to relax and his hands steadied. Then his eyes became heavy and he experienced nausea and a strange aching in his teeth. It felt to him as though a cure were coming too fast and changing his body at an overwhelming rate. It was still good, still right, but it was overtaking him, and he could not keep his eyes open.

Across the room, Adaiz scrubbed the rope harder on the clip, his motions no longer small and secret, for the other two were completely occupied.

Pruit felt the dizziness increase and fought to stay conscious. At last the suit receded from his ankle and began to fade back into her hand. Its work was done.

"It's finished," she said.

Jean-Claude released the garrote and it fell down along Pruit's chest. She quickly unwound it and dropped it to the floor. Jean-Claude clutched his stomach as nausea overtook him, then he vomited. He rolled over on his side and his eyes closed.

At last Adaiz felt the final binding fiber give. The rope released, and he slipped his hands free. He saw Pruit turning toward him, her own hands loose, her face looking tired and pale. She was free also. She knew him and knew his mission, and she would now do whatever possible to stop him. She was his enemy.

Just as Pruit focused her eyes on him, Adaiz rolled quickly

to the pile of weapons. He grabbed the closet one—one of Pruit's knives—and cut the ropes on his feet.

Pruit lunged toward him, forgetting that her own feet were still tied. She landed on her knees. Without hesitating, Adaiz threw the knife by its blade. Pruit's reaction was too slow. Before she could drop to the floor and roll aside, the knife arced through the air and embedded itself in the flesh of her left shoulder.

Her body hit the floor and Pruit felt the agony of the knife wound. Despite this, there was a good sensation, the sensation of her body moving into action. She could feel the heightened awareness as adrenaline entered her bloodstream and exhilaration swept over her.

Adaiz reached for Pruit's other knife and lifted it to throw. Pruit saw the motion and acted. With her right hand, she gripped the knife in her shoulder and pulled it out, then rolled, cutting through the ropes on her feet as she did so. The second knife arced through the air and landed in the rug, inches from her. Pruit jumped to her feet, grabbing the second knife with her left arm. Quickly she checked function of the limb. It was minimal. The arm responded, but with almost no strength. The skinsuit was tending to the wound, working to seal the severed muscles and arteries. But it could not move fast enough to prevent her from bleeding. There was blood running down her undershirt.

She faced Adaiz. He had recovered his own knife, and was now reaching for his gun. Pruit was unfamiliar with its type, but it did not appear to be a projectile weapon. Laser, then. That would make sense for a Lucien weapon. Projectile weapons would be taboo in a society that had grown up in enclosed asteroid colonies. If he managed to aim it at her, the fight would be over.

On the floor behind her, Jean-Claude was softly moaning, and had begun to move.

Pruit leapt at Adaiz before he could secure the gun in his hand. Her body hit his and sent him sprawling backward, into a long shelf up against the wall. They hit this together, then fell to the floor, Adaiz on top of her, his gun fallen. He drove a fist down into her wounded shoulder and Pruit screamed.

She twisted and unbalanced him, then made a slash along his ribs, a shallow penetration that began to bleed profusely. Adaiz reached for his guns, but she kicked them under the shelf and out of reach.

As Adaiz got to his feet, he felt the pain of the cut in his side, and the surprise at her strength and training. She now faced him with a knife in each hand and a wash of blood down her chest. Her breath was coming hard but her clarity and energy could not be mistaken. She was wearing only her underclothes and Adaiz found himself distracted by the lean lines of her body. He tried to clear his mind, tried to gain the clarity of the egani-tah. He must encompass himself and her. He must see her actions before she performed them, make her part of himself. He regulated his breathing.

I do not want to kill her. I must kill her. I have no love for her I am human in name only. I am Lucien I am one of the People I am enlightened I have known the stars and the universe they have passed through me and I have remained . . .

Adaiz tried to shut off these chattering thoughts, but they would not leave him. He tried to mentally touch her, but a wave of disgust washed over him, and he was pulled back into himself. She hated him and he could feel it. Pruit was laughing, and though he was not very familiar with laughter, it was clear she was deriding him.

"You are surprised that I can fight you," she said. "You don't know your own race. You've been told we are weak."

She was studying his motions. He was lean and fit, but the balance of his muscles was odd. His calves and legs were overbuilt when compared with the rest of his body. His stance and balance were good but not perfect. They spoke of a man who had been trained by a teacher who did not know human physiology. She would need this advantage, for she had only one arm working properly.

In a surprise move, she struck out and cut into his upper

arm. Blood welled up, and Adaiz stumbled back. She pushed him to the floor and lifted her right arm for the final blow.

But Adaiz was enraged now. The pain of this new injury achieved what he could not achieve with mental control alone—it had pushed everything else aside. He rolled back and kicked out. Both legs connected with Pruit's stomach, and she flew away from him.

Pruit landed hard on her back and Adaiz was on top of her. His knife came down at her heart. She blocked his knife arm and he screamed and rained down blows on her face and neck.

He lifted the knife again. Behind Adaiz she saw Jean-Claude, now on his feet and finally aware of the fight. Adaiz struck down at her, and at the same moment Jean-Claude pushed him, sending him off of Pruit. She lunged up to standing. Jean-Claude made a move for Adaiz, but he slashed out, cutting Jean-Claude's forearm.

Adaiz came at Pruit with full fury now. His mind had taken up its idiotic narrative again: *she is you and you are she and I must kill her and I am not a traitor I am not a traitor I am an adopted brother and have never been given anything but love!*

He pounded blows at her. Pruit fought him back, but she could feel her body losing strength. The shock of the shoulder wound was upon her. She was getting cold. Her head was pounding, from Jean-Claude's original blow and from the beating Adaiz had given her. He was backing her toward a wall. He was cornering her. Jean-Claude, not a trained fighter, was gripping his wrist where blood was freely flowing out and onto the floor.

Adaiz had only one knife, but he was wielding it like a madman. It was all she could do to block the blows. She felt something hard and cool against her back. The window. She was cornered.

No! she yelled in her mind. *You will not win!*

She drew on her last remaining strength, blocked him weakly with her left arm, and struck forward with her right.

She felt the knife go in. She could see a bloom of red on his side, just below his ribs. Adaiz cried out and fell back a step. Pruit lifted her arm for another strike.

Before she could bring her knife down, Adaiz felt his mind fill with the knowledge of his leg and foot and her body beyond them. He saw his muscles. There was pain, but it did not matter. He saw the path to follow. He would kill her. He would kill her now and worry about the technology later. He lifted his leg and felt the energy running through it. He kicked out with the foot. It connected with Pruit's chest.

Pruit felt the impact, and then there was another impact of her body with glass. She was falling. The evening air was cool and the dark shapes of buildings were moving past her. He had kicked her out the window. She would die. There was a shock wave of pain as she landed.

Up in the room, Adaiz fell back. It felt for a moment as though he was the one outside, falling through the air. He reached out a hand to steady himself, but there was nothing to grab. He felt his body hit the floor. He was losing blood. He was losing consciousness. He grabbed the rug with his hand, and then he passed out.

Jean-Claude saw Pruit fly out the window then Adaiz hit the floor unconscious. Jean-Claude had finally managed to stop his own bleeding just as the fight ended. She had saved him. She had freed him. And he had only sat there, huddled over his own wound as the other prisoner killed her.

For a few moments he watched a pool of blood forming under Adaiz, then he stood, scrambled for the guns and other weapons that he saw beneath the shelf, and tucked them into a small bag. He ran from the room and down the stairs. He took a dim, squalid hallway to the back of the tenement and found his way out into the narrow alley behind.

There were no lights here, but there was a bright moon above thin clouds and much reflected light from the city. A cool breeze managed to penetrate the space between the buildings, bringing some slight relief from the smell of urine and decay.

He saw her. She lay sprawled half on top of refuse, half on the dirt of the alley itself. Her eyes were closed. Jean-Claude looked up the building to the second-story window of his rooms. Her fall had been broken by the garbage. It was possible she was still alive.

He moved over to her and felt at her neck. He thought he could feel a faint pulse.

"I am so sorry," he mumbled to her in French. "I am so sorry."

Her knives were still in her hands and he put them into the bag with the guns. Carefully then, he picked her up and slung her body over one shoulder. She made no voluntary motions, but hung from him like a dead weight.

Jean-Claude whisked her from the alley. He could not take a taxi. He was a foreigner with a knife wound carrying a badly injured young woman. The police would become involved. He did not want police. He wanted time to think, time to find out who he was again.

Instead, he made his way through alleys for two miles, carrying her through the dark corners he had haunted for three years, past the brothels and the heroin and hashish dealers who infested the back streets of Cairo.

It was midnight when he reached the Sisters of Jude charity hospital. Pruit was moaning now, starting to wake. Carefully he set her down, propping her body against a wall outside the emergency admittance room, among dozens of other people huddled together, waiting for assistance. In light coming through the hospital doors he could see that she was looking at him.

Jean-Claude knelt down to eye level. He could not tell how lucid she was. "He will soon strike a deal," he told her.

Pruit's head fell to one side, and Jean-Claude put his hand under her chin and gently turned her face toward him. Her eyes were still open.

"He will soon make his deal," he repeated. "I believe he keeps only one copy of what you seek, and only he knows its location. When he makes his deal, he will give that copy in person." Could she hear him? It was difficult to tell.

After several moments, Pruit managed a slight nod. "Understand . . . ," she whispered.

Jean-Claude released her chin, and her head fell back against the wall.

"Thank you for my life," he said. "I am sorry I did not deserve it more." He put the bag of weapons in her hands, then left her, slipping back into the shadows.

Chapter 38

There were glaring lights and the smell of rubbing alcohol. There were sounds of pain and motion and feet and machines, and the feel of many bodies in close spaces.

Several men and women were gathered around her and there were bright lights shining in her eyes. Two of the people wore white cotton hats and small masks over their faces.

Pruit had just returned to consciousness and a world of pain. Her shoulder was aching and burning and throbbing, and her head pounded with slow violence. She was conscious of intense thirst. These people were trying to hold her down, and she found herself struggling. They were trying to inject her; they were trying to hook her up to an IV.

"Hold still!" someone shouted. "Hold her still!"

"No!" she said, trying to push them away. "No . . ." It was terribly important that she stop them. Why? She could not at first remember. Then it came to her—her skinsuit, they would not understand her skinsuit. They would discover it and they would know that she did not belong.

"No!" she pushed their hands away.

"Hold still!" a doctor yelled.

She had been yelling in Soulene and they were speaking Arabic. "No!" she yelled, remembering Arabic and using it. "I don't need your help!"

"Yes, you do, I'm afraid," said the young Egyptian doctor

with strained patience. They were pinning down her arms. She felt the IV going into the vein in her hand.

"Doctor, there's something wrong here," one of the nurses said.

It was her skinsuit, Pruit knew. It would be isolating the IV tube in a layer of cells.

"Inject her now! She is hysterical!"

She felt a needle at her inner elbow and then the painful tingling of a syringe being emptied into her artery. It was a painkiller, and she was thankful for it immediately. Her shoulder calmed. She knew she must get up off the table, but her eyes were closing.

"What is it?" the doctor asked, examining the tube.

"Look, sir, it's coming from her skin."

"No," she said again. "No . . ."

"It's some kind of tissue . . ."

"Look how fast it's growing . . ."

"Have you ever seen anything . . . ?"

"Quick, call in Dr. Faruk . . . !"

"No . . . ," she whispered.

Then, above the other noises issuing from the surrounding rooms, there were running footsteps and a bang as a door flew open.

"Pruit? Pruit?"

She knew that voice.

"Pruit!"

"Eddie . . ." She was only whispering. "Eddie!" It was all she could manage, but he had heard her. Through half-closed eyes she saw Eddie shove the doctor aside.

"What are you doing?" the doctor asked in Arabic. "Get him out of here!"

"This is my wife!" Eddie yelled in Arabic. "This is my wife, and I have a doctor for her at home!"

The doctor and one of the male nurses tried to grab him, but he executed a neat open-handed punch to each, giving the blows just enough force to push the men out of the way without actually hurting them. "I'm taking her. Let me go!"

"Yes," she mumbled in Arabic, so they would understand him. "He is my husband." Even in her half-conscious state she saw the intelligence behind Eddie's claim. The husband ruled in Muslim cultures. He could even deny his wife medical treatment.

The men moved toward Eddie again, but uncertainly. His frantic words were perfectly delivered and held them at bay. "Let me go! I'm taking her home!"

He yanked the IV from Pruit's hand and scooped her up from the table. They did not try to stop him. Pruit put her arms around his shoulders and he held her to his chest and helped her wrap her legs around his waist.

"Wait," she mumbled, gesturing toward the gurney desperately, her arm barely responding to her command. Eddie grabbed the small bag she was reaching for and Pruit clutched it.

"We're going," he said. "We're going!"

He backed out of the room's swinging double doors as the medical team stared at him. Then he was jogging down a narrow hallway with Pruit in his arms. There were people waiting in the hall, sitting on benches and the floor, with everything from minor wounds to serious injuries. There was a smell of disease and death. This was a hospital for the indigent, and many had made temporary homes in the passage.

Eddie picked his way over them, clutching Pruit, who felt insubstantial in his arms. Her skin was cold and damp. He reached the end of the hall and passed into a large reception area. Children were crying here, and it was a swarm of unwashed humanity. He pushed his way between, and then they passed through the outer doors and Pruit could feel the night breeze on her skin. She was still in her underwear and a shiver ran up her back.

A car was waiting. Eddie bundled her into the backseat, then slid in next to her. There was a blanket on the floor, and he wrapped it around her.

"Back to the hotel," he told the driver. He looked back toward the hospital. It was unlikely that anyone would follow them, but his eyes lingered at the door. The driver was staring back at his passengers. "Now!" Eddie yelled.

The car lurched into the street.

"Eddie . . . ," she breathed.

He leaned over her and examined her.

"What happened?"

"How did you find me, Eddie?" she asked, still in the pleasant grip of the painkiller.

"When you didn't come back and you didn't answer your phone, I started checking hospitals. . . . You're hard to describe, you know. Not exactly white, not exactly anything else. Why is the thing you're searching for always in the last place you look? Thank God I found you when I did. . . . Your shoulder!"

"I can fix it . . . I can fix it . . ."

He pulled the blanket more tightly around her, holding her upright. Her face and neck were covered with deep bruises. "Pruit, who did this to you?"

Her eyes were falling closed, but she knew she could not sleep. There was something wrong. . . . She remembered now. The human Lucien had been following her. She forced her eyes open. "Eddie, there's a tracer on me. They tagged me . . ."

"Who tagged you?"

"I'll explain later." It was difficult to speak. It was difficult to stay awake. "Check my back . . ." With her right arm, she began to pull off her undershirt.

"Check for what?"

"Something by the spine, something small and hard." The spine would be the usual location for a Lucien tag. That was one piece of Lucien procedure she had learned in training. Over generations of blockade, more than a few humans had been tagged by Lucien.

He did not understand, but he did as she said, helping her get the undershirt off and pulling the blanket up over her chest so she was not exposed to the other cars. Female nudity was frowned upon in Egypt. The hired driver was turning back to look at them.

"Mind your business!" Eddie snapped at him. The man brought his eyes back to the road.

Eddie studied her spine. "I don't see anything."

"Feel with your hands, next to the vertebrae."

He ran his fingers up and down her spine, carefully feeling each bone. There was something at her mid-back, something that felt wrong. "There's something here. But I can't see it."

"Get light," she said weakly.

"Stop the car!" The car pulled over beneath a streetlight and Eddie examined the spot on her back. There was something there, an almost imperceptible lump. "I think I found it."

She reached around and he put her hand on the spot. "Yes, that's it. Cut it out."

"What?"

"Cut it out, Eddie! They'll use it to find me."

"Who will?"

"Just cut it out! My knife . . ." She gestured to the bag she had made him take from the hospital.

"I can't cut you!"

"You can. Just do it. Don't think. No—wait." She activated her skinsuit control panel and turned the suit off so it would not interfere with his operation. "Now do it."

Eddie took her white knife in his hand. He did not allow himself to hesitate. Instead, he cut into her back, making a small incision just on top of the lump. Pruit gripped her knees. The painkiller was fading. Eddie touched the cut, and he could feel something hard inside. Pruit gasped as he prodded the wound.

"I'm sorry . . ."

"Pry it out!"

He took the tip of the knife and dug it beneath the lump. With a downward flick of his wrist, he pushed the tracer to the surface. It was small and oval, the size of a tiny ball bearing, covered in her blood. He pulled it out of her, then grabbed her undershirt and pressed it against the wound.

"I got it." He held out the tracer for her to examine. She glanced at it, hardly able to focus her eyes. "Throw it out."

Eddie rolled down the window and jettisoned it.

"Good," she breathed, leaning back against the seat, long past exhaustion. "Good . . ." Her eyes closed.

Gently, Eddie pulled her onto his lap, holding the shirt against her back to stop the blood, holding her body to his chest. He had been searching the city's dozen or so hospitals since the late afternoon, his panic level steadily rising. Even so, he had not realized how much he cared for her until this moment. He held her to him and knew suddenly that she was precious to him. "There's never a dull moment with you, is there, Pruit Pax of Senetian?" he whispered into her hair, kissing her head.

She let her head fall onto his shoulder, feeling his strength and grateful for it. Then she was asleep in Eddie's arms as the car took to the road again.

Chapter 39

Slowly coming back to consciousness on the floor of Jean-Claude's apartment, Adaiz tried to move. Pain made this impossible on the first try. The upper part of his left arm was burning, as was his left side, below his ribs. He could feel damage to his muscles.

He shut his eyes and rolled himself over on his back. The motion was agony, but he could also see the limits of his pain. Most of his body still worked, and he had not lost an excessive amount of blood. His recovery, Omani willing, would not be too lengthy.

He brought himself slowly to his feet, fighting light-headedness. There was a pool of smeared blood on the floor, but his shoulder wound had clotted. He studied it, then glanced around and found his shirt, which Jean-Claude had stripped from him. He picked it up, held it between his good hand and his teeth, and carefully tore it into strips. He wrapped his shoulder. With difficulty, he secured the bandages in a knot. Then he wrapped the long cut running under his ribs.

With his wounds bandaged, he forced himself to walk around the room. He nearly fainted several times, but he maintained consciousness by hanging his head low and holding onto furniture. As he approached the street-side window of the apartment, he heard a car pull up below.

Slowly he leaned his head closer. Down in the street a taxi

had stopped and out of it stood the gray-colored man Pruit had been following.

Adaiz moved as quickly as he could, pushing himself away from the window and moving along the counter to the old black phone which sat in the corner. He picked up the receiver and was relieved to hear a dial tone. He had taken time to practice with phones, and understood how they worked. He quickly dialed the number he had memorized.

There were two rings and then a hesitant voice at the other end. "Hello?" It was Enon-Amet, using one of the few English words he knew and pitching his voice low and quiet to emulate a human whisper.

"Brother, it is Adaiz."

"What's happened? Are you all right?"

"Yes and no," Adaiz said. "But I must hurry. The man Pruit was following is here and I have a plan."

"Where are you?"

"That can wait. Tell me, are the tracers on Pruit still working?"

"It appears she has discovered one of them, but the other remains intact."

"Excellent."

"Adaiz, are you safe?"

"I think so, Older Brother. And I believe I have two bargaining chips that will win us success in both aspects of this mission. I will be back at the hotel soon."

He hung up the phone. There were footsteps on the stairs.

Chapter 40

Nate sat with the Mechanic in the back of a taxi, heading through narrow streets toward Jean-Claude's old apartment. He was experiencing the tightening of his skin that heralded the onset of shivers. Soon his digestive tract would begin to cramp and the pain would come. He would start to moan, and this would annoy the Mechanic, perhaps even delaying his antidote. Silently he counted the seconds.

Outside the car, the seamier side of Cairo flashed by, hashish parlors and none-too-discreet brothels. There was an underground disco on this block, and young men teemed in front of it. Once upon a time, Nate would have been drawn to such a place. It seemed another life.

Next to him, the Mechanic said nothing, but Nate could tell he was pleased. Their meeting with the Chinese had gone very well. After several minutes of discussion, it had become apparent that the Chinese had already studied the sample formulas at length. They had, apparently, stolen them from one of the other countries negotiating with the Mechanic. They had already concluded that the technology was real and they had used this afternoon's meeting to make the Mechanic an offer. It had been very generous for an opening bid.

Nate anticipated a few counterdemands from the Mechanic, to which the Chinese would doubtless agree, then the deal would be sealed. Then . . . what? What would happen to him? He squinted his eyes as he felt the first cramp coming on.

Perhaps his fate would not be so bad. He had, after all, organized everything for the Mechanic: bank accounts away from
prying eyes, a nondescript safe deposit box where the manuals
were housed. He had even been the one to suggest that only
the Mechanic himself should know the location of that box.
The key for the Mechanic's future safety lay in holding no secrets. He would hand over the technology, all of it, and then
focus would shift from him to the technology itself. This was
facilitated because the Mechanic himself was not proficient in
the technology, a fact Nate had carefully made known to each
interested party. Once he handed over the goods, he would,
however, still be needed to translate the Haight manuals and
this would protect him.

In helping the Mechanic establish his plan of action, Nate
had asked him what he hoped to achieve from his negotiations.
The Mechanic's answer was simple: "To live like a god among
men." When asked to elaborate, he could not, other than to say
he wanted the means at his disposal to have anything he
wished.

In his dogged way, Nate had simply incorporated this desire
into the equation. To live like that, the Mechanic would need a
considerable amount of money, as well as protection. Thus, the
country that offered these in the greatest amounts would win
the negotiation.

China, with offers of immediate Swiss citizenship—something Nate had not known was possible, but which he was
convinced was a valid offer—as well as certain specified sums
and other accoutrements, would likely be the Mechanic's
country of choice.

The remainder of their afternoon and evening, however, had
been consumed by three additional offers from new countries,
countries who had materialized out of the woodwork. The Mechanic had listened patiently, but Nate was fairly sure he had
already made his decision.

The cramps were worse as the taxi edged up onto the sidewalk and came to a stop. Without so much as a glance at Nate,
the Mechanic left the car and headed into the tenement build-

ing. Nate paid the driver, then followed him inside. They had spent a week living in this apartment, and both knew the tiny, winding stairway by heart.

"Shall we see what the whore dragged home?" the Mechanic called back, moving quickly up the stairs.

The smell of urine and trash hit them as they reached the landing, but Nate was now too uncomfortable to hold his breath.

The Mechanic drew his handgun as he approached Jean-Claude's door. He saw that it was ajar and paused. No sounds issued from inside. He prodded the wood and the door swung inward.

Sitting in the room's single chair, bandaged at shoulder and side, was a young man. He held a knife casually in one hand. Neither the Mechanic nor Nate had caught a glimpse of Adaiz when he followed Pruit earlier that day, so he was a stranger to them.

"Who are you?" the Mechanic asked. The Mechanic's words were translated by his jawline device into English.

The young man smiled in a strange, mechanical fashion. "I have an offer for you," he said. "One that no country will match."

"What happened to the black whore?"

"He has been freed by the other prisoner. And that girl is part of my offer."

The Mechanic moved into the room and leaned himself against the low shelves along one wall, his gun trained on the newcomer. "I'm listening," he said.

Nate forced himself to take a seat on the floor. He took one of the cushions that lay scattered about and shoved it into his abdomen. His body had begun to double up. It would only be minutes before he began to moan aloud. He would suppress those moans as long as humanly possible. His pain must wait until the offer had been heard.

Chapter 41

2590 B.C.
Year 17 of Kinley Earth Survey

> The monarchs of the [Fourth] dynasty were gods: they
> alone after death were privileged to journey across the
> heavens with their retainers in the divine barque.
> —J. E. Manchip White
> *Ancient Egypt: Its Culture and History*

The foundation blocks had been laid over the preceding
weeks, and now the builders were beginning on the second
course of stones. The foundation itself covered thirteen acres
of sandy desert, sunk below surface level to rest on bedrock.
There was a large outcropping of natural rock near the center
of the foundation, which rose fifty feet above the desert
floor. This would serve as an additional anchor to the structure.

The courses on top of the foundation would rise up and inward, four sides forming a pyramid, sloping at an angle of
fifty-one degrees, to meet in a point nearly five hundred feet
above the desert.

The size of the individual blocks was limited by the maximum volume of mold in which a rock culture consistently
could be grown. Despite the Captain's attempts at preserving
Kinley knowledge, much of the Engineer's building prowess
had already been lost. This was inevitable in a primitive culture that turned technology into superstitious ritual, diluting
it in the process. Now, if they used too large a mold, the re-

sulting rock appeared uneven and artificial. The volume was
also modified by the shape of rock needed for particular locations in the structure, and the type of rock culture used.
For the granite that was to encase the primary interior room
of this building, the builders would produce slabs of over
fifty tons. Elsewhere, they would weigh as much as two hundred tons.

The Captain stood atop a wooden scaffolding that had been
erected to view the progress of the pyramid. He had aged, in
recent years, to a silver head of hair and a distinguished, mas-
culine face. He wore a robe of thick white linen, trimmed in
gold, and plaited leather sandals of the finest make. His hair
was oiled and braided behind his neck. He had become his
own vision of divinity in human form.

With him stood Khufu, the twelve-year-old king of all
Egypt and the Captain's blood son. Khufu had his mother's
brown skin, but his hair was light—not blond, but nearly so—
and his eyes had been muted from dark brown to gray. His
head already cleared the Captain's shoulder, and he was muscular for his age. He wore the tight, short royal skirt, with his
feet and chest left bare. On his chest hung a magnificent pectoral of a falcon, and there were gold and silver armbands on
his upper arms. The *nemes,* the royal kerchief, was over his
head, with a jeweled cobra arching up from his brow. His
young chin was adorned with the false beard for this public
outing.

Snefru, Khufu's legal father, had died the year before of an
intestinal ailment. Khufu had been the unquestioned heir to the
throne. His divine parenthood had been officially acknowledged and his mother, Hetep-heres, was queen of the highest
rank. With Khufu's youth, the Captain felt the reins of the empire settling into his own hands.

Behind them were their litters and two dozen guards and
servants who had accompanied them. Even so, this was a casual outing, a simple trip to check on the progress of the pyramid. There had been a huge ceremony, weeks before, to
commemorate pouring of the first block.

Beyond the scaffolding, the plateau slid downward to the Nile, filled with ships. On the other side was Memphis.

The Captain had built a pyramid for Snefru some fifteen miles to the south of this new pyramid. Though smaller in scale, it had the same proportions as the one now being constructed and had been the Captain's "pilot" structure. The Egyptians had a predilection for large burial monuments, and the Captain had obliged Snefru's wishes and gained building experience by creating that first pyramid. Though it served no useful purpose, the Captain was proud of it as a structure. Its limestone casing had a beautiful red cast, especially in the light of late afternoon.

The current pyramid, however, would stand out as an object of worship and pride for countless generations. He would encase it in white limestone. This would serve the dual purposes of making it perfectly geometrical and extraordinarily beautiful. He could already envision the limestone gleaming in the hot desert sun, visible for hundreds of miles.

It would truly be an impressive structure, a stone beacon capable of surviving almost any physical cataclysm and still carrying out its duty. The mechanisms of the transponder would be cast out of the Engineer's metalrock substance and housed within the stone around the central chamber. It would need no power source of its own. Vibrations hitting it would provide energy enough to stir it to action.

He had chosen this location for the pyramid because it was on a plateau within fifty miles of the sleepers' cave. Those had been the requirements of the Engineer.

"Father, they are starting," Khufu said.

At the center of the foundation, workers were pouring a new block. After ten minutes the thin crystal mold was removed, leaving what looked like a quarried block of brown granite. The Captain nodded, pleased. Soon he would order full crews of several thousand to work on the project day and night until completion. He had given his promise to the Engineer that he would erect this relay station. Despite all that had changed in the Captain's life, he intended to keep his promise out of respect for that man.

His determination with regard to the construction was more than that, however. In the part of his mind that held onto something of his former identity, that of Captain, decorated Herrod military pilot, and leader of a scientific survey mission, he knew that this building was created for a simple communications purpose. In the rest of him, though, it had taken on a new significance. He was Osiris. He was the god incarnate. Whether or not he had been born as such was irrelevant. As he had once said to his wife, what was a god but someone who inspires those around him? By that definition he had more than adequately proved his divinity, even to himself.

He was aging, but wasn't that appropriate for a god who had taken human form? To those from Herrod, he possessed no supernatural powers. Here, however, his knowledge of the physical world and how to manipulate it gave him godlike abilities in the eyes of those around him. As the god, he thought of the pyramid differently. It would cement his role as the center of Egyptian religion.

"Your genius at work, my lord and father," Khufu said, looking at the molded block.

The boy was excited, and why not? The Captain had told him that this would be Khufu's monument, the symbol of the first pharaoh with divine blood running in his veins.

"Where will it land?" Khufu asked.

"What, my son?"

"The divine barque. The ship that will bear us away." For this was the story that had grown up in the Captain's mind and spilled over into his son. Instead of a Kinley rescue ship coming to retrieve the sleepers, he now described a heavenly ship of gods that would bear away all the divine and deserving. A fraction of the Captain's being knew that this was not true, but he no longer cared. What he invented came to pass.

"The divine barque will land in the vicinity of the pyramid that calls it," he said.

Khufu's handsome young face became pensive as he scanned the plateau, trying to pick out a likely landing site. "I fear I will not be let aboard," he said thoughtfully, after several moments.

"Why do you say that?"

"I have thought this through, father. I am only a half-breed. My mother, the Lady Hetep-heres, though noble, is no god."

"Let me tell you a secret, Khufu," the Captain said, moving closer so only his son could hear him. "Hetep-heres is your human mother who bore you from her womb. She deserves all the honor due to a queen and the mother of a god. But your true mother, your spiritual mother, is Isis, my wife. I have hinted it to you many times, but perhaps it is better that I state it outright. You are our son. You are the incarnation of Horus."

"But my half-brother—he is called Horus as well."

"The Lion does not deserve that name," the Captain said slowly. The problem of how to explain his older son—a problem that had grown more pressing in recent years—suddenly resolved itself. In legend, Osiris had a brother named Seth, a traitor who plotted against Osiris and murdered him in cold blood. Seth was the embodiment of betrayal and evil. What if the Lion was not truly his son? What if the Lion were his brother instead? That would destroy his credibility and clear the way for Khufu to assume the role of Horus. "The Lion is not my son, in truth," the Captain said after a few moments. He was committing himself to this course and it felt right. "In another lifetime I took him as a son, yes. He is, in reality, my younger brother. He is the one called Seth, the one who feels jealousy when he should feel love. In my love for him, I adopted him as my own. But he has failed in demonstrating his respect and loyalty, and he is no longer fit for that role."

Khufu considered these words and studied himself. "I am honored by what you say, Father. But I do not know if I feel the holiness of a god. Perhaps I am also not worthy of being your son."

The Captain laid a hand on his shoulder and smiled gently. "That you question your fitness is a sign of worthiness. You will grow to be the man I know you are. Have no doubts, son."

"Thank you, father."

From the scaffolding, they watched for several hours as more blocks were placed and the pyramid slowly, slowly took shape before them.

Chapter 42

Present Day

In a small room in a business hotel in the heart of Cairo's commercial district, the Engineer lay on the bed, his eyes closed. His wife sat at a small table at one corner of the room, watching the unmoving dot that represented the Mechanic on the monitor they had brought from the cave. The Doctor did no more than glance at the monitor every few minutes, for the Mechanic had remained at his current location—another Cairo hotel—for some time. From small motions on the monitor they could see him moving about his suite of rooms, but he had not ventured out of the hotel in three days. Thankfully the signal from the Mechanic's tracer was clear from his present location.

Pruit and Eddie were waiting for the Mechanic to move, waiting for him to give some indication that he had struck a deal and would be handing over the manuals. But there had been no motion since the day Pruit had been captured.

The room was a gaudy mix of polished white marble and gold- and silver-colored fabrics. From the windows there was a view of the Nile River, a broad brown waterway bracketed by roads and crossed by dozens of wide bridges. Out on the water, modern feluccas plied up and down the river, their triangular sails adorned with advertisements for sodas and laundry detergents. On either side of the river were ugly high-rises whose busy geometrical forms stood out next to minarets and old churches.

Cairo was one of the most highly populated metropolitan areas on Earth, and on this warm day the polluted air of the city seemed to hang over the packed cars on the roads.

The Doctor was studying an Earth atlas, her eyes wandering through pictures of natives from every part of the world. It was an odd thing to see the planet she had lived on for several years, in its cultural childhood, suddenly grown up and at the verge of advancing into the universe. It was hard to feel that she was in the same place, yet the location of their old survey camp was less than fifty miles from this hotel.

The television was on with the sound low, for the Engineer often liked to watch it. Unheard by the occupants of the room at the moment, a newswoman reported cases of miraculous recovery from the Ebola virus. Infected villages were coming back to life throughout central Africa.

On the bed, the Engineer was not asleep. He was holding himself still in an effort to get his thoughts to do the same. His wife and those two others were chasing after the Mechanic. They were chasing him to get something. He should be able to help them. There was something he knew, or once had known, that would make all of this so much easier.

He brought his hands to his forehead and pressed gently. His thoughts faded in and out without pattern. There was the Mechanic. . . . There was the Lion. . . . Ah, the Lion, great and loyal friend. . . . And the Lion's father and mother—there was something bad about them, a feeling of sadness and confusion. There was a ship and a shaking and a cave and it was all disconnected and he was not even in the center of it, he was standing off somewhere looking at these thoughts as they blew by in a gale.

He lost himself again. It took several moments to remember the room and his wife.

There was a knock on the door, and his wife got up to let Eddie in. Yes, Eddie, he remembered that young man's name. Eddie leaned over the table and examined the little rectangular screen his wife had been looking at. They began talking, though the words meant nothing to the Engineer.

"Any motion yet?" Eddie asked.

"No, not yet."

"How's your husband?"

"Much the same," she said, her voice toneless.

Eddie squeezed her shoulder. "Here, I brought you some lunch." He set down the bag he'd been carrying. "Fresh fish from across the street."

"Thanks, Eddie."

He nodded and withdrew from the room.

When he had gone, the Engineer forced his body up onto unsteady feet. The Doctor turned and smiled at him. He came up beside his wife and dropped heavily to his knees. He grasped the monitoring device with both hands and shook it, willing himself to remember the significance of what he knew.

"We're monitoring the Mechanic," the Doctor said patiently.

The Engineer stared at the monitor, then back to his wife. He saw something in his own mind, something that almost made sense. He reached for it, but it was already gone. With a cry of anguish, he buried his head in his wife's lap.

The Doctor leaned over, hugging him.

"It's all right," she said softly. "It's all right."

But it was far from all right.

In the next room, Eddie walked in to find Pruit lying on the bed, a blanket draped over her. Her eyes were closed. She had been ensconced in her fullsuit day and night for three days, emerging only a single hour in every twenty-four to stretch and test her body and force herself to eat.

Eddie sat down next to her on the bed and her eyes came open.

"How are you feeling?" he asked. The bruises on her face and neck were gone. She looked tired but almost normal.

"Better," she said weakly. She nodded to her shoulder and he moved the blanket to look at the knife wound. It was still an ugly purple. He ran a finger lightly over it and she winced. "Still sore."

"I'm sorry."

"It's all right. I feel almost well. The Mechanic?"

"Nothing yet. He hasn't moved. Do you want water? Something to eat?"

"I should, but I don't feel like it right now."

He brushed a strand of hair from her face. "I'll get you water." He brought her a glass and helped her sit up to drink. When she had taken several small sips, she shook her head and he put the glass aside. She rested an arm on his leg and he held her other hand. Their motions with each other had become much more intimate after the hospital.

Eddie felt the warmth of her hand lying along his thigh. He gently lifted it and kissed her palm.

"I miss you while you're in that suit."

She studied his face and touched his cheek with her palm. In the half-sleep of her suit she had dreamed about him. "I know," she whispered. She said it softly and both of them knew that things between them were different.

"You know?" he asked quietly, looking down at her.

"Yes."

Pruit gently pulled him toward her. "Eddie . . ."

Their lips met, and it was clear to both of them that they needed this contact, that the last weeks had been building to this in a way neither of them had quite predicted. They began to kiss each other, very gently at first, then more deeply.

Pruit did not know when she had begun thinking of Eddie romantically. Was it that night in the cave when he had comforted her? Was it later, when he had saved her from the doctors at the hospital? She did not know the exact moment, but she knew that it was right. There was something peaceful about Eddie, and she felt pleasure in his presence. His life had been so different from hers. He had never borne the weight of his planet, of his race. There was an innate happiness in him that she could not understand, but which nonetheless made her happy to be near. And he was dedicated to her. That much she knew.

They broke away from each other and smiled for a moment

at the pleasant realization that human kisses spanned cultures and worlds and were the same for both of them.

Eddie moved the blanket aside, and his lips were on her body. She was pulling his shirt off, and the heat of their bodies against each other was blissful.

"Do you want this as much as I do?" he whispered in her ear.

"Yes," she breathed.

He moved carefully, and she could feel the length of his warm body on top of her. Then he was making love to her, gently and passionately, and Pruit had tears in her eyes at the intense pleasure of their union. It was somehow sad and strange and perfect and right.

Later, they showered and made love again, and then they lay in bed together, her head on his chest and his arms around her.

Eddie was in the grip of an epiphany that had started when he pulled Pruit from that filthy hospital and had only now reached its full magnitude. Something in him had altered its basic structure, and he no longer felt himself a disinterested observer of life. When he was with Pruit, he had a sense of the infinite, and felt that he himself was part of it.

"Do you remember your past lives?" he asked her quietly.

She could hear his voice vibrating through his chest, a pleasant, intimate sound. She lifted her head up and looked at him. Her reddish hair was tousled, and her face looked tired. Eddie thought she was beautiful. "Why?"

"I just . . . want to know."

"I remember some things," she said. "Not everything."

"Like what?"

"It's like early childhood. There are long stretches of nothing, and then a few very bright and clear images."

"Tell me."

She thought back, scanning through ancient memories. There were so many, and they had always been there, even when she was a child, a record of herself through countless incarnations. It was taken for granted, when she grew up, that everyone would have such memories. But on Earth such self-knowledge was not accepted by many religions. She could see Eddie reaching for understanding.

As she found the memory she would share, her face changed, became distant. "I remember the caves, before we built the dome," she said slowly. "I could feel the radiation getting to me. We could all feel it. We were dying. For months and months we were dying. My jaw ached and my stomach was cramped and my bones were turning to dust. We were eating anything we could chew . . .

"Later, maybe hundreds of years later, I remember the struggle to keep babies alive. There was a long stretch when we really were in danger of becoming extinct. The lab breeding wasn't working very well. The mortality rate was so high . . . I remember holding a baby as it died. For several minutes after birth he was fine, and then his organs simply didn't work." Her eyes became wet as Eddie watched her. "He just died, and I held him and I cried, thinking why does it have to be so hard?

"I remember a scouting mission. We had a ship that could travel in space, but it was so slow. It could barely crawl out of the atmosphere. The Lucien had quarantined us, and we were sent to run the blockade. . . . I was a man then, too short, but very handsome . . ." She smiled, then the smile faded. "They shot us, three shots that nicked the hull, then a direct hit. Their ships were so much better. . . . I remember the fire billowing through the tiny room. I was dying, and I thought, You haven't won, you won't win . . ." As she said this, her face took on the austere, determined look Eddie had seen many times before. "You won't win," she whispered again.

She shook her head and looked at Eddie, her eyes slowly coming back to the present. "There are more, but those stand out."

He put his hands gently on her face. "Pruit, I love you." He had not intended the words, but they formed regardless.

She looked down at him, his handsome face turned toward her, his body lying against hers. It was good to hear that he loved her, but she could not return the sentiment. She cared for him very much, but "I love you" was something she had only said to Niks. She let her head rest on his chest and kissed him there. "Why?"

"Because you're the girl who never gives up."

"There's no choice."

"Will you take me with you when you confront the Mechanic?"

"Yes." She said it without hesitating. He had come after her when Jean-Claude took her. He had hunted the city, then saved her from the hospital. He deserved her trust, and if he was willing to be her partner in this mission, she would gladly take him with her.

"Good." He stroked her hair and kissed her forehead. He could not tolerate the idea of her facing the Mechanic or the Lucien alone. He was still haunted by the thought of her lying unconscious in that filthy hospital. She was the girl who never gave up, and he would be the one who ran behind her, protecting her where he could.

Chapter 43

The Khan al-Khalili bazaar was a dense warren of old buildings covering more than twenty acres of land at the east side
of Cairo, about a mile from the river. Through this warren ran
cobblestone alleys, narrow dirt passages, archways leading
through ruined courtyards, and dozens of cement streets. On
any day but Sunday, which was taken by most shop owners as
a day of rest, the bazaar was packed with humanity. On Satur-
days, it attracted tourists, but for the rest of the week it belonged to locals. There were shops filling the bottom floors of
the bazaar's structures, and outside the shops were stalls, el-
bowing into the walkways. Everything from spices to clothing
to inlaid backgammon boards and jewelry to fresh catches
from the sea was sold. On the upper floors were dilapidated
apartments and offices, crowded into tiny hot rooms, many
with balconies overhanging the bazaar. The architecture was a
mishmash, as in all of Cairo, some brick buildings, some
wood, some plaster, most of it rickety but somehow still standing. Above it all was a blue-brown sky, choking with exhaust
fumes from never-ending traffic jams on all sides of the
bazaar.

On this morning, Pruit and Eddie threaded their way
through the crowds, following the monitor as they walked,
which Eddie held concealed in his hand. The Mechanic was finally on the move. They had been following his sporadic signal for an hour and were now closing in. His signal had been

strong since they entered the bazaar, as there was little electronic communications traffic to interrupt it in that low-tech environment.

"Go left," Eddie said as they reached an intersection of several alleys.

They turned left, entering a covered arcade where fishmongers displayed the day's fresh catches on iced platters. Despite the early hour, it was already sweltering hot, and the relative cool of this arcade was a relief. Women with covered heads leaned over the fish, arguing over prices.

Pruit had dressed like the local women, wearing a loose, flowing robe of black cotton, with a thick white shawl draped over her head and around her shoulders. Eddie had acquired brown contact lenses for her. With them covering the blue of her eyes and the shawl covering her hair, she was indistinguishable from the thousands of other women who thronged the Khan al-Khalili. She had cut long slits in the sides of the robe to allow her access to the gun and knife strapped beneath her ribs.

Eddie wore a gray gallabiya and a small white skullcap. With his deep tan from the days in the desert, he too could pass for a local on cursory inspection.

They passed through the arcade and emerged into an open cobblestone street, where the shops were given mainly to women's clothing. Specimens of this clothing hung from doorways and the bottoms of balconies and was laid out on folding tables and blankets on the street itself. The heat hit them again. Their robes clung to their skin, and Pruit wiped her brow on a sleeve. She scanned the street. For a moment, the crowd thinned, and she could see a long distance ahead. A hundred yards away was the Mechanic.

"I see him, Eddie," she said, nodding in his direction. Eddie's eyes found him as well.

The Mechanic was surrounded by the short American man who had accompanied him before and a tall, burly white man in his fifties who appeared to be a replacement for Jean-Claude. Around them was an escort of three local Cairo policemen in blue uniforms with machine guns. As Pruit and Eddie watched, the party turned a corner at the end of the street and disappeared from sight.

Pruit quickly checked her weapons. Then she turned to him, putting a hand on his arm. "Eddie, I don't know what will happen here. If he has the manuals with him, I must get them. There might be fighting. I don't know. If there are Lucien here, I will have to kill them."

"I'm ready," he said. He was nervous, but also elated. He felt the tough core of commitment in his gut, a new sensation, and this gave him strength. He squeezed her hand, then tucked the monitor into a small backpack and checked his own weapons, a knife and a gun, both strapped at his calves.

"Keep your eyes out for other Lucien. Either humans who look like me or true Lucien. They will be wearing full robes if they're here, I suppose."

He nodded, and they jogged after their target. They passed from the cobblestone street into a wide cement quadrangle, one of the central spots in the bazaar. The square was packed with vending stalls, and the crowds were heavy. For a moment, Pruit found herself faced with a group of elderly women and their grandchildren, slowly picking their way through the stalls and blocking her forward progress. She ducked around them, slipping behind a fruit seller, and saw the Mechanic again. He was heading to the far end of the square.

Pruit turned and saw that Eddie had been separated from her. His eyes met hers, and she gestured that they should split up and work their way up opposite sides of the quad. He nodded and moved away. Ahead of them, the Mechanic was only fifty yards away.

The Mechanic approached the meeting place, ensconced in his escort. Since Jean-Claude's disappearance, Nate had helped him acquire a new slave, Marcus. Marcus was a middle-aged German, built like an oak tree. It had taken a prodigious amount of the Mechanic's special solution to enslave him, but the need had ultimately been established, and Marcus lost all of his natural stature when his dose of antidote wore off.

Though the Mechanic was sweating in the morning heat, he took perverse pleasure in the fact that Nate was nearly drenched in perspiration, his dark suit jacket soaked through. Around them, at Nate's suggestion, were three Cairo police officers the Mechanic had hired.

Nate had advised against this meeting, but the Mechanic had ignored him. He was more than a little intrigued by Adaiz's offer. Adaiz had offered him two things. First he promised the Mechanic the Kinley girl who had been following him and who had set Jean-Claude free. According to Adaiz, this girl had come to Earth from Herrod. She would bring the Mechanic's past to haunt him and take vengeance upon him for stealing the Eschless technology. Adaiz would give her to the Mechanic to dispose of and thus save the Mechanic from her retribution. This was a gesture of good faith to demonstrate Adaiz's seriousness in his offer of negotiation.

Second, Adaiz offered the Mechanic mobility that no other country could give him. He had hinted that this would be a shuttle vehicle that would allow the Mechanic to travel off-planet. Naturally Nate did not believe this a realistic offer, but the Mechanic knew better. Like the girl, Adaiz had come to Earth from elsewhere. Though Adaiz had not been specific in revealing his point of origin, the Mechanic assumed it was some Kinley colony that had grown up over the last five millennia. Such a shuttle vehicle would do much to ensure the Mechanic's safety.

Most enticing of all was that Adaiz asked for no exclusive right to the technology. The Mechanic would still be free to sell it to the country of his choice. Such an offer, in the Mechanic's mind, was quite worthy of a face-to-face meeting. But he had acquiesced to the necessity of guards in case Adaiz turned out to be dangerous. He would find some way to get rid of these men when he sat down to negotiate terms.

Up ahead was the tiny café where they were to meet. It was little more than a room wedged between two taller buildings and kept dark by an overhanging awning. In front of the café were two men in full robes. One of these was Adaiz, and he stood with the hood of the robe drawn back, leaving his head bare. The other, taller man had his hood pulled over his head, completely obscuring his face. This man reminded the Mechanic of the nomadic desert tribesmen the survey crew had encountered in the Egyptian deserts. He felt a pang of worry as he looked at him. There was something ominous in his robed anonymity. Was the Mechanic overreaching himself?

Adaiz-Ari and Enon-Amet stood together in front of the tiny dining establishment they had chosen for this meeting, watching the Mechanic and his retinue approach. The restaurant behind them was empty of customers. The lone chef and waiter stood patiently in the shadows, waiting for the men who had rented their business for the afternoon. Adaiz had chosen the café because of its small size and its ready access, through a back door, to a narrow but clear alley that would lead them quickly out of the Khan al-Khalili, if that were necessary.

Adaiz stood stiffly, his wounds partially healed but still painful. He had performed daily healing meditations. These had helped greatly, but his body still needed time to repair. He felt vulnerable, both from physical weakness and from lack of a gun. His own gun and his favorite knife had been lost back in Jean-Claude's apartment. He carried only his spare dirk at the moment. Enon, however, was well armed.

He glanced at the underside of his gallabiya sleeve, where he had attached the thin monitor for Pruit's remaining tracer. She was closing in on them. On the monitor he had watched her reach the bazaar and then, over the past ten minutes, slowly wend her way closer. Her presence at this meeting would be essential to his own plans. He had found the Mechanic's weakness. The man was terrified of who he had been in his own past. Adaiz had used this to his advantage, creating, in the Mechanic's mind, an image of Pruit as a Kinley soldier who would do nothing less than try the Mechanic for his past misdeeds and punish him for stealing the Eschless technology.

He had frightened the Mechanic enough that it would now be a small matter to get him to kill Pruit. This would serve a purpose for both of them. With her dead, the Kinley would lose the Eschless technology forever, and Adaiz would be free of the questions she stirred in him.

She was no more than fifty yards away. Adaiz casually turned his head to the left and scanned the crowds. He could not see her yet. He waited as the Mechanic got closer, then scanned the faces in the crowd again, careful not to look concerned or eager.

He saw her. She was dressed as a native married woman and standing in front of a shop selling African beads, her face in profile to him.

On the other side of the square, Eddie approached. The Mechanic and his group had their backs to him. He threaded his way toward them. Their destination was now clear.

Eddie moved closer. In front of the café, he caught sight of two robed figures, one was a young man with bare head who looked like he could be Pruit's twin brother. The other was tall and thin and hooded. Eddie felt his heart skip. Was that one a Lucien?

He saw Adaiz, the human Lucien, surveying the crowd. What was he looking for?

The crowd had thinned as the Mechanic reached the café. This section of the square was populated with less desirable shops, and the main course of foot traffic passed it by for the most part.

As the Mechanic emerged from the crowds, guards in tow, Adaiz stepped forward to greet him.

"Hello, friend," Adaiz said. "Allow me to introduce my partner, Enon."

The Mechanic put out a hand, but Enon kept his arms folded in front of him, his right arm up his left sleeve, and vice versa. Instead of shaking hands he bowed slightly toward the Mechanic.

"Shall we go inside, out of the heat?" the Mechanic asked, his words being translated by the device on his jaw.

Adaiz glanced at his sleeve. Pruit was a mere twenty yards away. He dared not look for her, for she would certainly see him. "Before we go inside," he said, "I would like to make good on the first of our offers."

"Very well."

Adaiz turned to the three policemen. "Do not look yet," he said. "There is a young woman standing twenty yards away, on my left. She is wearing a black caftan and white shawl. If you pass through the café and down the alley, you can come out of the shop behind her. She is to be arrested and held."

The guards looked to the Mechanic for confirmation. Adaiz was happy to notice all three were sufficiently trained to avoid staring over at Pruit and giving themselves away.

The Mechanic nodded curtly, and the guards headed into the café.

Pruit watched as the guards were dismissed, then turned back to watch Adaiz and the Mechanic. Adaiz was still in pain from their fight, she noticed. She edged slightly closer, moving herself into a protected location behind a vending stall. She was not close enough to hear their words, but she could not approach further without exposing herself.

Fifty yards from her, Eddie was also watching the disappearance of the guards, but his attention quickly came back to Adaiz and his companion. They made no move to enter the relative privacy of the café. They seemed content, for the moment, to stand where they were. He wondered why.

After only a minute or two, the three policemen emerged from a tight passageway between buildings and closed in on Pruit's location.

Eddie saw them move, felt his legs jump into action as he automatically began to run toward Pruit. A moment later, the vending stall that had concealed her pitched forward and Pruit came into full view, grabbed by all three men, her legs kicking and her arms struggling.

Eddie pushed people from his path, heading for her.

The Lucien and the Mechanic turned to watch the struggle. The Mechanic played with the grip of the gun he carried beneath his linen jacket. Marcus flexed his hands, ready to draw his own gun.

Passersby stopped to watch. Pruit got one of her arms free and with it landed a punch in the neck of one of her assailants. He gasped and clutched his throat. Another of the men grabbed her right arm and her hair, yanking her backward.

Eddie was closing in. He saw that Pruit might well win this struggle. She used one man's grip on her leg as leverage and kicked him with her free foot, sending him sprawling to the ground. With her free hand she grabbed the knife at her ankle. Eddie was awed by her fighting ability.

The man she had punched was now drawing his handgun. He would shoot her, perhaps not fatally, but enough to stop her. Pruit got a leg wrapped around a man behind her and tipped him forward, throwing him onto the man with the gun. Both hands free, she armed herself with one of her own guns.

She would win, Eddie saw, but not without incapacitating those men. And if she did so, every policeman in Cairo would be after her.

The watching crowd was growing, people transfixed. Enon-Amet was anxious to have this business done so they could retreat to a private meeting, and Adaiz was equally anxious to get his brother out of the public square. The policemen were incompetent. Adaiz, having no gun of his own at the moment, turned to the Mechanic's tall bodyguard.

"End this, can you?"

Marcus nodded and reached for his gun.

Running, Eddie realized there was only one way to save Pruit. He veered from his course toward her and headed instead for the Mechanic and the men around him. The watching crowd was getting thicker, and he pushed his way roughly through.

He cut through the crowd thirty feet beyond the Lucien, then circled back behind them. Their eyes were on Pruit. One of the policemen fired at her. She leapt to the side, firing back and hitting the man in the leg. The other two policemen dove for her.

Eddie reached the hooded Lucien, coming up behind his robed back. Eddie's knife was already drawn. In a quick motion he grabbed the bottom edge of the Lucien's robe and slid his knife up from bottom to top, slicing the material cleanly through. He grabbed the ragged edges of the robe with both hands and threw them forward.

The robe fell away, revealing the silver skin and alien form of Enon-Amet. His chest and arms were bare, gleaming. His pointed face stared out at the square in shock.

There were several moments when little changed and time was slow. There was the chatter of the crowd with all eyes turned to Pruit. Then there was a high, long scream, as a child saw the Lucien. Eyes turned.

Adaiz saw that his brother stood exposed. Enon was paralyzed. This was the nightmare they had imagined since arriving on Earth. He was exposed as alien before a sea of barbaric humanity.

Even the police were looking at the silver Lucien. They had suddenly forgotten Pruit.

Enon looked wildly around.

"Adaiz!" he cried softly. "Adaiz!" He needed direction.

Adaiz had no idea what the reaction of the crowd or the policemen would be. But they would not stare in silence forever. In a moment, they would move to action. All he knew was he must get his brother out of this location as quickly as possible.

"Run!" he said in Avani, pushing Enon toward the café. "Run! Our escape route!"

Time shifted gears. Enon-Amet turned toward the café and began to run, but there was Pruit, heading him off, preventing his escape. She pointed her gun at him, aiming for the flesh of his neck, one of the Lucien's most vulnerable spots. She fired, and Enon felt the bullet sing by his head.

He veered aside, changing course as she fired again. He

could not follow the rehearsed route. Instead he ran across the top of the square, the crowd turning to watch, still transfixed. There were small numbers of people who continued to browse through vending stalls, unaware of the commotion. In moments Enon found himself in the middle of these. He gripped a woman's shoulder and thrust her aside as he sprinted for the end of the square.

There was an intersection up ahead, a smaller road leading off. He headed toward it, his gun now in his hand. There was a thick grouping of people in front of him, and he fired at them, spraying out bursts of laser. The crowd dispersed, several falling to the ground.

Pruit was after him. She wove her way through the crowd, people trying to get out of her way, and then she was in an all-out sprint to catch up.

Two of the policemen were intact. Watching the silver alien wreaking havoc on the crowds, they came back to themselves. They were policemen, this was their city, and no matter how fantastic this creature was, it was their duty to stop it and capture it if possible. If they did not, there would be thousands of witnesses to point out their failure. "Come!" the senior of the two yelled, then they too were running, their machine guns clutched in their hands.

Adaiz watched Enon run, and he looked wildly around, trying to make a plan, trying to figure out a way to save him. He cleared the pain of his wounds from his mind and grabbed the gun from Marcus, pushing the tall man away as he did so. Then he was running after his brother.

Enon ducked up a new alley, only to find it thickly crowded. He shoved and shot his way through. Pruit ran into the alley after him and saw the crowds, which were now in an all-out panic, trying to disperse, trampling on the bodies of the men and women who had been killed by the Lucien's gun. Her eyes flitted over a little boy crying and pulling at the hand of his dead mother. Near him a young woman was staring in shock at the body of her husband.

Pruit jumped onto a vending stall, grabbed the bottom of an

overhanging balcony, and swung herself up and out of the
melee. From here she looked across a series of haphazard balconies and roofs, following the route of the bazaar. She
jumped to a new balcony, surprising two small children napping in the sun, then grabbed the roof and hoisted herself up.
She was on corrugated aluminum, hot and smooth.

Below, she saw Enon still fighting through the square even
as people tried to get out of his way. Pruit's shawl had long
since fallen off, and now she ripped off her black robe, leaving
only light pants and a thin blouse. She felt immediate relief
from the heat, then was running again, finding her balance on
the uneven roofs, jumping from one building to the next.

For a moment, she lost sight of Enon. Then she saw him. He
was climbing to the top of the buildings opposite her. She
fired, using her projectile weapon. The shot went wild, rico-
cheting off an unlit neon sign across the alley. She dropped to
one knee and fired again with a steady hand. The shot missed
him narrowly.

Now Enon was atop the roof. He was running fast, his long
legs carrying him in what looked like an endless series of
leaps. He cleared the breaks between buildings with no effort
at all. He fired back at Pruit, but he was not stopping, and the
shots were off, searing the roof several yards from her.

Pruit could see the police in the alley below, pointing up
at the roof. They too fired at the Lucien, using rapid-fire
weapons that made up for lack of accuracy with sheer numbers of bullets. Enon tucked his head down inside his high collarbone to protect his neck from the shots, but he could not
maintain this position, for it prevented him from seeing his
way.

Then Enon was hit. Pruit saw him jerk forward, and there
were two brown splotches on his upper back where he had
begun to bleed. He did not stop running. She was familiar
enough with Lucien anatomy to know that the sheaf of bone
protecting his upper body would prevent those shots from
doing much damage.

Then she felt and heard a bullet sear the air by her own

head. She turned and found that Adaiz was on the roof behind her, heading at her in a dead run. Like the Lucien, he ran in great, strong leaps. There was blood on his shoulder and side where his wounds had reopened. He seemed ignorant of this, wholly consumed in chasing her. She fired back at him, still running, and missed.

Pruit jumped a span between two buildings and landed hard. A laser shot tore into the roof just in front of her hands—the Lucien was shooting again. Then another bullet from Adaiz, this one grazing her left arm. She leapt up and ran, as two more laser shots plowed into the roof behind her.

Adaiz knew there were only twelve shots in this gun. He had just used two. It did not matter; he would get Pruit. Something had happened to him as he chased her. He had found himself elated rather than angry. Though he was aware of the sore burning of his wounds, the pain no longer bothered him. He would get his chance to finish what they had started in Jean-Claude's rooms, and this time he would not be shaken by her.

Pruit leapt to a lower building and was out of Adaiz's sight for a moment. One of the policemen was on the roof with the Lucien now, chasing the silver being furiously. The policeman fired his gun with abandon, and Pruit saw several more bullets hit home in Enon's back.

Enon stumbled. As he lost his balance, he turned and fired at the policeman. The man collapsed, his leg hit. Enon fired again, and as he did, Pruit dropped to her knee and sighted on him. His head was up, his neck was exposed. She thumbed the trigger and shot. Enon's arms went to his throat, and she heard a scream issue from him, sibilant and awful.

Adaiz turned his head just in time to see his brother fall. Enon tottered for a moment, almost as though he were under control. Then his body collapsed in a twisting motion. He landed at the edge of the roof and toppled over, falling down into the alley below.

*   *   *

Confusion reigned in the alley. There were two dozen dead in the street. Children were crying. Men were pulling the bodies of loved ones away. A few unlucky victims were crawling about numbly, clutching laser wounds that would soon kill them. Most people were huddled at the sides of the alley and in shops. There were sirens everywhere, closing in on the bazaar.

Pruit turned to see Adaiz staring in shock at the dead Lucien. She fired at him, but he caught her motion from the corner of his eye and dropped to the roof in a move that must have been agony on his damaged shoulder. She ran toward him, and Adaiz fired from his prone position. She leapt to the side and they could both hear the shot whining away across the roof.

Adaiz fired again, but the gun was empty. He rolled to the edge of the roof and dropped off. He landed on a balcony and quickly swung his feet out and over its edge and dropped down into the alley.

There were still scores of people here, crouched in doorways, staring at the corpse of Enon, which was already fading to a dull gray, with brown smears of blood drying in the heat.

Adaiz hit the ground, and ducked under the cover of the balcony. The wound in his side was bleeding and he was nearly doubled over. Another shot from Pruit hit the cobblestones underfoot.

Pruit leapt down onto the balcony. Her eyes swept the alley and the buildings across from her. The final remaining policeman knelt over the Lucien's body, studying it for any signs of life.

She saw Adaiz dart across the alley and into a dark doorway. He was unarmed, Pruit realized. He would be looking for a weapon. She dropped over the balcony railing and landed in a crouch in the alley. People were huddled in a shop behind her, staring at her with frightened eyes. Pruit turned from them, her eyes on the doorway where Adaiz had disappeared. She walked toward it, gun and knife at the ready.

Adaiz slipped into the doorway and passed blindly down a hallway. It was walled by sheets of cheap particle boards that let in streams of sunlight. He could see her through openings between the boards. She was walking toward him.

Mentally, he neutralized the pain in his side. He stumbled over the bodies of three beggars who lay half-asleep in this stuffy hall, ignorant of the battle outside. He passed them and found another doorway back into the alley. Just outside were the policeman and the body of Adaiz's brother, lying in the street. Enon was dead, that much was obvious, but Adaiz could not grieve yet. He looked at Pruit and discovered he still felt the battle elation. She was there, he was here, and his path was clear.

He judged the distance, and saw her face turned to the first doorway where he had disappeared. He put his legs in motion, bolting from the passageway and back into the sunlight. There was a policeman, leaning over Enon. The man had two guns. The large one was gripped in his hands. The smaller one, the handgun, was in a holster at his side.

Pruit saw Adaiz as he emerged back into the alley. She turned and their eyes met, and as they did, Adaiz felt himself vaulted into the awareness of the egani-tah. He could feel himself, he could feel the alley, he could feel her.

As Pruit looked at him, she nearly lost her balance in a sensation of broadening awareness. She could not find herself. She was moving even while she was still. She was bigger than a single location.

And then she knew. She was not only herself. She was him as well. He had encompassed her. They were looking across at each other, and she could see both sides, and she had two minds. Suddenly there were thoughts, and they were pouring into her and out of her. She could not control it. He had created the connection, and she could only experience it.

I will kill him now.
I will kill her now.
She has killed my dear brother. I am alone to finish this mis-

sion. And I will finish it and I will bring the prize of that technology home. And in a few years the Plaguers will be no more.
  He will sacrifice me and sacrifice my race.

And then their minds were fully joined and there was only
one other thought, which they shared equally: *You will never
leave here alive.*

Pruit raised her gun. Adaiz grabbed the policeman from behind and jerked the handgun from its holster. In the same motion he pushed the man aside, and he and Pruit were facing
each other.

Pruit fired. Adaiz fired. Both of them and each of them were
aware of their hands on the triggers, and the final pressure.
The guns discharged.

Adaiz felt Pruit's thumb press her trigger, he saw the trajectory of her aim, and he was already twisting aside.

Pruit felt Adaiz's index finger pull back on the trigger of the
handgun. Through his eyes, she saw the gun and where it
pointed, she saw her own face down the barrel, and she was
already dropping to the ground, out of the bullet's path.

And then, as they each hit the ground, the egani-tah was
broken and Pruit and Adaiz were separate again.

The policeman jumped at Adaiz, swinging the barrel of his
machine gun around. In a moment, Adaiz was embroiled in
another fight for his life and had no attention left for her.

Eddie was there and he was pulling Pruit to her feet.

"Eddie? Eddie?" She was not sure where she was or who
she was.

"There are police everywhere!" he hissed, grabbing her
around the waist and sweeping her up over his shoulder. His
words did not really reach her. She was aware of a feeling of
dread and sadness.

Eddie started to run. The sirens had lessened, but there were
several hundred police pouring into the bazaar. He had spent
the last minutes misdirecting them, but he could see them entering the alley at both ends now. He ducked into a shop, pushing past the people within who sat on the floor, anxiously
waiting for help to arrive.

Pruit came back to herself somewhat. "I can run," she said.

He dropped her down onto her feet, and together they found their way out of the shop and into the tight alleyway behind. There were shouts as police converged on the body of the Lucien.

Eddie and Pruit walked several dozen yards then found another walkway secreted behind buildings, leading away from the commotion.

"We killed him," Pruit whispered.

"The Lucien?"

"Enon-Amet," she said, the name forming itself on her tongue as though she had spoken it all her life. He had a personality and she knew that personality. He had strengths and weaknesses, and a sense of honor and a desire for enlightenment and she was aware of these. "We killed him . . ."

"Pruit, we didn't have a choice."

She knew this to be true as well. There was no choice. "I know . . . ," she said. "I only wish . . ." What did she wish? She thought of the potential of Enon-Amet, a steadfast and meticulous mission leader, a loving brother, a man to be admired. Gone now. She put a hand to her head and whispered, "Blessed Life, what's happened to me?"

Chapter 44

The chapel was built of clapboard, painted bright white. It stood atop an outcropping of rock, with the Mediterranean gently breaking below. It was west of Alexandria, perched near the border between the fertile land of the Nile Delta and the wasteland of desert which stretched thousands of miles across the top of Africa.

The chapel was the first thing Jean-Claude had seen of Egypt. He had caught sight of it near dawn, as the cargo ship which had brought him from France sailed along the African coastline on the final leg before reaching port in Alexandria. The chapel had stood out against the twilight sky, peaceful and out of place, surrounded by wild grass. He had watched it from the deck for several minutes, a young boy leaning out over the ship's railing as the sun came up.

Jean-Claude had now found his way back to that spot, in hopes of reclaiming something of that fifteen-year-old boy who had still had a scrap of dignity.

Inside the chapel, Jean-Claude knelt before a small stone statue of Mary. He lit five candles for her and bent his head forward. He had made a full confession to the priest that morning. If the man had been surprised at the depth of Jean-Claude's sin, he had never let on, and for that Jean-Claude was grateful. Now, with his mind at peace, it was time to dedicate himself to what lay ahead.

Heavenly Father, he prayed, reveling in the clean heart

which allowed him to speak freely to God again. *Father, I am reborn. The priest has forgiven me, and I feel the debt of that forgiveness. Please give me the strength to care nothing for my own life. There is only one life that matters any longer, and I will find him . . .*

Jean-Claude's hand closed around the gold cross at his neck. He could feel God with him, and instead of shame there was pride.

"Nate?" Jean-Claude prodded the dirty blanket that lay huddled in front of Jean-Claude's old Cairo tenement building. Nate's sleeping face was just visible beneath the blanket, his cheek pressed into the sidewalk. It was nearly evening. The sun had gone behind buildings to the west, and the street was in shadow. Jean-Claude had set out from Alexandria that morning and made the long bus trip back to Cairo.

A low moan issued from Nate's mouth.

"Nate?" He prodded again.

Nate heaved upward in a scramble of limbs, and his eyes came open. "What? What?" His face was bloodless.

Jean-Claude squatted down, bringing their faces level. "It is Jean-Claude."

"Jean-Claude . . ." He said the name like he was grasping desperately at something that might slip away.

"Yes. What's happened to you?"

Nate twisted in a convulsion of uncoordinated pain. He began to laugh. "Nothing, nothing . . . I was shot! In the bazaar. Stray bullet . . ."

Jean-Claude reached out for Nate's jacket, filthy now, and pulled the lapel aside. On the blue shirt beneath was blood, much of it dried and black, but there was a fresh rivulet still dripping out of him. He had been shot in the chest near his left shoulder.

"I'll take you to the hospital." He moved to get hold of him.

"Why?" Nate asked, his head falling back, his arms feebly trying to push Jean-Claude away. He convulsed again. "They don't have what I need."

"He withheld your antidote?"

Nate laughed again, a high gleeful sound that seemed disconnected from his body. His right hand scrambled for something under the blanket and brought up a hypodermic syringe. "I have my own antidote."

His head fell back. Jean-Claude examined the syringe. Heroin. He had injected himself with heroin to kill the pain of his missing drug. Nate convulsed, and Jean-Claude saw that the heroin muted the convulsions slightly, but not much.

"I have plenty more," Nate said. "Enough to let me die."

"He left you here?"

"He has Marcus now! I'm so stupid, I explained everything to Marcus." The words came in a robotic rush, falling over each other. "I wanted him to take pity on me, I did everything he wanted. More. I made it perfect. I made myself disposable." The laugh came out of him again, mixed up in coughing as his body cramped and contracted.

"I'll get you to the hospital," Jean-Claude said, reaching for him.

Nate pulled himself away. His shoulder was bleeding more heavily. "Don't you dare!" His words were more coherent now. "I want to die here. Now. It's . . . my choice."

Jean-Claude looked at Nate's face. The man couldn't have been older than thirty, but he looked closer to sixty. Without the Mechanic's antidote, or the magic of Pruit's skin, Nate's body would slowly convulse itself into death. If Nate chose to let this happen without a fight, Jean-Claude supposed that was his right. He would not override the man's last action of free will. Nate had asked Jean-Claude to kill him once and he had refused. Now he could not.

"All right," he said quietly.

Nate nodded and clutched at his bleeding shoulder. He started to laugh, but it changed into tears, and he reached for his other syringe, the one that was still full.

"Where did he go?" Jean-Claude asked, pulling back the blanket and locating the hypodermic. He carefully tapped out the bubbles, thinking how pointless that action was in the present circumstances. He took hold of Nate's right arm. There was a belt around his biceps acting as a tourniquet. It was Nate's belt, once of nice leather used to hold up his dress pants, now cracked and ragged. Jean-Claude tightened it around his arm and sank the needle into the brachial artery.

Nate lay back as the drug entered his veins. This would be the last dose, he hoped. This would end it.

"Where did he go?" Jean-Claude asked again.

"Montreux," Nate whispered. The name was like something out of another life. He had been there once, with his parents, when he was a teenager. He remembered rain and sun, and the lake and mountains. They had stopped in Chillon to visit the famous castle. He had been impatient with the lines of tourists. Had that really been him? "Montreux. In Switzerland."

"I will find him. I will do something worse to him than this." As he looked at Nate, however, Jean-Claude was not sure that anything could be worse.

"I don't care," Nate muttered. "I don't care." His eyes fell closed. The dose had been far too strong, but at this moment, he was carried on its blissful gray cloud.

Jean-Claude watched his former slave companion enter what was surely his last high. Quietly, he said, "I do."

Chapter 45

> The most serious convulsion . . . was the fratricidal war
> between Osiris and Seth . . . From this . . . struggle the
> forces of the murdered Osiris, led by his son Horus,
> emerged victorious. Horus, avenger of his father, was
> ever afterwards held to be the pattern of the good son,
> and it was Horus who at the end of his life bequeathed
> the throne of Egypt to the line of human Pharaohs.
> —J. E. Manchip White
> *Ancient Egypt: Its Culture and History*

The house was a single story, built of wood, fine cedar im-
ported by traders in the Delta. It was a rambling house with
several enclosed courtyards. The roof was of bisected palm
trunks, overlaid with a mud, straw, and sand cob. The roof
rested on tall wooden pillars, carved like stylized sycamore
trees, and beneath it, on the north, was open space, allowing
the northern breezes into the house. There were many windows besides, and they had been built using clear sheets of
crystal left over from the survey camp, set into frames that allowed them to be opened and closed. These windows were
some of the few remaining artifacts from the camp. Most
everything from the camp had been cannibalized and disman-
tled over the past years.

Inside the house were dozens of pleasant, cool rooms, most
with brick or stone floors. The furniture was Egyptian, but had

been made more comfortable by thick down pillows on the couches and chairs. There were bathrooms, very rare in most of the country, where sluices drew away the waste and diverted it into a small sewage system. It was, altogether, a lovely home. It sat on the border of a sprawling farm, and it belonged to the Lion.

On this afternoon, he strode back to the house through his fields of barley and corn and his vineyards of wine grapes, brushing the dust off of his coveralls. He was in his late thirties now. His face was lined from years in the sun, but other than this there were not many other signs of aging. His shoulders were just as broad, and his waist as trim, as they had always been. He now kept his hair cropped short for coolness and his face was cleanly shaven.

The Lion had moved to the country to build a farm that would be a model for future generations. As he made his way back to the house, his eyes roamed over the planted fields, and the irrigation system he had spent years constructing. Until this farm, the Egyptians had only built canals to make transport easier. He was the first to build them solely for irrigation. Water was brought up from his new canals through ingenious water wheels. From there it was shunted into clay runnels, which spread it evenly throughout the fields. The workers supervised the plants, but did not have to spend the bulk of their time drawing water and carrying it by hand. As a result, they could farm a much greater acreage. The Lion had had almost ten years of excellent crops, even when the level of the seasonal Nile inundation had not met expectations.

The house sat on the western edge of the farm, close to the Nile, set in an enormous garden of trees and flowers and clear pools of water which were his wife Ipwet's love and work. The Lion reached the high wall that encircled home and garden and saw that the garden gate was ajar. This was unusual, but not unheard of, and he stepped through into the shade of the trees without giving it much thought.

Crossing the garden, he saw that their two gardeners were already gone for the day. There was no sound but the tentative song of a few birds up in the fig trees. The Lion reached the back verandah. The doors here were open as well. He stepped into the cool and quiet of the house. The servants were gone. This was odd, but his wife sometimes sent them home, to their own cottages along the river, when she wanted an afternoon alone with her son and her husband. The Lion smiled to himself. There was nothing more pleasant than coming home to find the house empty, their six-year-old son napping, and his wife waiting for him in their sunny bedroom with a cool pitcher of tea.

"Ipwet!" he called, keeping his voice moderate so he would not wake Isha. There was no answer. He crossed the entry and moved into the dining area, a wide room with several windows and cushions on the floor. A few of these cushions were out of place, as though someone had gotten up quickly and scattered them.

"Ipwet," he called again.

He moved through this room and out onto another porch behind, where a blue awning hung over cool brick paving stones. This was the most popular play place for Isha. But he was not there.

"Ipwet? Isha?"

There was no reply. He moved across the porch to a door at the opposite end leading back into the house. There he saw his son's favorite crocodile doll lying discarded. He picked it up and smiled. The Lion had made it for Isha himself. It was wooden, and the great mouth hinged open and shut and the tongue could loll out. He began to tuck the doll into one of his pockets when he saw that his hand had a smear of red across it. He looked at the red and rubbed his fingers together. It was blood. There was more on the underside of the doll, a thick smear of it. His stomach jolted. He quickly scanned the room, and to his dismay saw more blood, spattered on the floor inside the doorway. He ran inside, following the spatters, ducking into the nursery. In here were signs of a struggle. A ceramic vase was broken on the floor. A wooden chair was overturned.

"Ipwet!" He called her name frantically. "Isha!"

He passed through the nanny's room. There was nothing in there. He passed back out and ran down a wide hallway to his own apartment. In the sitting room were more signs of a struggle, and there was a small pool of blood on the floor. He burst through the far door to the bedroom.

He found them there. They were laid out side by side on the floor, their throats bloody, pools of blood beneath them, blood on their clothing. His wife's beautiful black hair was matted with it. The Lion fell to the floor between them. He slid a hand under her head and frantically felt for a pulse at her neck. She was already cold.

"Ipwet! Ipwet!"

He turned to his son. The little boy's face was gray. The Lion again felt for a pulse, but Isha had been dead for some time.

"Isha!" He grabbed up the little body and hugged it to him. The boy's cold face touched his neck, and the Lion felt his gorge rise. He bit his lip, looking at their faces. He was unable to believe that they were dead, unable to believe that they had been attacked and killed while he was away in the farthest field, unable to believe that he had felt no worry or danger at all while they were dying, that he had walked into the house minutes ago thinking of the warm embrace of his wife. He doubled over.

"Ipwet!" He clutched her hair, feeling the stone floor against his forehead. His skin was in her blood. It was all over his clothes now and in his hair.

It was some time later that he found himself standing up and staring at the wall. A long sheet of papyrus hung there, pinned by a knife whose blade was covered in streaks of dried blood. He studied the pictographs:

```
T   A   S   O   T   P
H   N   O   R   H   A
E   D   N   D   E   Y
            E   I   M
H   T   A   R   R   E
U   H   R       I   N
M   E   E   O   D   T
A       F   E
N   H   T   L   A   F
    A   A   O   T   O
M   L   K   R   H   R
I   F   E   D   S
S   B   N       S   S
T   R       O   E   L
R   E   B   S   R   A
E   E   Y   I   V   N
S   D       R   E   D
S           I       E
            S   A   R
                S
```

He stared at the notice for several minutes. At last a single word passed his lips. "Father . . ."

The next morning, the Lion entered the Captain's receiving room in the palace at Memphis. It was a great open chamber with high windows and murals of Osiris on the plaster walls. The Lion had shaved and washed himself scrupulously. He was dressed in native clothes—a short skirt of white linen, modestly unadorned, a leopard skin wrapped around his shoulders and chest, two small silver necklaces, and a few bracelets on his arms. He wore a formal wig of a light brown color, the straight tresses of which were arranged to frame his face and fall down in back below his shoulders. He had applied kohl to his eyes in the fashion of the nobility, making his handsome face look softer. Aside from his lighter skin and his blue eyes, he was the image of a typical nobleman.

His father had not yet arrived, but the Lion was already kneeling on the floor, his arms stretched out before him, his forehead resting on the ground in a gesture of complete prostration.

He held the position without motion. There were two guards in the room, and they stared at him uncertainly. It was not the attitude they had expected.

After a long wait, the Lion heard the footsteps. A door opened on the other side of the room, and feet entered—four guards and his father. He watched the feet of his father approach him and stop a few paces away. With his head on the floor, he could not see the Captain's face, but he could imagine him standing there, arms akimbo, staring down at his son.

Without looking up, the Lion cried out, "Father! What have I done to offend you so grievously?" He spoke in the local tongue. His father replied in their native Kinley language so the guards would not understand.

"What have you done? What have you done?" He had expected the Lion to charge in in a rage. He had not foreseen this submission. "A group of pilgrims came to your house last week, asking after your lineage, asking for an audience with my son. You sent them away, telling them they were mistaken, telling them they should examine their gods more closely!"

"I only told them the truth as I know it," the Lion replied, again in the local tongue. He kept his head on the floor. "Why have you punished me in this way?"

The Lion's use of the local tongue, and thus his refusal to keep the conversation private from the guards, coupled with the reminder of what he had said to those pilgrims, filled the Captain with new anger. He bent down and ripped off the Lion's wig. He grabbed his natural hair and forced the Lion to look at him. The Lion saw that his father was dressed in the fashion he had worn for years—a white robe, trimmed in gold, with his gray hair oiled and braided behind his head. He had gained weight recently.

With their faces only inches apart, the Captain hissed, "I warned you. So many times! Your mother warned you. You left me no choice."

The Lion stared back at him, his head held in place by the Captain's fistful of his hair. Slowly, in the Kinley language, the Lion said, "And you leave me no choice."

Before the Captain could react, the Lion shifted his weight backward, pulling his father toward him, pulling him off balance. The Captain fell onto his son and the Lion grabbed him by the throat with one hand.

The guards snapped into action, moving forward, but the Captain was now covering the Lion's body. The Lion shoved his free hand down the waistband of his shirt and withdrew the gun that had been overlooked by the Captain's guards. The weapon was small, fitting easily in the palm of his hand. It was one of several weapons he had secreted from the camp years before and laid away against an uncertain future.

As the guards paused, unsure how badly the Lion could hurt the Captain, he secured the gun in his hand and slipped his arm around his father's back. Then, still holding the Captain as a shield, he pressed the trigger. A jagged blue bolt of electricity shot out, finding the heart of the nearest guard with perfect accuracy. Without hesitating, the Lion swung the gun in an arc across the room. The guards tried to run, but he downed all six of them before they could take five paces.

The Lion pulled his father harder, unbalancing him again. With a quick shift of weight, he flipped over and pinned him to the floor.

"How dare . . . ," the Captain started. The Lion punched his neck, cutting him off and sending him into a paroxysm of gasps. The Lion lunged up to his feet and ran to the far door, sliding the heavy board into place to lock it. He could hear other guards running up as he did so. He crossed the room and locked the second door.

Then he turned and saw the Captain getting to his feet. He had drawn a knife and stood facing his son.

"You cannot do this."

The Lion felt rage nearly blind him. He ran at him, slamming his shoulder into his father's abdomen, thrusting him back across the room and into the wall. The Captain slashed at him with the knife, but he was weak from years of being a god. The Lion batted the knife from his hand, grabbed his father's shoulders, and shoved him back into the wall.

"I *can* do this!" the Lion screamed at him. "I *can* do this! I have stood idly by for years and years. I have thought that I could ignore you. I have made excuses for your insanity. I am a coward!"

There were guards shouting outside. The door shivered under an impact. They were trying to break in.

"They will come through that door and they will kill you."

The Lion punched him in the face. "You killed my wife and my son! Your own grandson! I came home to find them cold and lying in their own blood. He was just a boy . . ."

The door shook again.

The Captain was bleeding from his nose, but he spit at the Lion. "You spoke against me! You think my position here is easy to maintain? All I have ever asked of you is loyalty."

"Loyalty? This from a man who sends minions to murder his son's son." Tears ran down his cheeks.

Both doors shook.

"Your actions called for payment at a certain price."

The Lion gripped his father's neck and thrust his head into the wall again. "Do you remember me at age six, Father? I know you loved me then. Do you remember what that love was like?"

The Captain felt himself choking. Through constricted throat, he whispered, "You cannot kill me, Lion." In his voice was the quiet certainty of a man who was never denied in his smallest wish.

"You're human, Father!" the Lion yelled. With his hand he wiped blood from the Captain's nose and held it up for him to see. "Blood. Your blood. Human blood. Red, like mine. Like my son's. Like anyone's. You're not a god."

The doors shook again. Then there were shouts among the guards.

"I am a god," the Captain said. In that moment, he could not feel fear, he could not feel danger, he could only feel himself as Osiris, invincible.

"Then the god dies." The Lion shoved the barrel of the gun into his father's neck. He pressed the trigger, letting go of his body as he did so. There was a blue light at the tip of the gun, where it was wedged into the Captain's skin, and the Captain's body shook in random, wild jerks. His face contorted horribly. The Lion kept his finger on the trigger, sending a continuous bolt into him. A second or two would have been enough to kill any man, but the Lion could not release his finger. It was after a full minute, when there was a wet burning smell and curls of smoke, that he finally managed to command his hand to let go.

The Captain's eyes were frozen open, lifeless, but still twitching slightly. As the Lion pulled the gun away from his father's neck, the Captain slid down the wall and collapsed onto the floor. The Lion knelt beside him, feeling for his breath and pulse. There were neither. He stared at the Captain, thinking how prosaic and anticlimactic it was to see him lying there dead. After all the years building to this moment, it was so simple and quick. And right. Above his dead body sat the great Osiris of the mural, bearing the Captain's face, gazing out with equanimity on all that passed before him.

The Lion turned from his father. Only one of the doors was now shaking. The guards had concentrated their efforts. The Lion checked the gun. Its charge, drawn from kinetic energy of the user as well as sunlight, was still nearly full. It and the other weapons the Lion had taken were the only ones left from the survey crew's original stockpile. The others had been used over the first years of the survey and had eventually broken and been discarded. He was therefore more powerfully armed than any opponent he might face outside the doors.

As the far door continued to shake under impact from outside, the Lion grabbed his father's robe and dragged his body to the opposite door. Drawing on all of his considerable strength, he picked up the body and propped it up in front of him. As quietly as he could, holding his father's body against him, he released the locking board on the door and pulled it open.

There were two guards on either side of the doorway. They turned and saw the distorted face of their lord Osiris standing there. Before they could move or speak, the Lion shot them. The rest of the guards were on the other side of the receiving chamber, still attacking the door. The Lion eased his father to the ground, straightened his own clothing, then quickly ran down the empty corridor before him. Before the rest of the palace servants understood what was happening, he was outside, running through the gardens and away.

The tapestries were burning. The rooms of the temple were scorching hot and full of smoke. Guards ran from room to room, some trying to save others, some trying to save themselves. Those of the priestesses who were sober were also running. Many men and women, overcome by smoke inhalation, were lying or crawling on the floor. Others lay on couches or floor cushions, carried away on their opiate reveries, unable to mentally connect the heat and smoke to real danger.

The Lion walked from room to room, a torch in his hand, setting everything burnable aflame. There were no means of quick long distance communication in Memphis. Thus, the Lion had been able to run, unobstructed, from the palace, out of the city, to the desolate outlying spot of his mother's temple. He had killed a few guards at the outer doors and inside, and then the burning had begun. He had started with the rooms around the perimeter, burning toward the center of the building. He had torn off the leopard skin around his chest. His short blond hair was matted with sweat, and it stuck up wildly from his head. Barefoot and barechested, with only his skirt wrapped around him, he moved through the temple, bringing destruction.

There was screaming up ahead. He pushed his way through the great copper doors where his own likeness had been replaced with the likeness of his half-brother Khufu, pushed his way into his mother's bedchamber.

She lay on her bed, crying. The chamber was full of smoke from surrounding rooms. Several young women were screaming in a corner. They were all drugged, and the screams were high and insane. The Lion touched the torch to the nearest hangings, the beautiful tapestry renditions of his mother and father embracing each other. They sprang into flame. At the sight of new fire, one of the girls became partly lucid. She tugged the hand of another. When the second girl would not get up, the first ran, throwing open a door that led into a neighboring room, also ablaze. She plunged in regardless, trying to find the way out.

The Lion walked to his mother's bed. She looked up at him, tears of confusion streaking her face.

"I can't breathe," she said, her eyes trying to focus on the flames climbing the walls. "Son," she said, somehow recognizing him. "I can't breathe."

"You agreed they should die, didn't you, Mother? I know him. He would not decide such a thing without you."

She nodded, strangely coherent. "Yes. We had no choice."

The Lion felt tears burning his eyes. He threw the torch at the wall, igniting another group of tapestries, and scooped his mother off the bed, throwing her over his shoulder. She did not struggle.

He ran from the bedchamber with her, passing through burning rooms. The walls radiated intense heat, and the smoke was oppressive. The Lion felt his lungs giving out. He ignored the pain and ran, passing the women and men who had collapsed, passing blackened frescoes and smoldering furniture.

He reached the high doors to the outside, which now stood open, smoke billowing out into the sunlit air. There were people here who had escaped the blaze. They lay stunned and choking.

He dropped his mother to the ground. She did not try to move. Several hundred yards away, he could see a large group of men approaching at a run. They were coming from the city.

He fell to a sitting position next to her. Her eyes were open, staring up at him, still held by her drug.

"Tell me one thing, Mother," he whispered in Haight, the language he had learned from her when he was a toddler. "Did you really agree with him? Did you want all of this?"

Her eyes watered, and she turned her head away from him. She answered him in the same language, the first time she had spoken it in nearly ten years. Softly, she said, "I had no choice."

The Lion let his head fall into his hands.

"It is the Lady Isis, my lord!" someone called.

The Lion looked up. The group of men had arrived. There were thirty of them, breathing hard from a long sprint, all with spears and knives held ready. They stared at the smoke from the temple and the people lying outside. Khufu, now a strong lad of thirteen, was leading them.

The young king raised a hand and the men came to a stop. The Lion stared up at them, but made no attempt to move.

"Take him!" Khufu yelled, pointing at the Lion. The Lion still held his gun, but he threw it aside as several men took hold of him. He did not need it anymore.

Khufu knelt by the Lion's mother and tenderly placed a hand on her cheek.

"Are you hurt, Divine Mother?" he asked.

"No, my son," she responded, wiping her eyes. She took his hand. "I am safe now."

Khufu snapped his fingers and several of the men came forward to attend her. He walked over to his half-brother. The Lion had been pulled to a standing position. He regarded Khufu impassively.

"You have murdered the god," the young king said. His eyes moistened. "You have taken my father."

"He was also my father."

Khufu made a derisive laugh. "That claim wears thin. My father has told me of your true identity and your disloyalty."

This was, apparently, a new twist to the Captain's story. It did not matter.

"You have claimed my title," Khufu continued. "You have claimed to be Horus."

The Lion stared at the boy wordlessly. There was no need to answer.

Khufu went on: "Your life is insignificant, and so your death cannot possibly make up for the murder of the god. Still, I offer it as a small sacrifice on the altar of beloved Osiris. Het!" The last was a command, and five warriors sprang into position in front of the Lion, their spears held ready to strike.

"I am only a man, like my father," the Lion said quietly. "A single spear will be sufficient."

He held Khufu's eyes for a moment, then the boy made a downward slash with his hand, giving the signal to the warriors. Their spears came down with force, embedding themselves in the Lion's chest. The impact sent him backward, pulling him from the arms of those who held him. He hit the ground, five spears sticking up from his body. A single, long breath issued from his lips. Then he was silent.

Whatever the afterlife might be, the Lion only hoped his wife and child would be there with him and his father would no longer exist. No, perhaps his father would exist, but it would be his real father, the man who had raised him back on Herrod, the honest hero he had worshiped as a child. In the moment of his death, he thought: *At last it ends.*

Chapter 46

Present Day

The Mechanic and Marcus walked down a broad sidewalk bordering Lake Geneva. They were facing southeast, with the lake on their right and the café and restaurants of Montreux lining the street to their left. The Mechanic walked slowly, his eyes looking down at the pavement, which was dark after the rain showers earlier in the day. Marcus glanced around, his eyes skimming over the tidy buildings, old and new, that made up the town of Montreux. Above the buildings, the mountains were visible, half-hidden in mist. The day was cloudy, but the sun found its way through here and there, imbuing the air with a bright, rich quality, and putting hints of blue in the gray stretch of the lake.

There was a sprinkling of people in the roadside restaurants, most sitting inside, with only a few braving the chill of the patio tables. Pedestrians moved up and down the sidewalk in light jackets and hats.

The Mechanic glanced at his watch. He was dressed in a fine black wool suit, for which he had been fitted in Cairo. He wore a narrow-brim felt hat which cast his face in shadow, making his odd skin tone less obvious. He looked very much like a Swiss businessman out for a lunchtime constitutional. Next to him, Marcus also wore a dark suit, though he had left his head bare to allow himself unobstructed vision. With his tall, solid frame and weathered face, he looked a bit dangerous, even in his present clothing.

It was nearly time. The Mechanic would hand over the two manuals, the only existing copies of the Eschless Funnel technology. Once he had handed them off, all of this would be over and his life would begin. After the scene in the bazaar, he had realized that he was getting far too careless with his own safety. All that had mattered to him since waking was securing a pleasant life for himself, a life as good as the Captain's had been, maybe better. It was time to make the deal and put risk behind him, just as Nate had advised. The Mechanic had left for Geneva directly from the bazaar, ferried there by the Chinese, whom he had quickly informed that they were his buyers of choice.

He resisted an urge to look at his watch again. There were surely agents of the Chinese scattered throughout the local area, observing him at this moment. He turned to look out over the lake. Even out there, they were probably watching him from one of the boats on the water. He would not appear nervous. He put his hands into his coat pockets and stared ahead without expression.

"Do you see anything yet?" Eddie asked in Pruit's ear.

"No, just him and the tall man, walking," Pruit responded. She spoke into a tiny communicator hidden at her neck and in her ear. They had brought a pair of the communicators from the sleepers' cave. Their range was short, but sufficient for their needs today. She was walking down a street perpendicular to the lakefront, from which she had a view of the Mechanic and his bodyguard as they ambled along. As far as she knew, the Mechanic did not yet have the manuals. He had stopped nowhere since arriving in Geneva, except his hotel, and he carried nothing of any size on his body. Neither did Marcus. Where were the manuals?

Eddie was on a street parallel to the lakefront and a block away, slowly driving a rented car in pace with the Mechanic. Eddie had lobbied to be the one on foot, for there was a real danger that Pruit would be recognized by the Mechanic. Pruit had pointed out, though, that she did not drive cars with much skill, and her handling of weapons was better than his. Eddie had ultimately agreed. In this setting, wearing a sweatshirt and jogging pants, she looked nothing like that dark-eyed Muslim girl from the bazaar.

As she walked down a gentle slope in the street, Pruit was aware of the aching soreness in her lower back. It had been clear that Adaiz was expecting her in the bazaar and the obvious deduction was that the Lucien had planted a second tracer on her. It had taken Eddie a half an hour to locate it, concealed in the line of her lower spine, but he had managed to pry it out, and they had found no others on her body.

The Mechanic had left Cairo almost immediately, leaving no time for Pruit to sleep in her fullsuit and repair the wound. During the flight to Switzerland, however, it had not been the wound, but the thought of the Lucien Enon-Amet that occupied her. Where she once saw only differences between her race and the Lucien, her mind was now occupied with similarities. They had similar religious beliefs, similar knowledge of their spiritual nature. What else did they share? And why could she not hate them any longer?

Eddie passed the street she was on and saw her from behind as she headed down toward the lake. He mentally went over his weapons. Gun on right calf, knife on left, ready should he need them.

Jean-Claude sat on a bench, looking out over Lake Geneva. He was concealed in a stand of evergreen trees between the sidewalk and the railing overlooking the lake. His black skin stood out here, but no one seemed bothered by his difference. These were a tolerant people and they were pleased when they discovered he spoke French, even if he had a Parisian accent.

He wore a long overcoat and had dressed himself in nice clothing. Around his belt, concealed beneath the coat, were the three items he would need, ready for quick action.

To his right, several hundred yards away, was the Mechanic, slowly walking in Jean-Claude's direction. Jean-Claude had watched him for a quarter of a mile, but he now found he no longer had to look to know where he was. He could sense the man's proximity like hot light burning his skin.

Burning . . . , he thought.

It was almost time. He would not move until he saw those manuals. Those books had been the root of the Mechanic's power and his need for slaves. They too must go.

"Father, my moment draws near," he whispered. "'When you take the field against your enemies, you need have no fear of them, for the Lord your God will be with you . . .'" It was Deuteronomy 20:1. He had read it over and over in that chapel above the Mediterranean, spelling out the words until he understood them all. "I have no fear, Father. I have no fear . . ."

Pruit reached the lakeside street and casually passed by the patio of a café. Fifty yards ahead and across the small street were the Mechanic and Marcus, still heading slowly east around the lake. Beyond them, the railing at the edge of the lake curved away from the sidewalk toward the water, carving out a larger space where there were several tall trees. Pruit stayed on the opposite side of the street and picked up her pace.

"He's looking at his watch again, Eddie," she whispered.

"I'm moving down to your street," Eddie said.

"All right."

Up ahead, she watched a black sedan pull up on her side of the street, some distance beyond the Mechanic. From the backseat a small Asian man in a gray pin-stripe suit emerged. He crossed the street and began walking up the sidewalk toward the Mechanic. They were a hundred feet apart.

"It's happening, Eddie," Pruit said quietly.

A moment later, Eddie's car pulled onto the street behind her.

Pruit began to jog toward the Mechanic. Where were the manuals?

The Mechanic saw the Asian man approaching. The man did not look at him, exactly, though he did not avoid the Mechanic's gaze either. His demeanor indicated that he was interested in nothing but the fresh air and the view.

Where was the messenger? It was time. The Mechanic and Marcus continued walking toward the Asian. They were closing in on a stand of trees to their right.

Then, from behind him, the Mechanic heard a small, pleasant bell. He and Marcus turned and the Mechanic felt relief. Moving toward him at a quick clip was a young boy on a bicycle, wearing a blue jacket which bore the name of a local messenger service. He rang his bell again.

"Sir," the boy called out in French, as he closed the distance, "I have your package." He was holding a manila envelope in one hand.

The Mechanic stopped and let the boy reach him. He took hold of the envelope and nodded.

"Prepaid," the boy said, and continued on, crossing the street and heading back toward the center of town.

"He has them!" Pruit whispered. "Get ready!"

"I'm ready. I'll follow." He was just behind her in the car.

Pruit broke into a run that looked like a pleasure jog, heading for the Mechanic.

The Mechanic clutched the envelope. The Asian man arrived, smiling pleasantly. They shook hands.

"It's a pleasure," the Asian man said in English, his eyes glancing at the envelope for the briefest of seconds.

"For you," the Mechanic said, offering it to him.

Before he could hand it to the man, there was a scream. The Asian was knocked aside, and Marcus fell to his knees, clutching a red stain in his abdomen. The Mechanic found himself staring into the face of Jean-Claude, who had just made a mad dash from the trees on the right. In his hands was a long, curved knife, its blade red from Marcus's blood.

"Your time is here!" Jean-Claude screamed at the Mechanic in French. Then he thrust forward with his hand, burying the knife in him. Jean-Claude could feel it go in up to the hilt.

He pulled his knife out and felt his own body jerk. He had

been shot. There were bullets hitting him from several sides. He felt one of his legs give, but he did not care. His life was unimportant. Only one man's life mattered, and he was taking it.

He lifted the bottle of lighter fluid that was tied at his waist and clutched it with both hands, squirting the fluid all over the Mechanic, who had now fallen to his knees and was making an awful gasping noise.

The fluid soaked the Mechanic's clothes and the envelope in his hand.

Pruit was closing the distance now. "No!" she yelled. "No . . . !"

Jean-Claude felt two more bullets rip into him. He was shot in the chest. He was surely dead. But his hand found the third item at his waist, the lighter. He flicked it on and threw it onto the Mechanic. The man went up in a blaze.

Jean-Claude fell back, feeling the heat of the fire, feeling the shock of his own body dying.

"Your time is here!" he said again, trying to yell, but it came out as a hoarse whisper. Another bullet found his head, and he twisted to the side, falling. He hit the ground and was still.

Next to him, the Mechanic burned. He was still alive for several moments, trying to breathe, trying to scream. Then the flames consumed him and he fell to the sidewalk.

The Asian man beat a hasty retreat. His car pulled up beside him and he ducked inside. In moments, they were roaring away. It was often so in his profession. Countless times he had been close enough to touch something great, only to have it whisked away. He had learned to live with disappointment. He watched through the back window of the car as the Mechanic and the manuals burned.

Pruit ran up to the bodies and scrambled frantically for the envelope. Eddie ran up beside her. Where the envelope had been, all that remained was a stack of filament-thin sheets of carbon. Pruit stopped moving. She could faintly see the writing on those carbon sheets. The formulas were still visible there.

"Wait, Eddie!" She held her breath. Eddie stopped moving.

Then a breeze blew in off the lake and the carbon sheets disintegrated and scattered. She and Eddie knelt on the sidewalk, trying to grab the flakes, the bodies of the Mechanic, Jean-Claude, and Marcus lying around them.

A crowd was beginning to form. The few patrons of nearby restaurants were leaving their tables and moving across the street. There was a police siren in the distance.

Pruit clutched at the ashes, feeling them break up and become grit in her hands.

Chapter 47

Mission Officer Adaiz-Ari should have been lost. His brother and mission leader was dead. Enon-Amet's body had been carted off to be dissected, he supposed, by Earth authorities. Pruit had removed her second tracer and he had no idea where she was. He should have been defeated. He was not. Two days after the melee in the bazaar, he walked through Cairo with a clear destination in mind.

Despite his present circumstances, he felt a lingering sense of pride at his ability to enter the egani-tah during an actual battle. The state had not been fully under his control, for if it had, he would have been able to direct Pruit's motions as well as his own. Still, he had achieved it, forcing the joined awareness upon his enemy. Most masters of the egani-tah were not able to do this until a much older age.

For those brief moments, he had become Pruit. Her mind had been his. He now found his consciousness populated with people he had never known and filled with experiences he had not imagined. He had memories of training in the Sentinel, of great sheets of poisonous glass stretching away on every side of domed cities. He had memories of a young man named Niks and experiences of physical love. He could recall Pruit's journey to Earth and the crippling loss of Niks's death. He could feel the hatred she bore his people.

In a way, it was almost as though Pruit lived inside him. Though many of these memories had begun to fade, he was holding onto the few that were important. He would soon take time to write these down. They would provide much useful information to the Lucien.

Though it was difficult, he did not allow himself to be affected by the contents of Pruit's mind. No matter how strange and potentially unbalancing the visions in her head, he forced himself to categorize the information he had received only in terms of his own objectives.

There was one face in his mind that now mattered. It was a man called the Engineer. Pruit thought of this man as a broken repository of knowledge, but the knowledge she credited him with was great.

Another half an hour of walking—difficult with the stiffness of his muscles—and Adaiz had made his way through the commercial section of Cairo to a tall business hotel. He took an express elevator up and in a few moments had arrived at the Engineer's door. He knocked.

"Who's there?" came a woman's voice.

Adaiz recognized the voice from Pruit's memories. She was the Doctor.

"I am a friend of Pruit's," he said in English.

The woman's eye came to the peephole. Adaiz stood with a pleasant smile on his face. He looked so much like Pruit, he had no doubt he could gain entry.

After a moment the chain was drawn and the Doctor opened the door several inches. It was a shock to see her face and features match so perfectly the image in his mind.

"Hello," he said. She was wearing a jawline translator and could understand him. "My name is Niks. I am from the second Kinley mission. Pruit has asked me to see if I may be of assistance to your husband."

"You don't speak Haight?"

"No, I'm sorry," Adaiz said, using his recent observations of humans to make himself appear friendly and open. He had spent many hours practicing body motions that looked human. "I was not trained in that language. I have other . . . specialties."

It took several more minutes of convincing, but soon the Doctor stepped aside and invited him into the room. The Engineer stood leaning against the wall, looking at Adaiz as he entered. The Doctor explained Adaiz's presence, but the Engineer continued to wear an expression of pained confusion.

Adaiz approached him and felt honest sympathy for the man's condition. "I'm here for you," he said softly.

"He may not understand you," the Doctor said.

Adaiz smiled and took both of the Engineer's hands in his own. He was still surprised at the feel of other humans' flesh. It had a much different quality than Lucien flesh, slightly warmer and less resilient, and he had not grown accustomed to it yet. "It doesn't matter. Words are one of the lowest forms of communication. Come."

He led the Engineer to the center of the room, then helped him into a cross-legged position on the floor. Adaiz assumed the same position across from him. The Doctor watched this, surprised at her husband's willingness to follow the commands of a stranger.

"Now, you must relax," Adaiz said. Then, remembering the Engineer would not understand, he reached out his arms and gently shut the Engineer's eyes.

Adaiz began his breathing, following the steps of an Opening. After ten minutes, he had bridged the space between himself and the Engineer. He reached out to the spark he saw before him, then leapt inside, entering the man's mind.

Instantly, there was a maelstrom. Adaiz felt himself swept up in a hurricane of disjointed thoughts, which were pouring into each other, whirling around each other, forming eddies of nearly lucid logic, then falling away, back into randomness.

For a moment, Adaiz lost all sense of himself. He was caught in the motion and thrown, dizzily chasing after thoughts. With effort, he pulled himself back to objectivity and studied what he saw.

There had been a terrible, near-death trauma to the Engineer's body, and its ability to relay thoughts and commands had been damaged, almost destroyed. The thoughts and knowledge were still there, but any attempt to communicate them or study them rationally produced the hurricane.

Adaiz sent a feeling of calm to the Engineer. *I see you,* he thought. *I see you and I do not mistake you for the damaged functions you are living with.*

In response to this thought, he felt an outpouring of gratitude.

I am sorry for your troubles. Let me be the conduit to communicate for you.

Again there was gratitude, then eagerness to say something. This eagerness brought on another deluge of disconnected images.

Relax, Adaiz thought. *Let me look.*

The maelstrom quieted somewhat. Adaiz moved himself deeper into the man's mind. He moved through images of pain, waking from a great sleep, choking, and the first onrush of confusion. He moved to earlier images, and saw the construction of a cave, sleepboxes lined in a row. There was the Mechanic, and attached to that image was a feeling of distrust. There was another man, with gold hair down to his shoulders. And there were a man and woman who were somehow gods and somehow simply human.

Adaiz could feel the Engineer's attention growing stronger and more urgent. There was an image of his wife, packing her belongings, and the golden-haired man giving a warning. Adaiz was close to something important. He could feel the Engineer urging him on, and as he did, the images began to slip out of order, become confused.

Calm . . . , Adaiz thought.

The Engineer relaxed again, and Adaiz continued to work his way back. Beneath all the other images, which now seemed to move about each other in slow and random circles, Adaiz sensed something else, a central image. He reached for it. Attached to it was a gleeful sensation of outsmarting someone. He pulled it closer. At last, he saw the image clearly and understood it. With his eyes closed, he smiled. It was the first time the human expression had been drawn from him naturally.

He opened his eyes. So did the Engineer.

Very good, Adaiz thought. *I understand.*

The Engineer felt his words. His own mind was no more clear, but he knew that this man had found the thought that was important. He smiled at Adaiz.

Adaiz gently severed the link between them and allowed himself a moment of exultation. He would steal the Eschless Funnel from under Pruit's nose! He would steal it, and he would bring it home and the Lucien would become masters of space and all that was in it. They would put an end to the Plaguer threat and expand uninhibited throughout the galaxy. He would kill the questions Pruit had stirred up in his own mind. He would redeem the death of his brother by making the mission far more successful than anyone could have hoped. Enon-Amet would be honored as a hero.

He jumped to his feet. The Doctor was staring at him.

"Your husband has been trying to tell you something, Doctor," he said slowly. "There is something important we must do. And we must do it now."

She looked from him to the Engineer, who seemed calmer now and almost happy. She looked back at Adaiz. "What is it?"

"I will get my car," he said. "We will be driving."

Chapter 48

Adaiz was in the driver's seat of his green Jeep, maneuvering through Cairo traffic. They were on a street bordering the Nile, bracketed by city buses and taxis that pumped exhaust into the air. The Doctor sat in the passenger's seat, and the Engineer was in the back, along with the supplies Adaiz had hurriedly loaded into the car.

"Are you sure Pruit will know where we are?" the Doctor asked.

"She will meet us there," Adaiz said, his tone pleasant and reassuring.

The Doctor seemed satisfied with this. She was inclined to trust Adaiz, because of his resemblance to Pruit, but more important because the Engineer appeared to like him. It was the first time she had seen her husband happy, or nearly happy, since waking. She held a map and was navigating for Adaiz. This was a slow job at the moment. The cars on the streets of Cairo were moving at a crawl in lunch-hour congestion.

"We need to turn right at the next large street." She pointed up ahead. "That will take us to the highway."

Adaiz inched the car forward. Pedestrians walked freely in front of cars. The traffic lights seemed to have no relation at all to the motion of traffic. The Jeep was small and very hot with the noon sunlight beating down upon it.

At last, there was motion in the line of cars in front of them.

The whole lane moved forward at the green light. Adaiz pushed down the accelerator.

When he reached the intersection, however, the light had already turned red. Cars on the cross street were beginning to move. Adaiz still had his foot on the gas.

"Stop!" the Doctor said.

Adaiz did, just in time. He was sticking out into the intersection and had nearly driven them into cross traffic. The car lurched with the abrupt halt. "Sorry," he said. He had been distracted by thoughts of that cave. "I'm still new to this."

She smiled. "So am I."

Pedestrians were walking in front of them and behind them, threading their way to the other side of the street. There was a group of young schoolgirls in matching uniforms, all with long dark hair and dark eyes. They were led by two women in long dresses and shawls. There were men in gallabiyas and skullcaps, carrying crates. There were teenage girls in Western clothing. Adaiz watched them without really seeing. *They are not my kind,* he told himself several times. *They are not my concern.*

The light for the pedestrians turned yellow in preparation for turning green. A small boy on the sidewalk let go of his mother's hand and ran into the intersection wildly, chasing a small finch that hopped in the crosswalk. A moment too late, the boy's mother saw that he was gone. The boy was running around cars. He was so small he was difficult for the drivers to see. The bird he chased did not fly away. Instead, it continued to hop, picking at small bits of discarded food, careless of cars and humans.

The light before Adaiz turned green, and he stepped on the accelerator. The boy leapt in front of the Jeep just then, mimicking the motions of the bird. When his feet hit the ground, the boy realized his mistake and turned his head, startled and scared. For an instant, Adaiz and the boy looked at each other. The car jumped forward. Then Adaiz stomped on the brake with both feet. The car bucked, sending the passengers forward then back, but the vehicle, blessedly, had stopped. Behind them, a car screeched and narrowly avoided plowing into the back of them.

The boy stood completely still, looking in at Adaiz, paralyzed by his mistake. The grill of the Jeep was inches from his body. His mother ran at him, sweeping him up into her arms. She hugged him to her chest, burying her face in his neck as she carried him back to the sidewalk. The boy hugged her back and burst into tears.

Around the Jeep, traffic began to move. Adaiz did not take his feet from the brake. His eyes followed the mother and son back to the sidewalk, and lingered there, watching the way the woman set the boy down, then crouched to look him in the face. She smoothed back his hair and kissed him on the cheek. He was precious to her, and she had realized this anew. And the boy had been precious to Adaiz as well. In that instant nothing had been more important to him than saving him.

"Niks," the Doctor said. "We can go."

Cars behind them were honking. Adaiz tried to come back to himself. He was sitting in the Jeep, the Engineer and the Doctor were with him. He was on Earth, a human planet, eighteen years from his home. As he located himself, he knew that something had changed. He was now experiencing, long after the fact, the fruition of his egani-tah with Pruit. He had tried to reject the images he received from her, keep them separate from himself, keep them from inspiring emotion or feeling. Suddenly, he could no longer do this. That little boy had breached a wall within him, and Pruit's experiences and every feeling she had provoked in him since he had first seen her now stood out in a new light. Humans were not his kind. He was Lucien. This was still true. But it did not matter. They were the same. Human, Lucien, or some other race not yet discovered—all were alike. He could no longer pretend it was otherwise. Each race trying to survive. Children, like that boy, like any Lucien child, were precious. Each race hoped to make existence better for future generations. The ways of humans were imperfect much of the time. They, like Lucien, often made decisions that were incorrect. It did not matter. Each wanted the same thing: life.

"Niks," the Doctor said again. "We must go."

Adaiz turned to her. He was gripping the steering wheel, and his face wore a new expression. "My name is not Niks," he said.

Chapter 49

Pruit sat on the edge of the bed, her feet on the floor and her head resting in her hands. Her expression was blank, and she felt blank inside as well. Failure. This is what it felt like. Cold deadness. She could not cry or scream or do anything that might be an emotional release. There was no emotion. There was only the dread she had always felt.

She had sat numbly on the plane as they flew back from Geneva. Eddie had left her in silence. They were back in their Cairo hotel room now, and he was pacing slowly in front of her. She ignored him.

She had lost the Eschless Funnel. It had been there, in the Mechanic's hands, only yards from her, and she had lost it. The only copy of that most secret of secrets had burned before her eyes and she had been unable to stop it. Worse than that, she had brought on its destruction, for she had set Jean-Claude free and given him the strength to take out his revenge.

Back on Herrod they were digging deeper holes to bury themselves in when the Lucien attacked. Her father and mother and brother, did they know about the Lucien now? Had the Sentinel begun telling the population what was coming? Telling them that in a matter of years they would all be dead? She wanted to feel the energizing burn of hatred for the Lucien, but even that was denied her.

Suddenly, Eddie stopped pacing, and crouched down in

front of her, putting his hands on her knees and forcing her to look at him.

"Pruit, that wasn't the only copy of the technology."

It took her a moment to remember English and understand his words. "What?"

"The Engineer. He knows the Eschless Funnel. He built the ship they used to get here. The last copy is in his head."

"I've already thought of that, Eddie. But he's no help to us now." Her voice was flat.

"Maybe . . . maybe you can fix him. On your ship."

"I've thought of that too," she said. "But I have no access to my ship. My landing pod is destroyed."

"We can get to your ship," he said, becoming excited. "Somehow we can do it. We've already sent missions to Mars. We can reach Jupiter."

"How long?" She was not really interested. She knew how primitive Earth's space capabilities were.

"Ten years, maybe. The U.S. will do it, when they know your ship is there. Callen can help us, we'll talk to my father. We'll use your fullsuit to prove who you are."

"I don't have ten years, Eddie!" she snapped, finally roused to anger. "The Lucien attack is in fifteen years! Even if we could get to Jupiter, even if we could fix the Engineer, that leaves no time to get that information home."

Eddie stared at her for a moment, then he stood up and slapped her across the face. Pruit looked at him, shocked.

"What's the matter with you?" he yelled. "Would you rather give up?"

Pruit just stared at him, feeling her cheek smarting.

"We'll find a way!" he yelled. "We'll find a way. You're Pruit Pax. You don't give up!"

She looked at Eddie, seeing a man transformed. Where was the frivolous, lazy dilettante she had first met at the Cairo airport? He seemed to have disappeared and been replaced by this man, her mission partner. Suddenly, Pruit laughed.

"Why are you laughing?" he said, still angry.

"I don't know." She laughed again. The dread was receding. She did not have to face it alone. Eddie was with her.

Eddie studied her, then his anger disappeared and his face broke into a smile. He slid next to her on the bed and took her into his arms.

"I've never heard you laugh," he whispered.

"Well, you've never slapped me before," she said, hugging him tightly.

Eddie smiled into her neck. "We'll find a way to do this."

"I know." She drew back and looked into his face. "I know." They kissed each other tenderly.

There was a knock on the door, interrupting them. They drew away from each other slowly, both reluctant to end the embrace. Then Pruit moved across the room to look through the peephole, expecting a maid. Instead, standing just outside, was Adaiz. She drew back from the door.

"Who is it?" Eddie whispered, seeing her expression.

Pruit silently moved to the desk and picked up her guns, slipping them onto her hands. "The human Lucien."

"What do you want?" she called in Soulene.

"I want to make you an offer," Adaiz said, replying in the same language, his lisp coming through slightly.

Pruit studied him through the peephole. She could see the twin bulges of knife and gun at his waist. But she was well armed. She had been inside this man's head, and she was having difficulty maintaining a feeling of enmity. She could kill him if need be, but she was willing to hear him out. Behind her, Eddie took hold of his own knife and gun. She opened the door.

Adaiz stood in the hallway, one arm on the door frame, looking in at her. She gestured him inside with one armed hand, then kicked the door shut behind him. Adaiz glanced around the room, taking in Eddie and Pruit and the furniture with a cursory glance. He walked to the bed and sat down heavily on the edge, in just the spot where Pruit had been.

Adaiz ran his hands over his short hair. He sighed and looked at Pruit.

"I have what you want," he said. "At least, I know where it is. I can give it to you. I, a Lucien, will give it to you, my Kinley enemy. But first I would like to know what you have to offer me."

Pruit studied him. He was not suggesting treason. He was suggesting something else. She knew the answer, knew precisely what he wanted and what she could give. She wanted the same thing, had ever since their minds had been joined. "I can offer you understanding," she said. "For you, for me. For both of our races."

Adaiz smiled. Another natural smile. This time the expression showed a blend of exhaustion and satisfaction. "Good," he said. "That is what I hoped for."

Chapter 50

Pruit, Eddie, Adaiz-Ari, the Doctor, and the Engineer passed through the underground corridor leading to the sleepers' cave. They had arrived there together, after a day-long drive through the desert. At the end of the passage, Pruit entered the combination, and they moved through the two sets of doors and into the cave itself. Yellow lights came on around the walls to illuminate the space.

Adaiz stepped in front of Pruit and surveyed the room, his eyes coming to rest on the coffin-shaped stasis tanks. He pointed to one of the tanks. "This tank belonged to the Engineer." It was a statement, not a question.

"Yes," Pruit said.

Adaiz walked up to the tank and examined it. Behind him, the Engineer began to shift his weight excitedly. Adaiz smiled at him. "The Engineer was warned by the . . . the man with blond hair . . . ," Adaiz began.

"The Lion?" the Doctor asked.

"Yes, the Lion. The Lion warned him that the data crystals would be tempting." He knelt down beside the stasis tank and began to study the large, dark pedestal on which it rested. "There was another man, a man who was somehow a god?" The words sounded funny as he said them, but he knew they were correct.

"The Captain," the Doctor said.

"Yes, the Captain. The Engineer thought he might be

tempted to break into the cave, so he kept the entrance codes secret. Only the courier ship sent to Herrod had them." Adaiz ran his hands along the pedestal beneath the tank. Pruit came up beside him and knelt down nearby. "The Lion warned him about the Mechanic as well. So he made sure the Mechanic would remain safely asleep." He paused and turned to the Doctor. "How was the Mechanic able to wake?"

"He changed the programming. It must have been right before we went into stasis. Somehow he changed the number of the tank that was supposed to wake."

"Ah, that's too bad." He said it sincerely. He had seen the Engineer's mind and knew the man would be distressed that he had failed to prevent this small but profound treason. His hands were now feeling along the edges of the pedestal. "At any rate, the Engineer knew the crystals had to be protected. If rescue never came, they would need them to start a new life. And if rescue did come, he thought the Kinley might have lost some of their technology during the war, and the crystals could fill in the gaps. Either way, he wanted to make sure they would remain in the cave."

Adaiz ran his hands along the seam where the metalrock pedestal met the metalrock floor. Then he paused. He pressed on the side of the pedestal and moved his hands slightly in a jiggling motion.

As Pruit watched, the side of the pedestal seemed to retract a tiny fraction of an inch, then part of the smooth surface sprang up. Pruit caught her breath. The opened flap was about three feet wide and a foot high. Behind it she could see several rows of small boxes.

"So he made copies of every crystal," Adaiz said. "Secretly. Even his wife did not know." He pulled out one of the boxes from behind the flap and handed it to Pruit.

She took the box and touched a seam that ran along its side. The top smoothly flipped up. Inside was a row of data crystals, neatly packed.

"Great Life!" Pruit cried. "They were right under our noses." She and Adaiz quickly pulled the rest of the boxes from the hiding place. There were twenty in all. Written on the under-side of each lid was the name of the scientific discipline contained in the crystals of that box. Pruit opened them all until she found what she was looking for. Under the lid of one, the words read "All Ship Systems." She smiled.

Chapter 51

2564 B.C.
Year 43 of Kinley Earth Survey

> . . . may a place be made for me in the solar bark on the
> day when the god ferries across, and may I be received
> into the presence of Osiris in the Land of Vindication . . .
> —*Egyptian Book of the Dead*

King Khufu lay in his bed, his body doubled up upon itself,
the covers tangled around his legs. He was hot and cold at the
same time, the two discomforts vying for his attention. His
skin was clammy and his muscles had been lost, over the past
months, to fever weakness.

He was thirty-eight years old, a conqueror and a bringer of
peace, a man whose physical strength had always been a
source of great personal pride. Until the past year his body had
been as fit as any soldier's in his armies. Then, after a military
trip to the Sinai, he had been stricken with a stomach ailment.
His doctors had tried every cure known to them, but none had
been effective beyond briefly lessening the pain.

In recent months, the ailment had spread, consuming his entire digestive tract and even destroying his lungs. He could
breathe only with effort and knew that he was near the end of
life. It would be only a matter of days before death took him.

"Sire, we are ready."

Khufu was startled by the voice. He had thought he was
alone in the room. He moved his head with effort and saw his

chief retainer standing at the foot of the bed, dressed in a long, formal robe. Two of the king's valets stood nearby, also dressed formally. They were holding up a robe for Khufu.

Khufu nodded. "Yes," he said, coughing as he did so and feeling a hot stab of pain in his chest. "It is time. Let me go."

The servants wrapped him in the robe, then secured the false beard of kingship around his chin. The chief retainer placed a crown upon his head, the high double crown that represented his rule of all of Egypt. It felt too heavy.

Then they carried him to a litter and bore him silently through the palace. Men and women bowed as he passed, saying nothing. Khufu had already made his good-byes. The coronation of his son had been planned for months, and he had made him co-regent when his illness first took hold. Khufu's wife and the other women of his harem had begun to mourn him already.

Outside, Khufu was met by an honor guard of soldiers and moved to his long-distance litter. He slipped in and out of consciousness as the litter carried him through his gardens, through Memphis, then into the open land beyond.

By afternoon, he had arrived at the pyramid, the monument his father had built for him, the beacon that would guide the celestial barque to its landing spot. The curtains of the litter were opened, and Khufu squinted in the sharp sunlight. The pyramid stood before him, alone on its great plateau, a white edifice crowned with a golden pyarmidion. It was the most beautiful creation he had ever seen, breathtaking every time he laid eyes upon it. Its beauty was marred only by a brown swath running up one side, where a vertical course of casing stones had been removed to allow access to the inside.

The pyramid had been finished for more than twenty-five years. It was a symbol of the reign of Khufu, just as his father had promised. After the murder of Osiris, Khufu had ordered the construction to go on as planned. He had made only one change: he placed a stone sarcophagus in the central room. That was to be his own resting place.

The priests of Osiris and the priestesses of Isis were lined in two long columns, leading the way from the king's litter up to a scaffolding in front of the pyramid. They chanted incantations as Khufu passed, singing the code words he would need to be accepted onto the divine barque. Khufu mumbled these to himself as he walked.

His family was not present, for he had wished them to look forward only, to the glorious future of Khufu's line, and not to dwell on the unpleasantness of this day. He did not wish the elaborate rituals of a typical royal burial, for he was not dying, only going to sleep. Those present were merely well-wishers, seeing him off to a long voyage.

The scaffolding reached from the base of the pyramid to a point in its middle. There, where the casing stones had been removed, was an entranceway leading to the great chamber inside. Khufu was carried up the scaffolding, then helped across a long wooden ramp into the pyramid.

When he had crossed inside, the atmosphere changed immediately. The warmth of the sun disappeared as though extinguished. The inner corridors were lit only by small oil lamps, which released soot into the already stale air. It did not matter. He would be breathing the air for only a few minutes.

He was helped up the long passages and into the central chamber. The sarcophagus sat at one end of this great hall, simple and unadorned. It was filled with the fluid that would keep him alive. The dark liquid within had been concocted from notes written by the Engineer. This was a man about whom his father often spoke. The secret of the Sleepers, the gods who went into long rest as they awaited the arrival of the ship to bear them home, had not remained secret for long. The location itself was well guarded—Osiris had never hinted of it, even to his son—but what had been done in the cave became the subject of legend. They had gone into the sleep of death to await resurrection. And Khufu had found the recipe for the fluid that would make this possible.

His priests had not had all the ingredients to hand, but they had replaced what was not available with potions of the highest quality, potions that had been handed down from the time of his father's arrival. To ensure their potency, all ingredients had been repeatedly blessed, by priests who served his father Osiris and priestesses who served his mother, Isis. Their power was beyond question.

Even so, Khufu felt a surge of fear as he looked at the sarcophagus. What would he feel? Would there be dreams or would there only be silence? Propped nearby was the lid for the box, made of fine wood. He had not wanted stone, of course, for stone could not be lifted by the occupant. The wood was cured to last for generations and it was light enough for him to push aside.

More priests and priestesses were standing along the walls of the hall. As Khufu took his first step toward the sarcophagus, they began to chant in unison, "He enters the realms. He ascends to the sky. He is given new life." Their voices were eerie in this space, echoing into each other, reverberating through the walls. It was almost frightening.

On his own, Khufu walked the length of the hall. He reached the stone box and set his hands upon it, letting it support his weight. Within, the dark liquid was beckoning. It was time. His body was ready to give out. He would lie down in this sarcophagus and be preserved, resting peacefully, until the gods came to take him away. They would heal him and he would live a second life with them.

"I am ready, Priest."

They disrobed him, then took hold of his wasted body and gently lowered him into the fluid. It was cold and unpleasant. Khufu sank into it up to his neck, then slowly tilted his head back and let it sink below the surface. He felt the fluid covering him, felt it over his face, felt them pushing him to the bottom of the sarcophagus. He could feel the stone on his back now, cold. He must breathe in the liquid, that much he knew. He must take it into his lungs, just as the sleepers had. It would feel like drowning, but it would not be death, only sleep.

He did not want to take the breath. What if he was wrong? What if this fluid was only a foolish concoction? It was too late. They were holding him. He had ordered them to keep him under the liquid, even if he struggled. This was a leap of faith.

He inhaled. The fluid poured into his lungs, and it burned. He was drowning, he was dying. He struggled, but they held him pinned. He tried to gasp but only took in more of it. His muscles were gone. He had no strength. They held him, and there was no air. His lungs cried out, his body cried out, he felt a final convulsion of pain. Then he was dead.

When the king lay still, the priests in the chamber uttered the long, final incantation. Then the sarcophagus top was secured and the retinue moved out of the pyramid. Workers were already preparing to plug the entry with poured stone, for none belonged inside but Khufu himself.

Within weeks, new casing stones were grown in place and the pyramid gleamed white and perfect in the hot desert sun. Within it, the body of Khufu was slowly dissolved by the fluid, a mixture that had been half-right. Without the machinery of the stasis tanks and the tubes feeding his body, however, there had been no chance for him. Within a month, the body was eaten away, leaving nothing. The wood top too would eventually disintegrate.

None of this was known, however, and Khufu's entry into the pyramid and into the sarcophagus spawned an elaborate royal cult of the dead. For thousands of years, succeeding generations sought to emulate him, developing intricate embalming techniques to keep bodies intact for the life to come.

The technology of building the pyramid remained in use, unadulterated, for several generations, and was then lost forever, diluted by priests who turned science into religion, forgotten by mystics who wanted only something to worship.

Chapter 52

Present Day

The Lucien shuttle was just as Pruit would have imagined it. Its walls were a bright silver of polished metal, resembling the Lucien skin. The control panels were set into these walls in neat banks of monitors and lights. The craft was a squat cylinder, with three chairs grouped like petals in the center, facing out toward the walls. She, Adaiz, and the Engineer had trekked through central Africa, up into the cloud forest at the edge of the grasslands, and had found the shuttle that Adaiz and Enon had hidden weeks before.

Adaiz-Ari sat in the single chair that had been designed to carry a human. He controlled the craft from this seat. Pruit and the Engineer, strapped into the other two chairs, were merely passengers, and they were experiencing the discomfort of seats that did not well accommodate a human backside. The shuttle generated moderate gravity, enough to keep all three of them firmly in place.

From her position, Pruit could just make out the approach monitors. They were in the final stage of deceleration as they prepared to dock with Pruit's own ship.

"Adaiz, the dock is on the far side," she said. Adaiz moved his hands over the controls, to bring the ships together. He adjusted the docking mechanism, letting it expand and conform to the shape of the Kinley ship's hull.

They docked without incident, the craft making a gentle vibration as it connected with its target. Pruit watched as Adaiz deployed a variable airlock, creating a bridge between the hatches of their two ships. She had given Adaiz the docking code and her ship was ready to receive them.

"Secured," Adaiz said as the airlock clicked into place. They unstrapped themselves. The Engineer moved his arms to follow suit, but he could not manage the locking mechanism.

Pruit freed him from his straps and assisted him onto his feet. Then she shouldered the small backpack which contained their precious crystals. She helped the Engineer up through the round hatch in the shuttle's ceiling. Above them was the hatch into the floor of Pruit's ship. She reached it and pulled it open. There above her was the familiar room that had been her home for nearly twenty years. She guided the Engineer up the airlock's rungs, and soon they emerged together into the ship. Adaiz followed.

"Hello, Central," she said.

"Welcome, Pruit," the ship replied, returning to life instantly, as though she had left only a few minutes ago. It was Niks's voice coming from the walls. Pruit had forgotten it would be, and she was startled by the immediacy of the sorrow at the sound of his voice.

"Central, put the life systems computer on full alert. I have urgent business," she said, forcing herself to maintain composure. She looked around, her eyes moving over the cribs, their lids retracted, their inner wombs dry now, waiting patiently to be used for the return trip. Along the walls and at the ends of the ship were the two control centers, the exercise area, the medical and food stations, and the sentient tank, all in order.

"Adaiz, help me get him to the crib."

Together, they walked the Engineer to Niks's crib and undressed him. Pruit ordered Central to fill the crib, and biofluid began to pour in, hydrating the wombwalls which became orange webs of tissue. She quickly programmed the tank for medical examination, not stasis.

"I'm going to put you in the crib," Pruit said to the Engineer in Haight. She took her cue from the Doctor and never spoke down to him. She gestured to the biofluid, and the Engineer seemed to understand her intent.

She and Adaiz helped him down into the crib. Bioarms began to grow out of the walls, seeking out his body. The Engineer shied away from them, but Pruit squeezed his shoulder in reassurance. "It's all right," she said. "I think it will help you."

As the tank filled, the Engineer slowly settled back into the crib. A breathearm found its way down his throat. He gagged a little, then calmed. In moments, he let his head float beneath the biofluid. Adaiz watched in fascination at this demonstration of Kinley technology. *Kinley.* There, he had said it in his mind. He had not instantly thought of them as "Plaguers." It would take some time to get used to this change, but he was willing to try.

Pruit moved to one of the control centers, sank her hand into the putty pad, and accessed the life systems computer. Adaiz watched the screens in front of her with the varicolored cells that formed and reformed in nanoseconds to create the images required.

"Central, please coordinate with life systems and give me a workup on the man in Niks's crib," Pruit said.

She waited as the ship made a full examination of the Engineer. Then Central spoke.

"The prime problem is one of brain function, Pru." She struggled not to be affected by the computer's familiar tone. "He appears to have suffered extensive damage due to oxygen deprivation. This is a structural problem. Large blocks of cells have been destroyed and have not been able to regenerate."

"Can we fix him?"

"I believe so. It would be a matter of matching his body's cells and instructing his body where to place them. He has an unusual blood type, but still should be within ship capabilities."

"Please put all available resources into fixing him."

"Acknowledged. It will take some hours." The life systems computer, ordered by Central, began to work on the problem.

Pruit spent an hour loading the data crystals into a special crystal reader mounted in the control center, thus transferring all the Eschless Funnel data to the ship.

While she worked, Adaiz took a seat on the floor and let his eyes close. He was thinking of Enon-Amet, trying to find him. He thought he could sense him, his spirit, home, ready for his next life on beautiful Galea. In spirit form Enon had crossed instantly a distance that would take twenty years in physical bodies. *Good-bye, dear brother,* he said to him, *I hope I may have the honor of knowing you again . . .*

When Pruit was finished with the crystals, she found herself standing by the sentient tank. She was thinking of the future. How nice it would be to climb into the tank and talk things over with Niks. She would tell him everything that had happened. She would tell him about her plan, and the chance she saw ahead for the Kinley to free themselves. She would tell him about Eddie, and ask him if he minded that she had found someone else, ask him if he minded that she cared about him. She would tell him these things, and then she would ask him about the future and they would plan together.

But that was not Niks inside the tank, that was a computer with his voice. Niks was gone and the future was up to her. She put her hand on the tank and thought of him, the way he looked, his humor, his love. She found she did not need to cry; those things were still with her.

Softly, she said, "Good-bye, Niks."

After three hours of monitoring the life systems computer, Central spoke:

"The crib occupant is ready to wake."

"How did it go?" she asked.

"Structurally, he looks repaired. His brain function should be normal and continue normal. He may or may not have full memory, however."

Pruit moved to the crib, just as the plantglass retracted and the biofluid began to drain. As the bioarms released the Engineer, she reached in and took hold of his hand, helping him to a sitting position. His hands came to his eyes and rubbed them, then he opened them and coughed. He looked at Pruit and then at Adaiz, who was standing behind her.

"Do you know your name?" Pruit asked him softly in Haight.

"I'm the Engineer," he said, his voice scratchy.

Pruit smiled.

"Yes, you are. Do you remember coming here with me?"

The Engineer squeezed his eyes shut. "Yes," he said, as though the memory pained him. "Of course. I've been . . . living in a nightmare these past weeks." Then he opened his eyes and took hold of Pruit's hand. "Thank you."

She got a blanket for him. He stood from the tank and wrapped himself in it.

"Can you remember the Eschless Funnel?" she asked.

"Do you have something to write with?"

Pruit found him a stylus and writing pad. He took them in his hands and sat down on the floor. Quickly he jotted down a dozen long mathematical formulas, then did a few sample equations. Because of their complexity, this took him several minutes. Then it was his turn to smile.

"The core equations I still know by heart," he said, "The rest I can reconstruct."

"We have your data crystals," Pruit said.

The Engineer smiled again. "Then the Funnel is secure."

She returned his smile, then sent him to shower and dress. She and Adaiz moved to one of the control centers. "He can build me the ship I need," she said. "Are we ready to do this?"

"Yes," Adaiz replied.

Pruit accessed her ship's communication capabilities. There was a powerful broadcast transmitter aboard. It had been designed to send the Eschless technology back to Herrod. Transmitting the information in this way meant that it could be intercepted by the Lucien as well, but Pruit had a set of incredibly complex ciphers to use as protection. Now, however, she was not worried about the Lucien intercepting the information and eventually breaking the code. With the spies they had on

Herrod, that was, perhaps, inevitable in any case. She had another plan, one which she and Adaiz had agreed upon together.

With Central's help, she aligned the transmitter and prepared the ship to broadcast the manuals. When everything was ready, she returned to Adaiz again.

"Are you ready?"

Adaiz paused, then: "Yes. I may be called a traitor in my home for this. But I know my own heart, and I am willing to bear that personal burden."

"You are not a traitor. This is a new time, and the rules have changed. We will give the Funnel to both of our races. The field will ultimately be level for both."

"I hope you're right."

She turned back to the screen, double-checking her instructions. The data would be sent eight light-years through space, landing squarely in their home system. She was also sending the data to Earth, where it would arrive within a few dozen minutes of broadcast.

"Then here we go," she said. "Central, transmit."

There was a brief pause as Central executed her command. "Done, Pruit."

Pruit and Adaiz did not look at each other. They were thinking of the invisible beams of information traveling the speed of light, hurtling inexorably through the reaches of star systems, heading for home. And here, in the local neighborhood, Earth receiving stations in every country on the globe would soon be picking up an incoming message that would change the course of civilization.

At last, Pruit realized that she was not breathing. She let out her breath and drew one in. She would remember that breath for years, the first breath of a new life.

"Something is different," Adaiz said quietly.

Pruit knew immediately what he meant. "Yes," she agreed. "Everything is different."

Chapter 53

The bus was air-conditioned, and the cold air was very welcome after standing in the midday heat on the cement platform outside. Adaiz carried a small bag of belongings over his shoulder. He stared down the aisle, letting his eyes sweep over the people seated along either side.

The vehicle was only half-full. There were men and women of varying ages, some sitting together, some alone. A few glanced his way, but most were looking out their windows. He could smell them, not a bad smell, just a smell of bodies, mostly clean. There was also a faint chemical scent coming from the lavatory at the back of the bus.

Adaiz showed his ticket to the driver and worked his way down the aisle. He took a seat near the back. There was no one next to him. He set his bag down and glanced out the window as the bus gave a squeaky sigh and moved into gear.

This was the State of New York, in the United States of America, planet Earth. It was summer, and Adaiz was taking this bus from one coast of the continent to the other. It would be weeks before he arrived and joined Pruit.

Though a Lucien by upbringing and by loyalty, Adaiz had a human body, and he no longer resisted this. He wanted to experience humanity, wanted to be a part of it. Perhaps he could learn something about himself and teach something to his Lucien brothers as well. True enlightenment, he felt, had room to encompass all races.

He could feel someone's eyes on him. He turned his head to find a young woman looking at him from her seat across the aisle. She glanced away when he looked, a little shy, but he could see the beginnings of a smile on her lips. She was nice looking, he thought, with dark hair and fair skin. There was something unusual about the way she was smiling. With a flash of understanding he realized she was flirting with him.

He felt a tingling sensation in his abdomen. There was a feeling of attraction for her, and an excitement about possible contact. He turned his head away, unsure if he wanted these sensations. After a moment, he realized he did. They were part of humanity, and he no longer objected to them.

The girl was looking at him again. Adaiz turned and met her gaze. Slowly, he smiled. The woman smiled back, and Adaiz felt that nothing could have been more natural than that silent interchange.

His favorite chant from the Katalla Oman came into his mind unbidden, but the words were altered to describe the path he was now taking:

> *This world exists*
> *It surrounds me*
> *I will pass through it*
> *And become*
>
> *Awareness*
>
> *Light*
>
> *A point of knowing.*

Chapter 54

The cabin sat with oak and fir trees around it at the top of a hill in northern California. It was a large house, with an enormous common area that included a living room, kitchen, and dining room. Above this area was a balcony which led to several bedrooms. Off the living room were double doors leading to a garage which had been converted into a workshop.

This was a house that belonged to Eddie, left to him by his grandmother when he was still a teenager. It held his fondest memories from childhood, of the summers he had spent there with his family, daydreaming about anything he wished.

It was evening now, and a warm breeze blew in through the windows. Eddie was in the workshop with the Engineer and the Doctor, arranging the tables and equipment under the Engineer's direction.

Callen had arrived that afternoon, bringing her fiancé, a young man in a nice suit who sat on a kitchen stool with a somewhat bewildered look on his face. Callen was standing in the kitchen, talking into a wall-mounted phone and watching the television in the living room. A national news station was on, and the commentators, as they had been for the last month, were talking about the broadcast from Jupiter. "The government of Japan announced today that it is launching a program to study and develop the mathematical formulas broadcast to Earth three weeks ago. Japan becomes the fourth country to make such an announcement, following the United States,

China, and Germany. The source of the broadcast, which appears to have originated from the vicinity of Jupiter, is still unknown . . ."

Callen spoke into the phone, raising her voice to overpower the two other parties on her conference call. "Dad, Mr. DeLacy, I know you can get the broadcast information anywhere. But Eddie knows two people who can boost you ahead of anyone else. Everyone's expecting at least a decade to figure this stuff out. You could have a spaceship *built* within three years." That shut them up. "Yes, a spaceship. What do you think is up there making the broadcast? Yes, Eddie knows them," she said, answering a protest from Eddie's father. "Three years. We're in the summer cabin. Come out here and see for yourself."

Pruit was unpacking her small bag in the bedroom she and Eddie would share. The Engineer was going to build her an Eschless Funnel ship, and Eddie and Callen would ensure he had the help of Bannon-DeLacy. Securing that help would be easy, once the aerospace company realized it would get full access to the Engineer's knowledge. Broadcasting the Eschless data to Earth had been a teaser to ensure their interest and support.

The ship would be ready in three years, the Engineer promised her, and it would take only a few months to reach Herrod. She would arrive home long before the Lucien attack, with a fully built ship and plans to build more. The Kinley would have an edge, the ability to threaten the Lucien enough to stave off the attack, and even, perhaps, to move the entire Herrod population somewhere else.

In eight years—five years after she returned home—the transmission from her ship would arrive on Herrod, and arrive on Galea, the Lucien capital, as well. The transmission was heavily encrypted. It would take the Lucien a few years to decipher it, but they would eventually have access to all the Eschless Funnel data as well. Thus the Kinley would not have an opportunity to become aggressors and turn the tables on the

Lucien. It would be a level playing field and the two races would have to learn to coexist.

Later that night, the Engineer and Doctor were busy beginning work in the Engineer's shop and Callen and her fiancé were huddled in the kitchen, strategizing about the upcoming visit of Callen's and Eddie's fathers. Eddie snuck Pruit out of the house alone.

"Where are we going?" she asked.

"You'll see," Eddie said, a hint of a smile in his voice.

He was holding her hand and leading her through trees and tall grass. The night was warm despite the late hour. The moon was nearly full and bright enough to cast distinct shadows. After ten minutes, they made their way out of the trees, and in a few moments they came upon a wide road. It was midnight and there were no cars.

"This is the Pacific Coast Highway," he said, pulling her across it. "It only leads to good places."

"What do you mean?"

"You'll see," he said, putting a hand over her eyes as they reached the other side.

"What is it?"

"Stop asking questions!" He was laughing now.

He guided her down a short hill, then Pruit felt rocks beneath her feet. There was a rhythmic sighing sound in the air which she could almost recognize.

"All right," he said, and removed his hand from her eyes.

Stretched out before her was the nighttime expanse of the Pacific Ocean. It was blue-black, under a sky of slightly lighter color, and there was a wide swath of moonlight across it. She was standing on a low outcropping above the water, and the breakers lapped against the sand a few dozen feet below, almost at her feet.

"The ocean . . . ," she breathed. It was the first time she had seen an ocean in person. Even on their flights, the oceans had been obscured, by night or by clouds. Now, finally, here it was, water forever. "It's beautiful."

They sat together on the large rocks, watching the tide go out. Eddie leaned back and looked up at the sky. Despite the brightness of the moon, hundreds of stars were visible, for they were far from cities.

He took her hand and kissed it. Pruit wondered about love. Was it possible to love two people so different as Niks and Eddie? She leaned over and kissed him gently. Perhaps it was.

She lay back against the rocks and thought of Herrod, of its domed cities, of the Sentinel and her family. She would see them again. Soon. And there would be hope.

"It's going to be a new world," Eddie said softly.

Pruit looked at the stars. Within a generation, they would be within reach of three very different worlds. "A new universe," she said.

She was experiencing a strange physical sensation. There was a nervousness in her stomach, coupled with elation. It was a feeling she had never quite encountered before, at least not in this magnitude.

Eddie saw the look on her face. "What's wrong?"

"I don't know," she said. "I feel . . . strange. Like a weight has been lifted and the future is open. Like . . . like there's no longer a set path before me. Instead, there are possibilities, and they are limitless."

Eddie laughed and put his arms around her, pulling her close to him. "Pruit," he whispered, "you're happy."

She smiled, looking out at the horizon, where the ocean met the sky, feeling his warmth, feeling the life within her and the life ahead. She kissed him and whispered back, "Maybe I am."

Dramatis Personae/Glossary

Note: Ages given for the Kinley Earth Survey crew are the ages of the characters when they first appear in the story.

Adaiz-Ari (Mission Officer Adaiz-Ari) (uh-daz' ar-ee'): Twenty-two years old. Male. Kinley, fertilized and born in a Lucien laboratory, from stolen Kinley genetic material. Considers himself Lucien. Member of Clan Warrior and Clan Providence. Full blood brother of both clans. Raised in Lucien family, as younger brother of Enon-Amet.

Archaeologist, the: Forty-two years old. Female. Ancient Kinley. Archaeologist and member of the Kinley Earth Survey crew. Wife of the Captain.

Avani (ah-vah'-ni): The modern language of the Lucien.

Biologist, the: Thirty-five years old. Female. Ancient Kinley. Biologist and member of the Kinley Earth Survey crew.

Callen St. John: Thirty-two years old. Female. Earth human, Caucasian. Childhood friend of Eddie.

Captain, the: Forty-four years old. Male. Ancient Kinley. Military pilot with training in medicine. Leader of the Kinley Earth Survey crew. Husband of the Archaeologist.

Champion, the: The Kinley survey team's ship.

Clan Providence: The military organization of the Lucien people.

Doctor, the: Thirty-eight years old. Female. Ancient Kinley.

Doctor and member of the Kinley Earth survey crew. Wife of the Engineer.

Eddie (Harris Edward DeLacy III): Thirty-two years old. Male. Earth human, Caucasian.

Egani-tah (e-ga'-ni tah): A form of Opening practiced by members of Clan Providence. It involves a ritual battle in which the opponents have a full spiritual connection with each other. High masters of the egani-tah can also force this state upon their opponents during battle, encompassing an enemy within themselves.

Engineer, the: Thirty-eight years old. Male. Ancient Kinley. Member of the Kinley Earth survey crew, and designer of the *Champion,* the Eschless Funnel ship that brought the survey crew to Earth. Husband of the Doctor.

Enon-Amet (Mission Leader Enon-Amet) (ee-non ah-met'): Twenty-eight years old. Male. Lucien. Member of Warrior Clan and Clan Providence. Elder brother of Adaiz-Ari, and leader of the Lucien mission to Earth.

Eschless Funnel (esh'-les): An engine that can propel a space-faring ship at speeds greater than the speed of light. The Eschless Funnel was developed on Herrod and used to power the Kinley survey vessel that landed on Earth in the third millennium B.C.

Fifth Dynasty: 2498–2345 B.C.

Fourth Dynasty: 2613–2498 B.C.

Galea (ga-lay'-ah): The enormous asteroid that is the primary Lucien settlement. It lies at the edge of the Kinley star system.

Great Life (or Blessed Life): A modern Kinley imprecation. This curse derives from the generations of Kinley who struggled to keep the race alive.

Great War, the: The Kinley name for the ancient war between Lucien and Kinley that resulted in the near destruction of both races. Called the Plague by the Lucien.

Haight (hite): An ancient language of the Kinley, at one time the dominant language of science.

Herrod (hare'-ed): The home planet of the Kinley. It resides in a neighboring star system to Rheat, once the home planet of the Lucien.

Horus: Egyptian god, son of Osiris and Isis. He avenged his father's murder by slaying Seth (they had many legendary battles). He ruled over all of Egypt, and at the end of his reign turned over the empire to the line of human pharaohs.

Isis: Egyptian mother-goddess. Wife of Osiris and mother of Horus.

Jack, the: Forty-two years old. Male. Ancient Kinley. Member of the Kinley Earth Survey crew. Specialist in numerous disciplines, including the study of atmosphere and the interaction of humans with their environment. Known as a "Jack of all trades."

Jean-Claude: Eighteen years old. Male. Earth human, black. A French prostitute, working in the slums of Cairo.

Katalla-Oman, the: A collection of Lucien religious teachings emphasizing the individual's inherent ability to achieve unity with others around him and with the universe at large. Much of the Katalla-Oman is attributed to Omani, the god of wisdom.

Kinley (kin'-ly): The human natives of the planet Herrod. During an earlier incarnation of their society, they were quite varied in genotype, with over a dozen distinct races. After the Great War, however, the tiny remaining gene pool resulted in a homogenized race, in which every member shared the same basic coloring and bone structure. The modern Kinley has copper-colored skin, hair that varies from dark brown to reddish-brown, and blue, green, or gray eyes.

Lion, the: Twenty-one years old. Male. Ancient Kinley. Zoologist and member of the Kinley Earth Survey crew. Named "Lion" by the Earth natives for his resemblance to this animal. Son of the Captain and the Archaeologist.

Lucien (loo'-shen): A non-human, mammalian race that evolved in a neighboring star system to the Kinley. Notable aspects of their physical appearance are their silver skin, which becomes reflective when exposed to sunlight; the triangular, slightly insectile shape of their heads; the heavy sheaf of bone that provides protection to their chests; and their two knee joints, one bending forward and the other backward, which allow their legs to absorb much greater impact than a human leg could withstand.

The Lucien originally inhabited Rheat, but after the Kinley-Lucien war, Rheat was left uninhabitable and the Lucien society was thereafter based on the asteroid Galea at the outer edge of the Kinley star system.

Mechanic, the: Forty years old. Male. Ancient Kinley. Member of Kinley Earth survey crew.

Mother: The chief goddess in the ancient Kinley religion. Her name is often found in imprecations such as "Mother's Love," "Sweet Mother," or "Mother of All."

Nate Douglas: Thirty years old. Male. Earth human, Caucasian. An employee of the American Embassy in Cairo.

Niks (Sentinel Defender Niks Arras of Telivein) (niks): Twenty-five years old. Male. Kinley. Leader of the Kinley team sent from Herrod to Earth.

Old Kingdom: A period of Egyptian history encompassing the Third through Sixth Dynasties, approximately 2700–2200 B.C.

Omani (o'ma'-ni): The Lucien god of wisdom and unity.

Opening: A ritual meditation and mental exercise performed by Lucien. It involves expanding one's spiritual reach to encompass the surrounding environment and sometimes the mind of another person.

Osiris: Egyptian god. Ultimately became the god of the dead, and is believed to have been the first mummy. Osiris was murdered by his brother Seth, and eventually avenged by his son Horus. His wife and sister was Isis.

Plague, the: The Lucien name for the ancient war between themselves and the Kinley. It is so called because the Kinley's final action in the war was to release a specially engineered disease into the atmosphere of Rheat. This man-made plague wiped out the entire population of Rheat, leaving only the Lucien, who lived on asteroid colonies, alive.

Plaguers: A Lucien term for the Kinley. See **Plague.**

Pruit (Sentinel Defender Pruit Pax of Senetian): Twenty-five years old. Female. Kinley. Member of the two-man Kinley team sent from Herrod to Earth.

Rheat (ree'-aht): The original home planet of the Lucien. No Lucien live on the planet in the present day. It resides in a neighboring star system to Herrod, the home planet of the Kinley.

Saving Father: A modern Kinley imprecation. The "Father" referred to is the ancient genetic scientist who mapped out the recovery of the race following the Great War.

Sentinel, the: An elite military group charged with the ultimate responsibility for the future of the Kinley race.

Seth: Egyptian god, brother of Osiris, whom he betrayed and murdered.

Skinsuit: A web of cells that lives in the upper layers of the host's skin. The cells of the suit can retreat into the host's body, or rise to the surface to provide an additional layer of "skin" as needed to protect the host from microorganisms in the environment.

Soulene (soo-leen'): The modern language of the Kinley.